"On your back, please," Ned said.

Rosalind lay down, and ye cavorting cherubs, what a picture she made, hair a little untidy, lips rosy, clothing in disarray.

"You are a feast of temptations." Ned unknotted his cravat and began to unbutton his waistcoat and shirt. "An embarrassment of inspiration for the male imagination."

"Less talk, and more undressing, Ned."

He flung off his cravat and waistcoat and pulled his shirt over his head. "I had planned to read you poetry. Play you a few sentimental ballads on my fiddle."

Rosalind took his shirt, sniffed it, and rolled it up beneath her head. "We'll get to that part. Maybe not today."

Ned arranged himself over her. "Maybe not this year."

PRAISE FOR GRACE BURROWES AND THE ROGUES TO RICHES SERIES

"Grace Burrowes is terrific!"
—Julia Quinn, #1 *New York Times* bestselling author

"Sexy heroes, strong heroines, intelligent plots, enchanting love stories.... Grace Burrowes's romances have them all."
—Mary Balogh, *New York Times* bestselling author

"Grace Burrowes writes from the heart—with warmth, humor, and a generous dash of sensuality, her stories are unputdownable! If you're not reading Grace Burrowes you're missing the very best in today's Regency Romance!"
—Elizabeth Hoyt, *New York Times* bestselling author

"Adept and captivating leads."
—*Kirkus* on *How to Catch a Duke*

"Burrowes takes her series to new heights with this tender, turbulent romance."
—*Publishers Weekly*, starred review, on *The Truth About Dukes*

"A standout in the historical romance subgenre but is also a powerful story all on its own... Highly recommended."
—*Library Journal*, starred review, on *A Duke by Any Other Name*

ALSO BY GRACE BURROWES

THE WINDHAM BRIDES SERIES

The Trouble with Dukes

Too Scot to Handle

No Other Duke Will Do

A Rogue of Her Own

ROGUES TO RICHES SERIES

My One and Only Duke

When a Duchess Says I Do

Forever and a Duke

A Duke by Any Other Name

The Truth About Dukes

How to Catch a Duke

NEVER
A DUKE

A Rogues to Riches Novel

GRACE BURROWES

FOREVER
New York Boston

Copyright © 2022 by Grace Burrowes

Cover art and design by Daniela Medina. Cover images © Trevillion; Shutterstock. Cover copyright © 2022 by Hachette Book Group, Inc.

Forever
Hachette Book Group
1290 Avenue of the Americas, New York, NY 10104
read-forever.com
twitter.com/readforeverpub

First Edition: April 2022

Forever is an imprint of Grand Central Publishing. The Forever name and logo are trademarks of Hachette Book Group, Inc.

The publisher is not responsible for websites (or their content) that are not owned by the publisher.

The Hachette Speakers Bureau provides a wide range of authors for speaking events. To find out more, go to www.hachettespeakersbureau.com or call (866) 376-6591.

ISBNs: 978-1-5387-0698-5 (mass market), 978-1-5387-0699-2 (ebook)

Printed in the United States of America

OPM

10 9 8 7 6 5 4 3 2 1

To those who stand up

NEVER A DUKE

Chapter One

"She smelled like Hyde Park," Artie said. "And she were pretty."

Artie was the newest and youngest of the Wentworth bank messengers, a dark-eyed imp of indeterminate years with a curious affinity for soap and water. In Ned Wentworth's experience, cleanliness was an acquired habit for children consigned to London's streets.

Artie, unlike Ned himself, had taken to regular bathing with the enthusiasm of a schoolgirl shopping for hair ribbons.

"This woman smelled like horse droppings?" Lord Stephen Wentworth asked.

"Nah, milord. Not like the *streets*, like the *park*." Artie raised his little paw as if to wipe his nose on the back of his wrist.

Ned passed him a monogrammed handkerchief. "Do you mean she bore the fragrance of fresh air and greenery?"

"She smelled like spring," Artie said, snatching the linen and honking into it. "All sweet and sunny."

He folded the handkerchief and held it out to Ned. "Thanks, guv."

Stephen was *milord*, while Ned was *guv*, and thus it would ever be. "Keep it, lad," Ned said. "So the lady wore a lovely fragrance, was pretty, and passed you a note that you were to give directly to me?"

"Was she pretty like a fine lady," Lord Stephen asked, "or pretty like the women outside the theaters of an evening?"

Artie looked affronted. "She weren't no whore. She got into a fancy coach with crests on the doors and boot. Whores don't have crested carriages. She thanked me and give me tuppence for my trouble."

To a child like Artie, the thanks would mean almost as much as the coin. "You've done well, Arthur," Ned said, "and my thanks for your discretion. Keep an eye out for that fancy coach, and if you see it again let me know."

Artie had the most cherubic smile, all bashful and innocent, which was doubtless why the schools for pickpockets had been haggling over which one would recruit him. And Artie, already wise to the ways of the streets, would have considered that training vastly preferable to many other ways of earning his bread.

"On your way," Lord Stephen said, gesturing with his cane toward the door. "And keep mum, my boy. This is bank business."

The lads took pride in protecting the bank's privacy, as had Ned when he'd been a boy with a bottomless belly and little ability to safeguard himself.

Lord Stephen waited until Artie had withdrawn before taking a seat on the tufted sofa near the fireplace.

Ned's office was comfortable, not quite luxurious. The bank's owner, Quinton, Duke of Walden, didn't go in for ostentation in commercial establishments, or much of anywhere.

"So what does she say?" Lord Stephen, His Grace's brother and heir, didn't go in for allowing anybody privacy. He would not snatch the note from Ned, but only because his lordship relied on canes for balance, and Ned wasn't above shoving Stephen onto his handsome arse if the situation called for it.

The situation, alas, hadn't called for it for years.

Ned sniffed the note. "The wax is scented with roses." And the seal wasn't the usual reddish blob, but rather, lavender and sporting an impression of a rose. Ned slit the seal with a thumbnail.

Mr. Wentworth, if you will attend me at 2 of the clock today on the third bench along the Serpentine, I will make it worth your while.

Ned passed Stephen the note.

"A summons from a woman, Neddy? You aren't going, are you? We will never see you again, and Hercules will be bereft."

Hercules was a mastiff belonging to Stephen's wife. The canine would pine for a joint of beef longer than he would for Ned.

"You certainly heed any summons your darling Abigail issues," Ned said. That Stephen—brilliant, contrary, lame, and opinionated—had found wedded bliss two years past rankled. True, he was a handsome devil, charming when it suited him, titled, and wealthy, but still.

Stephen wasn't easy company, while Ned had worked tirelessly on his manners and deportment, and could make small talk with dowagers by the hour.

"Abigail is my dearest lady wife," Stephen retorted. "You have no idea who this woman is, or what her purpose is, if indeed, a woman sent that note. You don't need coin, so what could she offer you that makes such a risk worth taking?"

"That doesn't matter." Ned inventoried his appearance in the cheval mirror and smoothed down his cravat. "I can do with a walk, and it's a pretty day." Then too, walking meant his Meddling Nuisance-ship would remain at the bank.

"Stubborn," Stephen muttered. "Stubborn, opinionated, difficult, and too smart for your own good."

"You forgot handsome." Ned selected a mahogany walking stick with a lead weight secreted in the carved lion's-head handle. "Her Grace says I have slumberous eyes and a noble nose."

"You have shifty eyes and a great, arrogant beak. Be careful, Neddy. I don't like cryptic notes or assignations with women who drive about in fancy coaches."

Ned tapped his top hat onto his head. "You're jealous because I have a mystery to solve." He tilted the hat an inch to the left, a nod to his bachelor status.

"I fear for your life and you insult me. Take the dog. The lads are walking him for me."

"The lads are doubtless spoiling the beast rotten

and neglecting their duties." Bickering with Stephen was an old habit though no longer the pleasure it had once been.

Stephen held his forearm to his brow. "Not neglecting their duties! Heaven forefend small boys should get some fresh air on a fine day. Clap me in irons for corrupting the morals of a lot of budding thieves and pickpockets! Summon the beadle!"

Ned extracted another monogrammed handkerchief from a desk drawer and folded it into his pocket. "They aren't budding thieves or pickpockets anymore. Will I see you at supper tomorrow?"

Once a month, Ned endured supper with Stephen and his ducal brother at their club. The agenda was a combination of bank business and family tattle, though Ned had only a small ownership interest in the bank, and wasn't family in any biological sense.

"Her Grace will fret if her menfolk neglect their monthly supper," Stephen said, pushing to his feet. "I could go to the park in your place, Neddy."

"The note was sent specifically to me." Why? By whom? A lady fallen on hard times could have had Ned quietly call upon her at home, a service conscientious bankers routinely performed for valued customers.

Stephen took up his second walking stick. "Abigail says you need a wife."

"As it happens, she's right."

Dark brows rose. "You admit that holy matrimony would enhance your happiness?"

Stephen apparently intended to see personally that Ned took the dratted dog to the park.

"I admit that I am of age and of independent means.

The next move up the ladder of respectability is to make an advantageous match."

They quit the office, though Stephen's limitations meant their progress down the carpeted corridor was decorous.

"You make marriage sound like a step in the quadrille of social advancement," Stephen said. "That's not how it's supposed to be. And stop dawdling. My latest knee brace is the best of the lot so far, but I think ball bearings will improve it further still."

Stephen strode ahead, and Ned wanted to swat him with his walking stick. For as long as they'd known each other—well over a decade—Stephen had been troubled by a bad knee. He still used two canes, but his recent creation of braces for the knee meant he also moved more freely and suffered much less pain.

These developments were cause for general rejoicing, though Ned was honest enough with himself to admit to some resentment as well. One advantage he'd always had over Stephen was nimbleness. Petty, to look for ways to put himself above another man, but Ned had been a boy when he'd met the Wentworths, a convicted felon awaiting transportation.

Advantages and disadvantages could be the difference between life and death, and that was not a lesson Ned would ever forget.

"I'll have the lads deliver Hercules to you before dark," Ned said, for it was bank policy that the boys were in their dormitory by sunset. Their presence on bank premises protected the property, and denying the boys access to the streets after dark protected them too.

The better to entertain them, they were also subjected to two hours of lessons after supper. Since Ned had instituted that routine, he'd had much less trouble with boys sneaking out at night. That the lessons always ended with the tutor reading a rousing story or myth was merest coincidence.

"Will Arthur *do*, Neddy?" Stephen asked, as they emerged from the bank's side entrance.

Edward. My name is Edward Wentworth. Ned had had another name before being taken up for thievery as a child. A name he never spoke aloud.

"Time will tell," he said, pulling on his gloves. "Artie is canny, has a memory that won't quit, and has the knack of making the other lads laugh. I hope he stays."

Ned hoped they all stayed, though too often, they didn't. Achieving respectability was a long, hard, lonely climb, with many perils and endless temptations to lead a fellow astray.

One of the older messengers brought Hercules over from a patch of shade on the street corner.

"Watch out for our Neddy," Lord Stephen instructed the dog. "He goes to rescue a damsel in distress."

Or to put a silly woman in her place. Ned had little patience with spoiled society women, though he would always be polite to them. The terse note, though, had piqued his curiosity. He did not need money, he did not need another riding horse, or even a commodious home. His material wants were met to a degree that would have staggered his younger self.

So what could a wellborn lady have that would make troubling on her behalf worth Ned's while? He gathered up the dog's leash, bowed a farewell to Lord Stephen, and strode off for the park.

When he arrived, he was reminded of Burns's admonition about the best-laid plans, for on the third bench along the bank of the Serpentine sat none other than Lady Rosalind Kinwood in all her prim, tidy glory.

She was a stranger to distress unless she was instigating it, and she was the furthest thing from a damsel. Her devotion to various causes was both articulate and unwavering. Her ladyship of course occupied the one bench in all of London she should not occupy at the one hour when Ned needed her to be elsewhere.

He bowed and touched a finger to his hat brim. "My lady, good day. Might I join you for a moment? The water makes a lovely prospect and the dog could use the respite."

She twitched her skirts aside. "We haven't much time. I sent my companion off to purchase corn for the waterfowl, and she'll be back any minute."

Doom yawned before Ned, the same sensation that had enveloped him when as a boy, he'd been grabbed by the collar after a bungled attempt at snatching a purse. One blunder, and he'd been tossed into Newgate, his life over, his prospects forever ruined.

Lady Rosalind wasn't nearly so dire a fate, but not for lack of trying. She was the scourge of the fortune hunters, the worst nightmare of climbing cits, the subject of witty pub songs, and the despair of the matchmakers.

Ned unfastened Hercules's leash, and let the dog go nosing off along the bank. "You sent me that note?"

"Don't you dare sit," she snapped. "Your presumption

will be noted by every busybody in the Home Counties, and the gossips will have us engaged before Monday."

Clearly, an awful fate as far as her ladyship was concerned, and Ned agreed with her. "I heeded your plea for help out of an abundance of gentlemanly concern. Say your piece and nobody need fear Monday's arrival."

She huffed out a sigh, and because Ned was studying the curve of her resolute jaw, he noticed what he assumed half the bachelors in London had noticed late at night after a few honesty-inducing brandies: Lady Rosalind, for all her tart tongue and waspish opinions, was well formed, and her features would not have been out of place on a Renaissance tapestry. Beauty like that could entice otherwise wary unicorns to have a closer look.

The Almighty was nothing, if not perverse in His generosity.

She watched the dog, who snuffled about the reeds near the water's edge. "My lady's maid has gone missing."

"So you summoned a banker? Did she go missing in a Wentworth establishment?"

"Don't be odious. Bad things happen to young women who go missing."

"Elopements?" Ned replied. "New posts? A return to village life and the adoring swain who pined endlessly when his beloved left him for the blandishments of the capital?"

Lady Rosalind rose. "You trivialize a tragedy, Mr. Wentworth. I thought you would understand. Arbuckle is a village girl, but she's been in London long enough to know its dangers. She needed her wages, and believe me, the post paid well."

And she had the effrontery to leave your employ without notice? But no, Ned could not say that. He might never be a gentleman in the eyes of Mayfair society, but he could be civil to an obviously upset woman.

"What exactly is it that you expect me to do?"

Lady Rosalind gave him a brooding perusal. She was neither tall nor short, but she carried her ire before her like regimental colors. Her temper directed itself to bumbling younger sons, drunken baronets, the monarch's extravagances, and countless other targets. In the main, Ned agreed with her exasperation, as some of her peers doubtless did.

But a young lady did not remark on such matters until she was safely married and presiding over her nursery, and then she mentioned them only by delicate allusions in the hearing of her closest friends.

"I had hoped you could find her," Lady Rosalind said. "I cannot. I have tried, but the grooms and crossing sweepers won't talk to me. My brothers won't listen to me, and my father is threatening to send me to take the waters with Aunt Ida. Arbuckle has nobody else to worry for her, and she could be in very great danger."

Ned whistled for the dog, who trotted to his side like the well-trained beast he was. "And you believe the crossing sweepers and such will talk to me?" He'd been managing the Wentworth banks since finishing that purgatory known as university studies. He had some wealth of his own; he spoke French, German, and Mayfair passably well, and he was accounted a competent dancer.

But Lady Rosalind had sought him out because his native language was Cockney and his home shire was the stews. *Still.* Society never flung his origins in his face, but they never flung their marriageable daughters at him either.

"Arbuckle is pretty," Lady Rosalind said, gaze fixed on the mirror-calm surface of the Serpentine. "She has lovely features and a quick mind. She's sweet and quiet, not like me, and that means she's at greater risk of harm."

Ned sensed in Lady Rosalind's words an admission of sorts, an insight into the woman whom most of society invited to their gatherings out of unwillingness to offend her titled father.

"You fear for her."

"I do, terribly."

The calm façade wavered, as Hercules panted gently at Ned's side. For an instant Lady Rosalind looked not affronted, not impatient, not any of her usual repertoire of prickly expressions, but *desperate*.

Ned knew desperation well and hated it in all its guises. That Lady Rosalind, termagant at large and spinster without compare, was in the grip of desperation affronted him.

"I'll see what I can find out."

"Thank you." Two words, though like all of Lady Rosalind's other pronouncements, Ned believed she meant them. "There is more to the situation than I can convey at the moment, and I am beyond worried."

"I apprehend that your companion approaches." At

a good clip, just shy of a trot. "I will shop tomorrow at Hatchards among the biographies at ten of the clock. Prepare to recount for me all you know of the situation."

He snapped the leash back onto Hercules's collar.

"Thank you, Mr. Wentworth. Thank you so very much."

Ned tipped his hat and sauntered on his way, though some dim back corner of his heart put those words of thanks in a special hiding place, where they would be well guarded and much treasured.

* * *

The problem with Ned Wentworth was his eyes.

Rosalind came to that conclusion as she pretended to browse a biography of a long-dead monarch. She had come to the bookstore early, the better to ensure that her companion, Mrs. Amelia Barnstable, was thoroughly engrossed in the travelogues two floors above the biographies.

Ned Wentworth dressed with a gentleman's exquisite sense of fashion, and he spoke and comported himself with a gentleman's faultless manners.

But his eyes did not gaze out upon the world with a gentleman's condescending detachment. Rosalind's brothers, by contrast, had learned by the age of eight how to glance, peruse, peer, and otherwise take only a casual visual inventory of life, and then to pretend that nothing very interesting or important graced the scene.

Certainly nothing as interesting or important as her brothers themselves.

Ned Wentworth *looked* and he *saw*. His visual appraisals were frank and thorough, as if everything before him, from Rosalind's reticule, to a great panting behemoth of a dog, to a swan gliding across the Serpentine's placid surface, were so many entries in a ledger that wanted tallying.

His eyes were a soft, mink brown, his hair the same color as Rosalind's. On him the hue was sable, of a piece with his watchful eyes and sober gentleman's attire. On her the color was a lamentable brown, according to Aunt Ida. He was on the tall side, but not a towering specimen like the Duke of Walden, and not a fashionable dandy like the duke's younger brother.

Ned Wentworth's eyes said he'd somehow held out against domestication, unlike his adopted family, who had famously come from lowly origins to occupy a very high station. He prowled through life with a wild creature's confidence and vigilance, even as he partnered wellborn ladies through quadrilles and met their papas for meals in the clubs.

"She was quite the schemer, wasn't she?"

Rosalind turned to behold those serious brown eyes gazing at her. Up close, Ned Wentworth was a sartorial tribute to understated elegance. His attire had no flourishes—no flashy cravat pin, no excessive lace, no jewels in the handle of his walking stick.

His scent was similarly subtle, a hint of green meadows, a whisper of honeysuckle. Rosalind hadn't heard his approach, but she'd be able to identify him by scent in pitch darkness.

"Queen Elizabeth was devious," Rosalind replied, "but she died a peaceful death after nearly achieving her three-score and ten. We must account her a successful schemer."

"Are you a successful schemer, my lady?"

Rosalind closed the book and replaced it on the shelf. "Do you attempt to flirt with me, Mr. Wentworth?"

The biographies were unpopular, hence the conversation was not overheard. Had Ned Wentworth known that would be the case?

"If I were attempting to flirt with you, you'd likely cosh me over the head with yonder tome. Tell me about Arbuckle."

Rosalind withdrew a folded sketch from her reticule. "A likeness. I am no portraitist, but Francine Arbuckle was willing to serve as my model on many occasions. She has no family in London, and the last I saw of her, my companion had sent her to retrieve a pair of dancing slippers from a shop near Piccadilly."

"Specifics, please. What shop?"

Rosalind endured an interrogation, and Mr. Wentworth's methodical inquiries helped her sort recollection from conjecture.

"I told you I tried to talk to the crossing sweepers," she said, when she'd recounted all she could remember regarding Arbuckle's disappearance. "They acted as if conversing with me would turn them to stone."

"They might have had trouble comprehending your words, my lady. They know their Cockney and cant, and can recite you bawdy poems without number, but drawing room elocution eludes them."

"It eluded me for years as well. I developed a stammer after my mother's death. My governess was horrified." Rosalind was horrified. She never alluded to her stammer, while her brothers never let her forget it.

Mr. Wentworth frowned. "You stuttered?"

"For years. My brothers used to tease me unmercifully. Then my father hired a Welshwoman as my drawing master, and she taught me to think of speaking as *recitativo*. I do not stammer when I sing, and if I can hear a melody..." Rosalind fell silent, for she was prattling.

That her usual self-possession had deserted her was Ned Wentworth's fault, because after he posed a question, he *listened* to the lady's answer, and the whole time, he gazed at her as if her words mattered.

Very bad of him. "This isn't helping us to find Arbuckle," Rosalind said.

"Your secret is safe with me." He chose a book at random from the shelves. "Bankers learn more secrets than I ever aspired to know. We keep them close or soon go out of business."

He made a handsome picture, leafing through the book. Rosalind would like to sketch him thus, not that his appearance mattered one whit. "What sort of secrets?"

He turned a page. "Who has set up a discreet trust fund for a mere godchild. Who is one Season away from ruin. Who has abruptly changed solicitors, such as might happen when the first firm is unwilling to suborn a bit of perjury or sharp practice."

Polite society kept Ned Wentworth at a slight distance, and Rosalind had always attributed that lack of welcome to his past. He was rumored to have met His Grace of Walden during the duke's little misunderstanding with the authorities, the little mis-understanding that had landed His Grace on a Newgate scaffold with a noose about his neck. The duke had been plain Mr. Quinton Wentworth at the time, and appallingly wealthy.

His Grace was even wealthier now, but still Ned Wentworth's past did not recommend him to the matchmakers. Neither, apparently, did his present.

"No wonder they are all afraid of you," Rosalind said. "You could ruin the lot of them."

He turned another page. "You are not afraid of me."

They were wandering far afield from the topic of Arbuckle's disappearance, and Rosalind had more information to convey. And yet, to *converse* with Mr. Wentworth was interesting. Rosalind was usually re-duced to argument, lecture, small talk, or exhortation with men. That she gave as good as she got in each category only seemed to make the situation worse.

"Why would I be afraid of you?" Rosalind asked. "You are a gentleman and you have agreed to help me."

He closed the book. "Your oldest brother is habitu-ally in dun territory, Lady Rosalind, and your younger brother is barely managing on a generous allowance, very likely because he's trying to keep the firstborn son and heir out of the sponging house. I thought you should know this before I undertake a search for Miss Arbuckle."

The words made sense, but they were rendered in such polite, unassuming tones that Rosalind needed a moment to find the meaning in them.

"Do you expect me to *pay* you?" Rosalind had

money, because wasting coin on fripperies was beyond her, and Papa had little clue what it cost to clothe a lady, much less to run his own household.

"Of course not." Mr. Wentworth shoved the book back onto the shelf. "If your family is short of coin, then the sooner I put your mind at ease regarding remuneration for my efforts, the less likely you are to fret."

Fret? Whatever was he getting at? "You are being too delicate for my feeble female brain, Mr. Wentworth. Plain speech would be appreciated."

He selected another book, as casually as if he truly were browsing the biographies. "You promised in your note that if I heeded your summons, you would make it worth my while. A simple request for aid would have sufficed, my lady. You need not coerce me with coin."

Ah, well then. His pride was offended. Having two brothers, Rosalind should have recognized the symptoms.

"I beg your pardon for not being more clear. I meant to trade favors, Mr. Wentworth. You have agreed to search for Arbuckle, and thus I will share with you the fact that Clotilda Cadwallader is considering allowing you to court her. She's said to be worth ten thousand a year."

The book snapped closed. "She's *what*?"

"Said to be worth—"

He shook his head. "I know to the penny what she's worth, and it's not ten thousand a year. What else can you tell me?"

"She might allow you to pay her your addresses." Rosalind offered this news with all good cheer, though

Clotilda was a ninnyhammer. Men seemed to prefer ninnyhammers, alas. "You'd have to change your name to Cadwallader, but she says you aren't bad looking, you're solvent, and you would not be overly bothersome about filling the nursery." More delicate than that, Rosalind could not be.

"Because I have no title, and need neither heir nor spare, and what married couple would ever seek one another's intimate company for any reason other than duty?"

Mr. Wentworth's tone presaged not affront, but rather, amusement—and bitterness.

"I know little of what motivates people to marry, and as for intimate company..." Too late Rosalind realized that she'd sailed into a verbal ambush of her own making.

"Yes, my lady?" The amusement had reached Mr. Wentworth's eyes. He was silently laughing at her, which merited a good Storming Off in High Dudgeon, except that his gaze held only a friendly sense of fun and nothing of mockery.

He was *teasing* her. Rosalind's brothers had teased her, before a mere sister had slipped beneath their notice. Arbuckle had occasionally teased her. But when Ned Wentworth teased, his watchful, noticing gaze warmed to a startling degree. A smile lurked in the subtle curve of his mouth, and the corners of his eyes crinkled.

I must sketch him thus, must catch that near-smile. "We will now change the subject," Rosalind said, "because the alternative is to admit that I've mortified myself."

"Must we change the subject just as the topic is becoming interesting?"

"You are twitting me." Or perhaps he was flirting with her? Not likely, but Rosalind had so little experience with flirtation she could forgive herself for wondering.

"On the basis of vast *in*experience, you were preparing to lecture me about your complete indifference to marital joy. Of course I was teasing you. And as for the Cadwallader creature... You will please inform her that I want a very large family."

"Do you?"

He put the book atop the shelf. "If Miss Cadwallader asks, you may assure her I do. Can you tell me anything else about Miss Arbuckle? What did she do on her half days?"

"Came here, went to the park, wrote letters to her family in Somerset. She is a decent young woman, Mr. Wentworth. Her home village is a place called Cowdown."

An older couple descended the stairs arm in arm. Mr. Wentworth bent closer before they came too near.

"The decent young women," he said, "are the ones who don't see trouble coming, which is why most of Mayfair's belles aren't permitted to set foot outside the house unescorted. Shall I meet you here again next week?"

His scent changed up close, becoming more complicated and sweeter. "Why not Friday? I don't want to wait a week."

"Very well, Friday." He bowed and would have left, but Rosalind presumed to lay a hand on his sleeve.

"You should know that my last lady's maid also disappeared, Mr. Wentworth. I'll have a sketch of her for you on Friday."

The older couple was coming closer, and any minute, Rosalind expected to see Mrs. Barnstable parading down the steps with a new travelogue in hand.

"Until Friday, my lady."

He was halfway to the steps before Rosalind spoke again. "Be careful, Mr. Wentworth."

He saluted with his walking stick. "You may depend upon it."

He mounted the steps briskly, and Rosalind was left amid tales of the illustrious dead, wondering if Ned Wentworth truly did want a big family. She suspected he did, which was puzzling to say the least.

Chapter Two

"This woman wants you to find a missing lady's maid?" Stephen took a glass from the waiter's tray. "My dear Abigail might have some ideas about how to proceed with such a task."

Ned accepted a brandy for himself and passed the third drink to Quinton, Duke of Walden. When the waiter had bowed and withdrawn, His Grace set the brandy on the sideboard. For His Grace, the club's best private dining room was always available, while Ned had to make reservations well in advance.

"Does the lady's maid want to be found?" Walden murmured. "If she has eloped, then your efforts will be for naught."

"If she eloped," Ned replied, "she took nothing. Not a spare dress, not her hairbrush, not an extra pair of stockings." Ned moved to the fireplace, for the spring evening had a chill. "People who have little tend to value their possessions. Miss Arbuckle's greatest treasure was a locket with miniatures of her parents painted inside. She left that behind."

Stephen settled into an armchair. "Could she be the victim of a robbery gone awry?"

"In Mayfair? She carried no money, not even a parasol. She never reached the cobbler's shop, so she didn't have so much as a parcel to steal."

His Grace propped an elbow on the mantel and gazed into the fire. Quinton Wentworth had become of a piece with elegant surrounds like this room. He'd shed the trappings of poverty to fit in with Axminster carpets, staid portraiture, and fine brandy served in crystal glasses.

He did not simply play the part of a duke, he *was* a duke. How had he transformed himself to that degree?

"Thieves have been known to strip their victims naked simply to sell the clothes," Walden said. "A lady's maid in an earl's house would have decent boots, a bonnet, a cloak. That's all worth stealing, to some. If she fought against her attackers, she might well have been injured."

"Not likely, not seriously injured in any case," Ned said. "Theft usually merits transportation. Injury to the person in the course of a theft is more likely to get a fellow the noose." As could using any sort of weapon while committing a crime. English law was curiously sporting in that regard.

If a thief depended on only light fingers and quick wits, the law showed him a hint of clemency. Bring force or a weapon into the picture, and the clemency vanished.

Walden and his brother exchanged a glance. *Neddy knows of what he speaks.*

And not because Ned had studied law at university, though he had.

"You'll have a word with the abbesses?" Walden asked.

"I'll start that round of inquiries tonight." Though Ned dreaded anything to do with brothels and their denizens. If asked, he cited the disease rampant in such environs as his reason for abstaining, but disease wasn't the half of it.

"I can accompany you," Stephen said. "The ladies doubtless miss me now that I'm a happily married fellow. I will chat them up to aid your cause."

"Do you miss them?" Ned asked. Before marrying Abigail, Stephen had somehow parlayed lameness and eccentricity into attractive features where women of a certain ilk were concerned.

"Neddy, I will not call you out for asking me that question because you occupy the vast, stultifying darkness known as bachelorhood. You wander an airless and desolate plane, searching for you know not what, your heart relentlessly thirsting while you swill the waters of hedonism without surcease."

Walden found it necessary to consult his pocket watch, though the duke's shoulders twitched suspiciously at this description of *Stephen's* bachelorhood.

"I'll take that for a no," Ned said. "You have sense enough not to miss your erstwhile preferred foolishness. I have never swilled the waters of hedonism, and the closest I've come to stultifying darkness is the conversation to be had at most Mayfair entertainments. You have been married for less than three years, and are in anticipation of your second disruptive event. I would otherwise call you out for intimating that I am the same variety of idiot bachelor you were."

Abigail was six months gone with child number two, and according to her husband's faultless judgment, she grew more radiantly lovely with each passing week. To Ned's eye, the lady looked a bit tired and worried.

"If Miss Arbuckle hasn't eloped," Walden said, "and she hasn't been taken into a brothel, where else will you look?"

"Newgate," Ned said. "The jails, the sponging houses."

"Don't forget Marshalsea," Stephen said. "The sooner she's out of there the more likely she is to live to a happy old age."

Marshalsea, London's largest debtor's prison, was notoriously rife with diseases, as was Newgate. Crime could pay very well, but the punishment if caught was often lethal even when no noose was involved, to say nothing of the dangers of transportation.

"I will, of course, have a look among the debtors," Ned said, "but if you were a clean, well-spoken domestic going about your mistress's business on the busy streets of Mayfair, and you were taken up by the watch, what's the first thing you'd say?"

"I didn't do it?" Stephen suggested.

"No," Ned said, "because that's what every crook ever arrested says. You'd invoke the consequence of somebody who could inspire the watch to have a care. You'd tell them precisely who you worked for and what that august personage would do to anybody who interfered with the timely execution of your appointed duties."

"And you won't tell us who has tasked you to search for this missing maid?" Walden asked, slipping his watch back into its pocket.

"The matter requires discretion." Lady Rosalind would not want it known that she'd needed help only a convicted felon and former street thief could provide.

"You can trust us, Ned," the duke said gently. "You are donning a bit of shining armor and cloaking yourself in thankless decency. Sooner or later, you might need some henchmen, and we will be honored to serve."

"We'll rescue you," Stephen said, rising.

He need not add: *again.* When Walden had been pardoned by the Crown for a crime he'd not committed, he'd exercised a peer's consequence and hauled Ned out of Newgate with him. A boy facing transportation had never been more grateful or bewildered.

And Ned was grateful, still. Always would be, until his dying day.

"I must be going," Walden said. "Stephen, can you give me a lift?"

"Of course. I'll have copies of Neddy's sketch done by tomorrow morning, and I will put the mystery to Abigail."

"I will consult with my duchess," Walden said. "Jane worries about you, Ned."

"I am all of two streets over," Ned said. With the arrival of the fourth child to the Walden nursery, Ned had made a discreet exit from the ducal household and set up his own quarters. The privacy was marvelous, while the loneliness was...a bit, well, stultifying.

"Jane worries anyway," Walden said, passing

Stephen his second walking stick. "You are to call on her early next week. Don't put in a quarter-hour's penance at her at-home, call upon her. She hears gossip that would never reach male ears, and you are now the family bachelor."

"Is that a warning?" Ned replied, taking another sip of his brandy.

"Matilda and Duncan are coming in from Berkshire next week," Stephen said, "and Constance and Althea are in Town to do some shopping. Your fate is sealed."

Duncan was a Wentworth cousin, a sober fellow a few years older than Walden. Althea and Constance were siblings to Walden and Lord Stephen, and both had found husbands in Yorkshire. They had dragged their spouses south to remark the occasion of Stephen's wedding ball, and annual spring sojourns had followed.

"My fate was sealed when I was eight years old," Ned said. "With some help from His Grace, I unsealed it."

"You did," Walden said, extending a hand, "and I have ever been proud of you as a result." He thumped Ned on the shoulder as they shook, a display of affection that had become His Grace's habit right about the time of Lord Stephen's nuptials.

And every time it happened, Ned was surprised, pleased, and embarrassed.

"When the right lady comes along," Stephen said, "you will go meekly and gratefully into the wonderous light of her affection, Neddy. You will scheme to win her favors and bless the day she grants them. Trust me on this."

With the occasional willing woman, Ned went gratefully to bed, but as for the rest of it...

"Good night," he said, bowing to Stephen rather than extending his hand. When a man relied on two canes, handshakes could become awkward.

"You were born for domesticity, Neddy," Stephen said, tucking one cane under his arm and downing the last of his drink. "Jane and her legion of Valkyries will have you married by June. It's your turn."

No, it was not. "That reminds me," Ned said, pausing by the private parlor's door. "You were right, Walden. Cadwallader is rolled up. He's trying to marry off the self-same daughter whose entertainments have been bankrupting him for the past three years. Clotilda is vain, dimwitted, and chattery. Cadwallader isn't titled, so I don't see it ending well."

"He's old money," Walden said. "Somebody might take the bait in hopes of a title for a grandchild."

"He's apparently old debt," Stephen said. "How did you come by this *on dit*, Neddy?"

Lady Rosalind thought to thrill me with the news. "I hear things that don't reach titled ears."

"I'm glad you do," Walden said. "Cadwallader almost had me convinced to offer him a mortgage. We'll send him on to Barclays."

When Ned was once more alone in the cozy parlor, he took Walden's untouched brandy to the wing chair Lord Stephen had occupied. That last little bit, about Cadwallader, had been nice. To for once know something Walden or Lord Stephen hadn't yet learned was gratifying.

As the waiters cleared the table and Ned finished

the brandy, his mind wandered back to a question Lady Rosalind had asked him: Did he want a big family?

Of course not. Families were expensive and complicated. They required worrying about and feeding and keeping track of. Children especially were prone to getting into scrapes, and life was uncertain. What foolish god had thought it a sound plan for the human young to require years to reach independence when a parent could be carried off well before the child's need for that parent was at an end?

Besides, Ned had a family. He was a Wentworth in name and by association, and that should be enough family for anybody, certainly for gallows bait turned banker.

Ned finished the duke's drink and left the club, though he still had much to do before he could seek his bed.

* * *

"Miss Arbuckle is young," Mr. Wentworth said. "She's attractive and..." He waved a gloved hand.

Today he wasn't even pretending to search through the biographies. His eyes were shadowed, and he'd been five minutes late.

"She's smart?" Rosalind said. "Hardworking? Trustworthy?"

Mr. Wentworth dipped his head to speak very softly near Rosalind's ear. "Virginal. If the likeness is accurate, she has an air of innocence."

"I told you," Rosalind said, making no effort to keep her voice down. "Arbuckle is a decent girl. My father would only employ domestics of sound character, and the agencies we consult before hiring—"

Mr. Wentworth touched her forearm. The most fleeting brush, through three layers of fabric, but the shock of it, the intimacy, stilled Rosalind's tongue.

"I do not mean to impugn anybody's character or choice of domestics, my lady. I mean to suggest that to a certain unsavory business, a young woman with an air of innocence has particular appeal."

Oh. *Oh.* Rosalind paced off between the bookshelves. "You mean she's been taken up by an abbess?" One heard of such things, mostly in shocked whispers and bawdy jests, but it did happen. Otherwise, Rosalind herself might be permitted to cross the occasional street without her companion to her right and a muscular footman to her left and three paces back.

"I've asked questions," Mr. Wentworth said, following Rosalind deeper into the biographies, "but the answers will take some time, and every day the likelihood of finding her diminishes. She'd be traded up to York or the Midlands, possibly as far as Edinburgh or Dublin."

"Traded, like, like a horse or a pair of pistols?"

He nodded once, and today his gaze was all business.

"That's awful." That Ned Wentworth would know of such goings-on, and know how to investigate them, was also awful...and fascinating. "I've brought you a sketch of Arbuckle's predecessor." Rosalind withdrew the folded paper from her reticule. "If Arbuckle has an air of youthful innocence, Campbell is positively elfin. I doubt she is fifteen years old. Young enough that her disappearance could be attributed to an unsteady temperament."

Mr. Wentworth took the sketch, glanced at it, and tucked it into a coat pocket. "The next maid you hire must be plain and older, please."

"The less experience they have, the less they cost," Rosalind said. "And I prefer a lady's maid with some wit and mischief to her, provided she doesn't flaunt her wares at my brothers."

Rosalind had paced to the end of a row, right into a dead end. In the close confines of the shelves, Mr. Wentworth's height was more apparent, as was the immaculate care he took with his turnout.

George and Lindhurst could learn from his example. Rosalind's brothers fussed at great length about how their cravat pins rested amid the linen and lace of their neckcloths, but their gloves were often less than pristine, and they tended to smell of horse or tobacco, not of a sunny glade in an old, quiet forest.

"Your brothers would bother the help?" Mr. Wentworth asked. "Would they bother the help and then send a maid packing when she conceived?"

"You do not shrink from difficult topics, do you, Mr. Wentworth?"

"Would they?"

Rosalind sidled around him, which resulted in her skirts whispering against his breeches, her shoulder brushing his chest. The contact was fleeting, but...

But nothing, Rosalind sternly reprimanded herself. The topic at hand was Arbuckle, not Ned Wentworth's masculine splendor.

"George likes books and political debates," she

said, "and would have gladly taken holy orders. Papa wouldn't allow it, not until we get Lindhurst married off."

"Viscount Lindhurst is the heir," Mr. Wentworth said, this time following Rosalind more slowly. "He takes liberties with the domestics?"

The English language had too many ways to trivialize male philandering, and Mr. Wentworth apparently knew them all. "I've heard the housekeeper grumbling to Cook, but Lindhurst would not impose on my lady's maids. Even if he had, neither woman would leave her worldly possessions behind when she quit the household."

Mr. Wentworth gazed off across the room, which was deserted but for him and Rosalind. "You don't know that. Two pretty young maids going missing in the space of a few weeks is unusual, my lady. If your lady's maids got with child, Lindhurst's responsibility as a gentleman is to see to the support of his offspring. That's much easier to do if the mothers are willing to return quietly to their villages and dwell in rural penury."

Why had Rosalind not seen this possibility for herself? "I fear Lindhurst cannot afford to see to anybody's support. Word of his finances has reached your ears, which suggests his problems are chronic."

Mr. Wentworth's generally reserved expression acquired a cool edge. If Rosalind were seeking a loan from him, that glint in his eye would presage very strict terms indeed.

"Men who are profligate with their funds often cannot exercise restraint in other regards. Lindhurst might well have mis-stepped and taken extreme measures to hide his perfidy."

Rosalind moved to a different row of books. "If Lindhurst has ruined my maids, I will kill him."

"No," Mr. Wentworth said, sauntering after her, "you will not."

"A woman in service risks her position if she refuses the overtures of a scion of the house," Rosalind said, "and she risks everything if she accommodates him. Lindhurst can be charming, though, and I suppose love can make fools of even sensible young women."

Philosophers said that, most of whom happened to be men.

"Lindhurst wasn't offering your maids love," Mr. Wentworth said. "I will ask a few discreet questions and explore his potential culpability."

Mrs. Barnstable's voice drifted down the steps, a recitation of her preferred recipe for a tisane to settle the nerves.

"If Lindhurst is not to blame," Rosalind asked, "what is the next step?"

"I'm working my way through the sponging houses. I'll have inquiries made on the docks, and I've put the word out among my badgers. They notice much that otherwise goes unremarked."

"Badgers?"

"Flower girls, crossing sweepers, links boys, bank messengers, children at large, streetwalkers. They are the eyes and ears of London, and for a bit of coin, they will take a matter under advisement. I have consulted with a few of them, and they will compare notes with each other, but you must not get your hopes up."

Did Ned Wentworth have hopes? Rosalind's own hopes were limited to enduring the Season without becoming the butt of too much gossip, and hoping that Lindhurst would for pity's sake marry well. Maybe Clotilda Cadwallader would have him.

Mrs. Barnstable's quackery at the top of the steps was drawing to a close with admonitions to take care, mind the damp, and God bless.

"My hopes are not up," Rosalind said, "but when can we discuss further developments, Mr. Wentworth?"

"Shall I take you driving in the park on Monday?"

"That will serve." Though Rosalind hadn't driven out with a young man since...had it been two years or three? "Do you truly know those sorts of people, Mr. Wentworth? The links boys and flower girls?" *The streetwalkers?* Not even the London gossips alluded to him having connections such as that.

His smile was a little mischievous and a little sad. "Until Monday, shall we say one of the clock? And as for your question, my lady, I *am* those sorts of people." He bowed over her hand and strode away, just as Mrs. Barnstable began a dignified descent of the steps.

* * *

"I should be able to pay back the rest next quarter day." Evander, Viscount Lindhurst, smiled at George in his vanity mirror as if payment long overdue and short by half was a great benevolence between brothers.

Well, no matter. George was the Kinwood spare, and a loyal spare at that. "No rush, Lindy. Not as if I have the expenses you do."

"You don't have the amusements I do," Lindhurst said, wiggling his eyebrows. "I'm for Drury Lane tonight. Will you join me?" He selected a cravat pin from the jewelry box his valet, Higgins, held open for him.

A crumb of brotherly recognition was to be the interest paid on George's loan—on his loans, plural. Except that Drury Lane was silly, and George had seen everything on offer there at present.

"You'll fill the box without me, I'm sure. You could take Rosalind."

Lindhurst shuddered delicately on his vanity stool. "Please, George. My nerves. Rosalind expects to *watch* the performance. She's always shushing everybody and muttering the correct line when the actors blunder. The lads complain about her when they aren't composing odes to her unattractive attributes."

A spare's lot was that of peacemaker. Nobody had had to explain that to George, though Rosalind and Lindhurst made the job challenging.

"Perhaps the Cadwallader girl will favor you with a visit to your box."

"The gent does the visiting, Georgie darling." Lindhurst held up a gold pin tipped with lapis. "A bit daring for daytime, but it brings out my eyes, don't you think?"

George thought all of Lindy's sapphires had been pawned, and those gems truly had done justice to his lordship's Saxon-blue eyes. The gold would complement Lindy's beautiful blond curls, the towering maples in Hyde Park would accentuate his height, and the sun itself would attempt to rival his smile.

All the charm and looks in the Kinwood family reposed in the earl and his heir, leaving George to share Rosalind's dark hair and modest height. George had never stammered, but he'd never memorized entire plays either.

"Shall I fetch the matching sleeve buttons, my lord?" Higgins asked.

Lindhurst turned on his stool, so Higgins could insert the pin into the lacy cascade at Lindy's throat. Higgins managed this without brushing Lindhurst's chin, or otherwise presuming on the lordly person. The whole exercise of dressing, a ritual young men of leisure enjoyed performing before their peers, struck George as a reinvention of nursery routines.

Help me, Nurse, for my little thumbs cannot manage my own buttons.

"You should let Higgins dress you," Lindhurst said, rising. "And yes, Higgy, please do fetch the lapis sleeve buttons. One wants to be properly turned out, eh?"

George made do with the good efforts of Papa's valet, a venerable soul by the name of Coop. Coop looked after George's clothes, and George got himself into them on all but the most formal occasions.

"Will you pay a visit to the Cadwallader girl between acts?" George asked.

"I should," Lindy replied casually, rising as Higgins backed away with the jewelry case. "She's said to be worth ten thousand a year. No title, but titled families can be inbred."

The Kinwoods were titled. Had been for centuries. "Miss Cadwallader is pretty," George observed, which was surely an understatement. Clotilda's golden beauty outshone even Lindhurst's.

"They are all pretty, given enough time with the modistes and finishing governesses." Lindy held out one wrist, then the other, while Higgins substituted gold-and-lapis sleeve buttons for plain gold. "Clotilda could do far worse than to attach an earl's heir."

She could do better than to attach *this* earl's heir. Lindy wasn't a bad sort, but as Rosalind had observed, he was lazy. In her estimation, if a man could not make the effort to manage his own exchequer, how could he be trusted to oversee the management of a household, much less an estate, much less a share of responsibility for governing an entire empire?

Rosalind was afflicted with great stores of logic and exhibited them at the worst possible times, poor dear. She'd further opined that the Crown, perpetually in debt while reigning over the wealthiest nation on the planet, was the *apotheosis* of irony. Lindy had opined in his turn that women were not to use words of more than three syllables.

To which Rosalind had replied that for Lindy to boast of his ability to count all the way to five was beneath the dignity of a peer's heir, though she understood why he took pride in his accomplishment.

And that, blessedly, had been enough for Papa to send the combatants to their figurative neutral corners.

"You're off to lounge at shop windows?" George asked.

"As one does," Lindy said, slipping a cloisonné snuff box into his pocket, surveying the result in the cheval mirror, then removing the snuff box. "Ruins the line. Why must snuff boxes be so boxy?"

Higgins busied himself collecting the half dozen discarded cravats festooning the dressing closet.

"You don't even take snuff," George said.

"I know *how* to take snuff is the point, and one wants to offer same to one's friends. Lady Walters sent along an invitation to her Venetian breakfast. Do you suppose Roz will inflict herself on that gathering?"

That was a bit harsh. "On Thursday? I expect she'll go. Papa demands that she show the colors and collect the gossip." Papa also demanded that Roz serve as his hostess, which wasn't quite the done thing when Roz was neither a married lady nor old enough to qualify as doddering—yet.

"I can escort her," Lindhurst said, holding still while Higgins threaded three watch chains across his lordship's midriff. "Fraternal duty and all that."

"Enough of your martyred sighs," George said, though they were very convincingly martyred sighs. "Roz isn't eighteen anymore. She's learned how to go on, more or less."

"But she has her causes, Georgie, and she's infernally passionate about them. I've never heard a woman wax so strident on the topic of cockfights, and it's not as if gamecocks sit down to tea with one another when left to their own devices in the barnyard. Rosalind ought never to admit she knows of cockfighting, much less bring the topic up in polite company."

George was diplomat enough to let that declaration go unchallenged. Rosalind's theory was that Lindhurst's laziness had been indulged for too long. He wasn't stupid in her opinion, he was spoiled. He used his intellect rarely and only for the amusement of his friends—*bon mots* being the mark of a true man about Town—or for his own ends. Lindhurst would not tax his brain to solve a problem for another, unless doing so would amuse or impress his cohorts.

Once Roz had pointed out that pattern, George had tacitly watched for it, and seen the proof in Lindhurst's behavior—and also in Papa's.

"If you're for Almack's on Wednesday," George said, "a Venetian breakfast on Thursday might be a bit early for you." Those breakfasts were mid-afternoon affairs, and ghastly if the weather was disobliging. This early in the year, the weather was mostly disobliging. "I'll escort Roz."

"You're sure?" Lindhurst said, turning to present his trim profile to the mirror. "Do I carry the gold-handled walking stick or the plain mahogany? I vow I make more decisions before leaving my apartment than Parliament does in an entire session."

"Plain mahogany," George said, as Higgins maintained a discreet silence. "Understated elegance and so forth."

"George, your good taste does you credit. I'll let you do the honors with Roz on Thursday then, but only because you insist. Next time, it's my turn. I know my duty. Higgy, my hat."

Higgins opened a wardrobe in the corner of the room and produced a shiny black high-crowned beaver.

"For pity's sake, man, not black," Lindhurst said. "I'm carrying the mahogany walking stick, so I must have the chocolate fondant hat. Cream gloves rather than white. You are woolgathering, Higgy. Perhaps dreaming of the fair Mrs. Barnstable's ankles?"

Higgins produced a glossy brown hat of the same cut and dimensions as the black. "I'm sure I don't know anything of such an indecorous subject, my lord."

Lindy tapped the hat onto his head. "I'm sure you do, my good fellow. I would never begrudge a man an appreciative regard for the fairer sex. Gloves."

Higgins passed them over—palest cream—and the picture of sartorial perfection was complete. "Enjoy your outing, my lord."

"I always do. George, I wish you a pleasant day. See me to the door, would you?"

They left Higgins to tidy up the battlefield, which he would do well before the evening skirmish. By then, Lindy's daytime attire would acquire smudges on the gloves and ale stains on the lacy cravat. His coat would be wrinkled, his hat likely crushed, and his boots unfit for wear beyond the stable.

Higgins—and a steady supply of orders to Bond Street—would magically put all to rights. If Lindy's valet gazed adoringly at the somewhat embonpoint Mrs. Barnstable, he was due at least that much joy in life.

"You asked me earlier about Clotilda Cadwallader," Lindy said, as he made his way to the balustrade encircling the main foyer. "I tell you, George, I might have to consider her. Please keep a lookout as you make the rounds with Roz. If there's anything untoward about Miss Cadwallader, if I'm to have competition for a lady in her third season, if she has a secret penchant for faro, a fellow needs to know that before he does the pretty and makes an ass of himself."

"Isn't Rosalind better situated to unearth such information? I'm the spare, Lindy. I should be composing sermons in some rural parsonage." Thank heavens the business of war was at low ebb for the nonce. Papa might begrudge the church the use of his spare, but if the military had need of officers, George well knew what his fate would be.

"Roz has no patience for refined company. What's this?" Lindhurst peered over the balcony while pulling George back a step.

Rosalind herself, attired in a carriage dress, was greeting a caller at the front door.

A male caller, at whom she *smiled*.

"I do value punctuality in a fellow," she said.

The gentleman, who was exquisitely attired, bowed over Roz's hand and murmured something George could not catch. Then he and Rosalind were out the door.

"What the devil?" Lindy muttered. "What the perishing devil? I know that man. He's the Duke of Walden's lackey. Some say he's Walden's by-blow. Checkered past, received when necessary, but nobody's idea of a good catch. Goes by the Wentworth name, though he's not listed in Debrett's, if you take my meaning."

A duke with a by-blow? How utterly unexceptional. "Perhaps the fellow likes difficult women," George said. "Rosalind isn't anybody's idea of a good catch either." Roz was lovely, in her way, but she was too fierce and outspoken, and not witty enough to have made the ranks of Originals. She was too young to be a true spinster, and too wellborn to be unnoticed.

"Wentworth is a *banker*," Lindy said, his fine

golden brows knitting. "Has Roz gambled away her pin money? Papa won't care for that at all."

"Don't be mean. Rosalind does drive out with the occasional fellow, or she used to, and your friends are doubtless waiting for you."

"So they are. Do ask Roz what she's about, George, or perhaps I will. I meant what I said about escorting her to her next little outing. I know my duty."

Lindy touched a gloved finger to his hat brim, perched a hip on the curved banister, and slid down the polished wood to the foyer like a schoolboy showing off for his fellows. His dismount was graceful, like everything else he did.

But Lindhurst had not meant what he'd said about escorting Rosalind to her next social obligation. He would find an excuse, a scheduling conflict, a slight head cold, some reason why he could not be bothered to spend time in polite society with his own sister.

And perhaps that was for the best, all things considered.

Chapter Three

"We had a narrow escape," Lady Rosalind said as Ned escorted her to his curricle. "We very nearly collided with Lindhurst at the start of his appointed rounds."

A narrow escape in Ned's experience was being hauled out of Newgate by ducal decree hours before you were to be moved to the hulks, there to rot—or worse—while awaiting a transport ship.

"You and your brothers don't get along?"

"George is nice enough, but Lindy has an exaggerated opinion of his own cleverness. He is the heir, and thus owed the awe of his younger siblings and the world at large." Her ladyship climbed onto the bench nimbly, and Ned would not have been surprised to see her take up the reins.

"I thought siblings were to be protective of one another."

"I am protective of my brothers," she said, as Ned came around the vehicle and took the place beside her. "To the extent they'll allow it. What of you, Mr. Wentworth? Any siblings?"

"None." Ned took up the reins and considered letting that polite half-truth serve. He was driving out with the lady to discuss her troubles, not to burden her with his past, and yet...Rosalind deserved at least a three-quarter truth.

"I had an older brother. He did not survive his thirteenth year." Poor Robert had not been lucky enough to deserve transportation.

"I am sorry for your loss. When my mother died, I felt as if I was half-asleep for the entire period of mourning, and all around me, people were pretending...Well, it was difficult. To lose a sibling must be even worse."

Ned gave the horses leave to walk on, which at this hour of the day was about all they could manage. The streets were thronged with fashionable carriages, drays, cabs, pedestrians, stray dogs, and other effluvia, including a herd of a dozen geese flapping and honking along the green side of Park Lane.

"I love this," Lady Rosalind said. "Love the hum and bustle. There's no place on earth like London in springtime. What of you? Do you prefer country or city?"

This discussion had nothing to do with finding a missing maid—a missing pair of maids—and yet it wasn't quite small talk either.

"I am a banker," Ned said. "We ply our trade in or near the City, and in cities generally."

"I am an earl's daughter and must be dragged 'round the usual Mayfair blandishments each spring until I am too elderly to be presented as anybody's potential wife. That doesn't mean I enjoy any part of it."

They passed into the park proper, and into quieter and less malodorous surrounds. "You don't like turning down the room in a new frock?" Ned asked. "Don't enjoy sharing the latest tattle with other women?"

Her ladyship was quiet for so long that Ned realized he'd blundered. With Althea and Constance, the Wentworth sisters, he knew how to go on. But for a little teasing and a little blunt opinionating, they mostly left him in peace. They were married now and busily managing their adoring spouses.

The Duchess of Walden, Jane, had been as much at sea to find herself married to a duke as a very young Ned had been to find himself employed by one. Ned and Jane had rubbed along, with her taking the role of older sister and deportment instructor. Ned would die for Her Grace, but all his conversations with her revolved around Wentworth family business.

To genuinely converse with a lady was a novel challenge.

"One doesn't turn down the room in a new frock," Lady Rosalind said pleasantly, "unless one is asked to dance. That great blessing has befallen me in the past two years only if my partner is some widower or aspiring cit my father seeks to flatter or an aspiring cit's son. One doesn't exchange tattle with the other ladies unless one is included *in* their gossip rather than the butt *of* their gossip."

Ned hadn't merely blundered, he'd tromped on very sore toes indeed. He inventoried options—what would Quinn Wentworth do in such a situation? Stephen Wentworth?

The duke would change the subject. Stephen would recount all the gossip that he himself had caused. The final Wentworth male by birth, Duncan, was a former cleric turned country squire, and his inspiration proved the most helpful.

"My lady, I am sorry," Ned said. "I did not mean to make light of a circumstance painful to you. If you must know, I prefer the country." The curricle rolled along beneath maples leafing out in all their gauzy green glory, and Ned was reminded of Yorkshire, rife with sheep and fresh air, domed with a sky as big and blue as heaven. "The duke first took me north when I was a boy, and the sheer wonder of realizing that a great, beautiful world lay beyond London's filth and squalor still awes me. I've been back to Yorkshire a few times. The quiet grows on me."

Her ladyship sent him a curious glance from beneath her bonnet brim. "You don't care for London?"

"I live here. It's home, I suppose." In London, Ned had lost his parents and his brother, then his liberty and his birthright, as humble as that birthright had been. "The noise and chaos, the utter lack of compassion for one's fellow creatures, the stink and disease, the canting preachers, and canting politicians... All that is vile and contemptible about the species is concentrated here, no matter how many pretty churches we erect or parks we build."

Another silence ensued, this one more thoughtful. "But we have libraries, Mr. Wentworth. We have the foundling hospital, the newspapers, the charitable organizations. Campbell came to me from a Magdalen house. There is hope here, too."

The Wentworths embodied that hope, in their many charitable undertakings and in their refusal to risk their business for the sake of some peer's social convenience.

"The Magdalen houses work the women unmercifully," Ned said, "and pay them next to nothing. In some of those places, the residents aren't even permitted to speak as they work, and a matron drones scripture at them every waking hour. Campbell was lucky to find a post with you and probably very grateful for it." He turned the curricle down a shady lane, relieved to have the discussion back on safer footing.

Though what did it say, that kidnappings were safer footing than Ned's opinions about London generally?

"Precisely," Lady Rosalind said, untying her bonnet ribbons and setting her hat on the seat beside her. "Campbell had found a position she delighted in and would not have left me of her own accord. I came across a better likeness of her."

Her ladyship rummaged in her reticule and produced another sketch of a girl with a vivacious smile and big eyes. All the high spirits in the world beamed from those eyes, as did a certain arch, knowing quality.

Brothels would pay excellent money for Campbell's combination of innocence and sophistication. If she'd been in a Magdalen house at fifteen, she was no Puritan, though she had clearly sought to put that aspect of her past behind her.

"She's quite attractive," Ned said. Gorgeous, in precisely the wicked, beautiful, blameless manner of the best courtesans. At fifteen, Harriette Wilson had taken her first titled lover and done quite well for herself.

"Papa insisted I was daft to hire Campbell," Lady Rosalind said. "He claimed she'd nick the silver and be gone before Sunday services. Mr. Wentworth, she was a paragon. She tried so hard to be conscientious in her duties, and then she didn't come back from her half day. Papa still lectures me about my foolish attempts at charity."

Ned commenced lecturing himself: *Should have started with the brothels and cribs, should have begun with the opera dancers. Should have interrogated the streetwalkers right off, and to hell with wasting time at the sponging houses.*

"Were Campbell and Arbuckle able to read and write?"

"Yes. Why?"

"Because if the problem was indebtedness, the first stop is a sponging house. The people who run those establishments don't make money by delivering their prey to the debtor's prisons. They make money off debts paid, and services rendered while the debtor languishes at the sponging house. The first service offered is to send word to friends and family that the debtor has been arrested. The debtor is given paper and pen, and away the messages go."

"And sending those messages adds to the tally owed, is that it?"

"The debtor, impecunious to begin with, is forced to incur more debt for everything from daily bread, to water to wash with, or a blanket for a cot to sleep on. A small arrearage becomes ruinous in no time. Would the ladies have sent word to you if they'd been taken up for debt?"

"Yes, I'm sure they would have."

Ned drew the horses to a halt and asked the next

logical question. "Would you be permitted to *receive* such a message?"

Rosalind gazed at the sketch of the merry, pretty girl. "I hope so."

"But you don't know so."

"No, I don't. I can ask the first footman. Hicks will be honest with me."

"Ask," Ned said, "though I doubt the solution to the mystery is debt. A lady's maid doesn't have much opportunity to amass debt."

The shopkeepers never extended credit to mere domestics. *Should have started with the brothels.*

Ned was distracted from that dreary thought by the realization that Lady Rosalind had a lovely profile, also a few subtle freckles across her cheeks. The arch of her dark brows gave her face piquant charm. Foxes had the same alert, inquisitive air, as if creation owed them answers. Lady Rosalind's defined chin and jaw suggested her inquiries would be thorough, while that lush mouth...

I have no business admiring a woman's mouth, even if she does have a very pretty pair of lips.

"If my maids were not sent to the sponging house, what is the next reasonable line of inquiry?"

"Would you care to drive for a bit?"

That mouth that Ned had no business admiring turned up into a soft smile. "I would adore a turn at the ribbons."

"This is as steady a pair of lads as you'll find in the whole of London," Ned said, passing over the reins. "They have perfected the art of looking hot-tempered and half-wild, but they're actually quite lovely."

As Lady Rosalind's smile was lovely, beguiling even, which was of no relevance whatsoever.

She signaled the horses to walk on, and Ned was left with nothing to occupy his hands. Artie's words, about Lady Rosalind being all sweet and sunny, and bearing the fragrance of springtime, came to mind.

Canny little fellow, Artie.

"You didn't answer my question," Lady Rosalind said, feathering the curricle through a turn. "What next in terms of searching for my maids?"

Ned dreaded what came next. "For Campbell, it's probably too late, if she's been missing for weeks. For Arbuckle, it's time to inquire of the abbesses and street-walkers. I've already asked a few questions, and I'll follow up over the next several days." And nights.

The prospect was vile, but then, how much more vile was tenure in a brothel to a decently raised lady's maid who sought only to send some wages home to her aging parents?

"The situation is hopeless, isn't it?"

Yes. "Nothing is hopeless," Ned said. "You can give up all you please, but some corner of your heart will still hope." Hope that a miracle might spring a small boy from prison, hope that a brother condemned to die might be given a reprieve.

"Do bankers frequently deal in hope, Mr. Went-worth?"

"Never." Walden had pounded that lesson into Ned's head early and often. Ned had thus asked to be kept away from any aspect of the bank's dealings that related to extending personal loans, and His Grace had mostly obliged him.

"But you hope anyway," Lady Rosalind said. "I do too."

Ned liked that about her, liked that she had an indomitable streak, and if the discussion had proven anything, it was that Lady Rosalind was not the typical self-absorbed Mayfair miss. Ned wasn't sure exactly what she was, but he had gained some sense of what she was not.

The curricle rolled along through dappled shade and leafy pathways, birds flitting overhead. Ned's duties at the bank called to him, and yet, he resisted. An hour in the fresh air with Lady Rosalind was an unlooked-for gift, and if he could not bide in the country, he could at least enjoy this hour.

"I attended Lady Barrington's musicale last night," Lady Rosalind said. "The cellist was excellent, the pianist even better."

What had this to do with anything? "You enjoy music?"

"Some music." The horses shied at a darting squirrel, and her ladyship soothed them back into a placid walk. "Not bawdy songs that compare the fair Ros-a-lind to the full-rubbish-bin."

Ouch. "Tell me about the musicale."

"Miss Cadwallader's friend, Lady Amanda Tait, allowed as how she might consider your addresses, provided you agreed to join her uncle's shipping business."

Ye gods, the Yorkshire countryside was calling to Ned more and more strongly. "Somebody certainly ought to introduce the concept of management into Apollonius Tait's affairs. He rackets from feast to famine, and since Waterloo, the fare hasn't been feast." That much was common knowledge in the City.

Amanda Tait was another young lady who'd not bagged a proposal in her first Season. She was more sensible than most, but she gazed upon Ned as if she were considering bidding on him at Tatts. They all did. She was simply more honest about it than most.

"Then you might consider approaching Miss Tait?"

"I have no interest in Miss Tait, or in the thankless task of rescuing her uncle's business, but I appreciate the warning." Jane would likely have passed along the same warning had Ned paid a call on her.

"Do you appreciate the warning enough to escort me to a Venetian breakfast on Thursday? We could compare notes while I tend to a social obligation."

Ned was coming to understand that Lady Rosalind was honest about her opinions, but much less forthcoming about her feelings.

"My lady, I earn my bread as a banker, but you need not make everything a transaction with me."

She sat up straighter, which, given her perfect posture at the ribbons, should have been impossible. "I have no idea what you mean, Mr. Wentworth."

"You won't ask me to escort you outright, instead you have to offer me some sort of bargain. A bit of gossip for an hour of my time. You are a lady. You can simply say what you need, and any gentleman should be honored to oblige you."

That inquisitive, alert countenance cooled to a fascinating degree. "No, Mr. Wentworth, I cannot."

"With me, you can." A gentleman didn't argue with

a lady, but Ned had no desire to hear the terms upon which half the young women in Mayfair would tolerate his marital overtures.

"And tell me, Mr. Wentworth, what do you want?"

"I have everything I want."

Her ladyship guided the horses through another turn, so the curricle completed a pleasant loop through the park's less-traveled byways.

"Then tell me, Mr. Wentworth, what do you *need*?"

* * *

"I would give anything for a bath," Francine Arbuckle muttered. She had never realized how badly she would miss Lady Rosalind's insistence on cleanliness.

"For me, a nip of gin wouldn't go amiss," Catherine Campbell replied, dividing the deck of cards in half and passing a stack to Francine. "You know they're getting ready to move us when they start giving us the gin, or worse."

"What's worse than gin?" To Francine, raised among God-fearing country folk, all the wickedness in the world was epitomized by the drink so freely consumed in London. Gin palaces, in her limited experience, were as grand as any actual palace could possibly be. All gilt and polish, good cheer, and gaiety.

Her granny had described them as the gates of hell, and nobody with any sense argued with Granny Arbuckle. Francine hadn't ventured beyond the front door of any gin palace, though, and had come to grief all the same.

"The guards will give the flighty ones opium,"

Catherine said, tidying her half of the deck. "Puts them right to sleep."

"And where do they wake up?"

"If I knew, I'd tell you."

"You have your suspicions, Catherine."

Catherine began placing cards facedown on the table. "The same ones you do. The same ones we all do, but meanwhile, we have enough to eat, a place to sleep, and nobody's interfering with us."

Francine started laying out the cards when she wanted to fling them to the floor. If a woman gave in to hysterics, the guards subdued her and she was taken away.

She did not return.

And Catherine had a point. The place they were kept was a combination rooming house and jail, large enough for perhaps a dozen women, and comfortable enough as long as Francine ignored boarded-over windows and locked doors. The only hint she had of the house's location was the occasional whiff down the chimney of the river stink that pervaded much of London.

Who would have ever thought such a rank, damp smell could be a source of comfort?

"What's it like?" Francine asked, placing her own cards facedown in no particular order. "To be with a man?" For surely she and Catherine were on their way to a brothel in Manchester or Portsmouth.

Catherine made a face and rearranged some of the cards on the table. "Depends on the man. Not much bother usually, unless you get a lively one or a bloke who can't finish. We might not be headed for the brothels. They could have long since disposed of us that way, if that was the plan."

"Then what are we doing here?"

"Haven't a clue. Your turn to go first."

Francine made herself focus on the cards, though fear and worry were tearing her to pieces. "I've been here a week already. How much longer can they keep us?"

"I've been here better than a month. They took all the other girls away when I'd only been here a few days."

"You were spared because Hiram likes you." Hiram, the youngest and largest of the guards, spoke in the soft accents of the north and looked upon Catherine with obvious yearning.

"Hiram *wants* me," Catherine said, very pointedly not glancing in the direction of said Hiram, who lounged at his usual post by the door. "Not the same thing as liking. Will you play this infernal game, or do we pretend to read Mrs. Radcliffe's drivel?"

Mrs. Radcliffe's heroines would have been swooning by the hour to find themselves in Francine's shoes.

"How have you not gone mad?" Francine asked, picking up two cards at random—a knave and a seven.

"You know what nearly drove me mad?" Catherine turned over the same knave Francine had, and one other. "That Magdalen house. They about send you to Bedlam with their sermonizing and bad food and end-less laundry. We weren't paid a quarter what a laundress is paid, we weren't allowed out, we weren't permitted visitors unless they were from some rubbishing char-itable organization. I don't fancy another turn on the street, but I won't go back to that place either."

"You cheated," Francine said. "You peeked at the cards as you laid them down."

Catherine smiled, a startlingly warm-hearted grin. "Of course I did. I peeked when I shuffled, too. If you're going to play, play to win, me da always said."

"Show me how to peek." Granny Arbuckle would have disapproved, but Granny Arbuckle was in far-off Somerset, and Francine was unlikely to ever see her again.

She learned from Catherine how to cheat at Patience, and all the while, Hiram watched them from his place by the door.

* * *

One minute, Ned had been having a difficult, if necessary, discussion about the fates that could befall missing maids in merry olde Londontowne. The next, he was trying to come up with a polite answer to Lady Rosalind's entirely irrelevant query regarding his *needs*.

Her question flummoxed him. As a boy, he could have answered her: He'd needed his family to be well and for his papa to bring in enough work. He'd needed food. He'd needed a safe place to sleep. As short as the list was, every item on it had been cast to the wind before he'd turned ten.

Ned had been careful that nothing and nobody had become a *need* ever since.

"I need the good esteem of the Wentworths," he said slowly, an admission he would rather not have made. "I need to do well at my appointed duties." The bank relied on him, the duke relied on him, and the duchess in her way relied on him most of all.

Or so he liked to think.

"That's all well and good," Lady Rosalind replied, steering the horses onto the verge to allow another vehicle to pass, "but those are needs everybody shares— to get on with family, to exhibit some competence in daily life. What are the needs that make you who you are?"

Ned felt the strangest compulsion to leap from the vehicle and take off at a dead run. "I require respect for my privacy, I suppose. A banker hears all manner of confidences he'd rather not. To keep his own affairs in hand matters to him a great deal."

Lady Rosalind smiled as she drew the horses to a smooth halt. "Touché, Mr. Wentworth. I need my privacy too, and I'd go so far as to say, I also need solitude. My companion, Mrs. Barnstable, regards this as a sign of inchoate eccentricity, but she enjoys her hours at liberty nonetheless. Will you take the ribbons? I cannot go about Mayfair without my bonnet."

Ned accepted the reins, though that earlier question— what did he *need*?—had become a burr under his mental saddle. Annoying. Vexing. What sort of question was that, anyway?

"What of yourself?" he asked, as the lady dealt with her millinery. "What besides solitude do you consider a need?"

"That is complicated. I need to be taken seriously, to be seen as a person with a mind and heart as well as the usual feminine attributes. Napoleon said women are machines for making babies, and I suspect all too many Englishmen agree with him. If we're machines, why does reproduction so often kill us?"

Machines break down. Ned had sense enough not to say that, but he'd thought it, which proved the lady's point.

"A banker is supposed to be an abacus," he observed, clucking to the horses. "We look at the sum requested, the risks inherent in lending it, the security available to safeguard our interest, and we make a rational choice. When the result is a family's ruin, we shrug and say a loan would have only prolonged the inevitable and allowed them to sink deeper into debt."

"Unless that family is titled," Lady Rosalind said. "Then the debt can go uncollected for generations."

"Precisely," Ned said. "We apply one logic for the shopkeeper and another for the baron, and I find that inconsistency most trying." Thus he managed the bank's employees, and left the ruining and rescuing part to His Grace.

"You're a radical?" Lady Rosalind asked, as pleasantly as she'd ask how he took his tea.

Radicals in recent years had been the Crown's excuse for suspending habeas corpus, such that a man could be tossed into jail without charges being laid and then held indefinitely without any promise of a trial. And what dangerous, unreasonable needs drove those radicals?

Bread for their children, decent wages for their labors, housing that didn't collapse in a strong wind.

"I am not a radical," Ned said, "though like most loyal subjects of the Crown, I have concerns. John Coachman cannot be expected to manage the complexities of international trade, but I can't see that Parliament is doing a very good job of it either."

"Do you even *like* being a banker, Mr. Wentworth?"

"I like being a Wentworth," Ned said, signaling the horses to pick up the trot, "and thus I am a banker. His Grace saved my life, and I will repay that debt by loyally executing any task he gives me."

They crossed into Mayfair proper, with its attendant noise and chaos. Ned wanted to be rid of Lady Rosalind and her vexing questions, and he wanted to steer the horses back into the park's bucolic quiet.

"You are a loyal abacus," Lady Rosalind said. "If that's anything like being a machine for making babies, I don't envy you the post. Will you escort me to the Venetian breakfast, please? Lady Walters does like to show off her garden."

"I would be honored to accompany you." Ned gave Lady Rosalind the polite demi-lie a gentleman was bound to tell. Better that than more of the truths that came out of his mouth unbidden in her company.

"I wish I could accompany you on your inquiries," she said, when the stately Kinwood town house came into view seven eternities later. "I wish I could root through all those brothels and demand the return of my maids. I am worried sick about them, and I can do nothing but fret."

"I can make the inquiries safely, my lady, while your great good looks alone would put you in peril in such establishments. They'd dose you with absinthe or laudanum, and then I'd be looking for three missing women rather than two."

He drew the horses up in the porte cochere and

leaped down to assist the lady. She descended with his aid and stood for a moment, her gloved hands resting on his sleeves.

"You don't tell me not to worry, and you don't pretty it up for me. Thank you for that, Mr. Wentworth. At all times, I would rather know the truth, even the ugly truth."

No, she would not. She only thought she would. "I hope to have more to tell you when next we meet, my lady."

She stepped away and glanced up at the imposing façade rising to four stories. "You can't wait to get back to your ledgers, can you? I have that effect on most people."

Ned had not exactly enjoyed the past hour, but he did enjoy *her*. Liked her lack of small talk, her devotion to her missing domestics, her blunt speech.

"You challenge me," he said. "The only other women who do that are the Wentworth ladies. Their menfolk are better for being made to think on topics menfolk would generally rather avoid." His Grace, Lord Stephen, and Cousin Duncan would all agree with that observation. The womenfolk would merely smile at Ned for having stated the obvious.

Her ladyship looked only half-convinced. "I'm not simply a machine for making babies?"

"Far from it, and I am not merely a loyal abacus, though your reminder caught me by surprise." He took her hand and bowed over it. "Until Thursday, my lady."

She dipped a curtsy and Ned waited until she'd disappeared into the house.

As he took up the reins and signaled the horses to walk on, his mind presented him with another observation: Her Grace, the Wentworth sisters, Stephen's Abigail, and Duncan's Matilda would all brace Ned on any topic they pleased, however uncomfortable to him, and expect honest answers from him.

He might find the interrogations unpleasant, and even resent them, but he held each of those ladies dear and esteemed them greatly for both their integrity and their courage.

"Time to get back where I belong," he muttered, which set the horses' ears to flicking about. "Back to the ledgers I am paid so handsomely to mind."

Chapter Four

Venetian breakfasts were neither Venetian nor truly breakfasts. For Rosalind, they were a sort of outdoor penance, where she ran into people she'd rather avoid and had twice also acquired a bout of food poisoning.

"An orange," she said to Mr. Wentworth. "I will start with an orange."

He selected two from the bowl on the buffet. "Only an orange?"

"You will think me daft, but I don't trust Lady Walters's kitchen."

"What of her bread and butter?" Mr. Wentworth asked. "Safe enough?"

Safe was an interesting word in the context of Mr. Edward Wentworth. Rosalind had sorted through a year's worth of society pages and found no mention of him anywhere. The financial pages were equally silent, though his titled Wentworth associates were much commented upon.

Who was he? Who was he *really*? "A slice or two of

bread with butter will do," Rosalind said, "but not the croissants, please."

He assembled the food on one plate. "Let me guess: croissants are messy."

"As a girl, I loved them. I'd take mine to the garden to eat with jam and clotted cream, and no child ever indulged in such gustatory bliss. Let's find some quiet, shall we?"

The gardens stretching behind the Walters mansion were just beginning to come into their spring glory, with daffodils blooming in the occasional sunny corner and tulips still tightly furled in others. Pots of heartsease added color, and the new foliage on the birches and oaks stirred in the afternoon breeze. The setting would have been lovely, were it not for the traffic thronging the paths.

"This way," Mr. Wentworth said, turning down between two hedges. "I want to know what came between you and your gustatory bliss." He led Rosalind to a bench before a sundial, the hedges giving the place an air of seclusion belied by periodic laughter from the direction of the back terrace.

"Miss Tait is in good form today," Rosalind said, taking a seat on the sun-warmed bench. She ought to have asked Mr. Wentworth to find her a place in the shade, and she ought to have kept her parasol handy, and she ought to have declined this invitation, no matter how badly Papa would have fussed at her for doing so.

"One does not want to appear ungentlemanly," Mr. Wentworth said, taking the seat beside Rosalind, "but the lady does have a distinctive laugh. Rather like a coach horn with a stocking stuffed in the bell. Part bleat, part hoot. Shall I peel your orange?"

He offered his observation in such polite, bland tones that the analogy took a moment to bloom in Rosalind's imagination.

"Not a stocking," she said. "More of a hedgehog, desperate to get out."

"Just so." Mr. Wentworth passed Rosalind the plate and stripped off his gloves. "A hedgehog." He picked up an orange and began tearing the skin off, tossing the rind into the lavender border behind the bench. "Tell me about the croissants."

He would ask. "There's not much to tell, and everybody in polite society has heard the story, thanks to my brothers. I was enjoying my treat, as I usually did, but on the day of my ignominy, the crumbs attracted some particularly aggressive pigeons. I grew frightened because they would not desist, and I even suffered a peck or two. I ran crying into the house, a croissant clutched in my hand, only to learn that my brothers had observed the whole incident and found it hilarious."

The fragrance of the orange perfumed the air, and watching Mr. Wentworth dispatch the peel distracted Rosalind from an old tale that ought to no longer pain her.

Except it did.

"How old were you, my lady?"

"Eight."

"A difficult age, when we aren't as grown-up as we want to believe we are, or as our governesses insist we behave." He tore the orange into sections and set them on the plate. "Did you get even?"

"Even?"

He took up the second orange. "With your brothers, for their meanness. They should have raced into the garden to scare off the nasty birds. Not watched and laughed while a younger sibling grew frightened and flustered."

Ned Wentworth, aged eight, would have raced into the garden and sent those pigeons flapping for their lives. "How would you have evened the scales?"

He started on the second orange. "Retribution takes patience. I've watched Walden go about it, and with him it's always a polite financial transaction, sometimes years in the making. Personal slights he usually ignores, but anybody who attempts to cheat the bank is made to regret his folly. Walden is so calculating, so dispassionate about addressing a past wrong that it puts me in mind of how my father cut out a morning coat. Every snip exact, every seam perfectly straight, and yet the whole, thousands of snips and stitches later, was exquisite. Save for the color, the finished garment bore no resemblance to the bolt of fabric that had come in the door a fortnight earlier."

Rosalind took a succulent bite of orange. "Your father was a tailor?"

Mr. Wentworth paused in his peeling. "He was. I've been talking to the streetwalkers."

The subject had been unequivocally changed. Why? Was the forbidden topic the duke's interesting talent for retribution or Mr. Wentworth's patrimony?

"What have you learned?"

He munched a section of orange. "None of the ladies recognized the sketches. None of them have been approached by any new abbesses promising wealth and ease to young women willing to travel up to Manchester or over to Dublin."

"Dare I hope there's a *but*?"

He consumed more of his orange, and were his report not so worrisome, Rosalind would have marveled to find herself eating oranges in a sunny garden with a handsome and eligible bachelor.

"They know something," Mr. Wentworth said. "They suspect or fear something, but these women are nothing if not shrewd. They never work alone if they can manage it, always congregating in groups where gentlemen are likely to pass. They know that if presented with a selection, a man is more likely to make a choice than if he's given only one option. The question in his mind becomes *which one* rather than *the club or a diversion*?"

"I thought the ladies of the night worked in groups for safety," Rosalind said. "If a woman refuses an offer, she has two or three compatriots to chase the nasty pigeon away."

Mr. Wentworth peered at her, as if he might not have heard her aright, but he had.

Prostitution was a fact of life in London. Genteel women could ignore the reality, but they passed by it every day and every evening. Expensive brothels sat cheek by jowl with fashionable addresses, and a trip to the theater meant pretending transactions weren't occurring across the street from where the most elegant carriages waited.

"The ladies can't refuse many offers," Mr. Wentworth said. "But that's one advantage of working the street over employment at an established house. The streetwalker retains some choice of clientele and she keeps every penny of the proceeds."

Questions crowded into Rosalind's mind: Did the ladies ever refuse *him*? Did he patronize those established houses? A bleakness in his tone suggested perhaps not, and yet, Ned Wentworth was a man of means who had no attachments. Debauchery was his right and privilege.

"Are these women afraid to tell you what they know?"

He finished his orange and took out an embroidered handkerchief. "Perhaps. One learns discretion in their trade. If all they've heard are rumors and suspicions, they will be reluctant to say anything. I don't believe the women I questioned have seen Miss Arbuckle or Miss Campbell."

Rosalind finished her orange as well. "Will you make further inquiries?"

"Of course." He passed her his handkerchief. "I will explore farther afield. If your maids were snatched from the streets of Mayfair, prudence alone suggests they'll be employed in some other part of Town."

Some *unsavory* part of Town, where nobody knew or cared who Lady Rosalind Kinwood was, much less that she was missing her employees and worried sick about them.

"I wish I could do something," she said, scrubbing at the sticky juice on her fingers. "I feel the same way about the cockfighting and bear baiting and badger baiting. Cruelty for sport does not become a civilized society, and if we must exploit our base natures for the sake of profit, might we at least limit our violence to pounding on each other?"

"You are an advocate of the fancy?"

"Never, but grown men have choices that lowly animals do not. Do you know how dogs are taught to tear one another limb from limb?"

"As it happens," he said mildly, "I do, and I agree with you that the practice is barbarous. I'll have a slice of that bread, if you don't mind."

He agreed with her? *Agreed with her?* Rosalind passed over a piece of buttered bread. "You aren't planning to lecture me about natural urges and masculine humors and how dogs are born to fight?"

He tore the crust from his bread and stuck a piece into his mouth. Nothing with Mr. Wentworth was hurried, nothing spontaneous. If he sought to right a wrong, he'd be like the duke, relentless and methodical. If he kissed a woman, he'd be...

Well, that was neither here nor there.

"From what I've observed," he said, "dogs are born to cooperate with one another. They might snarl and snap or even nip at each other, but you seldom see a single stray dog loose on London's streets. They keep together, for warmth at night, for safety, for companionship. I've seen mongrels hunting rats, one dog chasing, one waiting at the mouth of the alley to snatch up the slowest rat. That is not the behavior of a species born to murder its kin."

Where had he seen such a sight?

Amanda Tait's laughter came again, closer this time. She truly did sound like an obstructed coach horn.

"While you are making inquiries, I cannot simply

sit at home sketching my cat. What can I be doing, Mr. Wentworth?" Rosalind smoothed her fingers over the embroidery of his handkerchief, surprised to see that the needlework was not a coat of arms or even a monogram, but rather, flowers.

Profuse, colorful, exquisitely precise flowers.

"You can make a few discreet inquiries of your own," he said. "Two lady's maids going missing might be a coincidence, or it might be the start of a pattern. Has anybody else mentioned a pretty, female domestic quitting without notice? Have you heard complaints about reliable help being harder to find?"

"Complaining about domestics is nearly as commonplace as remarking the weather," Rosalind replied, thinking back. "But then, I *attend* social gatherings, I don't particularly *participate* in them."

Mr. Wentworth gave her an odd smile. "You're participating in this one."

"Papa insists." Rosalind spread the handkerchief on her lap, marveling at the intricacy of the stitchwork. "He hopes that if he dangles me before enough bachelors, one of them will take me off his hands. Papa intimated at supper last night that Baron DeGrange is looking for another wife."

"*Another* wife?"

"DeGrange has buried two, and so far, has no sons to show for his marital endeavors."

"Are you tempted?"

She shook her head. "And Papa is only positing DeGrange as a hypothetical. Tonight he'll allow as how some silk merchant or pork nabob is looking to make an advantageous match for his firstborn son, and is willing to pay handsomely for the right bride."

"And do you owe it to your father to sell yourself to the pork nabob's piglet? With menfolk like yours, it's no wonder you expect to pay for every courtesy."

The disdain in Mr. Wentworth's tone was exquisitely veiled, also wonderfully gratifying. "George isn't so bad."

"Such a ringing endorsement."

The coach horn blasted again, closer still, and Rosalind, for the first time in memory, was tempted to laugh at a social gathering. Bad of her, when she had so often been the person laughed at, but Miss Tait never laughed like that in the retiring room, only in venues full of eligible bachelors.

"Hedgehog," Rosalind said. "I should never have said such a thing, but now all I can picture is a poor, wretched hedgehog."

Mr. Wentworth smiled back at her, the warmth in his eyes as brilliant and benevolent as spring sunshine. He really was quite handsome, and Rosalind really must stop looking at his mouth. She had tipped an inch closer to that gently curving, fascinating mouth—the mouth that did not argue with her and did pronounce her menfolk wanting—when she was interrupted.

"My gracious," drawled an amused male voice, "if it isn't my dear sister secreted behind the greenery with an unsuspecting fellow." Lindhurst sidled around the sundial, Miss Tait hanging on his arm, "Roz, do introduce us to your friend. I don't believe I recognize him."

* * *

Ned did not decide to whom the bank loaned money, but he did interview some of the parties seeking to borrow. Quinn, as the bank owner and resident duke, could not be troubled to conduct all of those interrogations, for impecunious peers were thick on the ground. Besides, His Grace insisted that Ned, as the closest thing to the bank's manager, be familiar with the lending process at least in theory.

Heirs and younger sons in want of coin were so numerous as to be the butt of humor among the clerks and tellers.

Baron Spender of Expectations and Inheritances.

The Earl of Misplaced Vowels.

The Honorable Mr. Abit Short and his younger brother Always Short.

Lindhurst might well have forgotten last autumn's tête-à-tête in Ned's office, but Ned easily recalled the interview. His job as a bank officer was to flatter and coax from the applicants as much information regarding finances as possible, thank them for the discussion, and assure them the committee would have a decision in due course.

The bank had been unable to extend credit to Lord Lindhurst, alas, and in his case, they hadn't even suggested that he put his request to another institution.

Lindhurst's titled father was in good health, while the viscount's finances were at their last prayers. And yet, here was Lindhurst, looking for all the world like the schoolyard bully preparing to enjoy himself at the expense of the new boy.

Ned considered lifting the viscount's pocket watch and then "finding" it at the bottom of the nearest birdbath. Lindhurst was owed some comeuppance for laughing at Rosalind all those years ago, wasn't he? But no. A respected banker—*a Wentworth*—ought to be above such a petty exercise.

"Miss Tait, Lindhurst," Rosalind said, popping to her feet and dipping a curtsy. "May I make known to you Mr. Edward Wentworth. Mr. Wentworth, I believe you know Miss Tait, and I'm pleased to acquaint you with my brother, Viscount Lindhurst."

Ned offered a bow. "Miss Tait, my lord. Good day. Beautiful weather for early in the Season, isn't it?" And was it on Miss Tait's account that Lady Rosalind's voice had taken on a subtle, lilting quality, or was Lord Lindhurst to blame?

"Too sunny by half," Lindhurst said, "and here's Roz without her parasol. What could you be thinking, sister dear?"

Miss Tait twirled the lacy confection resting upon her shoulder and swished her skirts gently. "Mature complexions are less likely to need protection from the elements, my lord. Her ladyship is wearing a bonnet after all."

Miss Tait's smiling perusal of Lady Rosalind's millinery implied that the bonnet barely qualified as such.

Ned's usual course when confronted with petty sniping in polite surrounds was to ignore the barbs, stick to platitudes, and escape at the first opportunity. He expected to serve as a target for belittling comments, because polite society could not very well aim its vitriol at the Wentworth family proper.

But Rosalind's bonnet was pretty, her freckles were charming, and Lindhurst was an ass.

"I actually prefer that a lady not hide away from fresh air and sunshine," Ned said. "Roses in the cheeks are so much more becoming than a cadaverous pallor, don't you agree, Miss Tait?"

Miss Tait, who had likely spent considerable coin on preparations intended to safeguard her cadaverous pallor, stopped twirling her damned parasol.

"Perhaps on a milkmaid, flushed cheeks are to be expected," Lindhurst said, "but I prefer refinement in a female companion."

Rosalind apparently found it necessary to stare past her brother's shoulder, her expression a polite mask.

"Refinement is all well and good," Ned replied, "but vanity quickly becomes tedious. Give me a lady who can command elegant reasoning and subtle humor, and spare me the die-away ninnyhammers with their obsession for passing fashions." He smiled blandly at Miss Tait, whose expression had become a trifle uncertain. "What qualities do you look for in a gentleman, Miss Tait?"

She took a firmer hold of Lindhurst's elbow and had gone so far as to open her mouth when Lindhurst spoke again.

"Miss Tait, being a lady in every sense of the word, wants a *parfit, gentil knight* in Bond Street tailoring, a fellow who will guard her with his life and brook no disrespect toward her."

Ned picked up his gloves from the bench and tucked them into a pocket. "I wish you good hunting then,

Miss Tait. The last time I looked, Mayfair boasted very few knights of the variety his lordship describes, much less in Bond Street tailoring. Lady Rosalind, shall we take a turn about the garden?"

He offered Rosalind his arm, and she took it.

"Good day to you both," she said, nodding graciously.

As he parted from the viscount and Miss Tait, Ned managed to brush against Lindhurst in the close confines between the hedge and the sundial. His lordship, predictably, pretended to ignore even that slight contact.

Ned and Lady Rosalind quit the vicinity at a placid stroll, and a silence ensued. Ned could not read that silence, a problem he mostly encountered with the Wentworth ladies. Among the gentlemen, silences could be angry, thoughtful, or even kindly, but the ladies remained a puzzle to him.

"I ought not to have antagonized them," Ned said, "but Lindhurst attempted to bribe me last autumn, and I take a dim view of such behavior."

"Bribe you?" Her ladyship sounded merely curious rather than appalled.

"In a business context."

They walked beside a row of birches, daffodils perfuming the air. The afternoon was pleasant, and yet, Ned wanted to be away from the garden. He should be back at the bank, though he didn't want to return there either.

Young men are restless in springtime, Jane would have said, and she didn't know the half of it.

"Let me guess," Lady Rosalind said. "Lindy applied to your bank for a loan, and you declined to waste your money. He tried to grease your palm, and you declined that folly as well."

"The bank has strict policies, and the decision wasn't mine to make." *Thank heavens.*

"But you could have influenced the outcome, couldn't you?"

"No," Ned said. "Walden applies a list of criteria and nothing outside that list sways a given case. Unlike private lenders, the bank can charge only five percent interest, so a loan in default creates significant difficulties for us. Your brother's tailors are apparently still accepting his custom, however, so he came right somehow."

"He always does. Lindy is a stranger to significant difficulties."

Ned strolled with Rosalind between another pair of privet hedges and came upon a birdbath. A half dozen goldfinches flitted around the water, several perched on the rim, others having a grand time splashing about.

"Do the birds bother you, my lady?"

"Not those pretty little fellows. I take exception to the gulls that pester the yachting parties or to the pigeons with their perpetual mess."

"I've always loved how much freedom birds have. They come and go as they please, and only God and the angels see the world as the birds do." Even in Newgate, the birds had flown in and out of barred windows, and scrounged for sustenance in the courtyard. They hadn't shunned the place, nor the crumbs left for them by a small boy who had moved beyond hunger.

"You are a poet, Mr. Wentworth."

"Hardly that." Though Ned liked to read poetry.

"You are upset with your brother." Lady Rosalind was no longer lilting her words. She had instead gone quiet, her gaze shuttered, and Ned could think of no other reason why that should be. *He* was upset with Lindhurst, who had behaved like the veriest boor.

"Lindy knew Papa expected me to put in an appearance at this affair," her ladyship said, "and had you not agreed to escort me, I would have had to apply to my brothers. I realize I am not in the first stare of anything. I am long in the tooth and too outspoken, but when Lindy planned to be here anyway..."

She fell silent, and the birds flew off, save for two little creatures who continued playing.

"Lindhurst wanted to accompany Miss Tait," Ned said, pulling his gloves from his pocket and making a little fuss out of putting them on. This minor commotion right beside the birdbath inspired the last two birds to fly onto a nearby branch and perch side by side. "Your brother put his own interests ahead of yours."

"As usual," Rosalind said. "I ought not to be surprised, and I don't particularly care that Lindy didn't escort me, but if he was planning to attend, he could have spared me the trouble."

"You truly don't care for social outings?"

"No," she said, studying the birds side by side on their branch, "I do not, though I find present company delightful and will thus ask you to join me on Monday for the Petershams' musicale. Very forward of me, but you did say I could ask."

Ned enjoyed music, and he enjoyed Lady Rosalind—found her delightful, in fact—and he indeed had said that she could simply ask him for what she wanted.

"I would be honored, and I might have more information for you by then regarding your maids." He would make the rounds of the brothels before Monday, and just get it over with.

Though London sported a deuced lot of brothels.

"Thank you," Rosalind said, shifting to take his hand. "Die-away ninnyhammers with an obsession for passing fashions...that was brilliant, Mr. Wentworth. Shall we find the punch bowl?"

"A glass of punch would suit," Ned said, winging his arm, then aiming a puzzled look at the depths of the birdbath. "*My gracious*, somebody dropped a pocket watch directly into the water. It looks rather pretty there, with the sunlight glinting off of it, don't you think?"

Lady Rosalind peered into the water, then at Ned. "That is my brother's..." Her features became luminous with mischief and joy. "He had his own miniature painted on the inside. I do believe that is Lindy's most favorite possession."

Ye cavorting nymphs of Olympus, that smile. That sweet, naughty, knowing smile. "What a shame his lordship was so careless with it."

"A pity," Lady Rosalind said. "A terrible pity." She kissed Ned's cheek, and Ned let her direct him back down between the privet hedges when all the while his insides felt as if the finches were leaping about where his vital organs should be.

Proper ladies did not press sweet little kisses to Ned's cheek. Such ladies did not think he was brilliant, much less approve of his lapse back into the larceny and rough justice of his boyhood.

Proper ladies did not ask him for anything—anything other than money—and even then, it wasn't his money they needed.

"Would you rather simply take leave of our hostess?" he asked.

Rosalind nodded. "How did you know?"

"I was ready to leave before the second blast of the coach horn." He patted her hand where it rested on his arm, though that did nothing to settle the riot inside him.

* * *

Ned Wentworth liked birds. His father had been a tailor. He did not use his influence at the bank to enrich himself. Best of all, he felt no temptation to linger among the parasol-twirling diamonds and rubies of polite society.

Rosalind felt like a bird herself, jealously snatching up crumbs about the man who sat so calmly beside her, guiding his horses through yet another thronged Mayfair street.

His silences were patient and self-contained, like landscape paintings. Much might be afoot within the scope of the scene depicted, but all the viewer saw was a single image, all elements of the composition in a pleasing balance.

"I suppose young ladies kiss you all the time." Rosalind hated—hated, hated, hated—the note of nervous uncertainty in her voice. Still, she hadn't stammered, that was something. Had not stammered when ambushed by Miss Amanda Tait either.

"The young lady most likely to steal kisses from me these days usually has to pull her thumb out of her mouth to effect her thievery. Her fingers are often sticky, and she has the sharpest little elbows a man ever did attempt to dodge."

"You have a daughter?" Ned Wentworth was handsome, more than solvent, and a scion of a ducal household, albeit informally so. That he had a by-blow should be no surprise.

"I refer to Lady Mary Jane Wentworth, youngest denizen of Their Graces' nursery. She has three older sisters, each of whom at some point regarded me as her favorite. Then Uncle Stephen or Cousin Duncan or—worst ignominy of all—some dog, kitten, or pony would come along and depose me. No amount of licorice drops or peppermint sticks can compete with puppies or ponies."

"You speak of these fickle damsels with great affection."

He turned the horses onto Rosalind's lane just as the breeze picked up. "I love them with all my heart, but then, who wouldn't? I have no sisters. My mother was gone much too young, and while I esteem Her Grace enormously, she has never climbed into my lap and demanded that I read her a story. The little girls, by contrast, besiege me."

That image, of Ned Wentworth patiently enduring the demands of small, determined females, did odd things to Rosalind's heart.

"Do you mind that I kissed you?"

He guided the horses around to the mews and drew them to a halt under the porte cochere. "Do I *mind* that you kissed me?"

"Young ladies are doubtless throwing themselves at you all the time, but you were so splendid with Lindy and Miss Tait, so self-possessed and at ease."

He wrapped the reins and leaped to the walkway. "While you were notably quiet. I exhort you to deliver a thorough scold to Windy Lindy when you have him behind a closed door. He was an utter dolt, and deserves to be charged a fortune for the repair of his watch." Mr. Wentworth came around and offered his hand to Rosalind. "Down you go, my lady."

Anxious to get rid of me? Rosalind had enough pride—barely—not to ask that question, and yet, when she alighted from the curricle, she made no move to retrieve her hand from Mr. Wentworth's grasp.

"If I had asked you to indulge me in another tour of the park," he said, "would you have obliged?"

"Yes." She would circle the park with him until the first snowfall, if he asked it of her. "Why didn't you ask me?"

He let go of her hand. "I am expected at the bank, my lady. Why did you kiss me?"

"Amanda Tait knows that I used to be afflicted with a stammer."

"Years ago. Years ago, I was an illiterate pickpocket. Even His Grace had difficulty pounding letters into my hard little head."

"The *duke* taught you to read?"

"Tried to. We both needed a diversion at the time. I had no use for the letters, but His Grace fascinated me. Tell me about the kiss, Rosalind, because that fascinates me too."

The porte cochere was a grand affair, arching over

the whole of the vehicle and ensuring the conversation had no witnesses. Rosalind was unlikely to have this much privacy with Mr. Wentworth in the foreseeable future, and the topic was best handled discreetly.

"To explain the kiss," she said, "I need to explain about Miss Tait. When Mama died, I developed a stammer, as I've told you. Papa sent me off to school, where a proper elocution teacher was to relieve me of that embarrassment."

Mr. Wentworth ambled up to the horses' heads, stuffed his gloves into his pocket, and loosened the near-side check rein. "How long had your mother been gone when you were banished to the land of elocution and deportment?"

Banished. Rosalind hadn't used that word, but that's exactly what it had been. "We hadn't started receiving condolence calls yet, so maybe two months. In any case, Amanda was the queen bee of the establishment, though she was two years my junior. I was an earl's daughter and thus a threat."

"Until you opened your mouth," he said, loosening the check rein for the second horse. "Then she had a weapon and could keep you in your place, not that you had any designs on her petty fiefdom."

The horses craned their necks and tossed their heads, clearly having needed a respite from the strictures imposed by their harness.

"Miss Tait made a game of me. Imitated my stutter and goaded the other girls into doing likewise. I see her now, and I can hear them all chanting my name, but stumbling purposely on the *L* in *lady* and *R* in *Rosalind*. They would swarm me like locusts, consonants buzzing, until I learned to retreat into silence. The headmistress did not notice the teasing, but she noticed that I'd stopped saying much of anything and sent me back to my father."

Mr. Wentworth stroked the neck of the nearest horse. "And now?"

"I see Amanda Tait, and the safest course for me is still silence."

"Then I wish I had dumped your brother headfirst into the nearest horse trough, and I am glad we did not tarry in Miss Tait's company. Is that why you kissed me, because I exchanged some small talk with her and his loathsome lordship?"

"Because you put her in her place," Rosalind said, "because you got even with Lindy for me, because I can ask you to escort me, and because you read stories to little girls and pine over their lost affections, and because..." Rosalind fell silent, appalled that tears were threatening.

Mr. Wentworth waited, patiently stroking the horse, who had calmed beneath his touch.

"You freed me from that situation with my dignity intact, Mr. Wentworth. I value my dignity." Though until that moment, Rosalind had never said as much. "I won't presume on your person again, but in the moment, I simply felt...I wanted..." She cast around for some way to end an increasingly mortifying confession. "You are so very kissable."

He took her hand again, and Rosalind was certain he was preparing to bow correctly and tool right out of her life. A polite note would arrive reporting no progress in the search for her maids, the postscript regretting an inability to escort her to any more musicales, break-fasts, or what-have-yous.

She'd find her heart glinting up at her from the bottom of the nearest birdbath.

"Once upon a time," Mr. Wentworth said, bending nearer, "I was a naughty, merry little boy, or so witnesses claimed. All the merriment and spontaneity were starved, beaten, and bullied out of me. I should never have sparred with Miss Tait, and never have lifted Lindhurst's bauble, but I could not resist the temptation to do a little mischief. That I yielded to my impulses does me no credit."

He framed Rosalind's face in his bare hands and paused, long enough for her to think *What is he about?*

"This is not an impulse, Rosalind. This is something I have considered at great length." He pressed his lips to hers, as softly as sunshine and as sweetly as joy. Rosalind sighed against his mouth and wrapped her arms around his lean waist.

Yes. Yes, yes, yes.

She had done very little kissing, but she had enough experience to sense that Ned was patient in this too, giving her time to settle into the moment. He tasted of citrus and his scent up close was honeysuckle and mown grass beneath that hint of cedar. The kissing was lovely, but even better was the pleasure of Ned Wentworth's embrace.

He knew how to hold a woman so she was enveloped in his strength without being overpowered. He was a sheltering edifice and masculine temptation all rolled into one, and Rosalind wanted to burrow into his heat and find all the mischief he yet commanded.

"Not here," he said, breaking the kiss and resting his forehead against hers. "Not now. I value my dignity too, Rosalind."

Rosalind remained in his arms, feeling as if she'd run a hard race and beaten all comers. That she could imperil Ned Wentworth's self-possession was a delicious thought. She allowed herself the space of a half dozen slow, deep breaths to linger in his embrace.

"Not here, and not now," she said, stepping back. "What did you mean?"

He let her go. "What I should have said was, *not me,* but you are kissable too, Lady Rosalind. Forgive me a momentary lapse, please?" His smile was all pleasantry and politesse, while Rosalind was still awash in wonder.

"A momentary lapse, Mr. Wentworth?" *But you said…*

"A very pleasant momentary lapse. I will look forward to our outing on Monday evening."

He did not sound as if he was looking forward to anything. He sounded all dutiful and friendly-distant, which was probably a demeanor unique to bankers.

Men in general confounded Rosalind, but she had a firm grasp of logic. Ned Wentworth had said his kiss was *not* the result of impulse, and now, two minutes later, he was calling it a *momentary lapse*. Those two descriptors were inconsistent, especially from a man who was neither flighty nor irrational.

A man who was eyeing the street as if calculating how quickly he could vault onto the bench and spring his horses.

"You need not fear that I'll descend into hysterics,"

Rosalind said. "I have been kissed before, Mr. Wentworth. The experience, while pleasurable, signifies nothing."

He pulled on his gloves. "Precisely. Pleasurable and insignificant. I do apologize for overstepping."

"I kissed you first."

He peered at her. "So you did, in a manner of speaking. Well, I must be off."

"To the bank." Rosalind waved a hand. "Duty calls."

He was on the bench in the next instant, reins in hand. "Until Monday, my lady."

"Your handkerchief," Rosalind said, extracting his linen from her pocket. "You must not lose so lovely an article. The embroidery is exquisite."

He looked pained. "Please don't trouble yourself. I want you to have it."

His hands being full of the reins, Rosalind tucked the handkerchief into his coat pocket. "Just tell me who did the needlework, and I will give her my custom as well."

The pained expression became one Rosalind herself had learned to cultivate, carefully blank, not quite bored.

"I did the embroidery myself," Mr. Wentworth said. "I will see you Monday evening, my lady." He clucked to the horses and they walked on toward the street.

Rosalind remained under the porte cochere, sorting theories and hunches. Mr. Wentworth had contemplated kissing her, and made a proper job of it, then regretted his actions.

Why? The first possibility was that she'd

disappointed him so badly that he was mortified to have indulged his fancies.

But *not here*, and *not now*, had been joined by *not me*. That suggested a second possibility: Ned Wentworth had found kissing her delightful, more than a passing pleasure, and he was *disconcerted* that it should be so because she had *exceeded* his expectations.

Interesting theory, and one Rosalind would test at the first opportunity.

Chapter Five

"Neddy, where the hell are you?" Lord Stephen spoke gently, his usual sarcasm nowhere in evidence.

"Sorry," Ned replied. He was sitting in his office at the bank, enduring a meeting that had no end. "I'm a bit distracted. You were saying?"

His lordship closed the blue-bound ledger book dearest to Ned's heart in all the world. "Your small investors' projects are generating twice the rate of return we see on the grander schemes. His Grace will want to know how you've done it, and how we can get the same profits for the larger clients."

Ned scrubbed a hand over his face, dragging his mind away from a stolen kiss and a lady who knew exactly how to handle a man surrendering to delicious folly.

"It's not like that," he said. "My small investors choose which businesses to support from the list I present them. In addition to investing, they give those businesses their custom. The investors take an interest in the venture and talk about it to their friends and family, who drop around to see what the fuss is about.

The business prospers, the investors see a return, and so they boast about that too, and the circle of prosperity widens."

Stephen sat back, brows knit. His lordship had been lamed in childhood by a father prone to excesses of gin and violence. Stephen had compensated by developing his intellect in architectural and mechanical directions. He was only recently taking more of an interest in the bank's activities, and Ned's feelings about that development were mixed.

Exceedingly mixed.

"And that scheme would never work among the swells," Stephen said slowly, "because talking about money and commerce is vulgar. Do you tell the clients to prattle on about their financial successes?"

"I insist upon it. Part of what the investors contribute is free advertising. I also introduce the merchants and shopkeepers to their investors, because I want every proprietor to know that if he or she fails, they will disappoint the hopes of people like the Misses Carruthers or old Mr. Lowell. The sense of investment has to go both ways."

"And among the aristocracy," Stephen said, gaze on the blue ledger, "that would never do. One invests and one reaps profits. One doesn't involve oneself in the tiresome financial details."

Stephen *was* the aristocracy—a ducal heir—and yet he spoke as if describing a curious culture in a distant land.

"Moreover," Ned said, "if some lordling's investments go well, he would never impart that happy news to his friends at the club, lest they invest in the same ventures, and dilute his profits. His objective is to narrow the circle of prosperity to one, and that one contributes only cash to the business. The person doing the work seldom knows his investors personally and if he fails, that's merely a risk any investor ought to assume."

Ned wanted this meeting to be over—he wanted this day to be over—but the small investors were the bright spot in his otherwise dull list of duties at the bank.

"How do you find the businesses?" Stephen asked. "How do you know which ones will turn more profit with a little extra capital?"

Ned *knew* because he'd listened to his father and mother talking late at night, when the children were in bed and parents could air their dreams and frustrations. He knew because he recalled the difference between Papa's shop and those of less successful tailors. He knew because he'd spent some long, hard years on London's streets, learning to assess who prospered, who was carefully maintaining appearances, and who was careening toward ruin.

"You look at the cart horse," Ned said. "Is he a solid, well-groomed specimen in good weight, or a skinny hack one delivery away from the knacker's yard? Are the womenfolk cheerful and energetic or listless and sullen? Do the apprentices serve out their terms or decamp for parts unknown after two years? Are the windows spotless, suggesting somebody has too much free time, or are they filthy, suggesting nobody has any care for appearances? You pay attention."

Stephen twiddled a quill pen. "I could study the

shops for ten years and never realize the successful enterprise has slightly dirty windows. Quinn would not come to that realization."

Ned smiled, because Stephen was right. "That bothers you."

"It puzzles me, but Quinn did manual labor in his youth, then he was in service, then he was a clerk and eventually, a banker. He never managed a shop."

"Neither have I." Though Ned had been born above his father's shop, and been given needle and thread before he'd been breeched.

"Abigail will adore your scheme," Stephen said. "Her Quaker leanings will approve of that bit about a circle of prosperity." And much of life, for Stephen, balanced on what Abigail liked or disliked. A man could have far worse lodestars.

"She gave me the idea," Ned said, "or the Quaker approach to banking did. They regard their obligations from a congregational perspective and are considered more trustworthy as a result, hence more people do business with them. The Friends back one another and rise or fall together."

"Their banks still sometimes fail."

"Not as often as most."

What did Rosalind think about mercantile ventures? How would she approach managing a bank? Did she have an opinion on the Corn Laws? Ned suspected she did, a well-thought-out, rational, and slightly unorthodox opinion.

"Neddy, something is troubling you," Stephen said, after a pause in the discussion had turned into a silence. "I realize you should figuratively draw my cork for prying, but Abigail would want me to ask if there's anything I can do to help."

"Abigail would want you to ask?"

Stephen tossed the feather aside and folded his arms. "Very well, I want to know. When the rest of the world was tiptoeing past my door for fear I'd go off into one of my tantrums, you taunted me to attempt a game of pall-mall. I'm returning the favor now. What's amiss?"

Ned had forgotten that exchange, had forgotten how upsetting he'd found the thought of a human being voluntarily shutting himself away from light and fresh air.

"You excel at pall-mall. You have the eye for it."

"I excel at nearly everything," Stephen replied, with what sounded like genuine exasperation. "My point is that we've never been delicate with each other, so what the hell is wrong?"

That kiss with Rosalind had been wrong—also wonderfully right. "I must pay a few calls I'm not looking forward to."

Stephen shot his cuffs. "You dread these calls."

"The brothels," Ned said, hating even the word. "I must canvass my connections in the brothels to learn if pretty female domestics are going missing from London's streets in greater numbers than usual."

"I'd relieve you of those errands, except Abigail would disapprove of me setting foot in such establishments. Most bachelors would leap at the chance to pay such calls."

"Most bachelors are idiots." Ned rose and locked the blue ledger in the glass-fronted bookcase beneath the window. "I kissed Lady Rosalind."

Stephen looked bored. "Proving that at least some-times, you do not number among the idiots."

"She's an earl's daughter, and she came to me for help."

"She's an adult with a brain in her head, Neddy. I hazard she did not swoon with disgust at your overture—unless you made a complete hash of the business?"

"I did not." *Nor had she.* "Most people think I'm Walden's by-blow."

"What matters, Neddy dearest, is what Lady Rosa-lind thinks of you. Your personal wealth recommends you to any woman short of royalty, as do your social connections. The problem is not Lady Rosalind's social standing."

Ned had suspected as much, though he'd not admit-ted that to himself. "I'm sure you will enlighten me as to the true difficulty?"

"Being generous of heart and brilliant of brain, of course I will. The ladies all eye you covetously. You are the dark-eyed Wentworth, the mysterious Wentworth, the quiet Wentworth. Byron's charms would pale be-side your manly allure, and yet, you never dally, never favor one lady over another. You treat all with distant, impeccable courtesy, and that drives them wild."

"You have a vivid imagination, *my lord*."

"I was pathetically jealous of you. Who can com-pete with that cool self-possession, particularly from the confines of a damned Bath chair?"

"So you became the idiot variety of bachelor."

"You are an idiot." Stephen rose and smoothed the crease of his trouser, which was fitted loosely enough to conceal the brace stabilizing his knee. "You aren't cool and haughty and all that other whatnot. You are simply indifferent. The belles and merry widows do not appeal to you. You see them as slightly tiresome, while they regard you as fascinating and forbidden."

The tiresome part was accurate enough. "To many of them, I am forbidden. In trade, baseborn, and so forth."

"Balderdash." Stephen collected his walking stick. "Money and ducal associations can elevate the prospects of the lowliest knight. In any case, your quandary arises not because you kissed Lady Rosalind, but because she kissed you back."

Oh, she had. Wonderfully, enthusiastically, generously. "You find that surprising?"

"Not at all, *but you do*, and therein lies the difficulty. She refused to adhere to your treasured prejudices and predictions, and now you are wrestling with hope and uncertainty. Being a mortal and tenderhearted male, you find those demons terrifying."

"Are you quite finished?" Ned asked, producing a yawn and a stretch.

"I am, and you are just getting started. You might consider offering a reward for information about the missing ladies. Make it quiet and confidential, and you might learn something."

"That is not a bad idea."

"Such high praise from you, dearest Neddy, will surely put me to the blush. When will you call on Jane?"

"Soon. Give Abigail my love."

"I will give her your fond regards, you blackguard.

Abigail is mine. Go find your own duchess." Stephen saluted with his walking stick and departed, closing the door silently in his wake.

Ned remained in his office, wrestling with hope and uncertainty, and with joyous memories of Rosalind's kisses too.

* * *

"My lady, with all due respect, you don't know who Mr. Wentworth's antecedents are." Mrs. Barnstable offered that vexing observation in tones of earnest patience.

"He is a member of the Wentworth family," Rosalind retorted. "How much more illustrious can antecedents be? Their Graces are not only titled, but also well situated, and Walden is said to have the ear of the Crown."

Rosalind was sketching, while Mrs. Barnstable worked at her embroidery. Both activities struck Rosalind as utterly pointless when each passing day could mean that Arbuckle and Campbell were in greater peril.

"I grant you," Mrs. Barnstable said, "he is attached to the Wentworth household and traveling under the Wentworth name, but the rumors about him are most troubling."

"What rumors?"

Mrs. Barnstable held her hoop up to the light of the morning room's east-facing window. "Unsavory rumors."

"I am not fourteen and ignorant of the world, Mrs. B."

Mrs. Barnstable resumed stitching, the sun making a golden halo of her blond hair. She was not yet thirty-five and surely qualified as an attractive widow. Rosalind liked her companion's penchant for books and her strong practical streak.

Also her firm grasp of the difference between a companion and a nanny.

"My lady, you are motivated to champion unfortunate causes, and Mr. Wentworth might fall into that category. Where does his wealth come from, for example?"

"He is a banker. Bankers, by definition, possess money."

"He *works* at a bank," Mrs. Barnstable corrected gently. "He is not a Wentworth by birth, or not by legitimate birth. Half the time when his name is mentioned he's referred to as Walden's by-blow, the other half the speculations run in even worse directions."

Rosalind took a moment to shade in her subject's eyebrows. They were dark, finely arched, and gave him a knowing air.

"How many FitzClarences are there?" Rosalind mused. "The heir to the throne can have ten by-blows, and they are lionized everywhere, but His Grace of Walden cannot have one?" Though Ned had said his father was a tailor. Had he meant his foster father? A stepfather?

"The FitzClarences are not said to have enjoyed the king's hospitality at Newgate. One does not hear jests about the FitzClarences graduating from picking pockets in Piccadilly to picking pockets in the City. I say these things not because I mean the young man any harm, but because somebody must keep your best interests in mind."

Rosalind's pencil stilled. "What are my best interests,

Mrs. B?" Lately that question, or a version of it, had been plaguing her. Lately since asking Ned Wentworth for help. "Am I to age into desperation, such that I finally accept a proposal from the likes of Lord De-Grange just to escape my father's household? Do I wait until I'm so close to my last prayers that when I write letters to the newspapers about the cruelty of badger baiting I become the object of jests?"

"No more letters," Mrs. Barnstable murmured. "Please, no more letters. The editors publish them for the sensation they create, not because anybody intends to pass laws for the defense of hapless badgers. Besides, Lord DeGrange is in every way an estimable *parti*."

"If he's so estimable, then you elope with him."

Mrs. Barnstable smiled, making herself look younger and altogether less staid. "If Lord DeGrange proposed, I would consider his suit. He has aged well."

But he had aged somewhat longer than Rosalind preferred in a prospective spouse. Then too, his conversation was limited to last year's adventures in the hunt field or this year's crop of foals. When he was in a truly lively frame of mind, he'd recount various cricket matches from his boyhood years at public school.

Worst of all, Lord DeGrange wasn't Ned Wentworth. He could not put Amanda Tait in her place with a bland word. He would never take on the challenge of finding a missing lady's maid, and he would never wonder why a woman had kissed him—and why would she?—much less ask her to explain her reasons.

"Until Papa calms down enough to stop heaving aging barons and unctuous cits at me, I won't be writing any more letters."

"Your father is concerned for you, my lady, as I am concerned for you. You drove out with Mr. Wentworth on Monday and permitted him to escort you again just yesterday. That will start talk."

"He has agreed to escort me again on Monday evening," Rosalind said. "George and Lindy should be overjoyed to be spared that duty. Moreover, Lindy appeared at yesterday's Venetian breakfast too, but never offered to escort me. Not well done of him."

Mrs. Barnstable's needle stilled. "My lady, please exercise caution. Gossip is unkind to women who violate convention."

And there sat Amelia Barnstable, a woman who personified conventionality, and society hardly esteemed her for her choices.

"Mr. Wentworth is neither silly nor vain nor self-absorbed," Rosalind said. "His manners are faultless, and he is received everywhere." Then too, his kisses were *amazing*.

"He is received, but not accepted. Please consider crying off on Monday night, my lady. Better still, tell Mr. Wentworth you will attend with one of your brothers and will not need his escort. If Mr. Wentworth is half the paragon you paint him to be, he'll understand he's been given his congé."

Logic, Rosalind's besetting sin, prodded her to leave off pondering Ned Wentworth's kisses long enough to consider Mrs. Barnstable's words.

"You are not making sense," Rosalind said, folding down a blank page over the unfinished sketch of Mr. Wentworth. "He is in demand as a dancing partner and escort. I've heard any number of matchmakers speculating about his wealth, and both Amanda Tait and Clotilda Cadwallader have admitted they would entertain his addresses. He is beyond eligible, and yet you disparage him."

"My lady, I applaud your independent spirit. You know I do, and I understand better than you think the allure of forbidden fruit, but Ned Wentworth isn't merely common, he's *questionable*. I urge you to greatest caution. Married to him, you too would be received but not accepted, and when a conversation paused at somebody's soiree, you would always wonder: Were they gossiping about your husband?"

As opposed to knowing, at least some of the time, that they gossiped about me?

But then, Rosalind was reminded of Ned's words to her: *Not me*. Was this what he'd meant? That association with him would come at the cost of society's dubious blessing?

If so, did she care? Rosalind drew a single line on the blank page, a line that happened to follow the contour of Ned Wentworth's upper lip. "He says it doesn't signify that I stammered."

"Of course it doesn't signify, particularly when you no longer suffer that affliction and haven't for years. What are you drawing?"

"Ideas for bonnets." Though Rosalind did occasionally still stumble over her words when she was tired, nervous, or upset. "I don't believe we've gone bonnet shopping yet this Season. Are you up for an outing?"

Mrs. Barnstable flashed that charming, mischievous smile again. "On a pretty spring day, what could possibly appeal more strongly than a shopping expedition?"

"Another visit to Hatchards?"

"Or *both*? Be still my fluttering heart." She gathered up her embroidery and closed the lid of her workbasket. "I'll meet you by the front door in ten minutes."

"And Gunter's," Rosalind said, closing her sketchbook. "Good things come in threes." That was a variation on the adage—*bad* things came in threes—but also suited to Rosalind's mood. To spend another afternoon sitting at home perusing the newspapers was beyond her.

"We should drop by Mrs. Abercrombie's and invite her to join us," Mrs. Barnstable said, pausing at the door, workbasket in hand. "Her new companion has decamped on short notice, and Mrs. Abercrombie has yet to hire another. She might appreciate some company and fresh air."

Mrs. Abercrombie was a widow of an age with Mrs. Barnstable, and not at all high in the instep. "The more the merrier," Rosalind said, getting to her feet. "How many companions does that make in the past year?"

"Three, but she does hire the younger, less-experienced women, and they are often less reliable too. You will consider what I said about Mr. Wentworth? You would not want to attract undue notice, my lady, especially not before your brother has attached a suitable bride."

And abruptly, the entire conversation fell into a rational pattern. "Lindhurst's pride is smarting because Mr. Wentworth wasn't cowed by his lordship's almighty consequence. Lindhurst put you up to warning me off Mr. Wentworth, didn't he?"

Lindy might even dimly suspect that the accident that had befallen his favorite watch—he had several—had not been an accident.

Mrs. Barnstable paused, hand on the door latch. "Actually, both your brothers mentioned their concerns to me, and just because they are your brothers doesn't mean you can dismiss everything they say. Your behaviors have caused them no little embarrassment in the past, my lady, to say nothing of the talk your father has endured on your behalf."

"And Lindy's inane bets? George's attempts at poetry that he wastes his allowance publishing in bound volumes? Higgins having to send the footmen out to bring Lindy home at all hours, dead drunk, pockets to let *again*? That's all simply amusing while my decision to allow the same man to escort me twice in a week has my brothers flying into the bows?"

Mrs. Barnstable sighed, the sound having a familiar, disappointed quality. Rosalind's tutors and governesses had frequently sighed like that, as did Papa.

"Your brothers are male, my lady. It's not fair, it's not right, but it's the way of the world that the male of the species in polite circles need not grow up unless or until he chooses to."

That surely qualified as an eternal verity, supported by observation and logic both. In the normal course, Rosalind would have apologized for being so vexatious and acknowledged the truth of Mrs. Barnstable's observations. George and Lindy were male, though compared to Ned Wentworth, they were hardly *men*.

But today, Rosalind's penchant for truth-telling beset her with particular intensity. "You live your entire life above reproach, Amelia Barnstable. You observe every rule and respect every protocol. Despite your exemplary existence, your husband's gambling left you without even your widow's mite. And yet, you defend the same conventions that rendered you impoverished and homeless. That is not right either."

Mrs. Barnstable shot Rosalind a look, one that hinted at fear and more subtly suggested the merest glint of rage. "I'll fetch my bonnet, and you will be careful where Ned Wentworth is concerned."

Rosalind let her have the last word. When it came to Ned Wentworth, Rosalind had every intention of being careful. He was the first man she'd noticed in a positive sense since becoming infatuated with the curate at the family seat in her eleventh year.

Ned Wentworth was honorable and kind, and so what if he'd had a rough start in life? His Grace of Walden himself had been to the gutter born, to hear the gossips tell it. Ned had made something of himself, an accomplishment far more worthy of respect than George's awkward poetry or the intricate knots in Lindy's cravats.

* * *

The most successful exponents of London's underworld rubbed along tolerably well with the most genteel. At the theater, a man of means might escort his mistress one night and be joined at the interval by his good friends.

The next night, those same friends would display equal cordiality to the man's wife when she occupied the same seat the concubine had previously. Other theatergoers observing these interactions ignored some and acknowledged others in a dance as necessary to polite society as it was tacit.

The best brothels enjoyed fine addresses in neighborhoods where crime was unlikely and clientele of means were close at hand. The best modistes were careful to schedule fittings such that wives and mistresses were never inconvenienced by undue proximity to one another.

Ned thus had to travel only two streets from his own lodgings to undertake the next phase of his investigation into the lady's missing maids. The premises were unremarkable from the outside, and on the inside, the appointments could have graced any well-to-do residence in Mayfair.

The number of wineglasses on a passing footman's tray and the unrestrained laughter from abovestairs suggested this residence was not quite as respectable as its neighbors. The faint odor of hashish in the air reinforced that suspicion, and nearly had Ned retreating into the chilly spring night.

But no. *Get it over with.*

"Please tell Mrs. Nimitz that Ned Wentworth requests a moment of her time." Establishments such as this one eschewed calling cards, though the butler wore an exquisitely tailored evening suit, and his dignity would have been sufficient for a ducal residence.

"Of course, Mr. Wentworth. Would you care to enjoy the refreshments in the blue salon?"

The laughter had come from the direction of the blue salon. "No, thank you."

"The music room is unoccupied at present, sir. Perhaps you'd like to wait there."

"The music room will do."

The music room was elegantly kitted out, the requisite great harp standing in one corner, a pianoforte with its lid raised in another. Closer examination of the painting gracing the open lid of the piano revealed a rendering worthy of old Hieronymus Bosch in a frisky mood.

A scene of cheerful debauchery involving men, women, farm animals, and fairies harmonized curiously well with the cherubs cavorting across the room's painted ceiling, and the half-naked goddesses depicted in the room's statuary. The parlor's unifying theme was gilt. Gilt on the pier glass, gilt on the molding, gilt on the picture frames, and gilt edging the piano's fantastic art.

"It's all of a piece, isn't it?" said a dark-haired lady standing in the doorway. "I want to make that point subtly, that how one views the naked form and what one does with it are mostly a matter of perspective and preference. You're looking well, Ned."

She advanced into the room and offered Ned her gloved hand. He bowed politely, though he knew that beneath her gloves, her hands bore scars from picking oakum by the hour. Her refined speech was the result of dogged schooling by a procession of elocution instructors, and she'd scrimped to hire the same modistes preferred by the most influential hostesses in Mayfair.

Mrs. Nimitz was a creation born of hard work and determination, much as Ned himself was. He respected her, as he could not respect many of the lordlings who pranced into the Wentworth bank in search of low-interest loans or easy profits.

He could never entirely trust her, though, any more than he trusted those lordlings. "You are in quite good looks too, ma'am." Only a few candles had been lit, the better to hide what cosmetics could not. Mrs. Nimitz was nearly ten years Ned's senior, and in proper lighting that fact would be obvious.

"Shall we sit?" she said. "I can ring for a tray."

"Thank you, no." Ned did not want to sit, did not want to observe the civilities. "My purpose here won't take long."

The lady smiled and settled into the middle of a blue tufted sofa. "As is the case with many gentlemen who call here. The ladies actually prefer a fellow who goes about the business with some dispatch."

Because the ladies could entertain more men per evening if their customers didn't tarry overlong upstairs. The banker in Ned grasped the concept, while the man who'd kissed Rosalind Kinwood suppressed a shudder.

"How is our duke?" Mrs. Nimitz asked, fingering a string of pearls arranged to cascade to just above her cleavage.

"Splendid, as always," Ned said, sorting the sheets of music stacked on the piano bench. Scarlatti, Mozart, Beethoven...A few of Burns's more sentimental pieces. "His Grace is more respectable by the year."

"Quinn Wentworth was always respectable, even in prison. Give him my regards."

"Of course." Ned would do no such thing, lest His

Grace confide to his duchess his concerns regarding Ned's female acquaintances. Her Grace would gently take up the cause, and Ned would be subjected to worried glances for the next three months. "You're faring well?"

"Business is good," Mrs. Nimitz said, running her palm over the sofa's velvet upholstery. "I bribe the requisite upstanding members of the constabulary, and see that others are offered free services. We manage. In another year or two, I can retire to the country, a proper widow of means."

"You've been saying that for five years. Why not give it up?"

Ned ambled along the mantel, which displayed a collection of porcelain figurines, some merely pretty, some lewd, all of them graceful.

Once upon a time, when a certain duke had been freed by royal pardon from a certain pestilential prison, that duke had insisted on taking with him not only Ned—his "tiger"—but also a would-be footman, and several of the imprisoned whores, his "maids."

In truth, during Walden's tenure at Newgate, he had paid those women to clean his accommodations—and paid them for only that service, much to their consternation. Upon his release, he'd offered the ladies domestic positions at the ducal residence. Mrs. Nimitz, in an earlier phase of her career, had been among those women.

She'd accepted the duke's offer long enough to clean up, fill her belly, rest, and don the decent clothing provided by Her Grace, and then piked off back to the Holy Land from whence she'd been taken.

"I have my reasons for staying in business," she said. "Good reasons, and besides, I excel at what I do. The women are happy and safe here, the customers even happier, and we mind our own business. Why do you stay at the Wentworth bank?"

Her reasons included two children, about whom Ned had never inquired. They were very likely receiving a genteel education at their mother's expense someplace in the shires, and using any name but Nimitz.

Ned took up a wing chair at an angle to the sofa. "I stay at the Wentworth bank because I am useful there to the man who saved my life."

Mrs. Nimitz twined a finger among the strand of pearls draped about her neck. "You weren't scheduled to swing, Ned. You would have been sent off to New South Wales, and being a canny lad, you'd have managed well enough."

No, he would not. He'd made his own plans in prison, and they had not included enduring months at sea being passed from one ship's officer to another.

"Transportation for some is worse than a death sentence, but I am not here to discuss our rosy past. I'm looking for a young woman."

Mrs. Nimitz made a face and left off playing with her pearls. "How young? I don't deal in children, Ned, not even for you."

"I am not searching for a child. I'm looking for two young women. Francine Arbuckle and Catherine Campbell. They were both lady's maids in an earl's household, and both have gone missing." He passed over Rosalind's sketches. "Have you seen or heard of them?"

Mrs. Nimitz studied the drawings. "Of course not. They will be Antigone and Electra if they've taken up the trade, or *Heloise* and *Mimi Delacroix*. Which earl?"

"Why?"

"Because some of the nobs are right bastards to their help and some aren't." A hint of the lady's native Cockney inflection colored that observation.

"They were maids to Lady Rosalind Kinwood. She's concerned for them."

Mrs. Nimitz passed back the sketches. "The earl stopped making the rounds years ago, and Lindhurst can't afford my rates. He's enough of a rat to get a maid with child and turn his back on her though, taking for free what he ought to pay for."

"Her ladyship says he leaves her maids alone."

Mrs. Nimitz snorted. "What would an earl's daughter know of her brother's sporting tastes? Maybe the maids simply did a bunk and are kicking their 'eels back 'ome in the village."

Ned saw, because he was watching closely, how those dropped haitches had mortified the speaker. She resumed playing with her pearls, but Ned now knew the topic of missing maids made his hostess nervous.

"Why leave an excellent post," he asked, "earning good pay from a prestigious employer for...ruin?"

The lady folded her arms, which accentuated her natural charms. "Some people—some women, and from what I can see all young men—like to fuck, Ned. Why not get paid for something so pleasurable? But you always were an excessively proper boy."

She hadn't known him "always." She'd known him

for a span of weeks at Newgate, and their paths had crossed from time to time since. Ned had never offered to handle her money, and she had never offered him much of anything.

Not that he would have accepted. "If you haven't heard of these two women, have you noticed an increase in the number of proper ladies abducted into the trade?"

"People exaggerate the dangers decent women face on London streets. Enough country maids, shop girls, and soldiers' wives sell their wares that nobody need bother the delicate flowers. They are more trouble than they're worth, truth be told."

"But a lady's maid is not a delicate flower. One of them had spent time in a Magdalen house."

"So Lady Rosalind is a reformer? Ned, you disappoint me. Next you'll be quoting scripture and closing down the print shops."

"Never that," Ned said, rising. "Will you keep your eyes and ears open for me? Her ladyship is very concerned, and neither woman was discontent with her post."

"Maybe they fell in love," Mrs. Nimitz said, getting to her feet. "Makes sensible people daft, I'm told. Try closer to the docks, Ned. Dora Hepplewhite likes the navy crowd, and if somebody's snatching proper misses from the streets, the fastest way to get the goods out of London would be on a boat."

"Not a cheering thought. I can leave the sketches with you."

She walked with him to the door. "Don't bother. I know where to find you. How is Artie doing?"

"Arthur is a work in progress. How did you know he'd come to us?"

"That child has a big mouth. He was bragging on his good fortune at the Pump and Tackle last night. Nebbins heard him."

Meaning Artie had broken curfew and returned to his old haunts. Like a dog to his vomit, to use a biblical analogy.

"I will have a word with Arthur about his nocturnal excursions," Ned said. "I'm off to put my questions to Mrs. Hepplewhite."

"She'd let you put more than your questions to her, if you asked nicely." Mrs. Nimitz laid a hand on Ned's arm. "I'll find Artie work in the stable or kitchen if the bank doesn't suit him."

"And he'll be back on the street, picking pockets before sundown," Ned said. "The temptations here are too great."

"You can't save them all, Ned, and you might be a jollier banker if you let yourself be overcome by temptation from time to time."

Well, no. He'd been overcome by the temptation to kiss Rosalind Kinwood, and since allowing himself that lapse, he had not been at all jolly.

But then, when *had* he been happy, much less jolly? A memory rose, of Rosalind smiling up at him, her lips rosy with his kisses, her eyes full of wonder.

At *that* moment, he'd been not merely happy, but joyous.

He bowed to Mrs. Nimitz and took his leave.

Chapter Six

"Do you play an instrument?" Rosalind asked, as Ned Wentworth handed her down from a sumptuous town coach. His vehicle did not boast the Walden coat of arms, but it didn't need to. Never had Rosalind traveled in such comfort. Never had she traveled in such *quiet*. The coach was like a little world, refreshment secreted here, pillows and lap robes piled there, the faint scent of cedar wafting pleasantly about the interior.

"I don't play with any proficiency," Mr. Wentworth said. "I pick up the fiddle from time to time." He saw Rosalind safely to the cobbles and assisted Mrs. Barnstable to alight. "What of you ladies? Do you have preferred instruments?"

Mrs. B chattered on about the flute not being as easy an instrument to play well as most people thought. Mr. Wentworth offered an arm to each lady, and they processed into the Petershams' impressive residence. Rosalind's escort continued conversing in pleasantries all the while, giving no indication that the addition of a companion to the outing in any way disappointed him.

Rosalind was disappointed. How was she to learn of Mr. Wentworth's progress among the houses of ill repute with Mrs. B holding forth so volubly about the Mannheim composers? How was she to convey to Mr. Wentworth that Mrs. Abercrombie's red-haired companion had left without notice? Calliope Henderson had been pretty, merry, and content with her post.

Bad things come in threes.

"I see Lord and Lady Nathaniel Rothmere are in attendance," Mr. Wentworth said. "Shall I introduce you? Her Grace of Rothhaven is with them."

Rosalind shuffled up a few more steps toward the top of the main staircase, where Mrs. Petersham was greeting her guests. A tallish dark-haired fellow was greeting the hostess, two dark-haired women flanking him.

"Those are the Wentworth sisters?" Mrs. Barnstable asked quietly. "Lady Althea and Lady Constance?"

"Lady Althea married Lord Nathaniel Rothmere," Mr. Wentworth said. "Lady Constance is wed to his brother, Robert, His Grace of Rothhaven. His Grace is not one for socializing, but the ladies never want for an escort."

Rosalind nearly stuck her tongue out at Mrs. Barnstable: *This is the man whose company you cautioned me against. He is on familial terms with not one but two dukes, and even you are impressed with his manners.*

Mrs. Barnstable's gaze said she was all but panting to add ducal siblings to the list of introductions she could brag about to her friends.

"I would not want to impose," she murmured.

"I would," Rosalind rejoined. "These people know all the best stories about Mr. Wentworth, and those, I am dying to hear. Besides, Her Grace of Rothhaven is reported to be a fine portraitist, and I do want her opinion regarding the many renderings of Lord Byron."

About which, Rosalind cared not one fig, but Mrs. B's demurral must be countered.

"We can sit with them if you like," Mr. Wentworth said. "The ladies and I haven't spent much time together since they arrived in London, and I'd like a chance to catch up."

So apparently would the Wentworth sisters, for they swarmed Mr. Wentworth—*How delightful! Our Neddy is here!*—and kissed his cheek and fussed over him as if he were the prodigal returned. Lord Nathaniel looked on with smiling patience.

"It's always like this," his lordship said quietly. "They embarrass the poor fellow without mercy because their own brothers are too delicate to endure such attentions. I have suggested to my wife that some restraint is in order, but that's like telling sheep to leave off grazing the Yorkshire hills. Cannot be done."

His lordship carried the sound of Yorkshire in his accent, and clearly, he carried a profound regard for his wife in his heart. His smile was doting, and he made no move to rescue Mr. Wentworth from the ladies' enthusiasms.

With Mrs. Barnstable looking as if she'd stepped into a fairy tale, the party found seats. The gentlemen took the outside positions, while Rosalind was tucked between Mr. Wentworth and Her Grace of Rothhaven. Mrs. Barnstable—waving cheerfully to every acquaintance in the room—nestled between Her Grace and Lady Nathaniel.

"You refer to them as Lady Althea and Lady Constance." Rosalind put the question to Mr. Wentworth quietly. "Is that at their request?"

He passed her a program. "Their insistence. When I met them, they were adjusting to being Miss Wentworth and Miss Constance. Then the titles befell them. The ladies eluded matrimony for years, until the Rothmere fellows came up to scratch. I gather Yorkshire appeals to them in part for its informality and relative peace. London airs are a trial to them both and to their menfolk."

A duke and his brother could be *menfolk*. Papa, George, and Lindy would have apoplexies to hear themselves referred to in such casual language.

"You like these ladies."

"I love them," Mr. Wentworth said, peering at his program. "I don't know Lord Nathaniel or His Grace of Rothhaven all that well, but what I do know of them, I find estimable. Althea and Constance have endured much and are entitled to expect much from their spouses."

"Have you endured much, Mr. Wentworth?"

He folded his program in half. "I suspect the soprano right before the interval will add to my burdens."

"We need to talk."

Mr. Wentworth glanced at Her Grace, who was chatting up Mrs. Barnstable on the topic of tisanes for nervous digestion.

"At the interval. Althea and Constance will keep your loyal vassal occupied, and if their good offices fail, Lord Nathaniel will escort her to the buffet."

"They will throw us together?" *How interesting.*

"At the first opportunity and as often thereafter as they possibly can. They will report what you say word for word to Her Grace of Walden, and she will discuss the particulars with His Grace. Lord Stephen will stick his oar in, after protracted consultation with his lady wife of course, and they will all—out of sincere concern—give me the benefit of their thinking."

"They will *meddle*?"

"It's what they do. As virtuosically as Walden manages money, the rest of the family manages one another."

And clearly, they included Ned Wentworth in the family fold. "This bewilders you."

"The Wentworths would bewilder anybody."

Just as clearly, Rosalind's escort saw himself outside of their family circle. Why? If she asked him that, he'd come up with some half-humorous observation about the guitarist taking her place at the front of the room.

Rosalind limited her mental agenda for the interval to what progress Mr. Wentworth had made questioning the demimonde, and the news of Calliope Henderson's disappearance.

Those were important matters, very important. That Rosalind also wanted more of Mr. Wentworth's kisses did not signify in the least, but it was uppermost on her mind for the duration of the first half.

* * *

Do not stare at Lady Rosalind's mouth. Ned's internal litany sounded very like Her Grace in a sermonizing mode. *Do not sniff her. Do not drop your program like some callow swain who needs the most obvious, pathetic excuse to bend nearer to the woman he's longing to impress.*

Do not glower at Althea and Constance. Do not surreptitiously tromp on Lord Nathaniel's damned toes.

Ned had all but elbowed his lordship away from Lady Rosalind's side. Only Althea's gentle hand on Lord Nathaniel's arm had spared the blighter some discreet parlor pugilism.

The guitarist strummed and plucked for six eternities. The duet thereafter lasted eight more, and the soprano was an undeserved penance for all in attendance.

"No more musicales," Ned muttered, rising at the interval to offer Lady Rosalind his hand. "I beg of you. I will endure your at-homes, walk dogs with you in the park, or steel myself for a literary salon featuring American poets on the subject of humanity's many ills, but no more musicales."

"Agreed." She put her hand in his and rose. "The accompanist was as enthusiastic as the singer, and they appear thoroughly besotted with each other. One fears for their children's hearing."

She smiled at Ned, and every rational thought departed his brain. The spacing of the chair rows meant he and the lady stood *quite* close, and—

"Neddy," Constance called, "spring the horses, would you? Nathaniel is determined to be sociable while my burning objective lies in the direction of the buffet."

Ned escorted Constance and Rosalind from the music room and across the corridor to the library, which had been pressed into service to house the buffet. Most of the guests had tarried at their seats, and thus Ned could make a flying pass down the offerings, holding a plate for each lady.

"Now seat us up on the mezzanine," Constance instructed. "We want privacy, but also to keep an eye on the proceedings. I'll find you."

She swanned off after aiming a particularly fierce look at Ned. She would find them at her leisure, but find them, she would.

"She's lending me her consequence," Rosalind said, winding her way toward the spiral steps that led to the library's mezzanine. "She's a duchess, and she need not favor anybody with her company. Your family is kind."

They are not my family. "In their way, they are very kind. Also ferocious. I haven't made much progress with our investigation."

Lady Rosalind preceded him up the steps, and Ned nearly dropped both plates.

"It has been mere days, Mr. Wentworth. If there's a scheme afoot to collect decent women from Mayfair's streets, we won't uncover it by surviving 'Caro Mio Ben' rendered as a marching song."

Ned found them a sofa with a low table before it. The library proper began to fill with guests, conversations blending into a dull roar. Constance had chosen well, for few would think to look up, though through the balusters of the banister, Ned had a clear view of the gathering.

Like perching in a tree in an alley to eat a purloined pie. The beadles and constables never looked up.

"I have called upon several parties likely to hear of a

scheme such as you allude to," Ned said, though Mrs. Hepplewhite had yet to receive him. "They all profess ignorance."

Rosalind settled on the sofa. Ned set down the plates and took the place beside her. Constance could make of that presumption whatever she pleased.

"Do you believe their protestations of ignorance?" Lady Rosalind stripped off her gloves and draped them across her lap. Though the action was brisk, Ned had not braced himself for the impact of her bare hands and arms exposed so casually.

He was in thriving good health and on excellent terms with his manly humors, and the sight of Lady Rosalind's wrists, of her building a sandwich from soft white bread, strips of cheese, and thin slices of ham...

Steady there, bucko. "I believe the women I spoke with lack particular knowledge, but they've heard something, they've seen something. A scheme is afoot, and they want no part of it."

"Then whoever crafted this scheme has power." Her ladyship passed Ned the sandwich. "Gloves off, Mr. Wentworth."

Gloves off, shirt off. Ned's imagination chose now of all times to torment him. He peeled off his gloves and accepted the food.

"Power in those circles comes in many forms," he said. "There's the kind of power polite society respects—wealth, standing, influence in the Lords. Your father is powerful, in that way. Then there's the simple power to take a life, to inflict suffering. In between those extremes is the power I see wielded at the bank, the power to ruin or rescue. For women trading on their charms, any of those sorts of power can affect them."

Her ladyship made a second sandwich and took a bite. *Do not stare at her mouth.*

"All of those forms of power are typically wielded by men," Lady Rosalind said. "The flesh trade is one we commonly think of as being more in the hands of women."

"True." A fact nobody much noticed unless to complain about it. "But to physically overpower young women in good health takes brute force. I've asked my badgers to make discreet—"

"Might we refer to them by another name?"

Rosalind was protective of badgers, bears, and vicious dogs—of any creature subjected to needless suffering for the sake of profit and amusement.

"My intelligence officers," Ned said. "Ignoring the children populating London's streets has become a virtue, my lady. If the Society for the Suppression of Mendicity has its way, nobody will feed, clothe, or house these children, and—so the Society insists—the beggars will magically cease their greedy, lazy ways, despite having no skills, no letters, no proper food to eat, and in many cases, poor health. The bank takes a different approach, employing and educating those boys who accept our terms." *And keeping the little imps safe, warm, and fed.*

A man's laughter drifted up, polite, genteel, cordial.

"Whose idea was this?"

Never explain, never apologize. Walden himself had laid down that edict to Ned many times when it came to the bank's loan decisions and its choice of employees or clients.

"Her Grace of Walden is a preacher's daughter," Ned said, "and genuinely charitable. She has causes, and she has His Grace's devotion. The badgers are the result of both."

Ned had offered a few suggestions when asked, but not until then. Management of the boys had fallen to him by default—or at the duchess's insistence, Ned had never been quite sure which.

"I want to know more about your bank boys and intelligence officers, but I need to tell you of a third disappearance." She summarized a situation much like that of her lady's maids. A decent girl in service apparently snatched from the streets on her half day.

"And she was pretty," Lady Rosalind concluded. "Well spoken. A companion is a step above a lady's maid. A considerable step. She had wages due and didn't collect those."

This was bad news. Very bad news. Questions piled up in Ned's mind: Was this woman melancholic? How proximate was the Abercrombie household to Rosalind's dwelling? Did the woman have any followers?

Was there any halfway innocent explanation for yet another disappearance? Before he could pose the first query, Constance appeared at the top of the steps and crossed the mezzanine with a stride more determined than the situation warranted.

"Neddy, you forgot our lemonade. Rectify your oversight, please."

Rosalind was on her feet in the next instant. "I can fetch my own lemonade, Your Grace, and I will be happy to bring you some as well. Mr. Wentworth's hands were occupied carrying both plates, and even he lacks the power to make glasses of lemonade levitate at will."

Constance did not enjoy an outgoing personality. Like Walden himself, she tended to seriousness and introspection. Her spouse, His Grace of Rothhaven, was a similarly reserved fellow and legendarily reclusive. Only Rothhaven, though, had the knack of confronting Constance and coming away unscathed.

Only Rothhaven, and apparently, Lady Rosalind, who stood, chin up, glowering at the duchess.

"My apologies, Lady Rosalind," Constance said, her smile startling for its warmth. "Hunger makes me irritable. I should have brought up drinks for all, but I wanted a chance to interrogate you. Neddy, be a love and find us some punch, won't you?"

"Come along, Your Grace," Rosalind said, offering her arm. "*Neddy* can be a love and guard the food while we fetch our own drinks, for I want a chance to interrogate you too."

The ladies departed and Ned sank back to the sofa, his knees curiously weak. The food sat forgotten while he wrestled with a daunting realization.

Lady Rosalind had been ready to do battle on behalf of Ned's dignity. She'd taken umbrage at Constance's preemptory words, when all Ned had felt was a passing annoyance.

Kisses were lovely, and Lady Rosalind's kisses in particular had much to recommend them. But kisses didn't explain why she made him want to laugh, cheer, applaud, and offer her his heart. Kisses didn't explain the half of it, and that was a problem.

Though a lovely problem indeed.

* * *

The Wentworths maneuvered so subtly that Rosalind didn't catch them at it until she was alone with Mr. Wentworth in his coach, the horses plodding along at a sedate walk.

"I did not see that coming," she said as the carriage drew away from the Rothhaven town residence. "I did not...One minute, Mrs. Barnstable was maundering on about her nerve tonic, and Lord Nathaniel was handing her up into the ducal coach..."

"The next," Mr. Wentworth said, "we're setting Her Grace down, and left with my own conveyance to ourselves. I will take you directly home of course."

"But Mrs. Barnstable will think Her Grace chaperoned me when in fact..." Her Grace had pleaded fatigue and asked to be dropped off first.

Mr. Wentworth hadn't objected.

Neither had Rosalind.

"I need to let you know something," he said, taking off his top hat and setting it on the bench beside him.

"Might you share the forward-facing seat when you do?"

His lips quirked. "Is that wise, my lady?"

The shades were drawn, the lamps turned down, but the mischief in his smile blazed brightly. "If you change seats, you will spare me the effort, Mr. Wentworth."

His gaze became considering, then troubled.

"You are afflicted by an excessive concern for propriety, sir. I was sent down from two finishing schools, and that's in addition to the one that rejected me because of my stammer."

"You were not sent down," he replied. "You were allowed time at home for a repairing lease. You were given leave to quit the term early. Earls' daughters are not sent down."

"In the first instance," Rosalind said, "I proposed that for one week, the students and teachers change places with the servants, in inverse order. Headmistress would become the scullery maid, while the scullery maid would have the running of the school."

"What prompted that mad flight?"

"Headmistress decreed that our debate topic for the term be the benefits and burdens of enslavement. Her family held property in the Indies, and her views on abolition were less than enlightened. Her brother was our vicar. The sermons he propounded made me bilious."

"Headmistress did not take your suggestion about switching places?"

"I proposed that firsthand experience with both powerlessness and authority would enrich the depth of our argument. Just as Wellington—a seasoned soldier—was regarded as an expert on the effective use of the military, nobody without experience being subjugated should support policies that perpetuate it. Headmistress opined that I had been reading too many philosophers, and was suffering a brain fever. I told her..."

Rosalind had shouted at her, in fact. Probably the last time she'd raised her voice to anyone.

"What did you tell her, my lady?"

"That a headmistress with so feeble a grasp of logic ought not to be permitted any role in the education of impressionable young females. My bags were packed for me, and I was on my way home the next morning, *before my condition worsened*."

Rosalind had never related that story to anyone, though the telling of it fortified her somehow.

"I thought my suggestion entirely rational," she went on. "You don't ask the butler to cook or the head stable lad to greet callers, do you? Why are people, particularly a lot of men, who've never beaten a rug or hoed a row of turnips..." She fell silent, for Mr. Wentworth's gaze had gone unreadable. "You will think me ridiculous."

Whatever he thought—and he was thinking *something*—he remained on the opposite bench. "What occasioned your second fall from grace?"

"I permitted the curate's brother liberties. He was visiting for the summer, which was a way of saying that he hadn't been welcome to holiday with the family that employed him as a tutor. He lent me books, and *The Wealth of Nations* was my downfall. I found it fascinating, but Mr. Woodhouse only let me read one chapter at a time, and to earn a chapter..."

"You had to part with some of your own riches?"

Rosalind nodded. "His French was atrocious, and his lovemaking worse than that. All the while he was about his pleasures, I was reading the titles on the bookshelf behind him, choosing which volume I'd seize upon next. He was found in a compromising situation with another girl. She implicated me, and my literary aspirations were disappointed."

Mr. Wentworth sat forward enough to take Rosalind's hands. "Listen to me, my lady. I don't care if you bore the curate and his brother six sons apiece. Just because the Wentworths have schemed to provide us some privacy doesn't mean..."

"Doesn't mean you want that privacy?" Well, blast and perdition. Heat flooded Rosalind's cheeks, and she held her tongue lest the moment provoke her to stammering.

"What I want shocks me," he said, letting go of Rosalind's hands. "And before you demand further explanations, you need to know that I've yet to speak with parties whose business puts them in frequent contact with naval officers and merchant captains."

Now of all times, Rosalind could not summon the rational capabilities she usually wielded with such ease. She had confessed her greatest transgressions to Mr. Wentworth, and could not tell if he was shocked, amused, impressed, or bored.

"You refer to another madam?" she asked.

"Her nom de guerre is Mrs. Dora Hepplewhite, though her given name is Tryphena, and her place of business is not far from the Pool. If somebody has been smuggling women out of London, she might know, but I suspect she's been avoiding me."

"Why would you suspect that?" And why would any woman avoid Ned Wentworth?

"I call upon her from time to time, and yet, she has twice not been home to me, as it were. That is unprecedented in all the years of our acquaintance."

"And thus your suspicion is reinforced that something dangerous is afoot." Rosalind did not allow herself to wonder *why* Ned Wentworth would have a long-standing relationship with a madam, because the answer was obvious. *Lucky Mrs. Hepplewhite.*

Mr. Wentworth switched seats. "It's not what you think."

"None of my business, Mr. Wentworth."

"I want it to be your business, and that..." He scrubbed a gloved hand over his face. "My father was an exquisitely skilled tailor, as was his brother. They could not tolerate each other as business partners, though they were devoted siblings. Uncle Amos set up shop in Portsmouth, while Papa kept to London. Papa was off in Portsmouth visiting Uncle Amos when the press gang took him up."

"Your father was impressed?" The practice had been so unpopular, the navy had abandoned it several years past. Then too, conditions were so awful on the merchantmen that a berth on a naval vessel was considered a step up by most sailors. "Why take a tailor out to sea?"

"The navy suffered a shortage of sailmakers, according to Amos, and would not hear of a wife and children in London needing Papa's support. One day he was a free man enjoying a pint with his brother, a week later he was at sea. I keep in touch with Mrs. Hepplewhite in hopes that I might hear something of the ship he sailed on."

"How long ago was this?"

The horses clip-clopped along, and bells tolled in the distance. "I don't know. Uncle Amos expired shortly thereafter. My mother was in poor health and could not manage the shop without Papa. I was *at large* for a time. I'm not sure how long, because there are no calendars on the street. What does a date matter or a day of the week when all a boy wants to know is where his next meal will come from?"

Mr. Wentworth spoke quietly, but Rosalind could hear the bewildered echo of that small boy in his voice.

"You don't know how old you were when your father was impressed?"

"I was probably eight. I could read a bit, though I was better at ciphering. I had been working in Papa's shop for some years by then. I might have been nine, and my brother was several years older than me. I was small for my age. We managed for a time, thanks to my brother, but my memories have gaps. I will turn a corner in some neighborhood I don't recognize and think, *I have been here before* ... but have no recollection of when. Matters, which were dire to begin with, deteriorated apace after my brother's demise."

The brother who had died in his thirteenth year.

Hence, the badgers at the bank. Hence the utter bleakness of Mr. Wentworth's profile. "You've been searching for your father all this time?"

"Not for him. He would have come home to us if he could. But I want to know ... Ships change names, they sink, they change flags, and get dry-docked. I knew what vessel he'd sailed on. I traced it to South America, from thence to the Sandwich Islands. Several years later it popped up in the Antipodes under a different name and a different captain, then disappeared again, though there's no record of scuttling or capture."

Rosalind disliked her father. The earl was too full of his own consequence, entirely lacking in affection for his only daughter, and his politics were the usual self-serving Tory bloviations masquerading as patriotism.

But he was *there*, a bulwark against many perils, a reliable constant and some check on Lindhurst's stupidities. To lose Papa would be...

"I am sorry," Rosalind said. "I am sorry for your losses, which have been many and tragic. What does the navy say happened to him?"

"Papa stopped drawing pay after three extended voyages, and none of those voyages would have brought him back to London. They lost track of him in Ceylon."

While his son, who could not state his own age reliably, had never forgotten him. "And now Mrs. Hepplewhite is trying to lose track of you?"

"Seems that way, and if I have consistently paid any party to gather intelligence for me, it is she."

Another silence bloomed, thoughtful, a little sad, but not uncomfortable. Rosalind marveled to think that she and Mr. Wentworth had confided in each other. The experience was novel and sweet, a little like a stolen kiss but more substantial.

More serious.

"I don't generally bruit my past about," Mr. Wentworth said. "I did spend time in Newgate and left the place only on the coattails of His Grace's pardon. His Grace was eventually exonerated of all wrongdoing, but Rosalind, I subsisted on thievery and begging for several years. The gossip in my case is based on facts."

He was being all noble and decent, dealing in the truth when he thought it redounded to his discredit.

The gudgeon. "Listen to me, Ned Wentworth. I am *glad* you begged, stole, and scrapped, *glad* you survived any way you could. A lesser person would have given up, would have died of grief or shame or some useless saintly emotion. But you didn't. You survived against all odds, and I am so proud of you I could..."

He regarded her, the faint smile again in evidence. "Kiss me?"

She nodded. "I want to *celebrate* you. When is your birthday?"

His smile became bashful. "I have no idea. Late spring, I think. My mother said the birds were singing as I was born, and that's why I like music. You are a very unusual woman, Lady Rosalind. I would like to celebrate you too."

I'd settle for a kiss. Rosalind nearly told him that, but with Ned Wentworth, maybe she didn't have to settle. As she pulled off her gloves and hauled him closer, her last rational thought was that maybe with Ned Wentworth, she could have more of celebration, and much, much less of settling.

Chapter Seven

I want to celebrate you.

Two days later—two days filled with bank meetings, ledgers, and more bank meetings—and Ned could still hear Lady Rosalind making that announcement, could still taste a kiss that had been full of both rejoicing and desire.

In defense of his wits, Ned had kept their indulgence brief. The instant the coach had rocked to a halt, he'd opened the door and handed the lady down. Her deportment up the steps to her home had been graceful and dignified, but as Ned had bowed his good night, she had winked at him.

And he had winked back.

Ridiculous, schoolboy, churchyard, puerile nonsense. Ned could not, in years of recollections, remember a Wentworth winking, ever.

"Lady Rosalind's coach is pulling up as I speak," Lord Stephen said. "You can stop pacing a hole in Abigail's carpets."

"And where is your dear Abigail? I wanted the ladies in particular to become acquainted."

"She's with our son. She will join us as soon as the demands of motherhood allow." Lord Stephen nearly preened at the words *our son*, so proud was he of two stone of darling boy.

On Ned's last visit to the nursery, the lad had already been babbling about the-pony-goes-trot-trot-trot, and that had made Ned feel old and wistful.

"So, Uncle Dee-Dee," Lord Stephen said, joining Ned at the hearth, "will you let Lady Rosalind get away after you've solved the riddle of the missing maids?"

"Bad enough you call me Neddy. Are you an infant now, to appropriate your son's nursery name for me?" A name Ned felt honored to have.

"You dodge the question, an encouraging sign. Abigail has consulted Jane on the topic of Lady Rosalind Kinwood. Her ladyship did not *take*, another encouraging sign."

Ned heard soft, female voices at the front door.

"How do you derive encouragement from polite society's failure to appreciate Lady Rosalind's many fine qualities?"

"Simple. Polite society tries its best not to appreciate the Wentworths as a family. Lady Rosalind already has the necessary originality and independence of spirit to join our ranks. Oh, my. You are giving me that somebody-ought-to-wallop-Stephen-with-a-pall-mall-mallet look. Haven't seen it for years. I feared Quinn had bankered that temper right out of you."

Jane had explained to a very young Ned that Stephen, often confined to a Bath chair, created drama for the sake of fixing attention anywhere but on his lameness. Stephen's temper earlier in life had made Ned look like the soul of decorum by comparison, which had fueled Ned's determination to acquire airs and graces that much faster.

"Abigail has earned the right to wield any and all pall-mall mallets where you are concerned," Ned said mildly. "We wish her the joy of that thankless office."

"You used to be fun, Neddy. You used to make Her Grace laugh and His Grace seize up with coughing fits that fooled no one. Now you are like a badger new to his livery, full of business and determined that everybody know it. That's not a very effective approach to lovemaking, if you want my opinion on the matter."

"Which no sane man would."

"Abigail finds my—"

The door opened and Constance, Her Grace of Rothhaven, swept into the room, Lady Rosalind trailing, and a resigned butler bringing up the rear.

"Her Grace of Rothhaven and Lady Rosalind Kinwood," the butler intoned, "as my lord can doubtless see."

"Don't pout, Rodgers," Constance said. "I was afraid they'd come to blows waiting for us. A tray with all the trimmings, please, and His Grace of Rothhaven should have a tray as well. You'll find him in the blue parlor pretending to read the newspapers. Stephen, don't stand there like a looby, greet your guest."

"Yes, Stephen," Ned said. "Greet your guest."

"We are acquainted," Lady Rosalind replied, dipping a curtsy. "Lord Stephen, a pleasure to see you. Mr. Wentworth, good day."

She wore a dark blue afternoon dress with lavender and green embroidery across the bodice. Not the colors a young girl would choose, and on her, they were luscious.

"Lady Rosalind." Ned bowed, and Stephen did likewise. "Thank you for joining us. You are looking well."

The butler withdrew, and Constance closed the door. "If her ladyship and I are to also make an appearance at the shops, we cannot waste time on pleasantries. Ned, have you learned anything more?"

Once upon a time, Constance had been the most retiring of the Wentworths, apparently content with her sketchbooks and cats. Her dark-haired looks had been unremarkable by design, though she was certainly dressed in the first stare of fashion lately. She'd married Rothhaven, and among the wedding gifts she had apparently found a duchess's ability to take charge of any situation.

"Your Grace," Lady Rosalind said, "I am not expected home until late this afternoon. We have time for pleasantries. Lord Stephen, thank you for hosting this call. I believe I met your lady wife last autumn at some at-home or card party. Her assistance will be greatly appreciated."

Before marrying Lord Stephen, Abigail Abbott had been a professional inquiry agent. Hence Ned's decision to enlist her aid.

The group assembled itself such that Rosalind was in a wing chair and Ned on the end of the sofa closest to her. Constance took a second wing chair and Stephen the opposite end of the sofa. The tea tray arrived on a wheeled barge, and Constance asked Lady Rosalind to do the honors.

"I have a sketch of Calliope Henderson," Rosalind said, when all had been served. "The likeness is imperfect, because she never sat for me, but it's close enough." She fished a page from her reticule and passed it to Ned.

"Pretty," Ned said. "Young, apparently without family in London, like the others." He handed the sketch to Constance.

"Neddy, fetch me a pencil. I've seen this woman. She was with an older widow. The girl was casting longing glances at a shop clerk while her employer sorted through various pairs of black gloves."

Ned procured Constance a sharpened pencil from the escritoire by the window. Constance made a few additions to the sketch and held it up.

"That is her to the life," Lady Rosalind said. "What talent you have, Your Grace."

"Since marrying His Grace, I have had much opportunity to refine the skills I was born with. What else do these women have in common, other than youth, looks, and a post in service to a London household?"

The conversation traveled a circular path Ned had worn flat in his own ponderings. Abigail joined them, which occasioned Stephen shifting to take the center of the sofa to sit between Ned and Abigail.

Maybe I am not the only fellow reduced to school-boy behaviors. Abigail was a statuesque brunette with a brisk air and an inexplicable fondness for her husband. She alone of all Wentworths was allowed to demonstrate protectiveness toward Stephen, an accomplishment Ned still marveled at.

Ned liked Abigail. He liked that she wasn't cowed

by the trappings of polite society and liked very much that she put Stephen in his place regularly.

"What these women have in common," Abigail said some minutes later, "is that they all knew Lady Rosalind, however indirectly. They all dwelled in a certain proximity to one another. They all were taken when on foot not far from their dwellings."

Well, hell. "You are right," Ned said, "meaning whoever is doing this has an opportunity to observe the comings and goings of senior servants from well-to-do households in a certain neighborhood."

"And," Lady Rosalind murmured, "they've been doing so for some time. Half days come but once a week, which is when two of the women were at liberty to tend to errands. Your Grace, do you recall which shop you were in when you saw Calliope with Mrs. Abercrombie?"

Constance named a glovemaker's within an easy walk of Rosalind's house.

"Somebody should chat up the handsome clerk," Lord Stephen said. "He might have crossed paths with all three women as well."

"I can do that," Abigail said. "I would enjoy doing it, in fact."

"What of the pubs?" Ned asked. "If I want to know what goes on in London, I ask the alewives and tavern maids. I was planning on making inquiries along the docks, and I would have started with the pubs."

"Not dressed like that, you won't," Abigail said. "And not alone. You will take Stephen, and you will exercise the greatest of care."

"I work better alone," Ned said. "Meaning no

disrespect, but Stephen's limp makes him too memorable."

"Ye of little faith," Stephen said. "My limp is barely noticeable these days. I'm better at disguises than you are. I'll squint and leer and swear, and nobody will have the least notion—"

"Neddy," Abigail began, "you cannot possibly think to venture—"

"He doesn't think," Constance observed. "Never has, and that is why Jane—"

Lady Rosalind stood and the Wentworths, much to Ned's surprise, fell silent.

"You will all do as Mr. Wentworth tells you to," she said. "He runs an entire bank and makes that look like a lark, and he knows London as you and I never will. If you do him the courtesy of attending him, he will keep you from mucking up the whole undertaking before a mystery becomes a tragedy. I asked for your help, and I am grateful to have it, but you...Excuse me. I need a moment."

She curtsied—to Ned alone—and withdrew.

"That," Stephen said, popping a bite of shortbread into his mouth, "is your duchess, Neddy. Lose all the lady's maids and companions in London, but don't lose Lady Rosalind."

"I won't have to lose her," Ned snapped, "you lot will horrify her into a permanent dislike of me. Stephen, I cannot frequent the clubs as you can. Sit among the lordlings and spares and listen for who complains of a lack of blunt or who is newly flush with funds."

"Excellent notion," Abigail said. "Stephen listens so very well."

No, he did not. He was a competent eavesdropper though. "Constance, I want to know every companion or lady's maid who's left without notice for the past six months. You have only recently arrived in Town. Send to the agencies for a companion and lady's maid, interview them all and see what you can learn. Abigail, what have I overlooked?"

She stared off into space. "I am stating the obvious, but the missing persons are all female. If there's a Lothario at large in the mews, then a call upon the neighborhood apothecaries is in order. It's possible the ladies all had a *reason* to discreetly leave Town. I can handle those inquiries."

"Thank you. I would not have thought to look in that direction. Now, if you will excuse me, I'll leave you to battle Stephen for the sweets remaining on the tray."

"You're going after Lady Rosalind?" Stephen called as Ned headed for the door.

Ned didn't dignify that query with a reply. The butler sent him upstairs to a guest parlor, claiming the lady had needed a few minutes of privacy, but Ned looked, and Rosalind wasn't in the guest parlor. She wasn't in the library, in Stephen's study, or in the family parlor either.

Where the hell could she be?

* * *

The parlor Rosalind barged into was done up in soothing, majestic blues, from the upholstery on the sofa and chairs to the velvet curtains, to the choice of art on the walls. Everything blended, everything brought to mind summer skies and bucolic tranquility. Potted ferns by the window added to the sense of repose, and a mild breeze wafted in from the back garden.

Rosalind very much needed that fresh air.

"How dare they?" she muttered, pacing across a carpet that featured more blue—irises and hyacinths, accented by green foliage. "*Neddy fetch me a pencil.*" She pivoted at the edge of the carpet. "*We haven't time for pleasantries.*" Another ten paces. "*Not dressed like that you won't.*" Pivot. "*I'm better at disguises than you are.*"

She gazed up at a ceiling painted to convey a sky of puffy clouds, swallows flitting across the firmament, doves perching upon blossoming branches at the corners.

"He's been disguising himself as a Wentworth for years," she said, "and the lot of them don't even notice the effort that takes."

Did *Ned* notice the effort that had gone into re-creating himself in the image of a ducal familiar? Not quite family, not quite a servant, not even fully an employee.

"I take it you refer to our Ned?"

Rosalind whirled to see a tall, dark-haired man leaning against a bookshelf. "Excuse me," she said. "I did not know the room was occupied. The butler..." Had he said the parlor was to the left or the right at the top of the stairs?

"Losing one's way when upset is easy. Rothhaven, at your service." He bowed with all the formality such a lofty station implied. "You are Lady Rosalind, and suffering a predictable bout of excess of Wentworths.

The cure for that malady is abundant peace and quiet. Ample helpings of humor also reduce the severity of symptoms. Shall we sit?"

"I am Lady Rosalind, Your Grace, also mortified." The duke was rumored to be reclusive, a throwback to the days when the aristocracy prided itself on its eccentricities. "I will leave you to your solitude. I did not make a dignified exit from the gathering below and must apologize to mine hostess for my rudeness."

Rothhaven ambled over to the sofa. "I made an undignified exit from society when still a boy. Society's loss. Come join me for a tea cake. If Stephen was among the horde you quit, you never stood a chance at any of the offered sweets."

This man's company was balm to Rosalind's soul. She ought not to be alone with him, but ought nots and should nots weren't very helpful when she was in a temper. She cared little what the Wentworths thought of her, but she cared a great deal for Ned's good opinion.

A tea service sat on a low table before the sofa. "I don't care for any tea, Your Grace, thank you just the same."

"Then bear me company," he said, patting the back of a wing chair. "I have, through diligent effort, trained my in-laws to leave me to myself, and as is typical of them, once they grasped the lesson, they became zealous in its application. My darling Constance reminds them of my need for solitude if they forget. I haven't yet found a way to convey to her that her zeal is sometimes more than the situation warrants. Watching her siblings scurry to do her bidding is too entertaining."

Her Grace had not struck Rosalind as in the least darling. "Your duchess is formidable." Rothhaven was more formidable, for all his talk of peace and quiet.

"She has had to be, as I suspect you have had to be. Tell me about your missing lady's maids."

Rothhaven had a way of making a command sound like an invitation, and Rosalind found herself settling into the wing chair and recounting the facts for him. She'd polished off a cup of tea and a piece of lavender shortbread before Ned peeked into the room.

"I should have known," he said. "Rothhaven, good day."

"Please join us," the duke replied. "Her ladyship sought an understandable respite from the melee. Stephen and Constance were in good form, I take it?"

Ned took the place on the sofa beside the duke. "Oh, of course, and Abigail is very much up to their weight. Lady Rosalind, I'm sorry they offended you, but I assure you, no insult was intended."

They *had* offended Rosalind. "I am unused to such rumbustious company. No offense taken."

Rothhaven passed Ned a cup of tea. "You sent them off on various goose chases, I take it?"

Ned glanced at Rosalind a little sheepishly. "Let's say they are pursuing peripheral theories."

"You manage them, and they don't even realize it," Rosalind said. "Don't you ever want to tell them all to go to blazes?"

Ned and His Grace both seemed amused by her question. "All the time," they said in unison.

"And they," His Grace went on, "grow similarly exasperated with us, and yet, our mutual regard is

great as well, else we could not so effectively annoy
one another. One learns to see the good intentions and
ignore the vexatious deeds, for the most part."

"They mean well?" Rosalind asked.

"They do," Ned said. "They invariably do, and I
would not have consulted them had I not thought them
capable of true aid at some point. Shall I escort you
downstairs, my lady?"

Rosalind wanted to linger in His Grace's company,
to bask in the warmth of his calm, and in his dry
humor and clear affection for a family Rosalind didn't
particularly like.

Also his obvious regard for Ned.

"Here is how you go on," Rothhaven said, rising and
extending a hand to Rosalind. "You enter from stage
left on Ned's handsome arm, and you smile at him as
if you're enjoying some secluded path at Vauxhall on
a lovely night. Thank the assemblage for their efforts
and suggest to my darling wife that you and she take
in the latest exhibition at the Royal Academy. Forget
about dragging her around to the shops. I will be in
your personal debt if you can endure the Academy's
offerings in my stead, and I always pay my debts, Lady
Rosalind."

Though his smile was slight, Rothhaven's eyes
conveyed warmth and a genuine request for aid.

"Are you managing me, Your Grace?" Rosalind
asked, taking the duke's hand and rising.

"Of course not," he said. "You strike me as a woman
who has had more managing than she can sanely
tolerate. I well know how that feels."

How could he possibly...? Rothhaven's earlier

comment came back, about having made an undignified exit from polite society in childhood. Rosalind was sure that departure had not been Rothhaven's choice.

"Have you any advice regarding our investigations, Your Grace?"

Rothhaven walked with Rosalind to the door, Ned on her other side. "I can tell you this, my lady. Those missing women need you to keep looking. You might be too late to save them, but if Ned's suspicions are correct, a scheme is afoot. That scheme will continue claiming victims until somebody puts a stop to it. The Wentworths are annoying in their vigor and outspokenness, but you could not ask for more loyal allies, and in this, I speak from experience."

He bowed over her hand, as courteously as if they were parting ways after Sunday services. "My advice is to *persist*. When you are daunted and overwhelmed, persist anyway. The ladies are counting on you, as am I."

Rothhaven delivered part of that speech while regarding Ned rather than Rosalind. Ned bowed to the duke before taking his leave and escorted Rosalind from the room.

"There isn't another duke like him in the whole history of the aristocracy," Ned murmured. "Jane claims Rothhaven and Walden understood each other from the moment they met."

"And yet," Rosalind said, pausing at the top of the stairs, "you and Rothhaven had the same rapport, didn't you?"

"I respect him."

"You like him and you trust him, and he likes you. I suspect he doesn't like many people."

Ned gazed back at the closed parlor door. "Rothhaven is one of the kindest people I know. Constance says that early in life he chose compassion over judgment, and I can see what she means. Rothhaven is nobody's fool, but neither is he haughty or arrogant."

"Early in life, he apparently lost his family and his home, just as you did. Of course you and he would have much in common. You have also chosen compassion over judgment, but I cannot like the extent to which the Wentworths trespass on your good nature. Will you accompany Her Grace and me to the exhibition?"

"Of course, but I draw the line at the milliner's."

"My companion subjected me to that trial recently. I would like to see your bank, Mr. Wentworth."

He led her down the steps, back to the parlor from which raised voices were now emanating. "It's not my bank, my lady. I merely work there."

He believed that. "If it's not your bank, why do you begrudge yourself every hour spent away from it? You might not own that bank, but the bank certainly has a claim on you. What was it His Grace said? Look as if I've been enjoying your company on a secluded path?"

Rosalind kissed Ned on the mouth, though fleetingly in light of the circumstances. Some disobliging Wentworth could exit the parlor at any moment.

"On a particularly lovely night," Ned replied, hand on the door latch. "I would like to show you the bank sometime. I mean that."

"And I would like to see it." Also to burn the place to the ground.

Ned kissed her, more lingeringly, and stepped back one instant before Lord Stephen yanked open the door.

* * *

I would like to show you the bank sometime.

For two hours, while the ladies had admired or criticized art, Ned had stood by and mentally kicked himself. *Show her the bank.* In the long and varied annals of swain-dom, that had to be the least romantic overture a man had ever made to a woman he wanted to impress.

But what else did he have to show her? His little town house, tucked away on a quiet street, would impress no one. His embroidery was a hobby for the idle hours of the evening. His fiddling was of the low sort—jigs, reels, ballads, and laments. He read music reluctantly, and Rosalind—veteran of endless musicales—would expect him to play perishing Beethoven for her.

Ned pondered his many shortcomings as he used the bank's front door rather than take the side entrance reserved for employees. The building was kept scrupulously clean at His Grace of Walden's insistence, which meant the main floor was full of light from overhead and clerestory windows. The whole of the lobby was ringed with a second story of offices and meeting rooms, while the bank's cellars were full of records, quarters for the badgers, and the clerks' hall.

Ferns added a bright touch, as did airy landscapes on the walls. Comfortable seating allowed the beldames and grandpapas to sit while waiting for a clerk or teller to attend them, and a bouquet of pink lilies graced both ends of the row of tellers' windows.

Ned had often thought that if a church could be cheerful rather than solemn, then it would more closely resemble the bank. The air of quiet industry was like a tonic, though the sight of Quinn Wentworth, His Grace of Walden, at the second-floor balustrade rather dimmed Ned's spirits. With each year, Walden became more the aristocrat, more involved with legislation and policy in the Lords. The sovereign conferred with him regularly, and Walden had recently expanded the bank's business to include a branch in New York.

His Grace would choose today of all days to monitor Ned's arrival.

Ned doffed his hat and took the steps at a decorous pace. No running in the bank, ever.

"Your Grace." Ned nodded and sauntered past. He'd nearly reached the door of his own office before the duke spoke.

"Enjoying the afternoon air, Ned?"

The question was pleasant—too pleasant. The little word *again* remained loudly unspoken.

"No, actually," Ned said, continuing into his office. "I was idling about the Royal Academy, listening to Constance and Lady Rosalind gushing about light and perspective and deuce knows what. Stephen avoids any outing that involves standing for long periods, and I gather Lord Nathaniel was otherwise occupied."

Rothhaven, it went without saying, was not to be subjected to the crowds, much less to the hurly-burly of London's streets.

"Constance no longer needs a chaperone," Walden said, following Ned into his office and closing the door. "She can hire a companion if she's of a mind to impress somebody with her knowledge of art. She can ask Jane to accompany her."

She could not ask her ducal brother, apparently. "Was there something else you wanted to say, Your Grace? If not, I have hours of work yet to do if I'm to be ready for tomorrow's meetings." Tomorrow was the day set aside for the small investors' progress reports, and Ned would be damned if he'd appear unprepared before the directors.

He was well informed regarding most of the accounts, but another review was still in order.

"You subjected yourself to Constance's artistic effusions," Walden said, "because you saw a chance to spend time with Lady Rosalind."

Ned wanted to sit at his desk and bury his mind in ledgers for a time. To push aside all thoughts of missing maids, Wentworths, and meetings, and occupy himself with work he was competent to do.

"Spending a pleasant hour or two with a young lady is now an infraction of some bank rule?" Ned asked, in tones as polite as those Walden had adopted. "Headmaster excuses me to attend Her Grace of Walden's at-homes without number, but I cannot escort a young woman whom I esteem on a pleasant errand?"

Ned had told Rosalind to ask him for what she wanted. That Walden would turn up cheeseparing now was unfair and unlike him.

Walden went to the window, inspecting for dirt, no

doubt. "You esteem Lady Rosalind, understandably, and she has asked for your assistance with the matter of her missing maids, but Ned, I know you."

"And?"

Walden swiped an idle finger across the windowsill. "All those years ago, Jane and I arranged a discreet exit from Newgate for you. The proper parties were in readiness, the way was clear. You refused to go."

"I was a boy. Boys are foolish." And Walden never referred to the circumstances under which he and Ned had met.

"You were loyal," Walden said, "and fierce, and principled, in your odoriferous, foul-mouthed way. You faced transportation with all the horrors attendant thereto, and I arranged a reprieve for you. You did not take that reprieve, and Jane has told me your reasoning."

Blast dear Jane to perdition. "What has this to do with my needing to get to work?" Ned did not want to sit while the duke prowled the room, and he couldn't seem to find anywhere to stand. He settled for a place by the hearth, though on such a pleasant day, the fire had not been lit.

"Ned, you refused to abandon me. You watched my hanging because you felt it unfair for me to face death alone. You had more conviction and principle as a boy than the entire English system of justice has amassed in centuries of trying."

The worst part of those memories was the sound of the platform dropping. The morning had been pretty as only springtime can be, sunny and peaceful, birds pecking at the dirt and chirping a greeting to the new day. By virtue of great expense, Walden had arranged for his execution to be private.

"You were innocent," Ned said, around an ache in his throat. "You were an innocent man, and what happened to you was wrong."

Walden prowled away from the window and stood two feet from Ned. "I never told you I was innocent. For all you knew, I was a killer."

"Guilt has a reek," Ned said, shaking his head, "a way of cramping a man's movements, shadowing his gaze. You were innocent of taking anybody's life. You didn't have to tell me that, I could smell it on you. You were solitary and hard and determined—I admired you for that—but you were not a killer. I did what I could to stand by you, little enough though it was."

"Precisely," Walden said. "For the sake of your stubborn notions of right and wrong, you threw away your own freedom. Now Lady Rosalind has involved you in another situation wherein the innocent are at risk for a bad fate, and you cannot help yourself. You are caught up in her cause, and you will jeopardize all you've worked for to aid her."

Ned sidled away. "No, I won't. I will do what I can, just as I did what I could in Newgate. It was precious little then, and I suspect it will be precious little now." Ned had had a plan of his own all those years ago, a plan that would not have ended in his transportation to a far-off land.

Walden ran a hand through his hair. "Women go missing from London's streets and alleys all the time, Ned. Some of them want to go missing."

Right now, Ned wanted Walden to go missing. "And

most of them do not want any such thing. I appreciate the warning."

"Jane told me to keep my mouth shut."

Ned took the place at his desk. "And just this once, you had to ignore your duchess's good advice and inflict your concerns on me?"

"Jane is worried for you too. She is well aware that locating missing women will force you into proximity with...bad elements."

Ned pulled a ledger at random from the stack on his blotter. "You've become a diplomat in your dotage. I've already started the inquiries at the brothels, and I will spend the evening along the river, assuming I ever get through my reports."

"Fine. You're a Wentworth. Stubbornness is emblazoned on your soul, but for the love of God be careful, Ned. Jane will be inconsolable if anything happens to you, and I will be..."

Ned looked up. "Yes?"

"I will be *deranged*."

The notion of His Grace not in possession of his wits.... Hyperbole, surely. The Wentworths were given to hyperbole.

"I will do my utmost to spare you any grief, Your Grace."

Had Walden lectured, exhorted, scolded, or otherwise resorted to displays of authority, Ned could have countered with silence, patient humor, and polite promises to address the duke's concerns.

Walden instead headed for the door without another word.

"How bad were the conditions of Rothhaven's

confinement at that asylum?" Ned asked before the duke could make good his escape.

"Awful, at least for a time. Why?"

"Imagine yourself a lady's maid, Walden. You were brought up to know your psalms and guard your virtue. You work hard, but you don't complain because you're glad to have your post and you do the best you can with it. Then you end up in hell."

Walden winced, but Ned wasn't finished.

"You are afraid," he went on, "without friends, your person violated, your good name gone forever. The pain in your body isn't the half of it, and nobody— nobody at all—knows or cares that everything you loved and everything you were has been ripped away from you. No laws protect you, no vestigial decency remains in the people exploiting you. Livestock and lapdogs have more value than you do, and are given more respect."

Ned stood because he finally had Walden's attention. "I will continue to pursue Lady Rosalind's causes, Your Grace, because nobody with the proper authority to do so can be bothered. My regards to your duchess."

Walden's gaze was unreadable, but he bowed slightly and took his leave.

That bow was still on Ned's mind hours later, when he closed the last ledger and realized he was hungry.

Famished, in fact, and the hour was too late to patronize the chophouse down the street. Ned donned his cloak and gathered up his hat, gloves, and walking stick, and prepared to spend the rest of the evening making inquiries in places low and bawdy.

"Good night, Mr. Wentworth," the watchman called

as Ned headed for the side door. "Mind how you go out there. Rain's on the way."

Brilliant. Ned detoured to the umbrella stand. "Are the boys all in for the night?"

The watchman, a former sailor by the name of Rawlings, shook his head. "The newest one, Artie, hasn't come in. He thinks I don't notice that he's left a window cracked, but I do, and it won't serve, Mr. Wentworth. Somebody sees him slippin' in the window, they'll slip in after him and have a look about."

Nothing of any value was left unlocked on the bank premises, but Rawlings had a point. The boys were valuable, Rawlings was valuable, and they could come to harm in the course of a failed robbery.

"I'll have a word with him," Ned said. "Another word. Any idea what he's getting up to on these nocturnal sorties?"

Rawlings looked past Ned, to the gloom beyond the door. "Says he has business to tend to, but you ask me, that lad is worrit something fierce."

Chapter Eight

"Neddy is managing us," Stephen said, rocking gently with the infant cradled in his arms. "Sending us off on harmless errands to keep us safe while he does the real work. This child will soon no longer be a baby."

The boy was marvelously solid, and thank all the minsters of heaven, he charged about on two sturdy legs as his father could not.

"He will always be our baby," Abigail said, "and you have, as usual, rocked him to sleep. Jane says Walden had the same skill. He could calm a teething infant when all the nursery maids and Jane herself could not."

"The ducal touch," Stephen said, kissing the baby's forehead. "The wee ones recognize it."

Abigail glanced up from her stitching. "The novelty of a father's affection. You show up at the end of the day, after that child has been fed, dressed, changed, entertained, scolded, and otherwise kept safe by women since dawn's early light. Of course he's fascinated with you. I miss you too."

The child sighed, the sweetest sound under heaven. "I'm at the bank more," Stephen said. "I know that. I'm not always sure what I'm *doing* at the bank, but Quinn is caught up in his parliamentary schemes, and the navy has little need for new cannons these days. I'm happy to assist Neddy with his mystery of the missing maids, but he's not really letting us *do* much, is he?"

Abigail was working on a quilt, stitching together squares of flannel into the Walden coat of arms. Stephen thought the design daft, but Abigail intended that the quilt become an heirloom, passed from one generation of Wentworths to the next.

"Ned has told us what we'll need to know should he require reinforcements," Abigail said, "and in the early days of an investigation, it's important to keep an open mind. The apothecaries might know something. The club gossip might yield a scrap of information."

"Neddy truly expects me to sit in the clubs twiddling my thumbs while he frequents the brothels and taverns. I don't like it, Abigail. Ned isn't a brothels-and-taverns sort of fellow."

She tied off her thread and snipped the needle free. "I don't like it either, Stephen. He's too alone. Always observing, always cordial and quiet. As a girl who didn't have friends, and as a woman who never fit in, I want better for him. What do we know of his family?"

"We are his family." Stephen shifted the baby so the lad was cradled against his shoulder. "Neddy is smitten with Lady Rosalind. I can't recall another occasion when he has been smitten."

Which was either a testament to extraordinary

discretion on Ned's part, or evidence of manly humors severely out of balance.

Abigail folded the fabric into a soft pile. "To hear Jane tell it, she was smitten with Ned as a boy. He was so fierce and so loyal to Walden."

"And so dirty," Stephen said. "Stank like a muck pit and at the mention of a bath he fought like a..."

"What?"

"A cornered badger. Ned wasn't wary of soap and water, he loathed it. Once Jane laid down the law to him, he would not allow anybody in the laundry when he was at his ablutions. He'd not only lock the door, he'd lock the windows and make Davies stand guard outside the laundry room. I found it hilarious."

Abigail looked thoughtful. "If your young son behaved like that, would you find it so entertaining?"

"No," Stephen said, "and the memory, as well as the recollection of my reaction, are both uncomfortable. We love Neddy, but we don't know his early particulars. He has more dignity than Walden in some regards, and one doesn't trespass on his privacy lightly."

"Maybe Lady Rosalind can be family to him," Abigail said, setting aside her sewing. "In her way, she is fierce too. I've never seen anybody else actually walk out of a Wentworth conversational affray, but the tactic was effective. We were on better behavior after that."

She rose and took the child from Stephen. He preferred not to carry the boy except in a dire emergency.

"This lad needs sisters," Stephen said, gathering up his cane and getting to his feet. "Sisters to make a gentleman of him in ways you and I cannot."

"He has girl cousins." Abigail managed the sleeping child and the door latch. "Didn't Ned have a brother?"

"He did, one who came to a bad end, apparently. Picking pockets is a hazardous profession. I gather that's how Ned ended up in Newgate. Either picking pockets or shoplifting."

"I cannot imagine our Ned resorting to larceny."

"He never begged," Stephen said, accompanying Abigail up the steps to the nursery suite. "He let that much slip after a few pints of summer ale years ago and hasn't alluded to it since. I didn't know if he was bragging, lamenting, or simply stating a fact." Stephen, by contrast, had been a very effective beggar boy with his little crutch and crooked leg.

"You aren't about to sit idling around in the clubs, are you?" Abigail asked, after they'd gained the warmth of the nursery and passed the child to a sleepy nurse.

"What do you suggest I do with myself instead?"

Abigail twined her arm through his as they made their way along dimly lit corridors to their apartment.

"You *should* lurk in the clubs," she said, moving from their sitting room directly into the bedroom. "Bankers and inquiry agents both must gather information from as many sources as possible. Ned's projects prosper in part because he listens to everybody—the tellers, the grannies, the flower girls, the nabobs, and the lordlings. If pet rabbits are becoming fashionable, Ned learns of it before anybody else, and that's an advantage."

"Pet rabbits?"

"Speaking figuratively. Good gracious, I am tired."

Stephen and Abigail had an evening routine, assisting

each other to undress, sometimes sharing a nightcap, sometimes reading to each other before the fire. If anybody had told a younger Stephen that he'd come to crave such domesticity, to need it more desperately than he needed his canes, he would have scoffed.

As he'd scoffed at young Ned, so determined to avoid the bath.

"I'm to lurk in the clubs as directed," Stephen said, undoing Abigail's hooks, "but might you also point me in a more productive direction? Ned finally presents us with a task he cannot accomplish entirely on his own, and I want to help."

Abigail unknotted Stephen's cravat. "Then you do something Ned cannot do for himself."

Nothing came to mind. Nothing at all. "For example?"

"Have a look into Lady Rosalind's situation. Two of the maids went missing from her household. Coincidence, perhaps, and perhaps not. Then too..." Abigail leaned in to sniff at Stephen's throat. "I love the scent of you."

"Then too?" Stephen prompted as Abigail unbuttoned his shirt.

"Then too, Lady Rosalind's father votes his seat. What does Quinn know of him, what does Jane know of the bachelor sons? Ned would not think to ask those questions, but you can."

Stephen had the vague sense his wife was managing him, as Ned had, but Abigail's management was thoroughly agreeable. She'd brought order, joy, and regular meals to Stephen's days, and as for his nights...

He kissed her. "I've missed you too, you know."

She stepped closer and wrapped her arms around him. In Abigail's embrace, Stephen felt secure. No need for canes, no need to lean against sturdy furniture or brace himself against a wall.

"Do you truly hope for a girl this time?" Abigail asked.

Stephen prayed simply that their baby would thrive. "Of course. Can't have the lad growing up spoiled."

Abigail insinuated herself more closely into Stephen's embrace, and how he loved, adored, and worshipped her sturdy abundance.

"Then let's to bed, Husband. Now."

"I am, in this as in all things, your willing servant."

Before Stephen finished undressing and joined his wife beneath the covers, he jotted down a note to himself: *Lady Rosalind's circumstances*. He did this against the certain knowledge that once he and Abigail embarked on their marital enthusiasms, every notion and idea would leave his head, save for thoughts of pleasing Abigail and being pleased by Abigail.

An exhilarating hour later, Stephen was drowsing in his beloved's arms, and a final question wedged its way past the sense of blissful repletion: What was *Lady Rosalind* doing for Ned that Ned could not do for himself?

* * *

Tryphena Dorinda Hepplewhite had parlayed tiny size and giant ambition into a thriving institution of venery two streets back from the docks. She was no longer young by the standards of her trade, and the passing years, in Ned's opinion, had made her ruthlessly determined to keep her riverside empire safe from all encroachments.

"Well, if it isn't my wee Neddy, come to call."

I am not now, nor have I ever been, your anything. "Tryphena, good evening." Ned did not bow, nor did he surrender his hat to the waiting footman-muscle. Tryphena had received him in the room that passed for her personal parlor, a shrine to gilt, hung silk, and what she doubtless considered imperial shades of red.

The result was a parody of grandeur, much as the gin palaces springing up all over London were parodies of the fine domiciles they aped.

"No word, Neddy," Tryphena said. "Hasn't been any word for years. You're like that Penelope fool from the Greek story, 'cept your pa won't ever come back."

She didn't bother mimicking the speech of her betters, and why should she? Her clientele had no aspirations beyond the next pint of ale or interlude upstairs, which Tryphena limited to thirty minutes, paid in advance.

"As it happens, I'm not here to inquire about my father."

Tryphena gave him a look that made his flesh crawl. She affected the appearance of a doll, from her use of bright red lip paint, to her hair done in elaborate ringlets, to a wardrobe in the pale colors chosen to adorn little girls still in the nursery.

The result, given her age and the knowledge in her eyes, was ghoulish.

"You aren't here to ask after your pa?" The leer she turned on Ned embodied both lechery and a coldness of soul so depraved it should have been recounted in Dante's description of hell.

She walked a slow circle around him. "I'd make an exception for you, wee Neddy. I have a soft spot for dark-eyed lads. A lot of my customers do too. You could give up all that nobbery and snobbery, come back to where you belong. I'd make you rich."

She reached out as if to pat his flank. Ned used his walking stick to gently deflect the caress. Not even provocation from her would tempt him to raise a hand to a woman.

"Somebody is taking decent girls from the streets of Mayfair, Tryphena. The young ladies aren't being held for ransom, they aren't taking up with some chance-met sailor or drover. These are lady's maids and companions, young women without family in Town and without lofty connections."

Tryphena stalked away and took a seat on a raised gilt chair upholstered in red velvet. Her perch was at such a height that she needed a stepstool to ascend to it, much as a child might.

"I ain't took 'em, so don't be askin' what I did wif 'em. The fancy ones are more trouble than they're worth. They don't know nuffink, and they don't hold up to the trade. Ask that Nimitz bitch wot she done with yer missin' maids."

"I won't be asking anybody anything, least of all you," Ned said, summoning all the icy hauteur he'd learned from watching Walden. "I am here to warn you, Tryphena. You have enemies without number. Every bawd in London despises you, your employees hate you, and the reformers would love to see your den of iniquity burned to the ground."

She sat upon her throne, the queen of indifference. "I'm an honest business woman, I am, running an honest business. I don't water me gin and me whores are willin'."

"Then why are your windows nailed shut?" Ned knew exactly why and how that practice had begun.

"Can't have the lads pikin' off with the goods, can I?" The goods, in Tryphena's estimation, were the women and boys she provided to her customers.

"Heed me, Tryphena. When it becomes apparent that somebody is preying on decent women, suspicion will turn on you. Informants will implicate you whether you have a hand in this evil or not. They will swear under oath that they've seen the missing women at your establishment, and there won't be a rock left in England that you can hide under."

"Talk never did nothin'. Billy will show you out."

Ned tapped his hat onto his head with every evidence of nonchalance. He had dressed for this occasion in worn attire, scuffed boots, and a hat with a slightly crumpled brim. No watch, no cravat pin, no rings. Just a knife in each boot and a peashooter in each pocket.

"You don't know who you're up against," he said, sending her a pitying smile. "You rile the Quality, and it becomes a matter of pride with them to seek retribution. Your guilt or innocence won't matter. You've committed enough wrongdoing generally that in their eyes you deserve their wrath. I know how they think, and you have but one choice if you want to continue on your puppet throne."

"Say your piece and get out." She tried for insouciance, but Ned saw the fear behind the façade. Tryphena had carved out a piece of turf for herself through grit, meanness, bribes, and determination, but she held that ground in a precarious grip. With her own kind, the truces were in place for now, but she couldn't indefinitely escape the notice of aristocrats and prosperous merchants determined to "clean up the docks."

"If you want to avoid the noose, you find these women, Tryphena. You listen to your sailors and dockhands, you ply the able seamen and bargemen with drink. Somebody has started a new game, right under your nose, and it's a game that bodes ill for your trade. When you learn something, you send Billy to me. No notes, no messengers I won't recognize. Find these women, find them fast, and don't think to involve yourself in whatever is afoot."

Tryphena stood on her stepstool, her glower almost convincing. "I ain't took 'em, and I don't know who did, and I don't wanna know."

"Yes, Tryphena, you do want to know. Because it's only a matter of time before whoever is behind this brings your little dollhouse crashing down around you. On that happy day, you will finally swing for kidnapping, among your many other trespasses. You are small, and your hanging would be a protracted entertainment for the mob at Newgate. I'll bid you good evening."

Ned turned his back on her without a farewell. As he reached the door, Billy abandoned his eyes-front impersonation of liveried statuary. The glance was fleeting and fraught, and confirmed what Ned had hoped to learn from this most distasteful interview.

Tryphena knew something. Unlike Mrs. Nimitz, who had probably heard rumors or caught a whiff of gossip, Tryphena *knew* something.

Ned knew something too.

He knew he would never return to this place. Not for any scrap of information, not for the pleasure of watching Tryphena squirm under the weight of a lifetime's fear and guilt. Not even for the profound gratification of seeing her arrested for her many crimes would he return to this hell.

He had proved what he had come to prove here and had nothing to gain by subjecting himself to more of Tryphena's cruelty.

Billy gave him the barest nod. Ned did not return the gesture. He stood out on the walkway, breathing the relatively fresh air of a chilly spring night. When he returned home, despite the lateness of the hour, he ordered a hot soaking bath.

Before leaving for the bank the next morning, he instructed his housekeeper to give the clothes he'd worn the previous night to the first beggar she came across on market day.

* * *

"I was hoping I'd see you here." Rosalind smiled behind her glass of punch, though the entire room should have noticed how pleased she was simply to behold Ned Wentworth.

"I am a regular fixture at Her Grace's at-homes," he replied. "I get a break from bank business, Her Grace has a tame bachelor on the premises, and before I leave I pay a visit to the nursery. Shall we admire the garden?"

Rosalind set her glass on the tray of a passing footman, a sizable blond specimen who was nearly the twin of the second fellow gliding regally among the guests.

Ducal consequence was subtly evident in Her Grace's formal parlor, from the matched pair of Viking footmen to the exquisite bouquets perfuming the air. Harp music drifted gently through the open folding doors of the adjacent music room, and guests chattered in convivial groups.

"The garden would be delightful," Rosalind said. "Her Grace introduced Mrs. Barnstable to some physician-viscount, and they are in raptures over the topic of nerve tonics."

Mr. Wentworth led her from the parlor and across the corridor to another parlor, this one clearly informal. An enormous mastiff rose from the rug to greet him with a sniff to his hand.

"This is Hercules," Mr. Wentworth said. "He is Abigail's sworn vassal. The garden here is much larger than what he enjoys at home, so he bides at the ducal residence frequently. Hercules, come."

Man and dog passed through French doors onto a back terrace blessedly devoid of guests. The day was fine, not quite hot, and the dog took off at a lope down the steps.

"He's going to pay his respects," Mr. Wentworth said. "Walden and I buried Her Grace's late pet, Wodin, in the back corner of the garden. Hercules supervised that undertaking."

"You and *His Grace* dug the grave?" Surely he did not mean that?

"Walden dug graves for a wage in his youth. The job is not as simple as you might think. If the grass and whatnot is to grow back, the bottom dirt must be replaced first, and so forth. His Grace has buried any number of family pets, and says the exertion helps ease the upset of a loss. For Walden, digging the grave was a way to be of use to his duchess and their girls. The ladies did treasure that dog."

"And you?" Rosalind asked, as Ned escorted her onto a walkway of crushed shells. "Did you treasure that dog?"

He gazed out over the garden, to where Hercules had disappeared beneath towering rhododendrons.

"Pathetically so. That beast saved my sanity, when I thought I'd expire of boredom or the sheer strangeness of wearing livery. I was His Grace's tiger for a time, then a clerk, then I had various duties at the bank. Throughout those years, regardless of my station, Her Grace would occasionally demand that I take Wodin out for some air."

"Wodin was your friend." Rosalind did not know what to make of such a conclusion. Ned Wentworth was personable, well spoken, well educated, handsome.... Why would he favor the company of a dog? And yet, what better company was there than a loyal canine?

"When I went up to university," he said, "I wrote letters to Wodin in my head. The letters I sent to Their Graces, to Stephen or the sisters, were polite drivel about natural philosophy and the symbolism in Greek mythology, but to the dog, I poured out my woes."

"I missed my mare like that," Rosalind said, linking her arm through his. "No amount of begging could induce my father to send her off to school with me. *Too expensive, Rosalind. Stop whining, Rosalind. Don't be impertinent, Rosalind.*" This topic had nothing to do with kidnapped maids, but it mattered all the same.

"Let me guess," Mr. Wentworth said. "Your brothers' ponies were packed off to public school with them."

"Horses, not ponies. Neither George nor Lindhurst went to Harrow until they were fourteen, and a four-teen-year-old boy must have a proper horse. Also a valet and tutor and regular baskets from home."

Rosalind and her escort had ambled some distance from the house, to a rose arbor covered in greenery. "Something has made you sad," she said. "Do you miss the dog?"

"Let's sit, my lady. Why do you say I am sad?"

"Your eyes, the quality of your quiet. You are self-possessed to a fault, but something troubles you today. If you are quitting the inquiry into my missing maids, you need only say so. You have already been of immeasurable help."

"Will you quit the inquiry, my lady?"

Rosalind thought back to the previous week's encounter with His Grace of Rothhaven. "I won't want to."

Beneath the arching rose arbor was a bench of wrought iron painted white. Rosalind took a seat, wanting the privacy, however forbidden.

Mr. Wentworth remained on his feet, which Rosalind

took for a prelude to a polite, entirely rational explanation of why they must admit defeat.

"The situation grows complicated," he said. "I have kicked over certain rocks, in certain low and unsavory locations. A scheme is definitely afoot, and whoever is behind it has the power to intimidate one of the most hard-hearted, ruthless, conniving people I know. My challenge is to be yet still more intimidating, which is difficult when I don't know who my enemy is."

"Sit with me?" Rosalind asked.

He glanced around the deserted garden, then flipped out the tails of his morning coat and settled beside her. The bench was small, and he took up rather a lot of it.

"The matter is now officially dangerous, my lady. If the abbesses and madams are afraid, then an earl's daughter has every reason to keep her distance."

"If the abbesses and madams are afraid, can you imagine how Calliope Henderson must feel? How Francine Arbuckle must feel?"

The dog woofed from some yards away, then came trotting up the path to sit at Ned's feet.

"Yes, actually," Mr. Wentworth said, "I can imagine exactly how they feel. Miss Arbuckle was off to fetch a pair of slippers one moment, and then her world came to an end. As far as she knows, nobody cares one whit about what has befallen her."

Rosalind slipped her hand into Mr. Wentworth's. "I would care very much if you disappeared."

"That's not what I... You ought not to say such things." And yet, he made no move to turn loose of her hand.

"Why not? My mother was there one day, and a

week later, she was gone. I was not permitted into her sickroom, and I never had a chance to tell her I loved her. When I was younger, I believed that if she'd known how much I would miss her and how much I needed her, she would not have left me."

Rosalind leaned against Mr. Wentworth, missing her dear mama all over again.

"Do you have a likeness of her?" he asked.

"My father has a miniature of her beside his bed. The servants looked the other way, and I sneaked into his room often enough to make a copy." While Ned Wentworth had nothing of his family, not a sketch, not a Bible, nothing.

"I keep at my embroidery for that reason," he said. "I would sit beside my mother when I was a small boy, and watch her make flowers with thread and linen while she sang the old lullabies and ballads. She showed me all the stitches and told me that when I could thread my own needle, I could have my own hoop. I poked more holes in my fingers than I did in the cloth at first."

"But you persisted, and now your stitchery is beautiful." And how Rosalind's heart ached for that small boy, fascinated with his mother's needlework.

"To become a tailor takes years, but I had the knack of embroidery fairly quickly. I want you to promise me something, Rosalind."

Not *my lady*, but Rosalind. She hugged that bit of familiarity to her heart. "I'm listening."

"Promise me that at no point will you take on the particulars of this investigation yourself. Somebody powerful, nasty, and determined has devised this scheme, and you are a pretty young woman."

My nose is too big. My hair is too dark. My opinions are too much in evidence and those are very unattractive qualities indeed. "I am not a companion or a lady's maid. I am safe."

Mr. Wentworth brought her gloved hand up, to rest his cheek against her knuckles. "I thought I was safe, Miss Arbuckle thought she was safe, as did Miss Henderson and Miss Campbell. If they can be snatched off the street, so can you, and I would never forgive myself if any harm befell you. Promise me you will be careful."

"You must promise me something too, Ned Wentworth. May I call you Ned?" Shockingly familiar of her, but she so wanted him to continue calling her Rosalind rather than *my lady*.

"My given name is Edward, and I will cheerfully answer to Ned. I'm not all that fond of Neddy, truth be told."

"If you refrain from calling me Roz, I will exercise a reciprocal courtesy and refrain from calling you Neddy. Promise me you will be careful. Not simply cautious as you are by nature, but inordinately careful. I would never forgive myself if any harm befell you."

He kissed her gloved fingers, and some of the bleakness left his eyes. "You are a marvel, Rosalind Kinwood. A blazing, beautiful marvel."

Had she leaned forward four inches, she could have kissed him for those words, but the dog chose that moment to spring to his feet, tail wagging, and warn them of approaching footsteps.

* * *

Ned hadn't brought Rosalind to the rose arbor on purpose, but the garden had only so many benches, and benches tended to be located in the shade, and her ladyship was, as Ned had noticed on countless occasions, ever so kissable.

Fate, in the form of two females whom he ignored at his peril, preserved him from taking that liberty.

"Uncle Dee-Dee can read me a story!" Lady Mary Jane Wentworth charged ahead of her sister and wedged herself between Ned and Lady Rosalind. "Nurse said."

Lady Elizabeth Wentworth, who no longer tolerated the nickname Bitty from any save her papa, sighed dramatically.

"Mary saw you from the nursery window, and what she sees she must have on the very instant lest we all lose our hearing. Nurse said the day was quite fine so the infant could take the air, and because I am exceedingly bored with my intolerably dull French verbs, I have made this enormous sacrifice. Am I not noble of heart? You should introduce me to Lady Rosalind, Ned. That would be polite."

Jane claimed that Elizabeth had reached the *excessive modifiers* stage of girlhood, when speech was peppered with *quite, exceedingly, very, vexatiously*, and other extraneous flourishes. According to Jane, the next phases would be wheedling for two straight years to adopt adult hairstyles, followed by the apotheosis of botheration, a fixation on boys.

"Read me the ass," Mary Jane said, opening her book. "The ass says hee-uhh-hee-uhh!"

Ned put Mary Jane on his lap. "Lady Rosalind

Kinwood, may I make known to you Lady Elizabeth Wentworth, long-suffering saint without portfolio and aspiring literary genius. Byron hasn't a patch on Lady Elizabeth's rhymes. This embodiment of all that is wonderful on my lap is Lady Mary Jane Wentworth, Mary the Magnificent to her mob of adoring friends. I suspect I will not be permitted to leave this bench without reading the indicated tale."

Mary Jane was growing like the proverbial weed, as was Elizabeth. Whereas Elizabeth had always been nimble and lithe, little Mary Jane was chubby. Elizabeth's coltish grace was lately accompanied by pronouncements alternately insightful and pompous, and by pensive silences.

She was at an age where her feelings were easily hurt, an age Ned found hard to even look upon.

"Make the ass, Uncle Dee-Dee!" Mary Jane demanded. "The ass goes heeee-uhhhh-heeee-uhhhh!"

The dog looked worried, while Lady Rosalind looked ready to burst out laughing.

"Ned does the best ass," Elizabeth said earnestly. "Papa is our best bear, Cousin Duncan is a creditable owl, and Uncle Stephen is a fearsome wolf. For a proper braying ass, we much prefer Ned."

"Then I must hear this story," Lady Rosalind said, in all apparent seriousness. "My own dramatic talents are limited, and I enjoy a well-told story as much as anybody."

"Elizabeth would be in your debt if you accompanied her back to Her Grace's parlor." More than that, Ned could not say without embarrassing Elizabeth. The girl longed to be included in her mother's weekly at-homes, while Jane insisted that there was time enough for *that nonsense* in a year or two.

Elizabeth had doubtless volunteered to bring Mary Jane to the garden simply for the opportunity to walk past the open parlor doors.

"Thank you, no," Lady Rosalind said. "I much prefer the company to be had here in the garden, and I'm sure Lady Elizabeth does too."

Elizabeth subsided onto the opposite bench, apparently concluding that having the notice of one earl's daughter was preferable to peeking through the parlor doors and risking Mama's wrath.

"You really must not let us keep you from socializing, Lady Rosalind," Ned said. "Perhaps I'll see you hacking out in the park some fine morning later this week." Tomorrow would serve nicely.

"Do the ass," Mary Jane said. "The ass goes heee-uhhhh—"

Ned put a gentle hand over her mouth. "You are scaring Hercules. Attend me." He could nearly recite the tale by heart, but for the child's sake trailed his finger along the written words as he spoke. "A donkey—that's *asinus* in Latin—out wandering one day came upon the skin of a lion left in the forest by a hunter. Desiring to graze in peace undisturbed by wolves, jackals, and other hungry beasts, the ass donned the lion's skin..."

The donkey of course fooled everybody until he opened his mouth to speak—Ned dreaded to read those lines before Lady Rosalind, but brayed his way through them anyway—in which case the fox laughed himself silly at the donkey's expense.

"*And the moral of the story…*" Mary Jane said. "You have to read the moral, Uncle Dee-Dee."

"And the moral of the story," Ned recited, "*Quod non es, nec te esse simules.* Do not pretend to be what you are not."

"Or the fox will laugh at you, and you will feel ashamed." Mary Jane closed the book and hugged it. "I try to be good so I won't be ashamed."

"You are good," Ned said, cuddling her gently. "Never doubt it, child. You are the best little girl in the whole wide world, excepting possibly your older sisters, and they have had longer to practice than you have."

Elizabeth smiled a knowing-older-sister smile at that nonsense.

"Uncle Dee-Dee says I'm good." Mary Jane stuck her tongue out at her sister. "Read me another."

"I must not," Ned said solemnly. "Nurse allowed us one story, and we should obey her if we're to catch up to your sisters in goodness."

"I want another story."

"Then scamper back to the nursery with Elizabeth now, and when I come for supper on Sunday, I will read you another. If you wished to be doubly extra-good, you could bring Nurse a daffodil or two to brighten the playroom."

"I'll bring her three!" Mary Jane was off the bench, her book forgotten, her sister's hand clutched in hers.

Hercules trotted after them, leaving Ned alone with Lady Rosalind, who had just heard him do his very best impersonation of a braying ass.

"My mortification," he said, "is without limit."

"As are your thespian skills. I had forgotten that story, if I'd ever heard it before."

She wasn't laughing at him outright. In fact, she was regarding him with a seriousness the moment did not warrant.

"I was so behind in my Latin when His Grace consigned me to the schoolroom that I had to start with simple tales. I began reading the English versions to Bitty—Lady Elizabeth, rather—when she came down with chicken pox years ago, and my fate was sealed."

Rosalind took his hand and leaned against him on the bench. He could not see her face and thus had no clue what she was about.

"Rosalind?"

"You adore those children. You would die to keep them safe."

"I would, of course."

"What am I to do with you?"

You could kiss me. Except the moment wasn't a kissing sort of moment. The moment was a Rosalind sort of moment. Ned wrapped an arm around her shoulders, and that seemed to ease whatever emotion gripped her.

They remained thus, his arm around her, her cheek pressed to his chest, until Hercules trotted up the path and sat at Ned's knee.

"Will you meet me in the park tomorrow morning?" Ned asked.

Rosalind nodded and swiped at her cheek with gloved fingers. "Weather permitting. The day after otherwise, and so forth. We must find them, Ned. Every day matters. I feel it in my bones."

"We will find them." He sneaked a kiss to her temple, not half so confident as he sounded. Tryphena Hepplewhite did not intimidate easily, and whoever was behind this maid-snatching scheme had her thoroughly cowed.

That dubious accomplishment spoke of both ruthlessness and the power to act on that ruthlessness.

"I'll see you back to the house and make my farewells to Her Grace," Ned said, removing his arm from Rosalind's shoulders. "I would rather tarry with you out here on a picnic blanket."

"Someday, Ned Wentworth, you will tell that bank to go to blazes, and when you do, I hope I am on hand with a hamper and blanket, and a gig waiting to take us into the countryside."

What a marvelous, tempting thought, and not because of a hamper full of sandwiches. "I'll live in hope then," he said, rising and offering Rosalind his hand. "I know a group of widows who have a thriving business making up picnic baskets. Say the word and I will put in our order."

Rosalind stood and hugged him. "Surprise me, as you have surprised me today." She took his arm before he could turn the hug into anything more and walked with him back to the house.

He parted from Jane on a promise to return for Sunday supper, though just once, he'd like to spend his Sunday enjoying a picnic in some secluded wood out in Surrey. He left the Walden town house as he mentally scouted locations for that happy occasion only to find a Walden groom walking Ned's matched pair of chestnut geldings.

"What happened to my tiger?" Ned asked, more worried than irritated that Artie would leave his post.

"Said he had to step around behind the mews," the groom replied. "That was three-quarters of an hour ago, Mr. Wentworth. I figured the lad was in the kitchen. That's where I'd have been at his age. Boy could use some extra meals."

"The boy will soon need a new post," Ned said. "Have a look around and send him out here. I'll circle past a few times, but if you can't find him, he knows to return to the bank by sundown."

"Aye, sir." The groom touched a finger to his cap and ambled off in the direction of the alley.

Ned dawdled for nearly thirty minutes, and still, Artie was nowhere to be seen.

Chapter Nine

"Did you and his lordship promise to exchange recipes?" Rosalind asked, tying her bonnet ribbons loosely.

Mrs. Barnstable accepted a parasol from one of the Walden household's Viking footmen. "We did, my lady, and I must say, the viscount's approach was very intriguing. Spices, of all things. I mean, one knows they have an effect on the humors, but his study of them has been most scientific. He avers that chocolate..."

She paused to extract gloves from her reticule. Rosalind noted that Mrs. B's gloves had seen better days. Ned had said the investigation had become dangerous, but allowing him and his Wentworth relations to take all the initiative had grown... vexing.

"Begging your ladyship's pardon," the footman said, "but Mr. Wentworth has said I am to accompany you home."

He spoke with a slight accent, German or Scandinavian. *Mr. Ventvorth.*

"Very kind of you," Rosalind replied, "but I'm sure that's not necessary. I thought to make a stop at the glovemaker's and who knows how long we might tarry there?" She tried for her gracious-lady smile and got exactly nowhere. This footman might have been the King of Sweden for all his dignity, and he was every bit as formidable a specimen as Walden himself.

"Then I will carry your packages."

Then I vill carry your peckages. Snapped off with a full complement of masculine implacability.

"Your name?" Rosalind asked.

"Ivor, my lady."

He was somewhat lacking in deferential manners, and Rosalind could not determine his age. Ivor could be a slightly weathered thirty or a splendidly vigorous forty, but no footpad with a brain in his head would test Ivor's mettle.

No kidnapper either. *You are a marvel. A blazing, beautiful marvel.* The words could have been teasing, but the look on Ned's face when he'd spoken them had been nearly reverent. Rosalind had no delusions about her desirability generally. She was not a young, comely lady's maid, but Ned Wentworth found her attractive.

Found her *marvelous*.

"My lady." Mrs. Barnstable stood by the door, bonnet and gloves on, parasol in hand. "One does not offend a ducal family by refusing the services of one of their domestics."

First, there was nothing domestic about this toweringly muscular footman. Second, to blazes with the ducal family, though Rosalind would not casually offend Ned Wentworth.

"Of course I appreciate Ivor's escort."

Mrs. B toddled along at far below her usual pace, doubtless delighted to be seen on Mayfair's streets with a footman in ducal livery. When Rosalind would have ducked down a shady alley, Ivor shook his head.

"No alleys, please, my lady. I am but one man with two ladies to safeguard."

Drat all cautious footmen. Rosalind would investigate the alley another time, for it was the route Francine Arbuckle would have taken to the cobbler's.

"The longer route then," Rosalind replied, ignoring Mrs. Barnstable's curious glance.

At the glovemaker's, Ivor assumed the usual post near the door. The proprietress took one look at him—and his livery—and hustled forward to greet Rosalind.

"My lady, good day. Have you come to complete your collection of spring gloves? We have the most delicious assortment of colors and fabrics, and I would be happy to measure either of you for future orders."

"Let's start with Mrs. Barnstable," Rosalind replied. "I believe she can use some new everyday gloves in the colors of her choice, several pairs of reading gloves, and an extra pair of evening gloves in preparation for the Season's social demands."

The proprietress's smile outshone the noonday sun on a sparkling sea. "Fabric choices first, then. If *madame* would step this way?"

Amelia Barnstable loved to shop, while Rosalind viewed it as a necessary chore. The purpose of the visit to the glovemaker's was not to procure gloves, but rather, to engage the young clerk re-arranging the offerings on a table toward the back of the shop.

"These are the less-expensive choices?" Rosalind asked him.

"Aye, ma'am. Just as well made, but without the embroidery and whatnot. Can I help you find something in particular?"

He was a handsome, brown-haired youth, and as a clerk at a thriving shop, he had a good post.

"You can help me find someone," Rosalind said. "Do you recognize this woman?" She passed him a sketch of Calliope Henderson.

"Is the young lady in some sort of trouble?"

"Not in the sense you mean. She isn't suspected of committing any crimes. She left her post without notice, and we fear for her safety. She did not collect her wages or gather up her belongings. Do you know her?"

Rosalind pretended to examine the stitching on a pair of black gloves. Their intended use was for reading newspapers and new books, to preserve a lady's hands from the ink. Rosalind didn't bother with gloves for reading, because they made turning pages nearly impossible.

Mrs. Barnstable did wear reading gloves. She was fluttering away about the differences between velvet and kid in terms of durability and warmth.

"I haven't seen this lady for some time," the clerk said. "Miss Henderson used to come in with Mrs. Abercrombie. Mrs. Abercrombie goes through black gloves at a great rate, but then, she is a widow."

"Can you think of any reason why Miss Henderson would leave her post?"

He passed back the sketch. "She had very fine eyes, Miss Henderson did."

Mayfair shop clerks were required to be friendly, attractive, attentive, and in some venues...more than that, where the female customers were concerned. This fellow had all the requisite qualities, but he was turning up bashful now.

"She is quite pretty," Rosalind said. "And I knew her to be charming. Did she attempt to charm you?"

The clerk went back to straightening up rows of gloves already quite tidy. "More the other way about. Part of my job, but..." He sighed, conveying bewilderment and defeat. "She let me slip the gloves onto her bare hands and take them off. Let me trace her hands on the pattern paper. But she was only playin'. I asked to take her for an ice on her half day."

Rosalind had never appreciated how sensual an undertaking glove-shopping could be. In the clerk's vast amorous lexicon, an ice was probably akin to a declaration of abiding regard.

"She was not receptive to your advances?"

He re-arranged the gloves, though Rosalind could see no pattern to their order. "Miss Henderson said she already had a beau. A fine gent who would offer for her as soon as the Season was over. She said she did not want Mrs. Abercrombie to have to change companions at the busiest time of year."

"A fine gent?" *Oh, dear.*

"Handsome as the day is long." His expression could not have been more mournful. "Dark and dashing, she said, and his family was wealthy. To be honest..."

The clerk pulled a pair of red gloves from a row of red gloves and set them aside.

"To be honest?"

"What fine gent marries a companion, ma'am? Miss Henderson is pretty, but she hasn't been in London all that long. Mrs. Abercrombie was her first post, and I had the sense the gent were stringing Callie along."

Callie. Perhaps the clerk had done more than trace the lady's hands. "You mean he had no intention of proposing?"

"Why wait for months to marry a woman like Miss Henderson? The Season is only getting started, and wouldn't he want to show off his sweetheart? Introduce her around? Mrs. Abercrombie has had companions before, and she'll have a new one soon enough. I tried to tell Callie that she was being foolish, but she laughed at me."

Rosalind suspected the fair Calliope was no longer laughing. "What is your name?"

"Allard Brock, ma'am. I'm London born and bred, and I fear for Miss Henderson. I can understand a woman with her looks and ways not settling for a clerk, but the fine gents aren't all gentlemen, are they?"

"No, they are not. Did Miss Henderson tell you anything else about her suitor?"

"All I know is, she thought he was Quality. A girl newly in from the shires wouldn't necessarily know the difference, though. Would not know custom gloves from ready-made. Wouldn't know a flash cove from a lordling or a cit's scapegrace son."

An interesting observation. "You think he was deceiving her as to his station?"

The clerk glanced around, though the proprietress and Mrs. Barnstable were still rhapsodizing over fabrics, and Ivor was at his post by the door.

"The Quality marry for business reasons, meanin' no disrespect. Money, standin', land, that sort of thing. A gent with real means don't look on a bride the way I might. Even if he does, his family don't look at marriage that way. Callie had nothing but her wages and her smile, if you know what I mean. A fine gent don't generally marry a gal for that, and if he's truly smitten, he don't wait months to speak his vows."

"You make a frightening degree of sense, Mr. Brock." Rosalind passed him her card. "If you hear of anything relating to Miss Henderson's disappearance, please send me a note. I am very concerned for her."

He slipped the card into a pocket. "As am I."

Rosalind offered him a coin, at which he shook his head, so she bought a pair of driving gloves, not that she was allowed to drive herself anywhere.

"Ivor will see me home," she said, when Mrs. Barnstable and her co-conspirator had switched to debating colors. "I will send him back for you, Mrs. B. You are not to stir from this fine establishment until Ivor returns for you—your word on that, please—and of course, your purchases will go on my account."

The proprietress beamed at Rosalind like a benevolent goddess, while Ivor's expression betrayed some relief.

"I will not set foot outside the door until Ivor is once again at my side," Mrs. Barnstable said. "Away with you, my lady."

"We will take the alley," Rosalind said, when she and Ivor were out on the walkway. "There might be only one of you, but there's only one of me as well, and if needs must, you will toss me over your shoulder and depart the company of any footpads. Or do I mistake the matter?"

"Mr. Wentworth will not like it." Ivor was smiling, a dazzling display of teeth that suggested a wolf lurked beneath all that velvet and satin finery.

"Mr. Wentworth is at his bank, and time is of the essence. Let's be off, shall we?"

The alley, of course, revealed nothing regarding Francine Arbuckle's disappearance, but it did confirm Rosalind's fear: With the trees leafing out, and high garden walls on both sides, a woman could be taken from many places along the route with no witnesses to remark her disappearance.

* * *

"I don't mind telling you, fatherhood leaves me terrified." Robert, His Grace of Rothhaven, did mind making that admission, but putting names to his emotions and speaking those names was part of the challenge he'd set for himself when he'd married Constance Wentworth.

She, oddly enough, had taken on the same challenge, and the sheer blinding intimacy of her confidences inspired Robert's courage and his admiration.

"Constance is your ally when it comes to parenting," Quinn Wentworth replied. Here in his bank office, he looked a little less the duke, but no less imposing. "She is your ally in all things, or do I mistake the matter?"

Robert, who had only his father's dubious legacy to go by for ducal conduct, studied His Grace of Walden at every opportunity. Walden excelled at interrogation by innuendo and raised eyebrow.

"You do not mistake anything, and yet, children… Neither Constance nor I had good examples when it comes to parenting. We are at sea, and the waters of uncertainty are vast."

"The stars," Walden said, pushing a set of documents across the desk, "are more vast by far. Navigate by the fixed beams of love and common sense, as my Jane does, and you will never go far off course. Sign at the bottom of each page, and you will become one of Ned's small project investors."

Robert dutifully signed, though there were a deuced lot of pages. While he scribbled away, Walden rose and wandered to the window, which overlooked the street running past the bank's side entrance. Walden's office was in a corner, the better to maintain surveillance over more approaches.

Robert knew exactly the sentiments that prompted such vigilance.

"Where the devil is Ned getting off to now?" Walden muttered.

Robert finished his task and joined Walden at the window. "It's a pretty day. Maybe he's taking a pretty lady for a drive." Robert certainly hoped so.

"With a picnic hamper at his feet?"

A picnic hamper, two blankets, and a fiddle case. "I am told, emphatically and repeatedly by those expert on such matters, that you are the best bear in the Walden nursery."

On the street below, Ned waited until a small boy in the bank's livery clambered up behind the gig's bench.

"What has my growling to do with the bank's manager nipping out again during banking hours?"

"Your manager doubtless dealt with pressing matters before leaving the premises and has a competent assistant on duty. Moreover, Ned is putting in more hours for you and your customers than you do yourself, Walden. Let the man have some liberty."

Walden glowered down at the street as if he wanted to commence growling and snarling. "Ned has done this more lately, and the inspiration for his truancy is a female."

"Gracious me, not a *female*. I must have a word with young Ned about the perils of consorting with *females*. Next thing you know he might be smiling a bit more, or—we *cannot* have this—laughing."

Ned and his minion tooled off, and Robert wished them godspeed.

"He has serious responsibilities," Walden countered, "and this particular female has the great misfortune to be the Earl of Woodruff's daughter. Woodruff does not manage his affairs competently, which only inspires him to sponsor the more draconian measures in the Lords for taxing the shopkeepers and smallholders."

Walden stalked away from the window, and it occurred to Robert that he was seeing his brother-in-law *upset*. Interesting.

"That explains your antipathy to Ned's courting aspirations," Robert said, "because we all know children invariably take on a father's worst traits. Excepting present company, of course." He smiled sweetly to emphasize the point.

Had a ferocious scowl, did His Grace of Walden, but nothing compared to Constance when a painting wasn't cooperating.

Walden resumed the place behind the massive altar to tidiness that served as his desk. "I liked you better when you lurked on the Yorkshire moors inspiring tales to frighten small children."

"You have me confused with my dashing brother, but never fear. Constance and I would not miss summer at Rothhaven for all the family drama in Mayfair. You have to let Ned go, Walden. You've done a fine job with him, but these last few steps back to civilization he must make on his own."

Walden twiddled a quill pen. "Ned is exquisitely civilized. Jane saw to that, and the battle took years."

The battle was not yet over, not for Ned. The last, highest hill remained before him. "Jane put the manners on him, and between you, you've given him a few people to trust. He must learn to trust himself."

The white feather stilled. "What the hell is that supposed to mean? Ned's judgment about investment schemes is nearly as…it *is* as good as my own, but in a different way. He sees long-term potential, and he knows how to build something sturdy over time from small parts. I know how to seize the larger market opportunities."

"And for you, investing has become a sort of game. If you make a few wrong turns, the result is that you are less fabulously wealthy. Like Stephen with a new mechanical challenge, you will move along to another project and chalk up any failures to experience. You might be more cautious, but you will not be ashamed as a result of a blunder."

Walden would never squirm, but he did shift back on his commercial throne and cross an ankle over a knee. "Ned is not ashamed. He works hard here, and both Jane and I are proud of him. He knows that."

Ned's gig turned at the end of the street and was lost to sight.

"Ned works hard," Robert said, "but does he *play*? Does he get down on all fours in the nursery and roar like a bear? Does he have sweet little jokes with an adoring spouse who teases him about his manly vanities? Does he sit around the dinner table with siblings telling fond stories of youthful pranks gone awry? Is he on a cricket team that spends more time drinking and singing than at the green? When was the last time you heard Ned Wentworth laugh?"

"Neither you nor I had those amenities at his age, and we managed."

"You've become a grouchy old man if that's all you have to contribute to the discussion." Robert had *not* managed. Most of the time, he'd clung to sanity by the slender reeds of hope and determination. He suspected that for Walden, those slender reeds had been the ability to make money and to provide for his siblings.

"Then I am a grouchy old man," Walden said, "because I do not see how neglecting his duties at the bank to lark about with Woodruff's daughter will result in Ned's lasting happiness. Woodruff has paraded Lady Rosalind before every encroaching mushroom and presuming cit to dangle after a titled connection. Ned won't fare well with a man like that for a father-in-law."

"In-laws," Robert replied, "are a cross we all have to bear. Ned needs a partner and playmate, a cohort in mischief, somebody who accepts him for all of who he is, not just the parts of him that fit the Wentworth profile. Have you heard him play the fiddle?"

Walden wrinkled the ducal beak. "I have not. He used to challenge Stephen to pall-mall. The point, I believe, was simply to get Stephen out of doors, and to create an occasion for foul language."

"You are an occasion for foul language, my dear duke. Ned needs to *play*. He needs to be himself, not simply the young fellow the Wentworths are so proud of. He needs…I cannot explain it to you, but I can tell you, a man who does not laugh with genuine merriment is not a well man. Your daughters love you, Walden, in large part because you saw the importance of making them laugh early and often."

Walden's brows knit as if he were working on a very complex investment scheme. "I am their papa. Silliness in the nursery goes with the job."

"Job. Right. Of course. Only you, Walden…"

Walden was regarding him with genuine puzzlement, so Robert tried again, this time with a story, for even small children grasped the essence of a good story.

"When I was at the asylum, the only laughter I heard was one of the residents in a fit of hysteria. Maniacal laughter, desperately unhinged misery turned inside out. Then one day, I came upon the new chambermaid, laughing at a cat that had taken up chasing its tail. The cat careened around the corridor, and the maid was bent over with genuine mirth. When she faced me, her smile was heaven's light manifest in human features. That smile was all that was good and holy about sanity itself.

"Ned can build all the thriving little businesses he pleases," Robert went on, "but if his future is to rest on a sound foundation, he must recover the courage to reach for joy. Let him frolic with Lady Rosalind, let him be truant from your damned ledgers, let him have a life beyond your aspirations for him. God knows, if you and I had limited ourselves to the paternal aspirations inflicted on us, we'd both be dead and disgraced."

"Not fair, Rothhaven."

"But true."

Robert let a silence bloom, and though Walden used silence well, Robert considered a capacity for quiet one of his greatest gifts.

"Ned was not doing well," Walden said, "not in Newgate, and not when he was taken up, if the warden is to be believed. I had the sense Ned allowed himself to be arrested. They let him go the first time, when they hanged his brother, but after his brother died, he lost heart for the struggle to survive, and then..."

Robert knew how that went, when the question became how to make surrender complete, rather than how to fight on.

"Then?"

"I don't know, but it was bad. I never asked for the details, and I hope Ned has forgotten them."

"He will never forget those early experiences, Walden."

"But the nightmares can become less frequent," Walden said softly, running a finger around the inside of his collar, "and the panics easier to hide. Then you realize one day that you haven't panicked since before the last baby was born, and you know you're through the worst of it."

For Robert, the nightmares were of never coming home, of being banished to the moors for the rest of his life, of darkness without end. Then he'd waken, feel Constance in the bed beside him, and focus on the sound of her breathing. On the bad nights, he fell back to sleep clutching her hand, her arms around him, but the bad nights were fewer and fewer.

"Ned has come a long way," Robert said. "But he deserves what you have with Jane, and what I have with Constance. If Lady Rosalind isn't his answer, then she's a step in the direction of an answer."

Walden rose and perched a hip against the desk. He was the picture of aristocratic self-possession, but for the worry in his eyes.

"Jane agrees with you." A grudging admission. "She says I'm not to meddle. She says her own father was a horror, my father was worse than a horror, and I am not to meddle."

"We are dukes," Robert said. "We do not meddle. I assume you have, though, had Woodruff's finances thoroughly investigated?"

Walden smiled, a flash of mischief that made him resemble his younger brother. "Of course."

"Then if you'll excuse me, I will return to Lord Stephen's abode, and dream of summer on the Yorkshire dales with my favorite picnic partner."

Walden laughed, a rusty, dry sound, but it was laughter, and thus Robert graciously quit the field of argument, having clearly won the contest, foot, horse, and cannon.

* * *

Ned had seen His Grace of Walden glowering down from his window at the bank.

That familiar sight had provoked dueling impulses. The first was to stop the horse, repair hotfoot up to the duke's office, and explain that every scrap of the day's work was done and the assistant manager was similarly caught up and ready to handle emergencies.

Ned's other impulse was to stick his tongue out at His Grace and urge the horse to a faster trot.

Ned had given in to neither, but of the two…the second kept his thoughts occupied until he was handing Lady Rosalind up into the curricle.

"You are prompt," she said. "I treasure that about you."

"What else do you treasure about me?"

From behind the bench, Artie snorted.

"I treasure how wonderfully discreet your tiger is, and how easy it is to forget he's even with us." Rosalind softened that rebuke with a smile over her shoulder.

"Sorry," Artie muttered, which was more than Ned had heard him say for three days.

"Artie is new to his post, and tact is not a skill easily acquired. I hope you're hungry."

"Famished," Rosalind replied, "and so grateful for

an excuse to be out of doors on this glorious spring day, that I could nearly burst into song."

"What would you sing?"

"Scottish ballads. They are so melodious and robust. What's in the basket?"

"Nectar of the gods, ambrosia, the water of life."

Artie shifted on his perch but held his peace while Ned guided the horse through a tollgate.

"Did your widow friends put that picnic basket together?" Rosalind asked when they'd finally cleared the worst of the metropolitan congestion and reached the quieter surrounds of Chelsea.

"They did. I try to patronize my customers' businesses when I can. My tailor is a bank client, as is my bootmaker."

Rosalind opened a parasol, and what a pretty picture she made, with the breeze tugging at her curls and sending her bonnet ribbons dancing.

"You don't buy from Hoby?"

"Hoby employs scores of cobblers, cordwainers, and apprentices. I'd rather do business with a fellow who knows me and values my contribution to his livelihood. I get boots just as good as or better than Hoby's and I don't have to pay nearly as much for them."

Rosalind undid the bow holding the lid of the hamper closed and peered inside. "And this feast will be as good as what Gunter's prepares?"

"Better. The ladies test their recipes and are always making improvements to their menus. They prepare to order, so they don't end up with excess inventory, and they don't maintain a shopfront in one of the most expensive neighborhoods in Town. If this Season goes well, they will expand to holiday baskets at Yuletide."

"They could also make baskets to give new mothers and baskets to send off to scholars at public school or finishing school."

"Himself has ladies making parasols too," Artie announced. "And there's widows that will do readin' and writin', all tidy and proper. And there's—"

Ned sent a pointed look at his tiger, though Artie was only trying to aid the course of true love.

"The parasol shop is Lord Stephen's idea," Ned said, "and the literary service is a new venture, but off to a good start. The women who began it realized that in every post as companions, they'd had to serve as amanuensis and scribe. One widow had spent years making fair copies of her playwright husband's dramas and realized that could also be a paid service."

Rosalind had questions about all of it—the literary services, the parasols, and the baskets—and Ned soon found himself talking of a widows' consortium, where the basket enterprise and the florists cooperated, and the literary ladies and those running a subscription library collaborated as well.

Ned took a turning that led into an orchard and brought the horse to a halt. The cherries were at their peak bloom, and the apples would follow soon after.

"My lady, will this spot do?"

"Splendidly." Rosalind hopped down and took charge of the blankets, leaving the violin case and hamper to Ned.

"Artie," Ned said, "take the horse back to the village at a walk, and I do mean a walk. Not a trot, not a canter. The hostlers at the livery will put him up for you, and you can grab a pint and a pie at the inn. You will come back for us in two hours, not one moment before. Questions?"

Artie scrambled onto the bench. "You want me to drive him?" He sounded half pleased and half terrified.

"You'll have little traffic to contend with this far from Town," Ned said. "The lane is wide enough that you can turn without having to back up, and there's only the one horse to manage. If you're not ready for the challenge—"

Artie unwrapped the reins. "I'm ready. We'll be fine, won't we, Hamlet?"

The horse flicked an ear.

"Walk on," Ned said. "Hamlet needs to cool out, and then he's earned some hay and water."

Artie turned the vehicle in a wide, slow circle and was soon headed back in the direction of the last village.

"I don't believe I've ever seen him sitting up straighter," Ned said. "And the choice of picnic spot goes to the lady."

Rosalind gave the matter serious consideration and eventually settled on a location some yards from the road, on the far side of a grassy bank that led down to a burbling rivulet. She spread the blankets and opened the hamper, then commenced unlacing her boots.

"Getting comfortable, my lady?"

"We have only two hours of privacy, Ned Wentworth. Join me on this blanket or I'll know the reason why."

He sat, letting the peace and quiet sink into him. Across the stream, a hedge of honeysuckle was beginning to flower. London might have been on the other side of the earth, and the road miles off.

"We have both wine and cider," Ned said, "Which shall I open and how will you explain an absence of several hours to your family?"

Rosalind passed him the bottle of cider. "I am driving with you in the park and then enlisting your aid on a shopping expedition."

"You are not a shopping-expedition sort, are you?" Ned extracted the cork and passed Rosalind the bottle.

She regarded him curiously, then took a pull directly from the bottle and passed it back. "That is good. Has a tingle to it."

"It's hard cider, you mean." Ned took a drink and had to agree. The flavor was excellent, a good balance between tart and sweet, much like the sight of Lady Rosalind Kinwood, drinking straight from the bottle.

"Why all the widows, Ned?" she asked, undoing her bonnet ribbons. "I know you also invest in enterprises run by men, but you seem inordinately willing to give widows your backing."

He could shrug off the question with bankerly prattle about diversifying a portfolio or some such rot. Instead, he gave his answer honestly.

"My mother was all but widowed when my father was hauled into the navy's clutches. She was skilled with a needle, but a seamstress can't earn what a tailor earns. She tried everything, even considered remarrying, but the only viable prospect did not get on well with my brother and me, and...eventually, she was just too exhausted and ill to keep trying. She could not fight both consumption and the Royal Navy's cruelty."

Rosalind set her bonnet next to her boots. "Coat off, Mr. Wentworth. The day is warm, and you won't scandalize me."

Ned pulled off his boots and shrugged out of his coat, though such dishabille was, of course, scandalous in the extreme—also delightfully comfortable.

"To speak of what my mother went through, on a day as lovely as this, in company as lovely as this, ought to be forbidden."

"Why?" Rosalind said, turning her face up to the dappled sunshine. "If you cannot speak of it to me, then I am a poor sort of friend, aren't I?"

Ned did not discuss those topics with his Wentworth family. "My small investment projects at the bank are regarded with amused tolerance, but Rosalind, if England prospers, it's precisely because we are a nation of shopkeepers and yeomen. Those who have little become resilient and wily, or they soon have nothing. And yet, we allow those who have always had much to run our nation. This puzzles me."

She regarded his boots, arranged next to her shorter, prettier footwear. "Are you a radical, then?"

"I am curious as to why people who have never had to solve a problem more pressing than which cravat pin to wear are in charge of everything from the poor laws to treaties to turnpikes. By breeding and experience, such men are not our most thrifty or ingenious thinkers, and yet, we expect them to handle the nation's exchequer and its most pressing difficulties. If Britain's government were in the hands of widows, you can bet the children would be fed and a great deal less would have been spent on making war."

He ought not to have said that. Ought not to have allowed a note of bitterness to creep into his voice. He was alone in the countryside with a woman he was attempting to woo, and spouting sedition never did win a fair maid's heart.

"Are your small investment projects successful?" Rosalind asked.

"They are. Not wildly successful, but consistently successful. I've had a few failures, but the failures aren't wild either. They are more disappointments than failures."

"I want to meet your widows." Rosalind stretched out her legs and leaned back on her hands. "I want to learn how they manage their businesses, and if other ladies could undertake the same degree of enterprise as successfully. London is full of widows, spinsters, wives with husbands off to sea, or women who simply need a decent livelihood. You are solving a real problem, Ned, and we will talk more about your ambitions, because if they matter to you, they matter to me."

Ned heard the words and hugged them to his heart, but he also watched Rosalind's lips, watched the breeze tease at curls coming loose from her chignon. He took another sip of cider and passed her the bottle.

"I am usually more than willing to discuss banking and commerce at great length," he said, "but right now, I am alone on a blanket with a woman who fills my every waking thought. Rosalind, might I kiss you?"

She took a sip of cider, corked the bottle, and set it aside. "I thought you would never ask."

Then she tackled him.

Chapter Ten

Rosalind pinned Ned to the blanket—or Ned allowed her to pin him—and straddled him. "Will he be all right?"

Ned's smile was a trifle bewildered. "The horse?"

"Artie. He's never driven before, has he?"

Ned cupped her nape with a warm palm and urged her down to his chest. "Not that I know of, but the gelding has worked out the fidgets and is a steady sort. Artie is equal to the challenge, and besides, I'm trying to sweeten him up."

Ned, lying on a blanket beneath her, was more sweetness than Rosalind could bear. She wanted to sketch him and devour him and...what she truly wanted might shock him.

"Why does your tiger need sweetening?"

"We're having a disagreement, as reasonable gentlemen sometimes do, but enough about that. I want to muss your hair and disarrange your skirts, and Rosalind, if you don't soon—"

She crouched over him and let the kissing begin.

They had time, two whole hours, and thus she made a thorough exploration of Ned's mouth and laced her fingers with his.

Ned was a good kisser, good at matching her mood, at making a kiss into a conversation.

"You are worried," he said, when Rosalind paused to catch her breath. "You need not fret, Rosalind. I will stop when you ask me to."

"I am more worried that you will stop when I *don't* ask you to."

He traced her eyebrows with his thumb. "What does that mean?"

Rosalind sorted through the riot of emotions and sensations crowding her mind and found a coherent thought. "You talk to me. You explain about your widows, about why they matter so very much to you. You boost a small boy's confidence. You buried Her Grace's dog."

And thus I must make love with you followed logically from those observations. Rosalind let the obvious conclusion go unspoken because she was too busy savoring the slow stroke of Ned's thumb on her forehead.

"I didn't want Walden to have to deal with the whole burial task himself," Ned said. "Wodin was a sizable—"

Rosalind put two fingers against his lips. "You are *a good man*, Ned Wentworth. I had nearly forgotten there were good men. My brothers are shallow, my father is arrogant, and the prancing bachelors…They have no ambitions other than idle self-indulgence. If I marry one of them, then I am to aspire to idle self-indulgence as well. My greatest challenge would be devising a seating arrangement for a formal dinner."

Ned wrapped his arms around her, and some of Rosalind's inner tumult quieted. She had needed to be held, simply held, and she hadn't realized that. Desire simmered too, but desire was not the sum of her longings.

"Are you in danger of marrying a prancing bachelor, my lady?"

"No." She mashed her nose against Ned's throat. "Yes. My father..."

Ned stroked her back in slow, easy caresses. "Talk to me."

She wanted to do so much more than talk, but talking mattered too. "Papa throws me at young men and not-so-young men with whom I would be miserable. It's as if by allowing the cits and younger sons to dance with me, Papa gains favors."

"You think they forgive his debts in hopes of gaining his approval as suitors?"

When Ned put it that way, the notion didn't feel as foolish. "Yes. Then Papa can blame my fickle nature when their aspirations come to nothing, which they always do."

"Your father plays a dangerous game, if that's so," Ned said, though his touch remained light and soothing. "Sooner or later, some ambitious fellow will feel entitled to trespass, and then your fickle nature won't come into it. You will be compromised, and marriage will become your only choice other than ruin."

Rosalind hadn't felt comfortable airing this concern with even Mrs. Barnstable, but it haunted her.

"I have tried," Rosalind said. "I have tried to like those fellows, to see their positive qualities, but they are such uphill work, and I am to be silly and superficial with them—or worse—grateful for their attentions. Then I spend time with you, Ned, and it's as if I have found my own heart. You have purpose and values, you work hard, you care for others, you have aspirations besides avoiding the sponging house."

His hand on her back paused. "I'm no saint, Rosalind."

"You asked what I treasure about you, Ned Wentworth, and the list is so long, I don't know where to start. Your honesty is near the top though, as is your sense of honor. I want to compromise you. You should know that. I want to compromise you so thoroughly that you are stuck with me."

"I have another suggestion," Ned said, framing her face in his hands. "Why not do as smitten couples usually do? Why not court for a time, and then become engaged? The progression is woefully dull and predictable, but I hope you'll consider it."

He was smiling at her, though his gaze was serious.

"Court for a time?"

"I'm told picnics qualify as courting behavior, as does driving in the park, calling upon a lady, escorting her socially. I realize we have other business that draws us together, and I might well be getting above—"

"*Yes,*" Rosalind said, an enormous weight of hope and worry lifting from her heart. "Yes, please. Let us court, and flirt, and make a spectacle of ourselves doting on each other in public, and then we will marry."

She subsided against Ned, felt his heart beating

next to hers, and let the enormity of the moment settle into her mind. This was not quite a proposal, but discussions like this were how proposals began. This was an understanding in the truest sense of the word. Ned understood her, she understood him. Intimacy in its rarest form.

"You have to promise me something, Rosalind."

"Anything."

"You have to promise me that you won't look with favor on my suit simply because you think I'm a reasonably decent fellow who can spare you from your father's machinations. I'm confident that between your own native wit and intervention from Her Grace of Walden, you could avoid ruin in all but the most difficult circumstances your father could concoct."

"Possibly, but Papa could easily pack me off to Aunt Ida's again or banish me to some Swiss hotel for months with only Mrs. Barnstable for company. Aunt Ida lives in Derbyshire. I treasure her for any number of reasons, but spending the rest of my life admiring scenery does not number among my ambitions."

"You fear your father will wear you down, you mean?"

"Yes." *Wear me down further.* "I am weary of his games, Ned."

"He doesn't know you very well, does he?" Ned's smile became sweet and mischievous. "He does not know that you are one part Damascus steel, one part ingenuity, and one part cool reason, all wrapped up in a big, courageous heart."

"When I am with you, I can be that person you describe, brave and smart and whatnot. I like who I am with you, Ned Wentworth, and if I look with favor upon your suit, which I will do, that's because I esteem you greatly too."

"Do you lollygag on picnic blankets with all the fellows you esteem?"

He was trying to lighten the mood, but Rosalind heard the thread of uncertainty in his teasing. Ned was a tad overwhelmed by the moment too, and that was lovely.

"I am not lollygagging," she said. "I am commencing a seduction. You will please seduce me back, and we will muddle through the business as best we can." And he doubtless heard the bravado in her voice too.

"Assure me, Rosalind, that you want *me*. Don't talk yourself into a courtship because it's the lesser of several bad options. That way lies disappointment and dashed hopes."

"You are so serious," she said, stroking his hair. "I adore that you are so serious, so substantial, and I promise you, Ned, you are who I want." How odd, that the right man was the man who did not try to bludgeon her with his charm or consequence, but rather, the fellow who insisted she think of and for herself.

Rosalind's assurances apparently sealed the matter for Ned, because his kisses changed, becoming heated and deliberate. He shifted from caresses to Rosalind's back to gradually frothing her skirts up high enough that he could stroke her thigh.

"No drawers, Rosalind?"

"The day is warm. I'm not wearing stays either." Two chemises and a set of front-lacing jumps. Rosalind could breathe freely, in other words.

Ned bowed up to hug her. "Truly, you were bent on seduction. I have never been seduced before. I suspect I'll succumb without much struggle. No struggle at all, in fact."

"Good." Rosalind undid the bow holding the décolletage of her dress closed. "That gives us more time to be wicked."

"Not wicked." Ned eased back to the blanket, taking Rosalind with him. "Loving. With you, only loving will do."

Rosalind's last pretensions to cool reason deserted her, for she wanted and needed Ned Wentworth's loving so very, very much. She had waited years in the hopes that such a man would come her way, and having found him, she would never, ever let him go.

* * *

Ned gazed past the lady's shoulder to the cloud of blossoms above and rejoiced.

Rosalind Kinwood wanted *him* for her own—Ned the banker, Ned the orphan, Ned the man who talked business with widows, and argued with his tiger. Ned who had no real family, but many familial obligations. She wanted all of those Neds, and—how this gratified him—she also *desired* the Ned who could be seduced on a picnic blanket.

That fellow was a new acquaintance to Ned himself. He was lusty. He had moved beyond the shadows of his youth, and delighted in being a healthy male in dear and willing female company.

He was a bit devious, that Ned, sliding a hand beneath

Rosalind's skirts to shape her hip and cup her delectable bum. Her skin was marvelously soft and warm, and she sank her weight against Ned's falls in a manner that conveyed enthusiasm approaching insistence.

"Patience," Ned said. "Savor this celebration."

"I want to be naked. I want to be naked now. I want you naked."

The images she conjured... "We'll start with a little nakedness," Ned said, undoing the bows of her jumps and the first of her two chemises. No fancy embroidery for his Rosalind, just plain soft linen worn almost translucent with age. "Near nakedness to allow me a touch of restraint."

He shaped her breasts, and she arched into his touch. When he used his mouth on her nipples, she *wiggled* and Ned had to pause and count backward from one hundred by visualizing Roman numerals.

"Your falls," she said, sitting back. "Time for you to be a little naked too, Ned Wentworth."

She had him half-unbuttoned before he assembled enough wits to realize what she was about. Even as part of him wanted her to slow down, to cherish rather than plunder, another part of him marveled that he had inspired her passion.

No dithering, no false hesitance, no practiced airs and posturing.

"Ned Wentworth." She rearranged his linen and took him in her hand. "You do want me after all."

"Had you any doubt?"

She stroked her thumb over the crown of his cock, and Ned had to close his eyes, which only made the sensations more immediate.

"You have depths of reserve," Rosalind said, repeating the caress. "I want to plumb them all, until you feel as desperate and determined as I am."

"My objective," Ned said, fisting his hands on the blanket, "is to visit upon you an experience of unbearable pleasure. If I'm to attain that—*merry hell, Rosalind.*"

She'd wrapped her fingers around his shaft and stroked him. "Did I hurt you?"

He had to get control of the situation before Rosalind's enthusiasm doomed him to humiliation, and he had to manage it without hurting her feelings.

"If you persist for another fifteen seconds, I will spend," he said, "and then I will wilt, and you will be disappointed. The first twenty years of our marriage will be taken up with me trying to compensate for a very poor first impression, though believe me, I'm tempted to worry about that later."

And what a wonderful twenty years they would be.

"Oh." She let him go, a relief and a sorrow. "Twenty years?"

"At least." Ned sat up, which left him a trifle dizzy. "On your back, please."

Rosalind lay down, and ye cavorting cherubs, what a picture she made, hair a little untidy, lips rosy, clothing in disarray.

"You are a feast of temptations," Ned said, unknotting his cravat and starting to unbutton his waistcoat and shirt. "An embarrassment of inspiration for the male imagination."

"Less talk, and more undressing, Ned."

He flung off his cravat and waistcoat and pulled his

shirt over his head. "I had planned to read you poetry. Play you a few sentimental ballads on my fiddle."

Rosalind took his shirt, sniffed it, and rolled it up beneath her head. "We'll get to that part. Maybe not today."

Ned arranged himself over her. "Maybe not this year."

He went still, the better to marshal his flagging self-discipline. They would have only one first time, and by allowing these intimacies, Rosalind was taking an enormous risk. He would withdraw, but she might still find herself with child before the vows were spoken.

Vows. With Rosalind. The joy was terrifying, matched only by the pleasure of kissing her, stroking her breasts, and exploring her sex, one glancing brush of his cock, one lazy nudge at a time.

"Ned, please. I need you."

The words resonated down through all the years when nobody had needed him, when he'd been the encroaching outsider on London's streets. When he'd tried to fit himself into a ducal household, when he'd made himself useful in every possible capacity at the bank.

"I need you too, Rosalind. Have needed you forever." He began the joining, and Rosalind sighed, her whole body relaxing beneath him. He put every sense on alert for a hint that she was uncomfortable, changing her mind, or in need of a pause, but she rocked up to meet him, and locked her ankles at his back.

The loving was so easy, so uncomplicated and *right*. The darkest corner of Ned's mind, where part of him always stood guard at a distance, finally surrendered its vigilance. He was in Rosalind's arms, she was in his heart.

"That is..." Rosalind eased her legs down along his flanks. "This is exactly... This is lovely."

"You are lovely." Ned lifted up enough to regard her, all rosy and warm beneath him. Bad idea—because the sight was too inspiring. Also a wonderful idea, because this Rosalind, all flushed and heavy-lidded, was his alone to treasure.

She went plundering, glossing fingertips over his nipples, stroking his arms, then clasping his wrists and adding some power to the undulations of her hips.

"How you make me yearn," she whispered.

Yearning was good. Moaning was better, though in Rosalind's case, the moans were more soft exhalations punctuating an escalating tempo. Ned set awareness of his own longing at arm's length, and instead focused on Rosalind. Her breathing, the urgency in her movements, the quality of her grip on his wrists.

Desire rode him hard, but this joining was about loving, not merely pleasure, so he held back, and held back yet more.

Rosalind in the throes of passion was a silent splendor. She bucked, she clung, and she shuddered all without speaking a word. Her body shouted her satisfaction more effectively than words could, and when she would have subsided into the bliss of fulfillment, Ned sent her over the edge again.

"What you do to me..." she murmured, kissing Ned's shoulder. "What unimaginable, glorious delirium. I had no idea."

"None?"

"Not a clue. I liked the kissing and cuddling. I liked the daring of breaking rules, but this is the opposite of breaking rules. This is...I can't find the words."

Ned snuggled closer, pressing his cheek to hers and withdrawing. He spent in the tight seam of their embrace, the satisfaction a promise of greater bliss to be had on their wedding night.

He was to have a wedding night. With Rosalind. The prospect thrilled and humbled and delighted. As Ned crouched over her, an eddy of cooling air whispering between them, he found the words Rosalind had been searching for.

This is home. You are my home. I am finally, finally home.

He produced a handkerchief and dealt with the practicalities, then subsided onto the blanket, and pulled Rosalind into his arms. They did not bother dressing, but merely tugged this and straightened that.

Under the benevolent spring sun, wrapped around the woman he adored, Ned closed his eyes, gave silent thanks, and slept like a soldier newly returned from the wars.

* * *

Rosalind marveled that she could share both the greatest intimacy known to the species with Ned, share a plate of sandwiches with him, and share a smile with him—ye gods, he was devilishly attractive playing his fiddle—and all of that sharing was of a piece.

She wasn't shy and embarrassed around Ned, she was pleased.

He wasn't strutting and flirtatious with her, he was tender. Ned did not need to make manly separations between affection, desire, cherishing, and friendliness. His regard for her was of whole cloth, a continuum of smiles, touches, silences, and considerations.

Rosalind was hungry for the food, which was quite good, and she was also famished for the closeness Ned offered.

"I don't want Artie to return," she said, when they'd packed up the hamper and donned their footwear. "Not until next spring." *Not until we're married.* She understood that Ned wanted to observe the outward proprieties, his version of gentlemanly esteem requiring that display, but the waiting would be nerve-racking.

"I want him to return punctually," Ned said. "Artie has been truant from work lately, and when I ask him what he's about, he glowers at me as only a boy upon his dignity can glower."

"You are worried for him?"

Ned passed Rosalind her bonnet. "He's too young to have a sweetheart. He's not dicing with the footmen or grooms. He's off on the king's business, but which king?"

Rosalind arranged her bonnet over a chignon Ned had helped her put to rights. He was competent at assisting a lady with her toilette, and how Rosalind envied the women who'd taught him those skills.

"Does Artie have family?" Rosalind asked.

"The badgers taken on at the bank typically don't, or no family who can claim them. Artie might have an uncle at the Marshalsea prison, or a cousin in service somewhere, but he doesn't talk about having family."

A boy without family would always give Ned Wentworth cause for concern.

Ned tied Rosalind's bonnet ribbons in a loose bow. "The badgers are answerable to me, and if Artie is up to no good, then I have chosen poorly."

"You don't care about that," Rosalind said, lying back on the blanket. "You fret that he's off picking pockets instead of earning an honest wage. If he ends up in Newgate, you will blame yourself."

Ned sat cross-legged on the blanket beside her, not touching. "Newgate is not the worst horror that awaits a boy on his own in London." His gaze was fixed in the direction of the road, as if he truly did worry that Artie would steal a vehicle he could barely drive and a horse he could not care for.

"You fear he'll end up transported?"

"Transportation is harrowing enough in theory, even for a lad in good health with stout boots and a warm cloak. But Rosalind, there are children all over London, miserable little wretches who would leap onto the transport ships if they only could."

His expression looked all the more bleak because he sat amid a blooming orchard, the afternoon graced with the music of a small stream and the chirping of sparrows.

And yet, Ned wasn't making sense. "Nobody leaps onto a transport ship unless the alternative is the noose, Ned."

"You are not in favor of transportation?"

That he asked her opinion meant worlds. Her father and brothers wouldn't bother, unless for the sport of belittling her views.

"For able-bodied men in good health, perhaps, as long as they leave no family behind, but I favor the notion that justice should have a rehabilitative aspect, else we are simply making the disaffected more bitter and dangerous. And for women and children, to subject them to such terrible hardship for the price of a stolen spoon? What we spend punishing them could be better spent teaching them a trade, but no, we must cast the unfortunates to the ends of the earth because our goods need markets and we need raw materials. And we call ourselves a Christian nation."

Ned rose and extended a hand to her. "I had a trade, or the beginnings of one. My brother was the equal of any journeyman tailor. England did not want our skills."

Rosalind got to her feet with Ned's assistance. She wanted to hug him, to ask him what memory haunted him, for clearly, the discussion had touched on old wounds.

Ned, though, was busy shaking out the blankets.

"What are you being too much of a gentleman to say, Ned? You listen to me. I am eager to listen to you as well."

He folded a blanket just so, such that the corners matched exactly, and passed it to her. "My sentiments on the behavior of London's good, Christian citizens toward its burgeoning population of starving poor do not bear repetition in polite company. What those children do to survive…"

He shook the second blanket vigorously, scaring the birds into silence.

Rosalind was about to ask him what *he* had done to

survive—what he'd done that was worse than picking pockets or mud larking—when the clatter of wheels sounded from the direction of the road.

"He's on time," Ned said, relief in his eyes. "He's trotting, but the little blighter didn't strand us out here in the shires after all."

As Rosalind and Ned came in sight of the road, Artie smoothly slowed the gelding to a walk and turned him into the orchard lane. The beast obligingly halted on command, and Artie was positively luminous with pride.

"Good lad," Ned said, passing the hamper and fiddle case into the gig. "You are punctual, and Hamlet appears rested. You found a meal?"

"Aye, guv," Artie said, hopping onto the back perch. "Caught a nap too. The grooms woke me in time to help them hitch up."

Ned took the blankets from Rosalind and stashed them in the vehicle. "You doubtless got in the way and reduced the stable lads to cursing. Pay attention to how I get us out of here. If you can tool along on the roads, your next feat is to master backing to turn. My lady, up you go."

Rosalind took a seat on the bench, feeling a little resentful of the boy perched behind. Of course Artie's accomplishment deserved acknowledgment. The lad had practiced a new skill and been conscientious about his duties, but what had passed between Ned and Rosalind in the orchard had been precious.

That such an experience was wedged between Rosalind's fibs about shopping expeditions and Artie's prattling was somehow wrong.

Before Ned picked up the reins, he touched a gloved hand to Rosalind's sleeve. "My thanks for a wonderful two hours, my lady. I can assure you, I've never enjoyed a picnic more." He bumped her gently with his shoulder, and the whole day came right again.

"Nor have I," Rosalind said. "Not ever."

Ned took up the reins. "Artie, attend me. When backing a horse in harness, you must give the beast a chance to comprehend what you're asking. You ask, then you wait. Then you ask again. Rather like giving a scholar a chance to recite before you repeat the query."

Artie had a thousand questions, now that he'd joined the loyal order of aspiring whips, and Ned was patient with him. When they passed through the village, Ned drew the gig to a halt outside the livery.

"My lady, will you take the reins for a moment? I want to make sure the bill was settled to everybody's satisfaction."

Rosalind took the reins, though she wasn't wearing driving gloves. "Artie and I will be fine. Be off with you."

Ned sprang down and strode off, while Rosalind admired the fit of his jacket across his shoulders.

"He's sweet on ye," Artie said. "He'll try to kiss ye, but if you tell him not to, he won't. Mr. Wentworth is a good sort."

"Your recommendation would mean much to him."

Artie appropriated one of the folded blankets and arranged it as a pillow for his perch. "He has blunt, buckets of it, though he don't lord it about like some. He'd never raise a hand to ye nor laugh at ye in front of yer mates."

Ned disappeared into the livery.

"If he's such a sterling character, Arthur, then why won't you tell him what has you so worried that you're jeopardizing your post by repeated incidents of truancy?"

Artie squirmed about on his seat. "Sissy used to call me Arthur, all prim and proper like you do. She's a chambermaid, or she was. Mostly."

"Mostly?"

Artie shot Rosalind a look much too mature for his years. "She's not on the game. Sissy's a good girl. We look after each other."

A chill goose-bumped down Rosalind's arms. "Has Sissy gone missing, Arthur?"

He ducked his head. "Nah. She'll show up soon. She must have a new post is all and she's waiting for her first half day. She wouldn't leave Town without letting me know."

"You've been looking for your sister?"

He nodded. "She had some fella panting after her. Sissy's pretty. She said this bloke was special. Ain't none of 'em special enough that she'd turn her back on me. She's not like that."

Hope and conviction colored Artie's words, the hope coming through most loudly.

Ned strode out of the livery. "They asked me where I'd found my groom," he said, climbing into the vehicle. "Said the lad had a nice way with the ribbons."

Where *had* Ned found Arthur? Rosalind would ask that when the boy wasn't shamelessly eavesdropping. She passed over the reins, though in future, she'd remember to bring her new driving gloves when on an outing with Ned.

"Arthur and I have been chatting," Rosalind said. "Arthur, you might be interested to know that my most recent lady's maid and the one before her have both gone missing. They left without collecting their wages or gathering up their things."

"Piked off?" Artie muttered. "Did a bunk? From a lord's house?"

Ned half turned to peer at Artie. "You know of a similar circumstance involving another party?"

Artie took a moment to translate that. "My sissy hasn't met me on her half day for two weeks. Sissy never misses a chance to check on me, not even when it's raining and cold and miserable. She sometimes brings me a meat pie or tuppence."

Ned stared off down the road, which wound out of the village past fields and hedges. "Tell us what you know, Artie, every detail."

Artie heaved a sigh, which to Rosalind sounded relieved. "I got to askin' around, and Belinda Crocker—she has the flower stand nearest the bank—said her cousin went missin' about the same time as Sissy. I'm that worried, Mr. Wentworth, but you mustn't say they went on the stroll. Sissy ain't a game girl, and I'd black your eye for insultin' her."

"Well you should," Ned said, giving the reins a shake. "But two heads are better than one, Artie, and I fear this problem is bigger than either of us knows."

Rosalind kept her peace all the way back into Town, but foreboding had cast a gloom over her perfect picnic. Ned asked the same thoughtful, thorough questions of

Arthur that he'd asked of Rosalind, and like Rosalind, Arthur had little enough to offer in the way of information. Nobody had seen his sister taken up by the watch, she wasn't in the sponging houses, and her friends hadn't heard from her.

Ned drew the horse up under the porte cochere, handed Rosalind down, and walked with her to the foot of the steps.

"I will make an appointment to speak with your father. As soon as he can see me."

Rosalind did not envy Ned that interview. "Papa will expect you to observe the formalities, and he will play the very devil over the settlements, but I know what my mother left me. I am quite of age, and the situation in truth should not require much discussion."

Ned bowed over her hand. "I will do this correctly, because you are deserving of every courtesy and consideration. Perhaps you might ride in the park on Friday morning?"

How she loved the warmth in his gaze when he posed the question. "I most assuredly will, one hour after sunrise."

He touched a finger to his hat brim. "Until Friday morning. Good day, my lady."

Rosalind wanted to watch him drive off, looking so handsome and dashing at the reins, but Ned would wait for her to safely enter her house, and thus she parted from him. The news Artie had disclosed was alarming, but also encouraging.

More disappearances meant more potential witnesses and more clues, and thus more hope.

And as for the picnic ... Rosalind removed her bonnet

and gloves, reliving memories of blossom-scented breezes, intense pleasure, and the sweetest lassitude.

I am in love. She made that announcement silently, while examining her reflection in the mirror over the sideboard. Her hair was still a plain brown, her figure unremarkable, her attire boringly proper, but her eyes were sparkling, and her heart...

In her heart was knowledge and wonder and love.

"Just where have you been?" Papa stood on the landing halfway up the steps, his query disturbing Rosalind's musing as effectively as a rifle shot. "The Wentworth whelp escorted you again, and for a woman who spent hours out shopping, you've returned without packages."

"I often find nothing to suit me," Rosalind said. "Mrs. Barnstable despairs of my finicky tastes, and for once, she did not have to accompany me as I browsed."

"Finicky," the earl said, descending the steps slowly. "Does Wentworth know how finicky you are?"

"He is a considerate escort, Papa, but I'm sure my preferences regarding gloves and scents hold no interest for him."

Papa gave her a brooding examination, one that was supposed to intimidate her into babbling, for which he would then rebuke her.

Rosalind passed her father on the stairs and assured herself that she and Ned would have a very brief, passionate courtship. If Papa thought it odd that she was more interested in escaping his company than removing her cloak, he kept his opinion to himself—for once.

Chapter Eleven

"I'm sure you didn't ask me here to discuss invest-ments, Ned. What is on your mind?"

Duncan Wentworth posed the question politely, for Duncan was always polite. He was a cousin to the Wentworth siblings, a few years older than Walden, and decades more reserved. While Walden exuded con-sequence, Duncan exuded nothing so easily labeled.

Not arrogance, not impatience, not humility, though Ned knew him to be a humble man. With his wife and children, Duncan was quietly doting, and with his cousins he occupied a place both in the family circle and entirely unto himself.

In the role of tutor to Lord Stephen, Duncan had years ago created a bridge between the most difficult Wentworth—which was saying something indeed—and the rest of the family. Ned had watched that process with a mixture of awe and envy.

"Thank you for heeding my request," Ned said. "May I offer you a drink?"

Duncan would never gawk, but in his reserved,

understated way he was clearly inspecting Ned's informal parlor—his family parlor.

"I'll have a tot to wash away the dust of the road. You favor botanical art."

Ned passed him a glass of brandy. "A man can't very well admit to a preference for having flowers on hand, can he?" At a bank, fresh flowers were a touch of graciousness. In bachelor quarters...

"Who did the stitchwork?" Duncan asked, examining one of Ned's more complicated flights of embroidery. "The blooms look vibrant enough to bear a fragrance."

"I needed something to cover up the seam in the wallpaper, and like you, I thought the work pretty so I had it framed. Shall we sit?"

Duncan took a sip of his drink, regarding Ned over the rim of the glass. Ned had prevaricated about the origins of the needlepoint, and Duncan knew it.

"I will be quizzed," Duncan said, taking Ned's favorite wing chair. "Her Grace will want to know if your housekeeper is maintaining standards. Stephen will ask if your libation was decent. Quinn will admit to general receptiveness regarding any reports I might make. My lady wife will ask if you are happy."

How to answer that? *I am in love* would never serve, and yet, it had become the defining reality of Ned's existence. He stared off into space while mentally recounting the most amazing two hours of his life. In his head, he calculated the minutes until tomorrow's sunrise, for sixty minutes after dawn, he and Rosalind would meet in the park.

When he wasn't praying that the weather would be

fine, he was fretting over how to approach Rosalind's father. Hence, this conference with the Wentworths' most accomplished strategist.

"I am thriving," Ned said, taking the end of the sofa. "As always. How are Matilda and the children?"

"Hoping you will soon come for a visit."

Ned's version of a visit now involved tooling along in the curricle, Rosalind at his side. Yesterday, that same visit would have meant making the journey alone, on horseback.

Nothing had changed, and yet, everything had *changed*.

"Ned, whatever it is, just get on with it. I wore a collar once upon a time. I know how to keep a confidence, even from my prying cousins. They are always well intended, but their concept of personal privacy can leave a fellow feeling like Prometheus, bound to the cliff face, raptors flapping about as they peck away at his peace."

Precisely. "You were clergy," Ned said, seizing on the least fraught aspect of Duncan's recitation. "In the course of your duties you encountered courting couples."

"I never progressed much past the disgraced curate phase of church work," Duncan said, running a finger around the rim of his glass. "I did not have a true vocation as it turned out."

And parting from the Church of England apparently troubled Duncan not one bit. "But you took holy orders."

"So I did, and I have not been defrocked, as it happens. Do you require last rites, Ned? Her Grace won't care for that idea at all."

What Her Grace wanted had become subordinate to what Rosalind needed, a curiously fortifying thought.

"How do I approach the father of my intended about gaining permission to court his daughter?"

The sole clue that Duncan Wentworth had been caught by surprise manifested in the manner in which he set his drink down on the side table.

"You have an intended."

"Lady Rosalind Kinwood. She has indicated a willingness to allow me to pay her my addresses."

And in his head, Ned heard Lord Stephen muttering about *fast work*, *airs above your station*, and *don't bungle this, Neddy*.

"Her father is the Earl of Woodruff," Duncan said. "Old-school aristocrat. Her grandfather was among the most enthusiastic about seeking enclosure acts for his common lands. The heir is a self-important fribble, while the spare fancies himself a poet. One will not envy you your in-laws."

"One must first marry the lady to acquire those in-laws, and Rosalind confirmed that her father will expect protocol to be observed."

Duncan rose and began a perambulation about the room. "Why her?"

"I esteem her greatly."

"You esteem everybody, from your urchins to the flower girls, to Her Grace's familiars, to the shopkeepers who flock to you for loans. One hopes you reserve a scintilla of esteem for yourself." Duncan paused before the other piece of framed embroidery, which depicted a tabby cat curled among a border of pansies. "I can almost hear him purr."

Her. Smokey had been a her, a friendly old besom who'd dozed away many an afternoon in Papa's shop window. She'd gone to her reward just weeks before Papa had been impressed.

"A gentleman shows courtesy toward all," Ned said, "but how do I inform Lord Woodruff that I intend to marry his daughter? I cannot approach him as a supplicant, for Rosalind paints him as a self-important boor who will sneer at weakness. I cannot condescend to him, or I will inspire his antipathy. I know how to discuss money, I know how to discuss final arrangements, I know how to tell genteel old women that they must sell their silver as soon as may be, but an earl whose daughter I seek to marry? I am at a loss."

Duncan took up a lean against the mantel, the posture reminiscent of Lord Stephen. Casual, elegant, thoughtful, and deceptively relaxed.

"If the earl is so difficult as all of that, then you must resign yourself to being disrespected. He has something you want badly."

"Rosalind is not a thing."

Duncan did not smile, but his gaze warmed. "Of course not. I allude to the tranquility of relations that ensue when a father reconciles himself to his daughter's choice of spouse. For Rosalind's sake, you want to get off on the best foot with the earl. What does the earl want that you can offer him?"

"I can offer him lifelong security for his daughter. Rosalind will have my utmost devotion and care. She will have the influence of the Wentworth family to call upon. She will have her own home to order and manage as she sees fit. What else could any man offer her?"

A nasty thought intruded: If the earl regarded Rosalind as a means of paying off his bills, then Ned's plans for her would disrupt that scheme for all time.

"I suspect," Duncan said, "if Lady Rosalind is the right choice, she would settle for your heart, and devil take the hindmost. The issue becomes, though, what does Woodruff need or want?"

"I fear he wants to dangle Rosalind before the cits and beer barons until she's at her last prayers."

Duncan eased away from the mantel. "You might consider eloping."

Of all the suggestions Duncan Wentworth might have made... "Eloping? That implies the lady has been compromised, or that I am not suitable."

"Has she been compromised?"

Thoroughly and delightfully, as had Ned. "Of course not."

"Then you are slower off the mark than the rest of the Wentworth menfolk," Duncan said. "Tell me about the missing maids, Ned, for that is apparently what brought you to her ladyship's notice."

Ned recounted what he knew, which now amounted to four young women in service disappearing from their posts, and three of them had recently kept company with a handsome young swell who had promised them marriage.

"And the fourth?" Duncan asked.

"Miss Arbuckle might have attached a follower as well, but we have no way of knowing." Or did they?

"And these ladies have not been taken up by the abbesses?"

"From what I can gather, no. This is a coordinated undertaking by somebody with considerable influence, and the usual procurers—who rarely venture to disturb the peace of Mayfair—are staying well away from it. I've posted eyes and ears to keep watch, and my pickets report only the predictable parade of drunkenness, debauchery, and despair."

"What do all these women have in common?" Duncan asked.

Ned recited the litany that kept him awake at night. "They are young, unattached, in service, attractive, in good health, and without much family in London. One of the missing ladies has a brother among the bank's badgers, but the lad is hardly in a position to apprehend kidnappers."

Duncan peered at Smokey's embroidered portrait. "And you are? This seems to be a matter for the authorities, Ned."

Duncan was no stranger to life's harsh realities, but in some regards, he was an innocent. Compared to Ned, all the Wentworths were innocents, despite their humble origins.

"The authorities might well have a hand in it, Duncan." In fact, they probably did, if only to the extent that they were ignoring the whole matter.

"Ah. Peculation and plunderage, of course." Duncan finished his drink and set his glass on the sideboard. "If the ladies aren't suffering the usual fate, then what has become of them? In other words, what happens to them if you fail?"

"What happens to the women? I can only speculate, and in distressing directions, but if we knew what fate awaited the women, we'd have an easier time finding them."

"What happens between you and Lady Rosalind if you fail?"

In Duncan's typical fashion, he was asking several questions at once. Was Rosalind's favor tied to Ned's success solving the mystery of the maids? Was Ned's interest in Lady Rosalind somehow dependent on that undertaking? How much was Ned willing to risk to unravel the situation Lady Rosalind had laid at his feet? Was rescuing unfortunate women to become Ned's lifelong quest?

In other words, *What the hell are you doing, Neddy?*

"I won't fail."

Duncan studied the ceiling, which sported no murals or frescos, and no cobwebs either. "The earl will not want to give you his blessing, Ned. Association with the Wentworths, in his estimation, does you no credit. Do you see this venture on Lady Rosalind's behalf as a means of forcing her father to respect you?"

"I undertook the search for the women without any thought of the earl's opinions."

Duncan regarded Ned, which was more unnerving than even Jane's inspections. "If you fall on your arse, get arrested for peeking in windows, or otherwise bungle the white knight role, where does that leave you with Rosalind and her father?"

"I hope it leaves me married to Rosalind and trying again to find the missing women."

Duncan eyed the parlor's humble adornments. "You hope." He ambled across the room, pausing only long enough to squeeze Ned's shoulder. "It's about damned time. Let me know what I can do to help, and yes, I will cheerfully stand up with you. You and her ladyship will always be welcome under my roof. Elope if you must, but be very sure the lady sees you as the wonderful fellow you are and not simply as an expedient minion who can solve a vexing problem for her. Be honest with her, about your family, about your past, about *all of it*. I will see myself out."

Meaning the interview was over, and Ned still had no clue about how to approach his prospective father-in-law. He did, though, have a damn sight more questions to grapple with.

And as for being honest with Rosalind about *all of it*…Absolutely not. Not ever, if Ned could help it, and certainly not before they'd spoken their vows.

* * *

Rosalind stopped by the library to check the time on the longcase clock, the most accurate timepiece in the house.

Forty-five minutes until her rendezvous with Ned. Perfect.

"Roz," came a groggy voice from the depths of the sofa. "That you?"

George rose, tousled and unshod. He wore no jacket, and his rumpled attire suggested he'd spent the whole night in the library.

"Good morning," Rosalind replied. "You were up late writing?" The desk held the usual detritus of one of George's poetry sessions—crumpled paper, open books, empty decanters.

"The muse was upon me," he said, scrubbing a hand through his hair. "I stretched out to rest my eyes, and then... *nescience*."

Unknowingness. One of his many arcane poetical words, which in this case referred to drinking himself into a stupor.

"Papa frowns on dishabille in the public rooms, George. You and your muse had best toddle up to bed."

He scratched his belly and stretched. "You're in a riding habit."

"I'm going for a hack. The weather is fair, and my mare could use the outing."

George peered at her owlishly. "You went to Her Grace of Walden's at-home. You've been shopping more lately. What's got into you, Roz?"

Don't call me Roz. "The Season has arrived. I'm out and about as Papa expects me to be."

George gathered up his boots and jacket. "That's not it. You went to that Venetian breakfast, and Lindy said you were on Ned Wentworth's arm. You dragooned Wentworth into shopping with you."

Why did George choose now of all times to turn up chatty and observant? "If my brothers were more generous with their escort, I wouldn't have to bother Mr. Wentworth."

George ambled closer, bringing the scent of stale to-bacco and an excess of spirits with him. "Is Wentworth bothering you, Roz?"

"Of course not. His company is congenial, and he's received everywhere. How could you think that he's been anything less than gentlemanly?"

George's eyes were bloodshot, his complexion sallow. More significantly his expression, usually jovially bland, was bleak.

"Ned Wentworth is received, but he's not *good ton*, Roz. He'll never be *good ton*. Rumors follow him from year to year, and when I was at university..."

Rosalind did not want to hear this, and yet, she needed to. "Yes?"

"Half the fellows said he was Walden's by-blow, the other half said worse things than that. Naughty things ladies aren't supposed to hear. Foul, naughty things about why Walden might keep a handsome lad close by."

"Your friends slandered Mr. Wentworth because they are a pack of foul, naughty boys. Go to bed, George. I'll send a footman in to clean up the desk and air the room before Papa comes down."

Rosalind had nearly made it to the door before George spoke again. "Don't let Wentworth develop expectations, Roz. You are softhearted, and leading him a dance would not be kind. He might be a decent enough fellow despite all the talk—God knows the gossips can be cruel—but he has a past and he's a banker. You'll be shunned if you show him marked favor, and then Lindy will have to deal with the talk. Until Lindy can convince some heiress to marry him, we can't have any talk. Surely you understand that?"

Rosalind considered George her harmless brother, while Lindy was the brother she'd learned to tread lightly around.

"Is Lindy in dun territory again?"

George went to the sideboard, put down his boots and

jacket, and poured himself a drink. "Lindy is always in dun territory, but lately he's had some luck at the tables. He will doubtless gamble away his good fortune rather than pay off his duns, though." He downed a generous portion of Papa's brandy at one go.

"No matter," George went on. "Lindy will have the title, so sooner or later, he'll charm his way up the church aisle with a suitably wealthy young lady. When that day comes, I might be able to find a woman to take a similarly charitable view of my own circumstances."

He saluted with his empty glass and set it on the sideboard.

"You could take holy orders, George. You're good-natured and every bit as handsome as Lindy, though less of a dandy. You have the requisite university education."

"Papa won't hear of me going for a parson, Roz. So here I am, composing odes to idleness and hoping you don't make a cake of yourself over Ned Wentworth."

Hoping she didn't complicate Lindy's finances, which Lindy himself had mucked up in the first place. "Get some rest, George. I must be off, or the bridle paths will be too crowded."

"You aren't listening to me," George said, a hint of real frustration in his tone. "Roz, if the talk is true, Ned Wentworth spent time in Newgate."

"So did His Grace of Walden. I don't see you giving him the cut direct."

"Ask him," George said. "Ask Wentworth if he's a former criminal, ask him if Walden put a pickpocket in charge of keeping other people's money safe. There's a reason the peerage tends not to bank with Walden, and Ned Wentworth is a big part of it."

"The boot is on the other foot, George: The Wentworths more often than not decline to do business with the peerage, but that is no concern of mine. Ned Wentworth has at least taken seriously my worries regarding the disappearances of both Campbell and Arbuckle."

George inhaled through his nose in exactly the same manner Papa did when he was preparing to lecture Rosalind about duty, expectations, and a woman's proper place.

"They simply abandoned their posts," George said, biting off each word. "For once, Rosalind, leave well enough alone. If you embroil Ned Wentworth in your cork-brained fancies about kidnapped maids, he could end up facing far worse than a few unkind whispers, as could you."

Today of all days, Rosalind did not have time to explain to George exactly how unkind the whispers about her had already been. *L-l-l-lady R-r-r-rosalind...*

"Mr. Wentworth has been nothing but proper with me, George, while you are tired and out of sorts. I'll leave you to seek your bed."

The longcase clock chimed the quarter hour, and Rosalind hurried from the library. She wasn't late, but she was upset. George handing out advice was unnerving enough, but that he'd taken note of Rosalind's comings and goings, and that he'd warn her away from Ned, was unnerving.

George's concerns were not, however, entirely logical. Rosalind assured herself of that as she settled into the saddle and took up the reins. Papa did not bank with

His Grace of Walden, but other peers did. The Duke of Elsmore was among the bank's directors, and His Grace of Rothhaven doubtless invested with the Walden bank.

Though Elsmore and his duchess didn't socialize much, and His Grace of Rothhaven attended only family functions, if that.

The groom trailed a respectful distance behind, while Rosalind's misgivings threatened to crowd out her joy to be seeing Ned again. She arrived at the park a bit early, and let her mare toddle up one bridle path and down another, and still, Ned Wentworth wasn't to be found.

* * *

Of all the excuses for tardiness or dereliction of duty that the badgers handed Ned—and their repertoire was vast and imaginative—the one Ned had the least sympathy for was, *I overslept.*

A lad could catch a nap in the afternoon, turn in early when exhausted, break his fast on the fly, and otherwise maintain punctuality. *I overslept* in Ned's lexicon equated to *I am unreliable*, which qualified as a mortal sin.

Ned was thus mentally berating himself as his horse was led out, for he was at risk for missing his appointment with Lady Rosalind. Duncan's warning—to tell Rosalind *all of it*—had wrecked any prayer of sleep. Ned had dozed off an hour before dawn, precisely when he should have been rising.

Rosalind would wait for him if he was a little late, but still...a gentleman was punctual.

Ned would normally have allowed his gelding a few minutes at the walk to limber up legs that had spent the night in a stall. He instead urged his mount to trot right out of the mews.

He was considering a canter as he approached the street, when a figure stepped out of the shadows at the mouth of the alley.

"Guv."

Not now. Ned drew the horse up. "Billy. Speak your piece. I'm late for an appointment."

Billy might have been thirty, he might have been fifty. His features were weathered and wary, his frame spare. He was exactly what Tryphena would have made Ned, given the chance.

A lackey, a broken spirit whose loyalty hadn't even a dog's dignity.

"Ye'll wait to hear what I have to say, guv."

"Then say it." Ned ought to be more diplomatic, for Billy had sought him out for reasons, probably Tryphena's twisted, criminal reasons. Still, Ned was at an impasse with his attempts to locate the missing maids, and Billy had taken a risk leaving his waterfront warren.

"You're all high and mighty now," Billy said, presuming to pat Ned's horse. "Quite the nabob with your own house, a groom, and a housekeeper."

In the parlance of the waterfront, that was a courteous warning that Ned's house and employees were at risk of harm.

"I've worked hard, Billy. I didn't gain what I have by stealing or extorting wealth from others." Ned tried for a flat statement of facts, but he stated only a convenient half-truth. He *had* stolen. If he'd remained in Tryphena's hands, then extortion, violence, and exploitation would have been all in a day's work.

"You think I don't work hard?" A world of ironic weariness colored the question.

"I know you do, Billy, and you've ventured far from the river to tell me something I need to hear."

Billy glanced about, though at this hour, the alley was deserted. "Something ain't right. Herself is worse than usual."

Tryphena worse than usual was a harrowing thought. "What has changed?"

"She's always been canny, but now she sees everything and everybody as a threat. No honor among thieves, if ye know what I mean. She talks crazy, and the look in her eye..."

"Has disease caught up with her?"

Billy shook his head. "I don't fink so. Tryphena stopped entertainin' years ago. This is sudden-like. She's scared and more than just the usual scared. She's done well for herself, played her cards right. You don't agree with her methods, but they was all she had."

"Old history, Billy. I'm willing to leave it in the past if she is. Have you noticed anything out of the ordinary besides her moods?"

Billy petted the horse again, and it occurred to Ned that once upon a time, had Billy been offered a job as a tiger or a groom, his life would have taken a very different turn.

"Herself owns doss houses. They bring in money. Not the fancy money the nunneries bring in, but it's steady, and as she says, folk need a safe place to sleep outta the wet. Besides, nobody comes after ya for ownin' a doss house."

The doss houses were safe, provided a man slept with a knife in each hand and one eye open. "Go on."

"I stop around every Wednesday to collect the take, but lately..."

"You think something is going on at one of these doss houses," Ned said. "Either nobody is seeking a night's lodging there, or Tryphena has found another use for that property."

The options were myriad: She could be holding stolen goods, leasing the place out to the river pirates and smugglers thronging the wharf, preparing to burn the house down for insurance money, or using the property as a gambling dive.

Or she could be harboring kidnapped women.

"She ain't sold the place," Billy said. "I'd know if she had. And it's one of her better houses. Could make a nice sponging house, but she won't listen to me when I tell her that. Says that's not honest work, holding up folk down on their luck for every pitcher of water or lump of coal."

"I applaud Tryphena's generosity of spirit, Billy, but which doss house has gone dark?"

A coach-and-four rattled by on the street. The minutes were passing, and Rosalind would not wait indefinitely.

"East of the City."

"A street?"

"Off Cuckminster Lane."

Ned did not know it, but then, the streets, alleys, lanes, and wynds in the older part of London often went through a series of names, depending on the trades plied along them.

"And where is that?" Ned asked.

"I told ye, near the Tower. A couple streets back from the river."

That last description was useful. "What does the place look like?"

"Looks like a doss house, Ned. 'Cept it ain't been a doss house since winter, and for all I know she traded it for some other property."

"She would tell you that because you'd have to read the contracts to her." Among Billy's many other duties, he was Tryphena's reader. "You know, Billy, if you ever wanted to leave that life…"

Billy shook his head. "She needs me, and she's all I'm good fer. She'll probably slit m' throat someday, but we're all put to bed with a shovel in the end."

And it would not occur to Billy to slit Tryphena's throat first because he was, in his way, a good man. "If you ever change your mind, a groom's life isn't half so dangerous as what you do now."

"Not half so excitin' neither." He gave Ned a cheeky grin and stepped back into the shadows. "Take care, Wentworth. You're a legend, you know. Wee Neddy turned honest, and ain't he just all the crack now?"

Ned was a man late for a pressing appointment. "Be careful, Billy, and save something for yourself against the day when Tryphena's empire crumbles."

"I come to see you, dint I? Somebody's moving against her. Somebody has an eye on her turf. She's scared, and I never seen her this scared afore. You take on her enemy, that's a problem solved for her, though she don't see it that way."

"Be careful," Ned said again. "Keep your bolt-hole well stocked, and your head down."

"You don't have to tell me, Ned Wentworth. Be off with ye. My reputation won't stand for bein' seen passin' the time of day with your kind."

Ned reached into his pocket, thinking to pay Billy for his considerable trouble.

"Keep yer coin, Wentworth, though I might ask you to return a favor someday. There's talk about cleaning up the docks, and God knows where an honest whore and her jolly boy will find work then."

"There's always talk about cleaning up the docks." Prim, condescending, simple-minded, virtuous talk that took no notice of how many people made their livelihoods on those vice-laden docks.

"You weren't on your own long enough to see how the times are changing, Neddy boy. In my day, the fancy lords went slumming in the lowest hells, the beggars were happier, and we took proper care of our grannies. Now, the poorhouse is worse than a prison, the temperance unions would take all our gin, and the transport ships send our grannies and kiddies to the ends of the earth. I've had a good run, but the reformers want to take it all away."

That sentiment—about a good run being a precarious form of success—was oddly resonant. "Then change your patch, Billy. Try your luck elsewhere, and drag Tryphena kicking and screaming with you if you must. She's good at both." Ned flipped him a coin, which he caught. "For luck. And you have my thanks, Billy."

Billy nodded. Ned saluted with his riding crop and cantered out of the alley.

Chapter Twelve

An hour after sunrise was an hour after sunrise.

Thirty minutes beyond the designated time, Rosalind had cantered and walked her mare sufficiently that a return home would be justified. The park was filling up, and the groom was doubtless wondering what all this fresh air was in aid of.

Rosalind's first thought was that Ned had simply meant something different by "an hour after sunrise" than she had thought. The horizon in London being obscured, the actual moment when the sun rose was inexact.

Not this inexact.

Her next thought was that Ned had been held up by pressing bank business, except no bank did business at the crack of doom.

She was inching up to the notion that Ned could have come to harm, when a rider on a dark horse cantered across the grass to intersect her. The dew had yet to burn off, and thus the gelding traveled over a sparkling green expanse, sunbeams slanting through the majestic maples, wisps of mist rising from the Serpentine.

Rosalind's heart sighed with equal parts relief and wonder. Ned Wentworth was magnificent, and he was hers, despite all the drivel George had spouted.

"My lady." Ned touched his hat brim with his riding crop. "You are a fine sight on this lovely morning. Will you walk with me while my horse catches his breath?"

"I would be delighted." Rosalind turned her mare alongside Ned's gelding. The groom dropped back a few yards, but only a few.

"I meant to be here earlier," Ned said, "but failed to rise on time. I apologize for my tardiness. How are you?"

If the groom heard that apology, he'd know this was not a chance meeting, and he might report that to Papa. More likely, the groom would grumble into his ale about her ladyship's flirtations in the park, and Higgins, who frequented the servants' hall, would overhear him. From Higgins to Lindy to Papa was a short distance.

One that had never much bothered Rosalind before, though she resented it keenly now. "I am glad to see you," she said, directing her mare down a path that was wide enough for two people to ride side by side. "You look a bit short of sleep."

"I am a bit short of sleep. I was up late reviewing loan applications."

Rosalind thought of George, getting drunk and calling it communing with his muse. "And you'd like to lend to them all?"

"No, not really," Ned said. "Too many merchants think that if they can only get their hands on some cash, then all will come right, but the ideal loan applicant is already doing well. His or her venture is competently managed, the customers and employees are happy, the goods or services are successful. The loan is not sought to come right after a bad patch, but rather, to turn a good patch into an excellent patch."

"How many of the loan applicants are ideal?"

"Next to none. Nobody wants to borrow money if they can help it, because defaulting on a loan can have such terrible costs. Borrowing is generally a desperate act rather than a prudent strategy, but Rosalind, I would rather not discuss the tedious business of banking on such a fine morning in such wonderful company."

"I don't find it tedious," she said. "How would you change things, if you were the King of Banking?"

Ned's lips quirked. "Like the Prince of Thieves? I'd make the rules for debtors the same for the shopkeeper and the lord. A peer cannot be imprisoned for debt, while everybody else can be. How is that fair?"

That was not a sentiment Papa would approve of. This was not a *conversation* Papa would approve of. "Ned, you must not air these thoughts before my father or brothers. Your theories approach sedition."

He held back a branch so Rosalind's mare could pass before his gelding. "When common sense approaches sedition, the nation has reached a sorry pass, but fear not. I will keep my financial theories to myself when I call upon your father. I brought you something."

"You brought me something?"

Ned unbuckled a saddlebag and passed over a bound book. "Your own copy of Mr. Smith's treatise. My copy is full of scribbling and marginalia, else I'd give you that."

"You are giving me a copy of..." She brought her mare to a halt. *The Wealth of Nations* was beautifully bound in red Morocco leather, the title embossed in gold. "You cut the pages for me. Is this why you were up so late last night, Ned?"

He gazed down the bridle path wending its way beneath the leafy oaks. "I needed something to occupy my hands while my mind eased away from the day's business."

"This was very thoughtful of you. I shall treasure it always." She would also read it, every word, probably many times. "I haven't any saddlebags. Could you bring it by the next time you call on me?"

"Of course." He accepted the book and returned it to his saddlebag. "Might we walk for a few moments?"

"I would enjoy a stroll," Rosalind said, signaling to the groom. Ned helped her to dismount, his assistance damnably correct.

"We won't be long," she said to the groom. "No need to loosen girths."

The fellow nodded and gave Ned a look that suggested her ladyship had best not come to any harm.

"We are in Hyde Park," Rosalind muttered when she and Ned had strolled a good ten yards down the path. "It's not as if you'd abduct..."

"Somebody is abducting young ladies, though so far, no women of your exalted station have gone missing. I want to kiss you so badly my lips ache, and yet

I also have information to impart, and yonder groom will not give us much privacy."

"Your lips ache?" The idea should have been humorous, and it was, mostly.

"My lips and a few other parts. I've had news."

"Tell me."

"An old connection who makes his living down near the wharves met with me this morning, which is another part of why I was so unforgivably late. He's had word of some doings that give me hope we might find your maids in one piece, and only slightly the worse for their ordeal."

The groom, damn him, was following on his cob at a discreet distance, leading the two riderless horses by the reins.

"You've found the women?"

"I can't say that. The fellow had few details, but this development is worth exploring. A doss house has abruptly ceased doing business as a doss house, with no explanation, and yet, somebody is using the place for something."

That did not sound to Rosalind like much of a development. London was awash in rickety overnight lodgings for rackety people. "Is your informant reliable?"

If Ned was aware of the groom, he gave no sign of it. "Yes, at least as regards this."

"But not in other regards?"

"Billy would not be received in even middling company, Rosalind, but I've known him since boyhood. I trust the accuracy of his information."

Ned Wentworth is received, but he's not good ton.

Drat George and his clumsy meddling. "How do you know him?"

Ned's smile was a bit pained. "I just do. He has no reason to lie to me."

"Unless he's setting a trap. Whoever has taken these women is doubtless doing so for financial gain. This Billy person might be in league with them."

Ned sauntered along for another few yards, to all appearances a gentleman enjoying a pleasant morning with a lady.

"I will not march up to the front door of this establishment and demand entrance, Rosalind. Present company, among many other factors, gives me sound motivation to remain among the living. I will use caution and call upon a few of my more arcane skills to effect reconnaissance. I must first find the place, though. Billy's description was less than exact."

Ask Wentworth if he's a former criminal, ask him if Walden put a pickpocket in charge of keeping other people's money safe.

"What arcane skills, Ned?"

"The ability to loiter about like a potted palm," he said, "looking so harmless and unremarkable nobody notices me. Came in handy at university and stands me in good stead at Her Grace's at-homes. Why?"

"Were you a housebreaker, Ned? Does something worse than a boy's thievery lurk in your past?"

His steps slowed. "The charge that first put me in Newgate, as best I recall, was petty larceny for a bungled attempt to pick a pocket. Polite society cannot seem to leave my ancient history in peace, though."

George certainly couldn't. "Twenty years ago, I was

still wetting my bed. Nobody feels any need to mention that, do they?"

"You are being logical, my lady. Polite society will choose vindictiveness over logic most of the time."

All of the time. "When can you speak to Papa?"

"Will he be in later today?"

Rosalind wanted to drag Ned by the arm back to the house that very moment. To have him accost Papa at breakfast, though Papa preferred to start his day with a silent meal spent in the company of the newspapers.

"Call upon him immediately after lunch. He should be at home, and not yet closeted with his man of business. I want a special license, Ned."

"Whereas I want to observe every courtesy. Her Grace of Walden might like to contribute to the planning of the particulars."

God, no. A meddling duchess would complicate what ought to be a simple and expedient exchange of vows. "I'd rather she not."

Ned gently nudged Rosalind with his elbow. "Let's quarrel, shall we? Have a rousing set-to right here in the park. That groom pretending not to spy on us will be agog, and tongues will wag."

"You are teasing me." A puzzling response to a difference of opinion, but at least he wasn't lecturing her.

"Rosalind, if we are to be married, I hope you will give me the benefit of your thinking on all matters of importance. We will differ, we will discuss, and sometimes, we will not mince words. Sometimes, I will be wrong and you will have to explain to me the error of my ways. Sometimes, you will be misinformed, and I will point that out to you. I, too, want to be married as quickly as possible, but our families would look askance at that choice. Right now, I am interested in how to win your father's approval, and a hole-in-corner ceremony isn't likely to do that."

"You make sense," Rosalind said, wishing he did not. "Do you really think we will argue?"

"I think," Ned said, bending near, "that once given a clear field to wield your considerable reasoning powers, you will delight in arguing with me. Read Mr. Smith. That should keep us exchanging verbal fisticuffs for a good five years. I will also delight in turning you loose on Walden and Lord Stephen, who think themselves the most rational of men."

The prospect of marrying into such a family, one that welcomed all comers to a debate, that entertained radical notions in a spirit of well-intended inquiry, boggled Rosalind's mind. No wonder she delighted so in Ned's company, and no wonder she wanted to make all haste to the altar.

"I adore you, Ned Wentworth. Now you have my lips aching too."

The path curved up ahead, such that if Rosalind were quick, she might be able to sneak a peck to Ned's cheek with the rubbishing groom none the wiser.

"I will call upon Lord Woodruff this afternoon," Ned said, "and then we can indulge in the liberties allowed a courting couple."

"No more aching lips?"

"Lips aching for all the best reasons," he countered, drawing Rosalind around the bend in the trail, and a few steps to the left. "Infernal perdition."

Rosalind followed Ned's gaze to the next curve in the path. Lindy rode along on his flashy gray, Clotilda Cadwallader up on a chestnut mare beside him.

"Roz, is that you?" Lindy called. "When one rides in the park, one generally involves horses, my dear. Wentworth, good day. I assume you know Miss Cadwallader?"

Rosalind handled the introductions, though the fair Clotilda was already acquainted with Ned. The groom came along with Ned's and Rosalind's horses, and Rosalind was compelled by manners to allow Lindy and Miss Cadwallader to escort her home.

Well, infernal perdition, to quote Ned, but at least Rosalind would see her intended that afternoon. She was home and changing out of her habit before she realized that Ned had only indirectly answered her question about the specific nature of his unfortunate past.

* * *

Ned had barely settled at his desk before His Grace of Walden strode into the office. The duke was immaculately attired, as always, and exuding more than his usual complement of impatience.

"Silas Cadwallader has an appointment immediately after lunch," Walden said. "You will need to handle that chore, for I have a committee meeting to chair. Cadwallader doubtless wants an increase in his line of credit, before his womenfolk spend him into the poorhouse."

"I'm sorry, Walden, but I—"

"Be noncommittal," Walden went on, as if Ned hadn't spoken. "Polite, deferential. Make the usual understanding noises, but hint that for a man of his station to go into debt over fripperies is an insult to him. Remind Cadwallader that his wife and daughters must learn to manage on a budget, though the ladies have likely been managing on pennies and prayers for the past three years."

"Walden, as it happens—"

"I've had word that Lord Woodruff's eldest might offer for Miss Cadwallader, which should make for an interesting match, provided the happy couple can remain afloat on the River Tick. Keep the meeting short, cite another pressing engagement, promise to schedule a second meeting if he wants to revisit the matter next month, and then—"

"No," Ned said, loudly enough to be heard in the corridor. "Or rather, I cannot handle this meeting. I have a prior engagement."

Walden's impatience coalesced into a scowl. "Driving in the park again, Ned? Going on another picnic?"

"And what if I were?" The question had come out: *An' waa' if I wur?* The Cockney had surfaced, which it did about once every three years, when Ned was losing his temper. He ought to be mortified, but he wasn't. Far from it.

Walden's expression became curious. "Are you perhaps venturing into the stews to find the missing women?"

"I am not." Not that afternoon.

"You lie poorly, which is a credit to you, according to Jane. I commend your nobility of spirit, if looking for needles in haystacks is the work of a noble spirit, but Ned, the bank is your—"

"The bank is my *job*, Walden. Lady Rosalind is my *future*. I am meeting with the Earl of Woodruff to ask permission to court his daughter."

His Grace, the imperious, imposing, fantastically wealthy and endlessly influential Duke of Walden, was rendered speechless, while Ned had more to say.

"I work twice the hours you do and four times the hours Lord Stephen puts in. If he is to be your successor as bank owner and titleholder, then his lordship must be able to do my job. He should know the tellers by name, if not the badgers, and he needs to spend time in the lobby as you used to, greeting the customers because your livelihood depends on them. If I want to go on a damned picnic twice a year, that is the least I am owed, considering all the at-homes and musicales I have endured in addition to running this institution.

"And if I must venture back into the stews," Ned went on, "to see decent women spared a future *your sisters narrowly escaped*, then into the stews I shall go, and you have nothing to say to it. I was managing on my own in those slums before you set one wealthy, booted foot on London's cobbles, which is why Jane charged me with looking after you, *Your Grace*, not the other way 'round."

In the ensuing silence, Walden prowled to the window for his usual reconnaissance, which meant Ned could not read his expression.

When the duke eventually faced Ned, he wore a glower that had probably intimidated everybody from the sovereign to the boot boy. "Are you quite finished?"

Ned inventoried his list of resentments and frustrations. "Stop having me followed."

"I am not having you followed, though bank policy requires that you take a badger with you, if you're on bank business."

Ned put down his pen in the very center of the pen tray. "I wrote the damned policy, *Your Grace*, and you violate it more than all the other managers put together. Lord Stephen comes a close second, but then, he's seldom on the bank's business because he regards this place as somewhere to go when he's bored with his clubs and inventions."

Another silence stretched as tight as a drum head. "Courting does not agree with you, Ned."

That might have been Walden's heavy-handed attempt at humor, or it might have been an equally heavy-handed warning.

Ned wasn't having either. "Perhaps banking does not agree with me." Not eighteen hours a day of it, six days a week, plus Sunday dinners, at-homes, and the occasional make-up-the-numbers appearance at Her Grace's insistence, to say nothing of stories on demand in the nursery, and let's-bury-the-dog.

"You are a very good banker," Walden said, propping a hip on the corner of Ned's desk.

"Too good, if you cannot spare me for a few hours here and there, Walden. What did you once tell me? An employee who cannot be replaced cannot be promoted. You would need three men to replace me, and they would be tired men indeed."

Walden's boot swung in a slow rhythm. "I'll hire you another assistant."

"Hire me a female this time. Somebody interested in more than currying favor with the widows. Tattinger is a good man, but he's so lonely he'd almost rather be a teller for the small talk involved."

"Hire yourself a female," Walden replied, "for clearly, you have the better grasp of what's needed. I'll have Stephen do the pretty with Cadwallader."

"Lord Stephen might not enjoy banking either, Walden. You should ask him. His mind is restless, and banking done responsibly is mostly for plodders."

"Your small investors don't consider you a plodder."

Ned rose, needing for this conversation to be over. He was anxious about his interview with Woodruff, frustrated with the investigation into the missing maids, and too weary in body and spirit to mend fences with Walden as he ought. Time enough to do that at the next Sunday dinner, assuming he was still welcome.

"My employer considers me a plodder," Ned said, "while I hope the Earl of Woodruff considers me a prospective son-in-law. Was there anything else, Your Grace?"

Walden rose and Ned realized that at some point, the duke had become distinguished. The touch of gray at his temples, the lines fanning from his eyes, the slight grooves bracketing his mouth made a fierce countenance more imposing. Walden was very much a man in his prime, but he was also no longer a dashing swain.

The thought was sad and sobering, for all too soon, Ned would no longer be a dashing swain either, if he ever had been. The years could march past, one quarterly directors' meeting, one monthly dinner at a time. If Ned did not seize the miracle of a life with Rosalind and hold it fast, he'd become another Tattinger, fawning over widows and fussing over which shade of carnation to affix to his lapel each day.

Ned had no desire to be a duke, but distinction in his later years would be...nice.

"I will leave you with this thought," Walden said. "Good luck with Woodruff. He's Tory to his bones and as land-poor as he is land-proud. He'll be the devil himself as a father-in-law, but if Lady Rosalind is your choice, we will welcome her with open arms."

Not what Ned had been expecting. "Thank you."

Walden ambled for the door. "Be careful, Ned. Jane tasked us with looking after each other, but when it comes to courting a lady, every gent is on his own. Lady Rosalind will be lucky to have you, as the Wentworths are and ever have been lucky to have you."

Walden left on those words, which was fortunate for Ned's composure. Ned closed the door after the duke, and went to the window, where he stood for a long time staring at the busy street below.

* * *

"Did I just hear our darling Neddy pinning your ducal ears back?" Lord Stephen Wentworth asked.

Walden took the place behind his own desk, a seat Stephen could never see himself assuming. But then, Stephen had never seen himself married, never seen himself as a father, never seen himself walking with relative ease, and look how delightfully those under-takings were going along now.

"Clearing the air," Walden said. "Ned has always had the knack of untangling knots. Knotted-up traffic, Bitty's knotted-up nursery dramas, and now, the knotty problem of Lady Rosalind's missing maids."

Something had derailed Walden's usual focus on bank business first thing in the day. Or someone.

"You have that I-must-discuss-this-with-Jane look about you," Stephen said. "What has Neddy in such a taking?" What had Walden in a much quieter but equally profound taking?

"I owe Ned my life."

Stephen refused on principle to occupy one of the chairs facing Walden's desk—supplicant seats, all too often. He instead appropriated the sofa beneath the window and helped himself to a tea cake.

"When you met Ned, he was a scrawny little thief with an impressively foul vocabulary." Which Stephen had envied him. "You have seen him educated and employed, while Jane has seen him scrubbed up and made presentable. How could you be indebted to him?"

Walden took out a nacre-handled penknife and began trimming one of the three quills in his pen tray.

"How good are your begging skills these days, Stephen?"

"You'd have to ask Abigail."

Walden's lips quirked. "Not those begging skills. The ones you survived on as a child when my wages were insufficient."

Truth to tell, Walden's wages had always been

insufficient. As a younger man, Stephen might have noted that point for the record.

"If I had to beg my way to a crust of bread now..." Stephen thought of his son, a sturdy little fellow with two sound legs. "Maybe for the boy, I could do it, or for Abigail. For myself, I haven't the knack."

"Exactly. We lose the knack. There I was in Newgate, all decked out in my Bond Street finery. Ned had to remind me that I should part with my gloves first, not to buy food, but rather, to buy pen and paper. Getting word to my family would solve the food problem and many other problems besides, but I had forgotten those priorities. I had also forgotten that nobody makes a good fist wearing his gloves."

"Ned reminded you of that too?"

"Within moments of taking me under his wing. The other inmates were still sizing me up, deciding how to relieve me of everything including my teeth. Ned swaggered up to me and appointed himself my general factotum. He negotiated with the guards on my behalf, amplified my reputation for violence considerably, and quite simply saved my life."

"You were five times his size, easily," Stephen said, picturing the Ned who'd been dragged, kicking and cursing, into the Wentworth household all those years ago. "You could have taken anybody in a fair fight."

Walden tested the point of the pen against his fingertip. "A fair fight in Newgate is one where the guards don't intervene. I was rusty, Stephen. I had worked for years to put aside my skills as a brawler. I craved refinement and *influence*, because the raw violence of the street fighter was too much of Jack Wentworth's

world. Ned was one-fifth my size, but he had ten times
my fight. In that, he was like you."

A compliment lurked well below the surface of
Walden's observation. Stephen would plumb the depths
for it later.

"What has all this to do with Ned telling you to sod
off now?"

Walden took up a second pen and began paring it
into serviceability. "Ned came back from the dead to
rescue me, though at the time, I fancied I was rescuing
him. He was starving himself. The guards explained it
to me later. Some prisoners, when faced with the prospect of transportation or the gallows, take matters into
their own hands. They choose the only option left to
them, on their own terms. Ned was feeding the damned
birds with his daily portion of bread or handing it on
to the other children."

Walden's knife had gone still. "Ned was nothing but
skin and bones," he went on, "and two bright, intelligent eyes that had seen far too much and all of it bad.
Jane says I was to be Ned's final act of charity."

As marrying Jane had been Walden's final act of
charity? "Either you took years of rescuing, or Ned
had occasion to rethink his plans."

"Both, I suspect. Ned sensed I'd been set up, and
thus had enemies willing to send me to an ignominious
death. This offended his sense of fair play, and so…"

Walden set the second pen back in the tray and took
up the third.

"And so…?"

"And so Rosalind Kinwood was right to ask Ned
to tilt at windmills on behalf of lady's maids and

companions. Her ladyship saw clearly what I had lost sight of. I gave Ned the life I wanted for myself from a young age—respectability, means, a position of influence, and a future full of profitable ventures. Ned has endured these impositions as graciously as he can, but he is still that fierce, righteous, wily fellow who took a future duke under his wing and never asked for anything in return."

Something about this fable wasn't quite running on all fours with the facts. "Ned was a housebreaker, pick-pocket, sneak thief, shoplifter, safecracker.... He was everything unsavory about London's underbelly." And how Stephen had envied him those adventures.

Walden shook his head. "Ned was a child surviving injustice, which is why he has taken such good care of us—because we were children who endured injustice. He never committed crimes of violence, never chose any but the affluent for his marks. Somehow, Lady Rosalind has deduced what I am only now realizing: Ned needs taking care of too. Not somebody to provide him a post, put him in fine tailoring, or teach him not to drop his haitches, but to *care* for him."

Abigail had alluded to the same notion, that Ned was in some regard still in prison, albeit surrounded by tellers, badgers, and clerks.

"I thought we did rather care for our Neddy." In some ways, Ned had been more of a brother to Stephen than Walden himself. "How should our regard be more in evidence?"

Walden swept the parings from the blotter into his palm and dropped them into the waste bin. "We start by sending him on more picnics with Lady Rosalind.

She sees Ned clearly, and Ned is willing to allow her that privilege. I do hope the Earl of Woodruff doesn't try to make things difficult for all concerned."

Stephen had been reading the file on the Cadwallader situation, including that little bit about a possible match with Woodruff's prancing heir.

"Woodruff is an obnoxious, self-important, old windbag who hasn't a feather to fly with, and Ned does not suffer fools. This might end badly."

"Precisely."

Chapter Thirteen

"Mr. Edward Wentworth," the butler said, bowing and withdrawing. He cast Ned a glance that suggested this call was not well advised, but foolish young men would rush in, and what was a mere butler to do about such goings-on?

Lord Woodruff sat at a desk that likely traced its provenance back to the Conqueror's desk, as Woodruff doubtless traced his lineage back at least that far.

Three acts of rudeness ensued—additional rudeness, because as a guest, Ned ought to have been received in a public room rather than an office.

First, Woodruff remained seated after a caller had been announced.

Second, Woodruff scratched away at some correspondence without looking up.

Third, he did not invite Ned to take a seat.

Fourth, fifth, ad infinitum, he was engaging in the petty displays of the pathetic bully. Ned remained politely by the door, while visually inventorying the earl's study. This was his lordship's sanctum sanctorum, the seat of his financial empire.

Ancestors who looked to be suffering a case of the wind frowned down from framed portraits, piles of correspondence and newspapers were stacked on the sideboard. The writing implements—wax jack, pounce pot, pen tray—were all silver, and the carpet Axminster.

And yet, the carpet needed a good beating, suggesting to the former housebreaker in Ned that the earl did not want footmen or maids in the room even briefly. The windows were far from pristine, which made no sense when the room's primary purpose was reading and writing. The candles on the mantel were beeswax, but the sooty stains on the wall behind them suggested those candles were for show.

Tallow candles were smokier than beeswax and would also account for the lingering stink Ned detected in the air.

Woodruff was either a penny pincher who could not trust the discretion of his domestics, or he was pockets to let. The lacy excess of his cravat, the riotous embroidery on his waistcoat, and the abundance of rings on his pale hands suggested the latter case prevailed.

As a boy, Ned had stood watch as a lookout, unmoving for hours in the shadows of foul-smelling alleys. His patience could outlast Moses holding up his arms to ensure victory over the Amalekites. He used the time to study Woodruff, who bore little resemblance to Rosalind.

The earl was fair, his hair having gone flaxen rather than gray. His locks were thinning around a widow's peak, and he favored an old-fashioned queue tied back with a silk ribbon. He had probably been a handsome young man, but fondness for the grape had taken a toll on his complexion. He was lean, and yet his countenance was jowly, and he had pouches beneath his eyes.

Ned could see a slight resemblance to Lord Lindhurst about the chin and jaw, but Lindhurst still had some charm. Woodruff, by contrast, was as cold as Puritan charity. Not an attractive man, but doubtless still confident of his own masculine perfection.

The earl ceased his little game after about three minutes and passed a merely curious glance over Ned. "Wentworth—if that is your name?"

"That is my name. Thank you for seeing me." Ned could not bring himself to append the deferential *my lord* to his greeting.

"I am a busy man, Wentworth. State the nature of your business as succinctly as possible. My solicitor will soon be here, and his time is precious as well."

This was precisely how the bank handled a presuming debtor, though bank managers exhibited a great deal more courtesy. Ned ambled over to the portrait hanging above the sideboard. The frame wanted dusting, and the artist's name was unknown to him.

"Lady Rosalind initially consulted me in the hope that I might assist her to find her missing lady's maids," Ned began. "My association with her ladyship has developed in more cheerful directions, and I esteem her greatly. My sentiments are, I believe, reciprocated. I have means, standing, and connections, and I am here to ask for your permission to pay her—"

Woodruff laughed, a well-bred cascade of mirth. "Has she led you a dance, Wentworth? Allowed you to develop ridiculous expectations? Not well done of her, but a woman must be permitted her diversions. Get out, and I will do you the courtesy of forgetting you ever presumed to call." Woodruff waved a hand toward the door, the lace at his wrist flapping over his knuckles.

"Lady Rosalind has not led me any dances," Ned replied. "She is too fine a person for such stratagems, and I have reason to hope she returns my regard."

"Do you?" Woodruff picked up a letter and slit the seal with a silver letter opener. "Do you really? Then you are as foolish as you are lowborn. I know who you really are, sir, and you no more deserve the Wentworth name than Quinton Wentworth deserves the Walden title. You're a gutter rat who scrapped and cheated his way from the sewer into a post he does not merit. You are the last man I'd allow to court Lady Rosalind. Leave now and I won't summon the footmen to toss you into the street."

Ned had expected to grovel, had expected lectures, and grudging, conditional permission. He had not anticipated this sneering dismissal.

"You cannot use Lady Rosalind as collateral for your debts for much longer without somebody expecting payment when due. I have means, Woodruff. Considerable means, and you are in need of same."

The façade of the genteel aristocrat cracked, revealing a rage that made no sense.

"How dare you?" Woodruff spat, getting to his feet. "How dare you set foot under my roof, casting aspersion on this house as you seek my daughter's hand. If you don't leave now, I will see you ruined, Wentworth, and I will send Rosalind back to Derbyshire. She should know better than to encourage the suit of an upstart bastard pickpocket with airs so far above his station as to suggest mental unsoundness."

Ned could not be ruined, because he moved in society only to placate Jane's need to parade him about. To be spared the waltzing and small talk would be a mercy.

But the thought of Rosalind enduring more banishment... "You cannot send Rosalind away again. You sent her away when she was but a grieving child. You sent her away time and again to receive an education she did not need. You sent her away when she could barely speak clearly on her own behalf. All she wanted was to take her place as a member of this family, and instead you left her to be bullied, teased, and baited—"

Like a badger cornered by dogs, like a bear chained to the wall while the pack attacked for the entertainment of a jeering crowd. No wonder Rosalind abhorred blood sport.

Woodruff tugged the bell pull. "This interview is at an end, and if you so much as glance in Rosalind's direction, I will see you derided from one end of Mayfair to the other. You come near my daughter again, and I will summon the watch and tell them you are responsible for those maids going missing."

Ned stalked across the room and had the slight gratification of seeing Woodruff take a step back.

"Rosalind deserves better than this family, and if it

comes to ruination, mind your own house, Woodruff, because you have tried my patience to the utmost."

"Out," Woodruff said, pointing to the door with a shaking finger. "Out, now."

Ned stepped back, bowed, and withdrew, furious— and relieved. He hadn't taken a swing at the old scoundrel, that was something.

"Ned?" Rosalind stood in the doorway of the parlor across the corridor. "I take it Papa was difficult?"

She was so composed, and so hopeful. Ned linked his hands behind his back lest he take her in his arms.

"He threatened to ruin me if I presume to peek at your hems, and he will not like finding us in conversation. I bid you good day."

"You'll run off? Just like that?"

She would doubtless allow him to run off, just like that, and endure the abandonment without complaint. Rosalind was nothing if not stoic.

"He threatened to send you away, Rosalind, and that was after I pointed out that a match between you and me could benefit Woodruff financially." Pointed that out by flinging it in the earl's face. Doubtless the worst possible strategy.

"Are you giving up?" Rosalind asked, staring past Ned's shoulder.

"Do you want me to give up?"

Lord Lindhurst chose then to poke his head out of a room two doors down. "I say, Roz, I'm in the mood for an ice. Tell Wentworth to run along, and I'll take you with me to Gunter's."

"I'll see myself out," Ned said, lest Woodruff summon the watch. "Don't provoke your father, Rosalind.

Something has him in a desperate frame of mind, and his bad mood must not be allowed to create further difficulties for you."

"But, Ned . . ." Rosalind sent a fulminating glance in Lindhurst's direction, though his lordship did not show any inclination to afford his sister privacy.

"I wish you good day," Ned said, then much more softly, "for now."

Rosalind grasped that hint, as Ned had known she would. "Very well, good day for now."

The urge to take her by the hand and drag her away from this temple to paternal conceit was nearly overwhelming. Ned offered a bow and left, snatching his hat from the butler and stalking out into the sunny afternoon.

"Tossed ye out on yer ear?" Artie asked, scrambling from the bench, where he'd been holding the reins, back onto his perch.

"As good as tossed me out. Woodruff needs money, I have money. Woodruff needs to see Rosalind married to somebody with connections, I have ducal connections. Woodruff doesn't love his daughter, I do."

"There's yer mistake," Artie said. "He has you by the balls, and he knows it. We going to sit here all day or are you headin' back to the bank?"

Ned did not want to go to the perishing bedamned bank. "How well do you know the waterfront, Artie?"

"I know enough to stay clear of it. Lads like me can disappear out to sea all too easily, and I've a fondness for the Old Smoke and dry land."

"As do I, but I need to find a certain house. Mind

the way we travel, because I might ask you to get the horse back to the bank without me."

Artie looked up and down the street. "Me and Hamlet will manage, but you ought not to be poking around the wharves on your own, guv. Not looking like that."

"I'll poke carefully." During the whole tangled, tedious journey along the Strand and on toward the City, Ned pondered what exactly had happened in the Earl of Woodruff's musty, stuffy study. Did Woodruff know his own son had sought funds from the bank?

Was that what the summary eviction had been about? The earl had gone from an aristocrat's everyday arrogance to hurling threats at both Ned and Rosalind. Something had inspired Woodruff to overshoot the mark of the imperious papa and slip into the posture of a bleating bully.

Something, but what? And how was Ned to deal with it?

* * *

"I say, Roz." Lindy ambled forth from the library. "If you are that hard pressed to find escorts, I could have a word with some of the fellows. You need not humor Wentworth to such an obvious extent."

The clatter of wheels on the cobbles told Rosalind that Ned had departed...*for now*. Those two words fortified her resolve. Ned had retreated in the face of enemy fire, but he had not abandoned her.

Yet.

"Mr. Wentworth is delightful company," Rosalind

said, "and in every way an eligible bachelor. You need not inspire your friends to charity on my behalf."

Lindy peered at her. If he took out his quizzing glass, Rosalind would smite him with it.

"No need to turn up shrewish," he said. "To have the regard of another party is flattering, isn't it? For your sake, I wish the party could be a little more the thing, though. A lot more the thing. Banking is worse than being in trade outright in the opinion of some."

"Lindy, would you please hush?"

Rosalind had spoken gently, but so unusual was her request that Lindhurst looked intrigued rather than affronted.

"Shall I take you for an ice?" he asked, looking as if the notion merited intense study. "Clotilda says an ice can cure all ill humors. The day promises to be fair, and I believe an ice would restore your mood wonderfully." He beamed at her, clearly pleased with his great inspiration. "I know Papa isn't always diplomatic with you, Roz, but he is getting on. You can be quite thick-headed, and allowances must be made. I am your brother, though, and I will take you for an ice."

Capital fellow that I have decided to be, for once.

"Clotilda?" Rosalind asked. Lindy had changed from riding attire to morning dress, though the dark red carnation he'd worn in the park again graced his lapel. The red carnation symbolized love and affection. For *Clotilda?*

"Miss Cadwallader," Lindy said, directing a fatuous gaze to the vicinity of the crown molding. "Anything you could do to encourage her regard for me would be appreciated. She's a capital girl, Roz, from a much-respected old family. She's also—if I might be blunt—worth ten thousand a year."

No, she was not, according to Ned. "Lindy, I'm sure Miss Cadwallader is everything lovely, and if she has won your heart, then she is to be envied above all other women, but I have reason to know that her situation isn't quite—"

The door across from the parlor opened.

"Rosalind." Papa stood in the doorway to his office, wrath rolling off him in silent waves. "I hope I did not hear you conversing with a man who presumed to call on me in private?"

Lindhurst's gaze ricocheted between Rosalind and the earl. Upon which pugilist would he have bet had some of *the fellows* been on hand?

"I greeted Mr. Wentworth civilly," Rosalind said, "as you expect me to greet every caller." Every caller, every nabob, mushroom, cit, and widowed viscount, to say nothing of the tabbies, gossips, and match-makers. "Lindhurst and I were discussing his plans for the day."

"Thought I'd take old Roz for an ice," Lindhurst said. "See and be seen, chat up the lovelies, take the air."

Old Roz. *Old Roz.* Lindy wanted to make a display of taking pity on his antidote of a sister. The rotten, sad truth was, his motives, while doubtless originating in a desire to polish his bachelor halo before the fair Clotilda, might also include a pinch of genuine pity for Rosalind.

"I'm not in the mood for an ice, Lindy, but thank you for the thought."

Papa strode out of his study to glower at Rosalind.

He had a way of inhaling through his nose that Rosalind usually dreaded, but today—perhaps because she'd been reminded of her very great age, perhaps because she and Ned had been reduced to whispered exchanges in the corridor—she found Papa's posturing annoying.

"If Lindhurst is kind enough to haul you about on his social rounds," Papa said, "you will fetch your bonnet and be grateful. As it is, I have reason to fear you encouraged Wentworth's marital aspirations, while you disdain the advances of more suitable parties."

"Ned Wentworth is more than suitable. He is respected, well connected, well-to-do, and in every way that matters, a gentleman. Why you'd think otherwise, Papa, I do not know."

"And that is the heart of the matter," Papa retorted, loudly enough to have been heard in the kitchen. "You do *not* know, Rosalind. You presume, you flounce about like a willful child, ignorant of the disaster you court. Wentworth is not suitable, he never will be, and there's an end to it."

Rosalind heard the voices of her every nanny, governess, and deportment instructor clamoring for her to apologize for her misguided words and promise to mend her ways. And what, precisely, had years of apologizing and mended ways earned her?

A father convinced he could sniff her into submission. A brother who tossed the prospect of an ice at her as if she were in truth the child her father accused her of being. Papa and Lindy stood in contrast to Ned, who wanted to hear her opinions, who considered her formidable, and who looked forward to watching her argue a duke into submission.

"I do not care for an ice," Rosalind said, "though I have cordially thanked Lindy for his consideration. You bungled that interview with Ned Wentworth, Papa. You gave offense to the dear connection of a ducal house, a man with more benevolent influence over London's commercial ventures than you could ever hope to have through your machinations in the Lords. I do esteem Mr. Wentworth. Anybody with half an iota of common sense would esteem him."

"He's a bastard, upstart, presuming—oh, never mind. Go to your room, Rosalind, and don't come down to dinner. Contemplate the splendors of your Aunt Ida's dower house, because you will soon find yourself there if you don't learn some decorum. And be warned: Viscount Dinkle has spoken of you quite favorably. If he were so misguided as to offer for you, I'd let him take you off my hands."

"I would not marry Lord Dinkle if he were the last bachelor in Mayfair." The words were out of Rosalind's mouth before the chorus in her head could rail against them.

Lindy winced.

Papa tried his sniffery again, and even drew his hand back as if preparing to deliver a slap.

Rosalind stared at him, letting him see every scintilla of contempt his high-handedness inspired.

"I tell you this," Papa said, lowering his hand, "for your own good, Rosalind. Continue with your willful departure from proper deportment, refuse my guidance regarding the company you keep, and I will see

Ned Wentworth's name dragged through the foulest sewers. The Wentworths will realize the error of their association with him, and you will see what a fool you've been."

Papa made a grand exit, shutting the office door behind him with a bang.

Lindy turned a frown on Rosalind. "What the hell has got into you, Roz? If I'm to court Clotilda, and believe me, that project is well under way, then you can't be provoking Papa like this."

"I provoked *Papa*? Lord Dinkle is three times my age, four times my girth, and he's already buried three wives."

"Old Dinky needs sons, Roz. Don't be petty. Best run along to your room. I'll make sure the kitchen sends you a tray before nightfall." His tone said Rosalind did not deserve that much consideration.

"It might surprise you to know, Lindy, that I can operate my own bell pull."

"But you cannot govern your temper. I must agree with Papa: Learn to behave, and stop throwing yourself at unsuitable parties, or I will second the motion to return you back to the shires."

Rosalind curtsied to his bedamned lordship. "I wish you and Miss Cadwallader every joy, Lindhurst. If you'll excuse me, I have some letters to write."

She left at a decorous pace, though another instant in the company of her father or brother, and her ungovernable temper might get the better of her in truth. Before she sat down to write her letters, Rosalind took a moment in the solitude of her bedroom to consider what had just transpired.

Ned had attempted to gain Papa's approval of a courtship, and Papa had been ridiculous. Ned had made a tactical retreat, the course of a prudent man. If Ned had any sense, he'd send Rosalind a polite note tomorrow turning tactical retreat into a complete abandonment of the field.

Ned had a lot of sense, but he had even more honor. Rosalind's whole future was entrusted to his honor.

She, by contrast, had pointed out to Papa the inconsistency of his behavior. She was no great beauty, and her settlements were merely respectable. Papa played his little games in the Lords, though he was certainly not among the most powerful peers.

Rosalind's marital prospects had thus never been more than good. Ned Wentworth was everything Papa should have leaped at in a suitor: wealthy, well placed, with some influence of his own. Ned was a vast improvement over Lord Dinky and his ilk.

And yet, the prospect of a match between Rosalind and Ned Wentworth had sent Papa into a tantrum. Papa's reaction was absurd. Perhaps *Papa* had been refused a loan from the Wentworth bank?

Rosalind pondered that conundrum while she penned a short note to Ned. She rang for a footman, passed him the sealed note and a package she'd chosen the previous day. Then she took out a fresh sheet of paper and sent off a lengthier epistle to Aunt Ida.

* * *

Ned rumpled his cravat, rubbed a smudge of mud onto his boot, added some dust to the back of one coat sleeve, and generally affected the demeanor of a weary traveler. In that guise, he inquired in a half dozen wharf-side taverns about where a fellow newly returned to London could safely spend a night or two on the cheap.

The same several lodging houses were suggested over and over. Ned called at four of them, asking after a brother—Robert Taylor—who'd come through London three months ago. In the first three cases, he was told to inquire at one of the other doss houses.

The landlady at the fourth house, an old woman a trifle tidier than her predecessors, added that earlier in the year, Mr. Taylor might have stayed at the place on Grapeshot Court—number twenty, it was—but that establishment no longer took in boarders.

Ned got directions to Grapeshot Court, which was a dog's leg off a dead end not far from Cuckminster Lane, and made his way through lengthening shadows to the designated neighborhood.

London changed moods between one street and the next, with seedy dilapidation yielding to respectable terraces, or venerable Tudor dwellings sliding into disreputable tenements. Grapeshot Court clung to shabby pretensions of respectability. One determined housekeeper had put potted pansies on her stoop, though Ned was certain those pansies were taken inside before sunset each evening.

The rest of the court was tattered around the edges, with grass springing up between flagstones, evidence of pigeons speckling the walkways, and a scrawny one-eyed tabby perched like a vulture on the lid of a rain barrel.

Ned withdrew to the narrow space between two houses on the court and watched number twenty for more than an hour. Nobody came or went, and on this fine spring day not a single window was cracked. Not on the ground floor, not on the upper stories, which would be getting warm this late in the afternoon.

Ned knew better than to be on unfamiliar turf after dark. He rapped on the front door of number twenty, which was arguably foolish of him. If Tryphena's thugs were up to no good here, they might recognize Ned.

The young man who opened the door an entire six inches was large enough to qualify as one of Tryphena's henchmen, and had the requisite broken nose and wrinkled finery, but Ned didn't recognize him.

"Wot yer want?"

"Lookin' fer me bruvver," Ned said. "Came through earlier in the year and mighta stayed here. Name a Robert Taylor."

"We don't take in boarders no more."

"But he mighta stayed here when ya did, and if I knew that, then I'd know Bobbie made it to Lunnon."

The door eased back another two inches. "Can't help ya, mate. This place offered a cot for a coin, no names needed."

"What about regulars?" Ned asked. "If I could find somebody who stayed here back then regular-like, maybe they could tell me if Bob passed this way?"

"This ain't my patch," the fellow replied, shaking his head. "I wouldn't know about any regulars from months back. Ask at the Dog and Dam, maybe they might know, but I can't tell you nuffink."

Ned adopted the requisite frustrated expression and touched a finger to his hat brim. "Thanks all the same. Where's the Dog and Dam?"

He was given directions, and he shuffled on his way. A glance over his shoulder told him that the door to number twenty did not close until Ned was almost at the end of the lane.

He turned in the direction of the Dog and Dam, though he didn't need to make any inquiries there. He needed to get back to the genteel environs of the bank before the sun set, and he needed to sort through the disappointing interview with Lord Woodruff earlier in the day.

Not for all the wedded bliss in England would Ned risk causing Rosalind to be banished again, but neither was he about to give up on the quest to find her missing maids.

The windows at number twenty had been nailed shut from the outside, and Ned knew of only one reason why that might be.

* * *

"If you are officially courting Lady Rosalind," Walden said, setting aside the bank policy he'd been reading in the fading afternoon light, "you might want to tidy up a bit before venturing forth in public."

Ned's attire was uncharacteristically scuffed and wrinkled, considering that the bank was still open for business. Ned himself had an impatient, annoyed air as he stalked into Walden's office.

"I ventured into surrounds where too much tidiness

is an invitation to get your pocket picked. Where is Artie?"

Walden rose from the settee beneath the window. "He's a badger. How the hell should I know?"

"He's the badger assigned *to me*, and thus you keep an eye on him. I sent Artie back with the curricle more than two hours ago."

Ned was even moving differently, prowling across the carpet in a loose-limbed gait that bore little resemblance to the straight-backed posture of a gentleman in polite company.

"Where exactly did you go," Walden asked, "and why did you go there?"

"I might well have found Lady Rosalind's missing maids." Ned opened the sideboard cabinet, extracted a bottle of the best brandy Walden kept on hand, and poured himself a generous portion. "You joining me?"

Ned would not normally take strong spirits before dark, much less help himself to Walden's finest brandy. He would not be seen on the bank premises in less than pristine turnout, and he would not serve himself first.

Something seriously untoward was afoot. "I believe I shall."

Ned poured Walden two fingers and passed him the glass. "Lord Woodruff all but summoned the watch on me."

And what was more seriously untoward than a thwarted swain? "Does his lordship yet draw breath?"

Ned's lips quirked. "For now. He could bastille me three times a day and I wouldn't much care, but he threatened to send Lady Rosalind back to the shires if I pressed my suit."

A mere refusal would not have Ned swilling brandy and roaming London's backstreets by the hour. "Was that bombast?"

Ned took another considering sip of his drink, the movement casual and curiously elegant. "No, it was not. Woodruff has banished her previously for bad reasons and no reason at all. Because she stuttered, because she stopped stuttering, because she grieved, because she mastered her grief. When he allows her in Town, she's expected to stand up with every cit or nabob her papa owes money to. When she behaves badly—such as when she expresses an original thought, for example— she's sent off to her widowed auntie in disgrace, like a twelve-year-old caught smoking her papa's cigars."

Walden considered that litany, and considered how Ned, who'd lost his family early in life, would react to a father treating his daughter so cavalierly.

"What if he does banish her? You simply steal the lady away, take her off to Gretna Green, and live happily ever after." Jane would approve of that course, under the circumstances.

Ned appropriated the chair behind Walden's desk. "And what will people think, Your Grace? First, that Lady Rosalind anticipated her vows with me and must marry me in haste. Second, that she's taken leave of her senses because Woodruff will be within his rights to keep her settlements if she marries without his approval."

"Not necessarily. If she's of age, the portion that comes to her through her mother's settlements isn't subject to Woodruff's approval."

"She's of age," Ned said, though this seemed to bring

him no comfort. "And I can provide for her handsomely enough, but the gossips won't recollect that."

Walden took one of the chairs opposite the desk, an unusual perspective. "I doubt Lady Rosalind cares what the gossips think." Nor did Ned, usually.

"She cares," Ned said, setting his drink in the center of the blotter. "She has to care. Her brothers have yet to marry, and the scandal of her running off with me would affect Lord Lindhurst's situation especially."

Walden snorted. "The fact that Lindhurst's father is nearly rolled up will have a much greater impact on his lordship's marital prospects."

"*He's what?*"

"Woodruff disdains to sully his hands with trade, even to the extent of eschewing mercantile investments. He's sinking fast, and his acres are overrun with sheep in the usual desperate fashion."

"That explains the tallow," Ned muttered. "How long does he have?"

"He might be able to bluff his way through another Season or two, but I feel as if I'm watching two carriages careen toward each other from opposite directions on a road that crests a hill. The coachies can't see each other, and a spectacular crash looms ahead for both."

"Who's in the other carriage?"

"The lovely Clotilda Cadwallader, her mama, three younger sisters, and a boot full of unpaid bills. Cadwallader was in here earlier today bleating to Stephen about an expected improvement in his daughter's circumstances, and the family's prospects magically coming right as a result of her good fortune."

Ned held his glass up to the sunlight slanting through the window. "It can work like that when a cit's daughter marries into a titled family. The cit is eventually accepted into the better clubs, the titled family gains a share in viable businesses, the younger sisters get all the right introductions."

"It can work like that, given enough time and money. Cadwallader and Woodruff have neither. Which idiot declared that putting people in hard chairs discouraged them from taking too long to state their business?"

"Some cork-brained duke or other. Woodruff might have tossed me out because he knows Rosalind will have to marry money."

"You *are* money," Walden said, finding it curious that Ned would need to be reminded of that. "Compared to the average younger son, you reek of money. You could be wealthier still, but you lack for greediness."

"A serious shortcoming, I know."

Ned looked good in the big chair behind the big desk. He looked at home, confident, competent. He was managing the bank, but he was also... *in charge* of the bank, in a manner Walden hadn't quite admitted to himself. Walden managed the large-scale investing, and a directors' committee made the bigger loan decisions, but Ned managed *everything*. The people, the building, the policies, the day-to-day dramas.

When had that happened, and did managing a bank make Ned happy?

"In a banker," Walden said, "a lack of greed is a strength. A greedy man is owned by his venal ambitions. Shall I buy Woodruff off for you?"

Ned swirled his drink. "Buy him off?"

Such delicacy. "Determine his price, arrange the settlements, and get him out of your way. Make a wedding present to you of some estate or other. That sort of thing." Jane had been agitating for Ned to have some acres of his own for years. Every other Wentworth did, ergo, Ned should have an income-producing property too.

"I am"—Ned peered at his brandy—"touched at the offer, but as regards my courtship of Rosalind, I doubt that Woodruff has a price. Part of his outrage toward me was apparently genuine aristocratic shock."

A diffident Ned was an unusual sight. Ned could be considerate, discreet, and even diplomatic, but he was a stranger to shyness.

"Why the hell would the prospect of you paying addresses to Lady Rosalind outrage anybody?"

"Woodruff said he knew who I was, Walden. He made allusions to Newgate, and he sits on at least one committee that oversees the prisons. I had the sense he'd read every official document attached to my criminal past and was prepared to see them all published in the *Morning Gazette.*"

Walden had never asked Ned about his childhood. What Walden knew was bad enough: a brother hanged at too young an age, theft undertaken simply to keep body and soul together...and then Newgate and the possibly lethal prospect of transportation.

"Woodruff cannot have read any documents relating to your past," Walden said. "I haven't read those documents. Nobody has."

"Why not?" Ned finished his drink and ambled back to the sideboard with his empty glass. "I would certainly like to know what the constables and magistrates had to say about me."

"Jane asked that I arrange to have those documents destroyed, Ned. I left Newgate on good terms with the warden and at least one of the guards, so no record of your incarceration exists. Not yours, Davies's, or any of the ladies who left that place with us. I thought Jane would have told you this. She was insistent."

"No record?"

"None. Not in the magistrate's office, not in parish records, not at the prison. In any case, you weren't using the Wentworth name at the time, so connecting those misdeeds to Lady Rosalind's suitor would be impossible."

Ned moved toward the door, pausing before leaving. "So Woodruff was bluffing? Making empty threats regarding my past?"

"He had to be."

"Interesting."

Ned left the office and Walden took the seat behind his desk, though he was fairly itching to discuss the whole exchange with his duchess.

Chapter Fourteen

"You know the girl who arrived last night," Catherine said, keeping her voice down.

Francine shuffled the deck and passed Catherine half the cards. Lately, all the women had taken to speaking quietly, and Hiram barely said a word.

"I think I recognize her," Francine replied. "She looks like a lady's companion I've exchanged a few words with. She's lost weight if that's the case."

Calliope Henderson had lost more than weight. When Francine had passed the time with her at the milliner's or glovemaker's, Miss Henderson had been friendly, inordinately so given that a companion ranked above a lady's maid.

Miss Henderson had claimed that her cheerful disposition was part of why she'd been hired, and that the last thing a widow needed around her were long faces. Calliope wasn't cheerful now. She hadn't so much as spoken since Hiram had ushered her into the parlor last night. She'd sat reading or—more likely—simply staring at a book.

At breakfast, she'd barely eaten. She'd sipped at the weak tea and nibbled her toast, gazing at nothing in particular.

"Who knows where they were keeping her before," Catherine said. "That dress hasn't seen an iron or a washtub in a fortnight at least. Poor thing has probably been ill-used."

That Catherine could allude so calmly to rape chilled Francine as the thin blankets and leering guards had not.

"If we're to be shipped off to brothels, I wish they'd get around to shipping us."

"Set out your cards, Francine," Catherine said. "We'll learn soon enough what they plan to do with us."

Francine made herself begin placing the cards one by one facedown on the table. "How soon? Has Hiram told you something?"

Catherine shuffled her half of the deck, her movements deft. "I know that the last time the house was full up, all the other women were sent somewhere else the next day. I heard something about the count having to match, and that's when they told me to go back upstairs. Hiram said I wasn't the kind to give them any trouble, just my luck."

Hiram was watching them, his gaze brooding. He generally regarded Catherine with frustrated longing, but this morning, his homely face was sad. Pitying, even.

"You think they're getting ready to ship us off?"

"This is not a charitable institution, Franny. They are getting ready to do something."

The windows were never open in this godforsaken dump, but Francine heard boots on the walkway below.

"Stay where you are, ladies," Hiram said, going to the window and peering down. "Nobody so much as twitches until I tell you to."

The front door creaked open one floor below, and masculine voices drifted up. Three men, at least. Francine's meager rations threatened to rebel.

"I'm scared, Kitty."

"No point being scared, Franny. Don't fight them, and they eventually leave you in peace."

Catherine sounded composed, but she'd stopped dealing her cards, and she was watching Hiram as if he were her last hope of salvation.

"I want to jump out the window," Francine said. "I have a really, really bad feeling."

"You'd have a worse feeling with your brains splattered all over the cobbles. If they wanted to hurt us, they'd have done it by now."

That was not reason. That was desperation trying to sound logical. "They've hurt us already," Francine said. "Lied to us, snatched us away from our posts, forced us to stay here." Apparently done worse than that to Calliope Henderson.

Boots tromped up the stairway, and Calliope seemed to grow smaller without moving.

Catherine put down her cards and gathered up those that Francine had spread on the table. "For the love of God, shut your mouth, Franny, and keep it shut."

The men were now at the door to the parlor, and Hiram conferred with them. Francine had the thought that they couldn't toss her into the Thames in broad daylight.

"Ladies, lend an ear," Hiram said. "Time to collect

your things and bid this palace farewell. You'll be veiled and bound, but nobody needs to get hurt. Just do as you're told, and we'll all get along."

"I don't want to do as I'm told," Francine muttered.

Catherine didn't answer, but was instead engaged in some visual battle of wills with Hiram. The other women rose and shuffled toward the door, while Francine considered the drop to the cobbles beneath the window.

"Come along, Kitty," Hiram said. "Time to go. They won't hurt you if you behave."

Catherine rose. "Francine is right. We've already been hurt, Hiram, and I hope you suffer the nightmares of the damned."

The first to leave the room was the new girl, Calliope. Tears streamed down her pale cheeks, though she made not a sound. Did she even know she was crying?

"Take the cards with you," Hiram said. "They'll help you pass the time." He gathered up the deck. "Go on with you. Set a good example for the others. They look to you for that."

He held out the deck of cards, and Catherine took them. "Every time I play a game, Hiram, I will think of you and curse your name."

He smiled crookedly. "See that you do. Step lively now. You've a busy day ahead. A very busy day and a great adventure."

"Come along, Franny," Catherine said. "We won't soon forget the stink of this place."

Hiram laughed and winked, and Francine all but ran from the room rather than be left alone with him.

* * *

Rosalind took a breakfast tray in her room rather than risk further annoying Papa.

Or Lindy.

Or George.

Or *herself.*

She had tended to more than a little correspondence the previous day, though, and wanted her letter to Aunt Ida on its way. She waited until Papa would be reliably off to smoke and gossip away the morning at his club, then took herself down to the front foyer.

"Your ladyship was busy with her pen," the butler remarked when Rosalind added her letters to the stack for Papa to frank. "Will you or Mrs. Barnstable need the carriage later today?"

Rosalind was very tempted to call on Ned at the bank. He'd not elude her there, but she'd have to take Mrs. B with her.

"I might, when Lord Woodruff returns from his club."

The butler was a staid old soul, a fixture from Rosalind's girlhood, and she had learned to read him of necessity.

"What is it, Cranston?"

"Lord Lindhurst has ordered the carriage for his afternoon social calls, and Mr. George has an appointment at the hatter's this morning. The carriage might well be in demand, your ladyship."

Of course, two reasonably healthy young men could not be bothered to walk five streets to their appointments.

And Cranston could not simply tell her that, once again, she'd be on foot if she needed to go out.

"Then I won't need the carriage after all." She spied a sizable parcel sitting beside the umbrella stand. A sealed note had been tucked beneath the string securing the parcel's wrappings. "I thought that would have been delivered by now." More annoyance, to think the package she'd ordered delivered to Ned yesterday had sat in plain view in the foyer all this time.

"I'll have it sent around immediately, your ladyship. We were a bit at sixes and sevens while you were catching up on your correspondence. Mr. George and Lord Lindhurst had a difference of opinion, and Lord Woodruff intervened or tried to. I'll take care of your package if I have to deliver it myself."

"Your personal attention to the matter would be appreciated. It's important to me."

Cranston bowed. "At once, your ladyship, and I apologize for the oversight." He collected the package and marched off toward the stairs.

Rosalind's general ire with the day acquired an edge of despair. Ned could not very well answer a note he hadn't received, and if he were prudent, he'd never marry into a family like Rosalind's.

Papa was a pompous old boor who might well see Ned ruined. Lindhurst was a boor in training to the extent a simpleton could aspire to such status. George had no prospects and was content to scribble and drink himself into a nightly stupor.

The glorious sons of Albion, indeed.

"While I am..." Rosalind fell silent. She was *one part Damascus steel, one part ingenuity, and one part cool reason, all wrapped up in a big, courageous heart.*

She was also vexed past all bearing, and torn between the certain knowledge that she must let Ned go and the equally firm conviction that she must not.

"Did the cat chew your slippers again?" Mrs. Barnstable came down the steps, looking obnoxiously cheerful in a lavender sprigged muslin ensemble.

"Something like that. I hope supper last night wasn't too unbearable."

"You should have a word with Cook," Mrs. Barnstable replied. "The roast was nearly inedible again, the meat was so tough. Your menfolk were too busy glaring daggers at each other, I don't think they noticed the food."

"What set them off?"

Mrs. Barnstable glanced about, though no footman was on duty at the front door so early in the day. "Lindhurst made an unflattering remark about a young lady. George leaped to her defense, and off they went, like a pair of boys scrapping in the schoolyard. Were you truly indisposed, my lady?"

"I was suffering an excess of paternal guidance. Papa is unhappy with me because I prefer the attentions of Ned Wentworth to those of Lord Dinkle."

"Old Dinky isn't a bad sort, though I admit Mr. Wentworth is far easier on the eye. Does Mr. Wentworth have the ability to keep an earl's daughter in proper style?"

"Most assuredly." Ned Wentworth had many varieties of wealth. He was honorable, smart, kind, resourceful, discreet, and much too lovely a man to suffer the fate

Papa had threatened. He was also probably quite well heeled, about which Rosalind frankly did not care.

More of her willful departure from proper deportment.

"This talk of suitors reminds me of a question I wanted to put to you," Rosalind said. "Did Francine Arbuckle have a follower?"

Mrs. Barnstable's cheerful expression turned thoughtful. "Let's continue this discussion in the family parlor, shall we?"

That was a maybe, if not a yes. Rosalind crossed the corridor and preceded Mrs. Barnstable into a room where privacy was guaranteed.

Mrs. B closed the door. "Francine Arbuckle was a good woman, my lady. She guarded your interests belowstairs and she did not gossip."

"But?"

Mrs. Barnstable made a circuit of the room, smoothing a table runner, straightening a candle listing from its holder. Watching her, Rosalind realized that Mrs. B longed for a home of her own to tend, a home—however humble—such as she'd once had.

"But a life in service is lonely," Mrs. Barnstable replied. "Servants take their consequence from the people they serve, and thus Higgins has greater standing than the footmen, but Lord Woodruff's valet has greater standing than any save Mr. Cranston. Cranston's authority is a matter of custom and also derived from the fact that he served the previous earl."

Rosalind knew all of this. "You're saying Arbuckle's situation was difficult because I garner little respect in my own home."

Mrs. B took particular care straightening a portrait of Lindy on the momentous occasion of his breeching. "Arbuckle had to be careful not to cross swords with the cook or housekeeper, and not to offend the maids. The male servants all regarded her as inferior, and I daresay any fellow offering her a sympathetic ear would have heard a complaint or two."

Was anybody offering Mrs. Barnstable a sympathetic ear? "Francine had found such a fellow?"

Mrs. Barnstable took out a plain handkerchief and ran it along the mantel, then flapped the linen about, sending dust motes dancing in the morning sun.

"I cannot say for certain, my lady. I detected an air of happy secrecy in her eyes. She hummed when going about her duties, and she seemed less upset with the usual sniping in the servants' hall. She was happier, and her joy had an element of…"

"Yes?"

"The same element I see in you when Mr. Wentworth is about."

"If Ned Wentworth is ever about again, Papa will ruin him."

Mrs. Barnstable tucked her handkerchief into her cuff. "Mr. Wentworth has apparently overcome much to get where he is, and I'm sure he holds his achievements dear. What will you do?"

In other words, Amelia Barnstable believed Papa's threat was genuine. "I thought I would begin by discussing the situation with Mr. Wentworth. He should know Papa is his enemy, regardless of other considerations."

"I understand that a banker's reputation is his most

cherished asset, my lady, but if Mr. Wentworth can be so easily cowed, is he truly the sort of man you want to spend the rest of your life with?"

"You think Lord Dinkle is the greater prize?"

Mrs. Barnstable's smile was surprisingly winsome. "I like Lord Dinkle. He's not too proud to ask a companion to dance—such as he can totter about— and he doesn't take himself too seriously. Yes, he's stout, but he does not have a wife to take his menus in hand, and gout and inactivity further complicate his health. He has known much sorrow, my lady, and yet, he doesn't wear his grief on his sleeve. You could do worse."

"You are the voice of common sense." Not the voice of courage, though. Rosalind entertained the peculiar thought that common sense alone, however rational, was not adequate to address all challenges.

"If you do meet with Mr. Wentworth again," Mrs. Barnstable said, "please be very careful, my lady. Somebody could well have lured young women to their doom in this very neighborhood, and I would not want you to come to harm too."

"Mr. Wentworth is trying to find the missing women," Rosalind retorted. "He would never wish harm upon an innocent."

"But he hasn't found them, has he? Your father might well see a connection between Mr. Wentworth and the missing women where none exists. For your own sake as well as Mr. Wentworth's, please exercise the greatest of care in your dealings with him."

Rosalind's tea and toast threatened to rebel, because Mrs. Barnstable's caution was appropriate. Ned was dark and dashing, he had an unfortunate past and knew people in low places, he was charming...

"A frank discussion with Mr. Wentworth has become urgent," Rosalind said.

"A frank, discreet discussion," Mrs. Barnstable replied, going to the door. "I was hoping to have a letter from my sister this week. I don't suppose you've been through the morning post yet?"

And thus the subject was changed, and any hope of support from Mrs. B dashed. "I haven't been through the post yet."

"Let's have a look, shall we?" She crossed to the foyer, took up the stack of correspondence sitting in the letter tray, and held up one slim epistle. "Here we are. Veronica is not the greatest wit, but she has a way of bringing to life all the personalities back in the village. If you do pay your aunt Ida a visit, perhaps I might look in on my sister while you're traveling?"

"You heard Papa's threats?"

She passed Rosalind the rest of the letters. "The whole household heard him. I'm sorry, my lady."

Sorry, and already planning an expedient departure from her post, for which Rosalind did not blame her. "Fortunately, I love my aunt."

"But you do not love the idea of more months ruralizing so far from Mr. Wentworth. As a widow, I can tell you this, my lady: Knowing that I would end up without children, without a home of my own, the nearest thing to a poor relation, I would still marry my Derrick and still be grateful for the few years we had together. He was my husband, my best friend, my confidant, and my conscience. My only regret is that he was taken so soon."

She brandished her letter and disappeared up the steps.

Rosalind pondered those parting words and felt all over again the magnitude of the loss she'd endure if Ned quit the field.

Or if Rosalind sent him away, which would be the kinder course.

She had riffled through a prodigious number of bills and invitations before coming to a note addressed to her. The note hadn't come through the post—no franking—but had apparently been delivered by messenger and slipped through the letter slot.

The hand was tidy, the seal plain. Would Ned part from her by note? She hoped not.

She slit the seal and read:

Come alone and at once to the Dog and Dam, on the corner of Cuckminster and Chickering, Wapping, if you want to learn what became of your maids.

* * *

Stephen found Ned in his office at the bank, which was where Ned was ever wont to be. His Ned-ship was not wielding the abacus at a speed even Walden envied, nor was he penning policies in that tidy, infernally precise hand he produced so easily.

Ned was staring at a box positioned upon his desk blotter, a pretty cherrywood box that looked to Stephen's expert eye as if it held no particular puzzles.

No hidden compartments, delicate locks, false bottoms, or double linings—unlike dear Neddy.

"It's a box," Stephen said, sauntering over to Ned's desk. "Boxes are usually employed as containers for sundry items. If I'd known you were so easily fascinated with them I'd have—what's that note?"

Ned passed him the little missive without comment, which display of meekness should have earned the *Morning Gazette*'s front-page headline.

Mr. Wentworth,
I have chosen today to remark the miracle of your arrival into the world and your survival of all subsequent perils. Please accept a token of my esteem on this most joyous anniversary.
R.
PS Additional celebratory gestures to follow when next we picnic.

Stephen opened the box. "Did Lady Rosalind confuse you with her companion? This is embroidery thread, if I'm not mistaken. A colorful array, I grant you, and the scissors, hoop, needles, and thimble are artfully displayed, but...embroidery?" The case even held a sizable quizzing glass, tucked along one side.

Stephen set the note atop the thread, for surely Ned would treasure the epistle more than the box itself.

"Is today your natal day, Neddy?"

"Apparently so."

A nonsensical answer, from a very sensible fellow. "And will the occasion be remarked with another picnic out in Surrey?"

Now Ned speared him with a look. "Did you have us followed?"

"Artie was boasting of his success at the ribbons. To hear him tell it, he beat the sovereign's record to Brighton. Is somebody following you?"

"Yes. Jane must have had a word with Ivor or Sven, but I was certain I wasn't followed when I drove out with Lady Rosalind. The Earl of Woodruff might be gathering dirt on me, but I took enough extra turns that I know my picnic at least was private."

"You have no dirt to gather," Stephen said. "In my younger days, I pursued the joys of the flesh with dedicated profligacy. You were a Puritan by comparison."

"Not always," Ned said softly. "I didn't learn to open safes by reading the Book of Common Prayer."

"Neddy, are you preparing to do something noble and blockheaded like returning this lovely box to Lady Rosalind?"

"I should. If I love her, then I want only her happiness. Woodruff will see her transported to Derbyshire if I'm caught skulking about behind the hedges in her vicinity, and that's bad enough."

Stephen considered the pretty box, which made no sense to him. Ned was a banker, not a seamstress. "What's worse than a little ruralizing with the dowagers?"

"Marrying me and seeing every door closed in your face, hearing every rumor become more vile with each telling. Rosalind thinks I'm some sort of gentleman because I can speak the lines and wear the costume, but I am not a gentleman. I am..."

"Yes?"

"I am gallows bait dressed up in banker's clothing."

"Then what is Walden? If I recall correctly, he's the fellow who actually wore the noose."

"Walden was innocent. I knew that from the first moment I beheld him delivering that freeze-you-to-death stare to the guards. I am not innocent."

Something distant in Ned's gaze suggested he wasn't referring to safecracking or picking pockets. He was referring to some personal version of original sin, and Stephen well knew what that felt like.

"Then tell Lady Rosalind what a scoundrel you are. Lay it all at her dainty feet. Just as she has decided when your birthday is, she can decide if you're too great a fiend to claim her heart."

"Duncan said the same thing. Said I should tell her the whole of it."

"And yet, here you sit, after having consulted the Oracle of Berkshire himself. If you have to call Woodruff out, I will cheerfully serve as your second."

Ned closed the box. "What would Abigail say about that?"

"She would offer to serve as your other second, and she would make a proper job of it too, Quaker leanings notwithstanding. You belong to us, and we will not let you go into battle alone. Word of a Wentworth."

That little sermon had come out with just the right amount of condescension and humor, if Stephen did say so himself. To emphasize the point, Stephen scrubbed his knuckles across Ned's crown, and kissed the top of his head.

"Walden offered to find me a few acres for my own,"

Ned said, finger-combing his hair back into order. "A wedding present."

"A birthday present too, apparently. Neddy, go talk to your lady. She sent you a lovely present and now you are supposed to thank her."

Ned rose, though he first put the box into the bottom drawer of his desk. "I embroider," he said, producing a handkerchief awash in bright flowers. "My mother taught me the basics. I like the feel of the fabric and thread. I like the colors. I like threading the needle....I like the memory of Mama singing to me as I sat beside her by the window and made the most crooked seams with the most uneven stitches...." He folded his beautiful handkerchief and tucked it into a pocket. "Woodruff thinks I'm illegitimate. I'm not."

Hidden compartments and double linings, and Ned had apparently handed Lady Rosalind the key to them all.

"What matters legitimate or illegitimate when you're a Wentworth?" Stephen countered. "Woodruff is a donkey's arse, and Lady Rosalind would be well shut of him."

Ned opened another drawer and took out a book bound in red leather. "I have a present for her ladyship."

"Maybe it's her birthday too," Stephen said. "Deliver it in person. If Woodruff sent you packing, her ladyship needs to know you'll try again."

Ned went to retrieve his hat and walking stick from the stand by the door. "What is the worst thing you've ever done, Stephen?"

"The list of my transgressions is long and impressive...."

Ned fixed him with a stare not quite in league with a ducal freeze-you-to-death stare, but full of weary forbearance.

"I wasted years blaming myself for saving my own life and the lives of my sisters. Abigail sorted me out, which gives you some idea of the magnitude of the task."

Ned tapped his hat onto his head. "Jack Wentworth?"

Stephen nodded. "Commended him into the keeping of his Maker, or more likely into hell's privy. Abigail approved. Emphatically." Acknowledging the past, even to Ned, required fortitude.

"I approve emphatically too. Your father was a blight upon the species. Wish me luck."

Ned collected his book and walking stick, and to Stephen the moment seemed to call for more than luck. "If Lady Rosalind turns up her nose at your boyish peccadillos, she's an idiot."

"You don't know the extent of my boyish peccadillos."

"I don't need to know, *not ever*, and you are dithering. Be off with you."

Ned saluted, propped his walking stick against his shoulder like a soldier on the march, and stalked out.

* * *

"Don't interfere," Walden said, letting the curtain drop. "Don't let Mr. Wentworth see you, don't put yourself at risk of harm, but keep him in your sight at all times."

Artie did not need a perishing duke to tell him his job. "On it, guv."

"That's Your Grace, Arthur, and Ned's instincts on the street are uncanny. Be invisible or he'll spot you before the first intersection."

"On it, *Your Grace*," Artie said, scampering for the door. "I'll turn sideways and disappear."

"I mean it, Arthur. Do not put yourself at risk of harm. Your job is to send for help if need be, not to slay dragons."

Artie waved a hand and slipped out the door. The duke was a good sort, not too high in the instep, not too familiar with them as didn't deserve his notice. But even Walden should grasp that no child survived on London's streets without doing in a few pesky dragons from time to time.

Chapter Fifteen

Rosalind had no intention of going anywhere unsafe alone, and she knew only one person whose escort would serve. Ned Wentworth would find a way to accompany her without being seen, or he'd ensure that the Dog and Dam presented no hidden hazards.

A quick consultation with a map in the library showed that establishment to be squarely situated among the venerable and none-too-prosperous environs of Wapping, on the north bank of the Thames. If Rosalind went to the bank first to collect Ned, the journey could take a good two hours on foot.

She changed into her plainest dress, the one reserved for supervising the annual dusting of the attics. She appropriated one of the cloaks kept near the kitchen stairs for the maids and donned a straw hat she reserved for wearing in the garden.

Escape was surprisingly easy. Mrs. Barnstable was at her correspondence, George and Lindy had not yet stirred, and Papa was off to the club. Rosalind tucked a few coins into a pocket, put only her Book of Common

Prayer into her reticule, and was soon slipping out the garden gate into the alley.

She was preoccupied with the notion that she really ought to have left Mrs. Barnstable a note, when a man stepped out of the mews. He was a sizable dark-haired specimen, dressed as a groom. She did not recognize him, but he was an attractive fellow with a genial expression, and she thus felt in no danger.

The man raised a hand as if to touch the brim of his cap, and the next thing Rosalind knew, his arm was around her neck and something sharp prodded her in the ribs.

"Not a peep, milady. Not so much as a loud breath, and no harm will come to ye. Make a fuss and ye'll regret it."

"I excel at not making a fuss."

He smelled of horse and ale, and there was nothing friendly about the arm nearly choking her.

"Himself said you was the sensible sort. Now just walk along to the next turning, and get into the coach what's waiting for us there."

If I get into that coach, I will never see my home again. That thought was not as disturbing as it should have been. The Earl of Woodruff's house was a dwelling, a place to sleep and eat and draft letters. More upsetting was the thought that Aunt Ida would wonder what had become of her niece, and most unnerving of all was the thought of Ned Wentworth.

Papa could well blame Ned for Rosalind's disappearance.

And Ned would blame himself.

That Rosalind could not bear. "Where are we going?"

"Don't bother your pretty 'ead about that, milady. Just do as yer told and ye'll live to see the next sunrise."

Do as you're told. Rosalind hated those words, but she had only herself to thank for her present dilemma. Her sole comfort came from the realization that kidnapping an earl's daughter was a far bolder step than snatching a maid from an alley.

The objective was probably to hold her for ransom.

Thus the pertinent question became, could Papa pay a ransom, if he even wanted to?

* * *

A growing sense of urgency hastened Ned's steps, for Lord Woodruff might well have already bundled Rosalind into a coach and banished her to the shires. Ned did not trust the earl farther than he could toss a cow.

Rosalind would hate being dispatched like a prisoner of war to an obscure parole town, there to be forgotten for years.

Ned dodged down the alleys and cut through the private squares, *The Wealth of Nations* bumping against his thigh as he leaped fences. If he and Rosalind were to be parted, he at least wanted to wish her farewell and tell her...

Tell her that he loved her? Of course he loved her. Loved her wit and spirit, loved her ability to view life with pragmatism and humor. Loved her passion and her smiles...

But telling her so would serve no purpose.

He dodged through wynds and alleys, taking short-cuts he hadn't used since boyhood, surprised at how easily he could still navigate London with both speed and stealth.

He soon crossed into the alley that would take him behind Rosalind's house, only to feel the prickling at his nape that told him his shadow was again on his heels. Whoever tracked him had stayed far enough back to remain undetected, or they were expert at prowling London's streets.

Ned slowed his pace, fished Mr. Smith's book from his pocket, and opened it to a random chapter. He sauntered along, leafing through pages as if searching for a particular quote, and then turned into the arched recess of somebody's garden gate.

Ten seconds later, his shadow sauntered past the gate, a nondescript fellow of indeterminant years. Wiry, not much above average height, and moving with the light balance of a man anticipating an ambush.

Ned stepped silently from the shadows and tapped the fellow on the shoulder. "You fell for the oldest dodge in London, though you're quiet. I'll grant you that."

The man turned slowly, hands up. "I carry no weapons."

"You don't need to," Ned said. "Your fists, your feet, your teeth, your hard head . . . they are all weapons. Did Woodruff set you to spying on me?"

The fellow lowered his hands slowly. "If you mean the Earl of Woodruff, I've never had the pleasure."

His speech was neither refined nor Cockney, though he had the planed-down leanness of the hardworking class. He looked to be a weathered thirty-five and his complexion suggested he'd spent time in the tropics. His attire was clean enough, though in want of ironing, and his gaze as he studied Ned was neither afraid nor arrogant.

"Who the hell are you?" A Newgate connection? The place had been bursting at the seams with youths and boys, all crammed in with the worst of London's malefactors.

"That doesn't matter. What matters is that your young lady was taken from this alley not five minutes past. She was bundled into a hackney, a knife at her side unless I miss my guess. The horse in the traces was a piebald, the hackney number 617. Took off in the direction of the Strand, the beast moseying along so as not to attract attention."

"How do I know you're telling me the truth?"

The man's lips quirked. "You don't, but if I am being honest, then you are wasting precious time."

And if the fellow was lying... Something about his attire plucked at Ned's memory. Something subtle and elusive.

"What were you doing in this alley?"

"I was on my way to fetch you, Ned Wentworth, because Lady Rosalind needs rescuing, and I lack the standing and skills to pull that off."

This stranger also lacked... furtiveness. He was not afraid of Ned, and he wasn't trying to intimidate anybody. A tail, possibly, set on him by the duchess or the duke.

Ned touched his hat brim. "We'll meet again."

The fellow nodded, and Ned left him in the alley, a puzzle to be solved on another day.

* * *

Rosalind's first reaction to being abducted had been terror. Reassurances that she'd live to see another day had been little comfort, but the longer she was jostled and bounced along in the malodorous hackney, the more her fear was supplanted by anger.

How many times had Papa seen her tossed into a coach and sent speeding off to a different school? A few months later, Headmistress would toss her into another coach and send her home in disgrace. How many evenings had she climbed into a coach, steeling herself for hours in the company of leering bachelors or nervous widowers?

How many times had Papa summoned her away from Aunt Ida's, just as Rosalind had resigned herself to a life of rural obscurity?

Men and their damned coaches.

Her abductor hadn't joined her in the hackney any longer than it had taken to bind her wrists, affix a blindfold over her eyes, and tie what she assumed was a heavily veiled bonnet atop her head. The door had no interior handle that Rosalind could find, the windows did not open. He'd climbed up onto the perch behind, if the rocking of the coach was any indication, and he remained there for the duration of the journey.

London at midday was choked with traffic, and the frequency of the coach's stops told Rosalind she was being taken across Town, not out into the countryside to the north or west. When the coach door opened, the stink of the river was strong, though Rosalind could not hear water slapping against a pier or dock.

A firm grasp closed around her arm. "Mind your step, milady. Wouldn't want you to trip."

"My hat," Rosalind said, emerging from the coach. "Please don't leave it in the hackney." If he'd turn loose of her for even a moment, she might be able to elude him long enough to raise a hue and cry.

"Nice try." What felt like a shawl was draped over her bound hands, and then the grip on her arm became tighter. "Move along now. We ain't on the fancy end of Town, so don't think you'll be any safer running about on yer own."

Rosalind could not see, and thus her progress was halting. She was directed across a cobbled lane, then onto an uneven walkway.

"Steps ahead," her escort said a handful of yards later. "Three, and then you can have a nice sit-ye-down."

Rosalind managed the steps, then heard a key scraping in a lock. She was ushered into a space that smelled of tallow and gamey bacon, though the place was quiet. No footsteps, no banging doors, no voices.

"In here," the man said, turning her by the arm. "I'd fetch you a cuppa tea, but you'd probably throw it in me face."

If the tea was hot enough, Rosalind would have thrown it at his crotch. "Now what?" she asked.

"Now you sit and keep yer gob shut." The shawl was taken from about her wrists. "Be a good girl, and nobody gets hurt."

Be a good girl.

Be a good girl.

Rosalind sat, clutching her reticule and holding fast to her temper. She was debating whether to posit a fictitious plea for the chamber pot—a lady could not exactly hoist her skirts while blindfolded, could she?—when a delicate scent tickled her nose.

Beneath the stink of cheap bacon and cheaper candles, Rosalind caught a whiff of honeysuckle and scythed grass. All the benevolence and warmth of a summer day in the country.

Ned was here. That could not be, and yet, his scent was unique to him, and Rosalind would recognize it anywhere. He had been in this room recently or he was nearby, waiting for the right moment to intervene. Her relief was enormous, though tempered with caution.

If Ned was on hand, Rosalind needed to let him know that she was aware of his presence.

"My good man," she called. "I must trouble you to direct me to the necessary."

"Hush, milady. Won't be much longer and we'll be joined by my associate. I don't mind tellin' ye, he aims t' put the fear of damnation in ye. Ye've been meddlin' where you oughtn't and makin' life difficult for 'im. He's not a patient sort, but that's the Quality for ye."

"Nor can I afford to be patient," Rosalind said. "I lack the ability to embroider on the truth regarding a matter as indelicate as a lady's bodily functions. Do you honestly believe I'd admit to such a need if it weren't becoming a dire necessity?"

"Such fancy talk. I could listen to you go on all day."

"And I would give the wealth of nations for a moment's privacy with a chamber pot."

Perhaps her captor consulted a pocket watch, perhaps he peered out a window. "If he's not here in a quarter hour, I'll walk ye out to the alley, and ye can take a piss like the rest of the regular folk do. I'll even hold yer skirts up for ya, gent that I am."

In which case, Rosalind would knee him in the nose. "The matter is urgent, I tell you."

"Oi, now. Urgent, is it? Everything with the Quality is urgent. Cease pesterin' me, and don't even think to whine to himself. Has a temper he does, and a fine lady, all delicate and proper, might not survive the places he could send ye. Be a good girl for another quarter hour, promise to cease pokin' yer nose where it don't belong, and you can go back to pickin' out bonnets."

Ned had been right, then: Somebody with a great deal of influence was behind the disappearances, and now that influence was directed toward intimidating Rosalind into submission.

"I have never much cared for picking out bonnets, and I have lost—utterly—my patience for being a good girl."

She swung her reticule in a circular arc, hard, and had the gratification of knowing she'd hit her target. A scuffle ensued, during which Rosalind tore off the veiled bonnet and blindfold.

Ned Wentworth stood over a large heap of downed villain. "Well done, my lady. Clocked him on the side of the head and he never saw it coming. Are you well?"

"I want to kick him in an unmentionable location."

The fellow groaned.

"So do I," Ned said, untying the bindings at her wrists, "but not when he's down. Street rules forbid it. If his reinforcements are on the way, we'd best make haste away from here."

"I have things to say to you, Ned Wentworth."

"And I have things to say to you, Lady Rosalind, *but not here*. Give me your blindfold."

Rosalind passed over the requested item, and Ned gagged the specimen on the floor.

"What about his hands?"

Ned produced a wickedly impressive folding knife, cut strips off the curtains, and bound the villain's hands and feet.

"That won't hold him for long, but we only need a few minutes. Let's be off, shall we?"

"The front door is locked," Rosalind said, retrieving her reticule. "I heard him lock it behind us."

"The doors are locked, the windows are either nailed shut or boarded over, and the neighbors can be relied upon to mind their own business. I've already had a look around upstairs, and there's nobody living here at the moment."

Rosalind stepped around the groaning form on the floor. "Then how do we get out?"

"I came in through the coal chute, which nobody thinks to lock in warm weather, but we'll go out the kitchen door."

Ned led Rosalind down a narrow, dusty set of steps to a dingy kitchen, then past a gloomy pantry and scullery to a door that opened onto a set of steps below ground level. A stout boot applied to the lock sent the door creaking open.

"When we get to the street, we saunter along," Ned said, "a besotted couple enjoying a stolen moment on a pretty afternoon. We have eyes only for each other." He held the door open for Rosalind, who preceded him up dank, uneven stone steps into an alley so narrow the houses on either side seemed to lean in to blot out the sky.

"The brains of the operation was due to arrive in a quarter hour," Rosalind said. "I want to see who that is."

"And if he brings two more bully boys, all of them armed?" Ned said. "In this part of town, nobody would interfere with them, Rosalind. We need to put distance between us and your abductor."

"He said I'd be let go." Rosalind allowed Ned to lead her up the dank stone steps. "The objective was to frighten me into minding my own business."

Ned stopped at the top of the steps, which opened onto a narrow, trash-filled walkway between number twenty and its nearest neighbor.

"I don't mind telling you, Rosalind, the past hour has seen me more terrified than I have been since the watch took me up for picking pockets." He offered his arm. "You might well have been told a tale to keep you from bolting or resisting. Who knows what fate awaited you? Look like you've just stolen a kiss."

Rosalind kissed Ned's cheek and wrapped her hand around his elbow. She wanted to throw herself into his arms, but he was right: time to move.

"Thank you for coming, Ned. I should be terrified, I know, and I will be soon, but I am too angry. Angry at myself, among others. I fell for a simple, stupid note. I thought to take it to you at the bank, and enlist your aid, but it never occurred to me...He simply walked up to me in the alley and *took possession* of me, telling me to come along like a *good girl*."

"You weren't thinking of your own safety," Ned said, pausing before directing Rosalind onto the walkway. "Look sharp, and if I tell you to run, Rosalind, run like hell and scream as loudly as you can."

This version of Ned was as ruthless as he was careful, and yet, he walked along down a street too narrow for wheeled traffic, not a care in the world.

"Say something," Rosalind muttered, when they emerged onto the wider thoroughfare. "I am so upset I could spew invective loudly enough for all London to hear."

"Please don't."

Two words, though they held enough banked emotion that Rosalind could tell Ned wasn't quite as self-possessed as he seemed.

"Ned, whoever is stealing those women knows we're onto their scheme. They know we're getting close. Now is not the time to turn up missish."

Ned escorted her around the corner and down the street, where the Dog and Dam appeared to be doing a thriving business.

"That man whom you wanted to kick," Ned said, "travels under the name of Reggie Sharp. Sharp is a reference to his facility with a knife and his penchant for keeping souvenirs carved from the bodies of his victims. He has a whole collection of ears, if rumor is to be believed."

"He did not kidnap those women for their ears."

Ned came to a halt. "Rosalind, you are an eminently practical woman. Be practical now. If the likes of Reggie Sharp are involved, then somebody is willing to kill to keep this scheme afloat, whatever its particulars.

This investigation grows too dangerous, and we must desist before greater harm befalls you."

Ned was speaking reason. Rosalind knew he was, and yet, she also knew that if she gave up, more women would be snatched from more alleys, and nobody would care.

Nobody would ever care.

"I cannot stop now, Ned. When that man took me captive, it occurred to me that I might end up in a brothel. Assuming I survived that experience, I'd be ruined beyond any prayer of redemption. Do you know, I think my father would be *relieved* to see me ruined? He would not have to part with my settlements, and he could disown me with a clear conscience. Aunt Ida would take me in, and that would be the end of me. Nobody would notice, save for Mrs. Barnstable, and she's already planning for my next banishment."

Ned's gaze was tired and somber. "I would notice, but why would Woodruff disown you? If he wanted you off his hands, he'd have allowed me to court you, and if you're ruined, he can't use you to placate his creditors."

"Because Woodruff is not my father." A family secret, one Rosalind should have taken to her grave rather than disclose on a busy street in an ungenteel part of London. "My mother was indiscreet, though she'd already provided the requisite heir and spare. Papa informed me of my antecedents after her death, and I suspect that had something to do with my words becoming garbled. I know I ought not to burden you with this...this truth, but I have more in common with the maids and companions than you might think. I will not give up on them, Ned."

Ned's eyes went colder than a winter night in Derbyshire. "You must. Woodruff apparently would welcome anything that puts you into disgrace, and I am only giving him more opportunities to treat you poorly." He put two fingers to his lips and whistled shrilly.

"What are you saying?"

"We need to end this," Ned said. "The investigation, the courtship that never began, the everything. I will not be the cause of your death, ruin, or banishment." He fished a book from his coat pocket. "*The Wealth of Nations*. Please recall when you read it that I wanted only the best for you."

A hackney coach rattled up to the curb. "The best for me is to be abandoned, left friendless without an explanation? Ned Wentworth, what on earth are you about?"

"Artie, see the lady safely home and pay the jarvey." Ned flipped a coin to Arthur, who had materialized from beneath the awning of the Dog and Dam.

"You think to *bundle me into a coach* and just stroll out of my life?"

Ned bowed with a courtesy that Rosalind found frankly bewildering. "I think to *keep you safe* from all perils, my lady. I have a record of failing badly when it comes to the safety of those I care about, but I've learned my lesson. I wish you good day."

Artie opened the coach door, and Ned began to walk away.

"Fine, then. Run along, Ned Wentworth, and I will continue this investigation on my own. The worst peril, the very worst peril, is to believe nobody cares and to have evidence of that belief on every hand. Go back to your damned bank if you must, but I care about those women, and I will not be deterred by Reggie Sharp and his perishing collection of ears."

To her utter horror, Rosalind's eyes filled with tears, and thus she could not have seen to blunder her way into the coach even if she had been willing to heed Ned's bedamned dismissal.

* * *

Go back to your damned bank.... Go back to your damned bank....

Except it wasn't Ned's damned bank and never would be. He had never aspired to own a bank and could not foresee the day when he would.

A ladylike sniffle stopped him halfway to the Dog and Dam, where he would make a futile attempt to drown his sorrows.

The sniff was followed by a delicate gulp, and Ned was back at Rosalind's side in an instant. "Don't cry." He pushed a handkerchief into her hand. "Rosalind, please, you must not cry."

"You made her cry," Artie muttered. "Turned your back on a lady in distress. I'm that ashamed of you."

"Arthur," Rosalind said, dabbing at her eyes, "there's no need for dramatics. I've merely had a trying day, as has Mr. Wentworth."

"Bawlin' 'er eyes out," Artie went on. "In front of half of London, and Reggie Sharp on the loose and lookin' fer a fight. Mr. Wentworth ain't the only gent to have a tryin' day. I go to work for the great man himself, the famous Ned Wentworth, from Newgate to new money, that Ned Wentworth, and he turns out to be dicked in the nob."

"I ain't got all day," the hackney driver called down. "Somebody climb in, or I'll find another fare."

"Artie," Ned said, "take the coach to the bank. Tell Walden or Lord Stephen that I've come to no harm. Lady Rosalind is out shopping with me. She's perfectly safe."

Artie glowered with all the ire of a boy in the presence of adult foolishness. "She's got her heart broke being perfectly safe around the likes of you."

"Arthur, please do as Mr. Wentworth says." Rosalind sounded composed, though her eyes held a world of hurt. "We are all not ourselves, but His Grace and Lord Stephen will worry about Mr. Wentworth."

"They oughta lock Mr. Wentworth up, you ask me," Arthur said, climbing into the coach. "He's gone queer as Dick's hatband, and that's puttin' it kindly."

Ned slapped the side of the hackney, and Artie was still hurling imprecations as the coach pulled away.

"You have acquired a champion," Ned said.

"I've acquired two," Rosalind replied, turning a glittering gaze on Ned. "Only one of them is convinced he must protect me from ruin by banishing himself from my life. What on earth bedevils you, Ned, that you'd conclude the dubious tolerance I endure in Woodruff's house is preferable to any status I could hold at your side?"

She would ask that, and she deserved an answer.

Stephen Wentworth had confessed to his Abigail

that he'd committed murder, and that good lady hadn't batted an eye. Walden had been facing the noose for taking a life when Jane had agreed to wed him. Duncan Wentworth, when he'd been as bruised in spirit as he was vigorous of intellect, had captured the heart of a duchess.

Even the half-daft Rothmere brothers had found safe havens in the arms of their respective wives.

"I am a thief," Ned said, "a housebreaker, pick-pocket, shoplifter, and safecracker."

"You *were* all those things," Rosalind said, folding his handkerchief and tucking it into her reticule. "Those descriptions no longer apply."

"And at the time," Ned said, "those were my better qualities. My brother died because of me, and even that's not the worst of it. We should leave this place." Though nobody was setting up a hue and cry, no mamas were appearing to whisk loitering children back indoors.

A pair of mongrel hounds snored away in the shade, crows strutted about picking at the gutter before the house across the road. The signs of a neighborhood going about a normal day were all in evidence, if Ned recalled how to read them.

Rosalind took him by the hand. "We should leave this place and go where? Papa will pack me off to Derbyshire if you're seen taking me home, and I will not part from you without saying what I have to say. Is the Dog and Dam halfway respectable?"

"Of course. The fare will be simple and the company humble, but it's a decent enough place." At this time of day. "Besides, you aren't interested in the food. You want to linger at the window and watch for a crested coach to pass, but Rosalind, whoever had you kidnapped won't be that foolish. They'll slither away unseen and resume their mischief once you've been banished again—banished because of me."

Ned wanted to spirit her off to the Walden residence, there to keep her safe, except that would be kidnapping, and Woodruff would probably have him arrested and hanged for it.

"Let's have a pint," Rosalind said, "and you can tell me how horrible you are."

Ned toddled along at her side and felt the old partitioning in his mind take hold. He was both hand in hand with Rosalind and drifting a short distance from himself, watching with bemusement as Lady Rosalind Kinwood sat down to enjoy a lady's pint at an ancient and none-too-grand dockside tavern.

A few streets away, Reggie Sharp was waking up with one hell of a headache, and doubtless trying to concoct a story that would explain how a blindfolded woman had walloped the daylights out of him.

"Tell me about your brother," Rosalind said, when a loaf of warm bread, along with butter and cheese, had been brought to the table. "What was his name?"

Tell me about your brother. The Ned vaguely noting that Rosalind was abroad without a bonnet—surely a cause for dismay—heard her command as a novelty. Nobody asked about a boy done in on the end of a rope years ago.

The part of Ned who could not remain at a distance from Rosalind for long heard an invitation to put down an old and heavy burden.

"We were named for kings and saints," Ned said.

"Edward and Robert. Ned and Bob, and we were thoroughly rotten boys."

"Of course you were." Rosalind buttered him a slice of bread and passed it across the table. "How did he die?"

"I let him down. We were doing a jostle-and-bump. The better thief picks the pocket, then passes off the take to the boy who most convincingly looks earnest and innocent. The hue and cry follows the thief, who cannot be found guilty of anything because no stolen goods are located on his person. The other boy has long since left the scene with the goods. His job was simply to walk along, looking late for an appointment with a meat pie."

"Which you doubtless were."

"I was constantly ravenous. We'd sometimes go three or four days without eating, and in winter..."

He ought not to be telling Rosalind this. She was a lady, and for all the tribulations she'd endured, Ned hoped she'd never known hunger like that. Hunger that turned a boy into a beast.

"In winter?" she said.

"I tried to sell my boots, but the cobbler wouldn't take them. He knew I could go another day without food, but not another day without boots. Gave me a piece of bread with butter. Told me an army does not march on its belly, it marches on its feet. I split the bread with Bob, and it was the best..."

Ned had to look away from the steady regard in Rosalind's eyes. Had to look away from the memories, from the half a loaf sitting on the cutting board in the center of the table.

What that boy had nearly done for a crust of bread . . .

"Bob was taken up, because I fumbled the handoff. He kept the take, though the crowd was already shouting. He could have passed me the goods, and I would probably have been shown leniency because of my age if the constables had thought to arrest me. I didn't see him again until he was hanged."

"You saw that?"

"I did not want him to be alone. I owed it to him to be there, but I could not get to the front of the crowd. I saw enough. I heard enough. I hope he knew I was there."

As spindly as Ned had been, as thick as the crowd had been, he hadn't seen the actual hanging, but he'd heard the platform drop, he'd heard the crowd. Some had decried the execution of a boy, most had jeered.

"I cried," he said, very softly. "I cried for a good brother who'd only done what he'd had to do to keep us alive. I cried because it was my fault. I would gladly have switched places with him. I was a burden to him, and Bob never once complained. I cried, and Rosalind, it didn't matter. *I* did not matter, Bob did not matter, my father, my mother. . . . We simply were of no moment to anybody in a position to make a difference."

Rosalind glanced around the common, then rose.

Ned accepted that he'd asked too much of her. It was one thing to know in theory that a man had a criminal past, it was quite another to learn that his bungling had seen his brother dead at the end of a rope. Ned stared hard at the bread, denying himself the impulse to reach for Rosalind's hand and call her back.

He'd walked away from her, after all. Tried to,

anyway. He was no better at leaving her than he'd been
at picking pockets.

Rosalind came around to Ned's side of the table
and slid onto the bench beside him. "Damn them all.
Damn them, damn them. You were a pair of hungry
boys, no parents, no family. The Royal Navy snatched
your father away, and you had nobody to take you in,
nobody....Oh, just..." She wrapped her arm around
Ned's waist and laid her head on his shoulder. "Damn
them all to eternal, flaming hell."

The sight of the bread blurred. Ned put an arm
around Rosalind's shoulders and closed his eyes. He
did not know how long he sat there in the humble
tavern, where lovers being too familiar was of no
moment, but something inside him eased at the feel of
Rosalind tucked close.

Sorrow, rage, guilt, despair...he did not have to
name the burden to know that it would never again
weigh on his heart so heavily.

"I grew mean after that," he said. "Tough and determined. It helped."

Rosalind took his hand. "Tell me the rest of it."

Chapter Sixteen

How much heartache and injustice could one man endure? Ned's story put Rosalind in mind of the animals tormented for sport. The dogfights, cockfights, bear baitings...Perhaps there was something fundamentally wrong with the human character, that it could ignore the suffering of children and delight in the abuse of mute beasts.

What manner of society could end a child's life, because he sought merely *to eat* in a city that claimed to be the wealthiest on earth?

Ned kissed her fingers. "The rest of it is equally ugly and not half so excusable. I grew bolder and graduated to stealing property. I had a talent for getting into and out of dwellings undetected, and I had a nose for where valuables would be stored. I began to work alone and was too adept at my trade. My competitors saw me taken into the keeping of a house of ill repute that caters to a certain clientele."

Rosalind sorted through blunt translations. "A molly house?"

"Ladies aren't supposed to know of such places."

"I read Latin, Ned. I hear my brothers gossiping. Aunt Ida is not one to mince words."

"I hope to meet your Aunt Ida one day, if you'll still have me."

Rosalind looked around. A pair of old sailors sat knitting in the snug, and a bag of canine bones snoozed before a cold hearth. In the corner, a gent of no particular description wearing a hat of equally unimpressive provenance nursed a pint, and at the bar, a maid wiped down tankards and hummed a tune that probably had bawdy lyrics.

"I will *have* you, Ned Wentworth, at the next available opportunity."

He laced his fingers with hers. "Will you, Rosalind? Will you have me? I spent one night in that molly house. I was too stupid to realize the soup would be drugged. I woke up in the same bed with an older boy. He had a pretty little speech all rehearsed, about regular meals, warm blankets, nobody the wiser, and why work like a dog only to end up in jail, when a little frolicking would result in all the security a boy ever needed?"

"Did he violate you?"

Ned pulled Rosalind close and kissed her temple. "The windows were nailed shut, so I broke the glass with my fist. Tossed my clothing and boots out before me and left that place mother-naked in the dead of winter. I have never been so frightened in all my life. Not when Bob went before the magistrate, not when I landed in Newgate, not when I was sentenced to transportation. The last thing that was mine on this earth—my very body—was to be taken from my control."

He hadn't put that into words before, hadn't admitted the depth of his fear.

"This," Rosalind said, "is why I could talk you into looking for missing women, because you were nearly forced into the flesh trade yourself."

He took a sip of ale, though his hand shook slightly. "You did not talk me into anything. You asked, and I could not countenance the notion that you'd go poking around the stews on your own."

Rosalind covered his hand with hers and brought his mug to her lips. "They serve good ale here. Exactly how did you end up in Newgate?"

"I was set up, of course. The same people who'd turned me over to the molly house arranged for stolen goods to be found at my lodgings. My sentence was transportation, but I well knew what that would mean for a boy on a long voyage. The whores did what they could to protect the children, but I'd heard the stories, and I wasn't about to...I stopped eating."

"You excelled at going without, I suspect."

"Precisely. If the great and the good of London thought I was not worth feeding, then I would simply oblige their pious wishes that I be admitted into heaven's benevolent light. I exercised the one right left to me, the right to abandon the hell to which I'd been consigned. I missed my family, and all I could think was that a benevolent Deity would surely allow me to see them again. If Walden hadn't come along, looking so fierce and so lost..."

Ned offered Rosalind a bit of cheese, then finished

the slice himself. "I knew the bewilderment Walden hid so well, knew the utterly paralyzing confusion of a life knocked arse over ears. I could not leave him to the tender mercies of the Newgate regulars. I decided I could always starve myself to death later."

How different Ned's feelings for his family were from Rosalind's. "I want to see Aunt Ida again," she said, "but as for the rest of the Kinwoods…"

"If you marry me, Rosalind, Woodruff will likely ensure you're ruined. He'll get only close enough to you to give you the cut direct."

"Ruined." Rosalind disentangled herself from Ned's embrace. "Is that when I no longer have to flatter aspiring cits who think marriage to a titled lady, any titled lady at all, should be the zenith of their ambitions? When I'm ruined, will I be spared the speculative leers and execrable dancing of the aging widowers?"

She waved a hand in the general direction of May-fair. "In a ruined state," she went on, "will my evenings be my own, or will I have to continue to hare about at my father's whim—my father, who is not my father—and will two brothers continue to gossip about my many shortcomings behind my back? Explain this dire state of ruination to me, for I suspect ruin has much to recommend it."

The fellow in the corner had glanced up at this tirade, as had the dog. The old sailors paused in their knitting, and the barmaid was no longer humming.

"That sounds about right," Ned said, as several other patrons paused at the entrance to the common. "And in your ruined state, you might not even be married to a banker. A banker's fortune rests upon his reputation, and my clients tend to be folk of middling means and sound morals. If Lord Woodruff digs deeply enough into my past, I could well end up out of a job, Rosalind. Walden destroyed the documents, but he can't destroy people's memories."

Rosalind buttered a slice of bread and passed it to Ned, then buttered a second one for herself. The bread and butter, like the ale, were exceptionally good at this humble inn.

"I doubt Papa has the tenacity or connections to unearth the worst of the traumas visited upon you. What will your ducal family do if Papa proves difficult?"

Ned took a bite of bread. "From your tone, I gather they'd best take my part against Woodruff."

"You gather correctly. Given that Papa is a mere earl, and the Wentworths are a ducal family allied with the Rothhaven dukedom as well, Papa had best tread lightly."

Though to a surprising degree, Rosalind did not care how Papa trod, provided his steps took him someplace far, far away. And may George and Lindhurst join him in that distant location.

"Rosalind," Ned said, "I am not a good bargain as a husband. I have a wicked past, my own family died in penurious and scandalous circumstances, and I have prospered only because of the charity of people who owe me nothing. But I promise you this…"

The other four occupants were goggling at him, as was the dog, and the newcomers remained in the doorway half-obscured by the afternoon shadows.

"I will love you to my dying day," Ned said, "and

I will bend my every effort to keeping you safe and making you happy. You might not have the finest coach, but you will have my constant devotion. I will never forsake you, and if we have differences…"

"We will resolve them," Rosalind said, "and without anybody being banished, imprisoned, arrested, or starved."

"Marry him," the barmaid called. "Marry him quick, or I'll steal him away for meself. A man talks to you like that, you don't let him get away."

"Heed the lass," one of the sailors added. "And lad, get yonder miss before the parson posthaste."

"Will you marry me, Rosalind? For I most assuredly do want to marry you."

The setting was all wrong, with strangers for an audience, bread and ale for a meal, and an old dog presiding over the whole scene, but the right man was asking.

"I will marry you, Ned Wentworth. And if we end up keeping body and soul together by opening a tailor's shop, that will suit me splendidly. Your embroidery alone should fetch a fortune."

Ned kissed her, a sweet, sumptuous press of his lips to hers, which inspired a round of applause from the onlookers.

"Took ya long enough." Artie swaggered forth from the door, plucked Ned's bread from his hand, took a bite, and set it back on the table.

"Artie." Ned got to his feet and offered Rosalind a hand. "And Walden and Lord Stephen. My lady, we have company, or possibly, reinforcements."

"You are damned right you have reinforcements,"

His Grace said. "My lady, good day. Ned, what the hell is going on?"

Lord Stephen was looking about with unabashed interest, while the dog had risen to sniff at Artie's boots.

Ned kept Rosalind's hand in his when she took the place beside him, which was just fine with her.

"The situation is complicated," Ned said, "and more than a little dangerous."

Walden swept the room with a gaze that should have left ice on the exposed surfaces. "You propose to a genteel lady in surrounds like these, abandon your duties at the bank without a word, and send young Arthur back to us spouting mendacious nonsense. Then Arthur lapses into lurid tales involving abductions, ears, and known felons, and we find you here, swilling ale and announcing your past to Wapping's hapless denizens. Her Grace will not be best pleased with this state of affairs, and I am more than a little dismayed. Explain yourself, and be quick about it."

Ned seemed amused at this tirade. "Thank you for *Her Grace's* concern, but—"

A gent with a battered hat had sidled up to Ned. He took off his hat and speared Walden with a look that promised dire consequences to loquacious dukes.

"But you do not harangue my little brother like that in public, sir, I don't care who you are. The lady said yes, and her opinion is all that matters. Ned, tell this fancy bugger to sod off, or I will. The Taylor boys don't tolerate disrespect. That hasn't changed. Apologies for my language, Lady Rosalind."

Ned's grip on Rosalind's hand became desperately

tight. "The Taylor…Robert? Robert?" The silence in the inn became as vast and fraught as the open ocean. "You are dead. I attended your hanging."

Robert stood a little straighter. "I was sent to New South Wales. Earned my ticket of leave, though it took half my life. I never forgot you, Ned, never forgot how hard you scrapped, how loyal you were. Broke my heart to think I'd abandoned you to the wicked streets of London. Then I come back to find you're a fine gent, toolin' around Town in your own coach, and I wasn't sure you'd want your convict brother calling on you."

"Your buttonholes," Ned said, fingering Robert's lapel. "You finish them counterclockwise and never start in the corners. I have only ever known one person to sew them in that style." Ned closed his fist around Robert's coat and pulled him close. "I thought you were dead. I thought…"

A long moment passed while Ned and his brother held tightly to each other. Rosalind fished out her handkerchief while Walden and Lord Stephen looked anywhere but at the embracing siblings.

"I could use a pint," Artie said, a little loudly and to no one in particular. "And some tucker. This is a nice dog."

"Have you a private dining room?" Rosalind asked the barmaid as Ned and his brother simply stared at each other, Ned still gripping Robert's coat.

"Fine notion," Lord Stephen murmured. "Let's withdraw to less public surrounds and feed the boy. Could use a pint myself."

The barmaid dabbed at her eyes with her apron.

"Back this way. Cost you extra. The dog's name is Nelson."

Nelson trooped along with them to the private parlor, where Ned took a place at a settle with Rosalind on one side and Bob on the other. Walden and Lord Stephen appropriated the chairs opposite, and Artie repaired to a window seat, the dog accompanying him.

Was there any greater joy than finding a lost loved one thought long dead? Rosalind could feel the wonderment radiating from Ned, at the same time she mourned for brothers separated so long ago. So much had been taken from them, and yet, Robert had come halfway around the world in the hope that his brother still lived.

No other lady being present, and the gentlemen appearing to have no clue how to go on, Rosalind posed a question when the ale had been served.

"You were sentenced to hang, Mr. Taylor. Was your sentence commuted?"

"'Twasn't." Bob blew the foam off his ale and the dog ambled over to lick it from the floorboards. "Ned, you recall Coffin Tommie?"

"Had consumption," Ned said, "coughed all the time, hence a rather unkind nickname. You switched places with him?"

Robert nodded. "Tommie had a mortal fear of burial at sea, or worse, burial in a heathen land. The whole thing was his idea. We traded clothes, the guards kept mum if they even noticed, and I was hauled off to the hulks at Deptford to await the next transport ship. Tommie got a quick end on the gallows and burial on his home soil. I had no time to get word to you, and I wouldn't have known where to send a message anyway. Haven't known where to send a letter, for that matter—assuming you were still alive."

"How bad was the voyage?" Ned asked.

"The voyage was *long*. Took us the better part of a year with layups in Rio de Janeiro and Table Bay. Our captain was a decent sort, and when the first mate realized I could sew, he assigned me to assist the sailmaker. The sailmaker gave me the officers' uniforms to look after, and when we landed, the captain put in a word for me. I was spared the worst of the hard labor and have my own tailor's shop in Port Jackson."

"How did you recognize me?" Ned asked.

"I asked around. The tailor's boy turned nabob has a reputation in certain circles. Then there's your walk. You have this half-strutting, half-sauntering walk. You have the same eyes, Ned. You still observe the world from a careful place. You're a damned sight better looking than I thought you'd be, but we both know what good tailoring can do for a fellow."

Rosalind watched this exchange and realized she might well have found Ned only to lose him. Banking was a job to him, not a calling, and his only blood kin now dwelled in the Antipodes. Would she travel that far to stay by Ned's side? Would he give her that chance?

"Neddy has gone thoughtful," Lord Stephen said. "This bodes ill for somebody."

"Women are scarce in New South Wales, aren't they?" Ned asked.

"*Scarce* puts it mildly," Robert said. "It's not as bad as it was twenty years ago, but still…Bachelors outnumber the available ladies by a considerable margin."

Walden swore softly, and Arthur looked up from entertaining the dog.

"You think the missing maids are bound for transportation?" Rosalind asked.

Ned nodded. "They are young, healthy, comely, *unmarried*, have no family on hand to object, and they can be substituted for women too old, young, or sickly to manage the challenges of transportation, or for women already married. Some of those bachelors in Botany Bay have significant means, and somebody here in London is being paid handsomely to put the wrong women on board the transport ships."

"And," Lord Stephen added, "the women spared transportation are not about to complain to anybody in authority. They are probably told the court has allowed them clemency owing to their age or infirmity, and off they go, remembering the mercy of the court in their prayers."

"This is corruption," Walden growled. "Corruption in the governance of the penal colony, corruption in the administration of justice here in England."

Robert sent him a curious look. "Ned, where did you find this bright fellow?"

"The bright fellow is a duke," Ned said. "Found him wandering the common wards at the stone jug. It's a long story, but if His Grace of Walden takes a notion to investigate corruption, then eighteen committees and forty-seven milords will soon be bleating about the need for reform."

"All very well," Rosalind said, "but what about my maids? Is it too late for them?"

The men exchanged a look she could not decipher, but clearly, they expected Ned to answer her question.

"Let's find out," Ned said. "Artie, ask mine host when the next transport ship is expected to sail."

The boy darted off, the dog trotting at his heels.

"The convicts are typically taken to the hulks to await a transport ship here or in Portsmouth," Ned said. "The swap will take place as the convicts are rowed out from the hulks to the transport ship. Once aboard, there will be no retrieving them. The ladies have been taken somewhere, but the question is—"

Artie barreled back into the room. "Transport ship over at Deptford has been taking on supplies for the past fortnight. The *Tantalus* is due to sail on tonight's tide."

* * *

"You are wrong, you know," Walden said, as the ducal coach inched across London Bridge. This late in the day, with the City disgorging hordes bound for Southwark, nothing moved faster than a crawl. Deptford was several miles downriver, and those would be congested miles too.

Rosalind dozed against Ned's shoulder, suggesting she wasn't used to imbibing strong ale. Bob had chosen to ride up top with Artie, the better to take in a metropolis that had changed much in recent years. Lord Stephen was on horseback, his preferred mode of travel.

"I am frequently wrong," Ned said. "Fortunately, my Wentworth relations delight in pointing out my errors to me. I still think you and his lordship should leave this to me and Bob."

Rosalind stirred, then subsided. She'd agreed to marry him. That miracle, compounded with Bob's resurrection, had yet to feel real to Ned, but the danger to innocent women facing transportation was all too immediate.

As was the danger to any seeking to free those women.

"I agree with you that her ladyship's safety could be imperiled by this errand," Walden said, "but I agree with Lady Rosalind that women facing transportation on top of abduction aren't likely to trust a pack of strange men brandishing weapons."

"She is so brave," Ned said. "Has had to be so brave. Did you know Woodruff isn't even her father?"

Walden opened a compartment in the side of the coach and extracted a pair of long-barreled dueling pistols, setting one on the bench beside him. He'd taken the backward-facing seat, a show of deference to Rosalind, who kept hold of Ned's hand even in sleep.

Walden set about cleaning and loading the first pistol. "Jane intimated that the late Lady Woodruff had taken the usual liberties after presenting his lordship with an heir and spare. Thank heavens for Stephen's preoccupation with fortifying our vehicles. You have a knife?"

"Two, and a sword cane, but Walden, you are too big to pass unnoticed in these surrounds. The docks are for the trades and laborers, humble folk who do not typically reach Viking proportions."

"You aren't exactly dainty. What's your plan?"

"Stephen will stay with Rosalind. He's armed to the teeth, willing to kill to protect those he cares for, and easy to underestimate."

Walden paused with the rammer down the mouth of the barrel. "Told you about that, did he?"

In true Stephen Wentworth fashion, he'd made disclosure of patricide into a casual remark. "His lordship's past needs no further discussion."

"While yours does," Walden said. "You told her ladyship that you prosper as a result of charity, Ned, and in that you are mistaken. Take this."

"Firing a gun will bring half the Royal Navy running to apprehend me for disturbing the peace."

Walden started cleaning the second pistol. "We might need to summon the Royal Navy, which is when having a duke underfoot will be an advantage. Now attend me, for I will not repeat myself. At no point has my interest in you been charitable."

Ned was mentally working out the details of freeing women from a well-coordinated team of kidnappers, monitoring Rosalind's breathing, and wondering if Bob had returned to London for good when it occurred to him that Walden had gathered his courage to make some sort of proclamation.

"I work for my wages now," Ned said, "but all those years ago, you did not have to drag me from Newgate and take me into your household. That was an act of charity and one that saved my life. I thank you for that."

"When I met you in Newgate, you had given up," Walden said. "I know that. Your affairs were in order, and like that Scottish king from days of yore, you had turned your face to the wall in anticipation of death."

"James V." Who had lived long enough to know his line was secured by a child then only six days old. "Newgate did not agree with me. What's your point?"

"*Life* did not agree with you, for which you cannot be blamed, but Ned, you were..." Walden loaded the second pistol. "Honorable, in how you went about your self-destruction. You gave your food away to the other children, left the crumbs for the birds. Then you saw me and decided you had one more little bird to tend to."

"You are more of an eagle, or perhaps a hawk, and there was nothing little about you. I think I know who engineered these kidnappings."

"He or she will be far, far removed from tonight's business." His Grace finished with the second pistol as the coach lurched onto the cobbles that signaled they'd reached the Thames's south bank. "Forget your many kindnesses to me in prison, Ned. Forget that you refused Jane's efforts to get you out of there because you did not want me to die alone. Forget that you also stood the same vigil for your brother at an age when no boy should be anywhere near the gallows."

"I have tried to forget all of it, but you insist on dredging up the past."

"Forget it if you must, but recall this: When I was so determined to confront my enemies at the first opportunity, my tiger—a mere boy, who should have left me to my folly—had the sense to summon those who'd take my part. You roused the watch, Ned, and brought me the allies I needed to win free of a very bad situation. You were just a boy, and you already knew what I had yet to learn: If you have family, any kind of family, you are never alone. That's what family means."

Ned wanted to see Rosalind's maids to safety because that would right an injustice, but he also needed for this day with all its drama and disclosures to be over. He needed to sit with Rosalind in the quiet of his own house, embroider a few irises, and settle his nerves. He'd stitch his pretty flowers and look up every two minutes, just to make sure Rosalind was still there, still real.

Still his.

"You gave me the Wentworth name," Ned said, quietly. "Just handed it to me, when my own name was lost to me. Then you marched off, alone, blind to your own danger.... I could not lose you too."

"You never will. Emmigrate to the Antipodes, set up your own merchants and widows bank, end up back in Newgate, and I will still be proud to call you family."

Ned gathered Rosalind close, because he needed to hold on to her. "And would Her Grace agree with that sentiment? Woodruff is promising to make trouble for Rosalind and me."

"Jane will put Woodruff in his place without so much as looking in his direction. Depend upon it."

Rosalind had seen that possibility, but to hear Walden say the words was reassuring. A duchess's silence could be more lethal to a man's consequence than all the loaded pistols in London.

"I do not know if I want Woodruff put in his place," Ned said, stroking Rosalind's hair. "He is Rosalind's father, as far as the world is concerned, and she is ever kind to dumb beasts."

"You don't have to know," Walden replied, as the coach horses swung into a trot. "Rosalind will sort that out for you, just as you are sorting out a few pesky kidnappers for her. Abigail and Jane will envy us this adventure, and Elizabeth will immortalize you in one of her grand stories."

"You sent word to Her Grace?"

"Badgers are ever so useful when I recall to follow bank policies and actually keep one handy. When does the tide turn?"

"We have less than two hours."

Not much time to arrange a rescue that could set off a scandal the likes of which would reverberate halfway around the world, and yet, holding Rosalind, enduring Walden's ill-timed sentimentality, and knowing that Bob was perched up top…a weary, lonely part of Ned's soul began to hope that somehow, it might all come right.

It might all finally, finally come right.

Chapter Seventeen

Rosalind dozed, the weight of a trying day pressing on her mind and body. She heard Ned's voice, felt his warmth beside her, and rode the steady rise and fall of his breathing as the coach swayed along.

When the coach halted, she roused herself, though it was an effort.

"You will stay with Lord Stephen," Ned said, when he'd handed her down from the carriage. "Bob and His Grace will come with me, as will Artie."

"Arthur will be your scout?" Rosalind asked.

"Nobody notices boys," Arthur replied. "I'll turn sideways and disappear."

"Nobody notices women either," Rosalind retorted. "I will keep my head down and have no need to disappear."

Lord Stephen handed his horse off to a groom. "You are too pretty, my lady. Every tar new to port and every man putting out to sea will notice you."

Rosalind had never before been accused of being too pretty. Lord Stephen was dissembling for the sake of gallantry.

"Those men will notice the ladies whose demeanor and attire signals a willingness to be friendly. I am tired, I have much on my mind, and—"

"And you have no bonnet," Ned said gently. "I know you want to help, but his lordship is right—for once. You are too conspicuous."

Ned had chosen the more honest words. The men were trying to keep her safe. How could they not realize she wanted to keep them safe too?

"We are wasting time," Walden muttered.

"Mr. Taylor," Rosalind said. "Give me your cravat."

To his credit, Ned's brother complied without protest. Rosalind took the two yards of wrinkled linen and fashioned it into a sort of turban.

"Artie can come with me," Rosalind said, "and I will scold him so unrelentingly that nobody comes near either of us. Other than my missing maids, what exactly should I be looking for?"

"Look for the *Tantalus*," Ned said, his gaze on the many ships at anchor mid-river. "Listen for any mention of it. It's out there in the Pool somewhere, not very far from shore. But Rosalind..."

Rosalind loved this man and loved very much that he'd take on the challenge of freeing kidnapped women, but she also loved him enough to be honest with him.

"Ned Wentworth, if you tell me, ask me, or suggest to me that I should get back into that coach and wait for you to take on this entire challenge alone, I will be disobedient. I am safer with Arthur's escort than you are dressed in your Mayfair finest and looking ready to break heads."

Arthur took a knife from Lord Stephen as casually as if he'd been passed tuppence. "Better listen to her, guv. She can argue all night, and then where will we be?" The knife disappeared inside Arthur's jacket.

"The lad has a point," Mr. Taylor said. "And if her ladyship does reconnaissance to the north, I'll amble along the docks to the south. I'd say, based on the crowds, that the transportees will be rowed out from that pier there."

A knot of women and children stood along one of the many wooden piers jutting into the river. They were humble folk, some were in tears, and most of the children were silent and glum. Bundles sat along the edge of the dock, a last gesture of hope for the well-being of the convicts.

"Arthur," Rosalind said, taking up her reticule. "Let's be off, shall we?"

Artie skipped ahead, adopting the posture and attitude of a younger boy, and making it look convincing.

"Your gait should be a trifle uneven," Lord Stephen said, "as if you've tromped the whole way here from the City, miles of hard walkway, noise, and crowds, and you'll do the reverse journey again before the sun rises. That boy wears you out, and you are nearly too tired to eat."

"But you love him," Ned said, "so you don't lose sight of him."

Walden looked amused at all this theatrical advice.

Rosalind kissed Ned's cheek. "I love you."

She made an exit worthy of Mrs. Siddons—she hoped—trailing in Arthur's wake along the narrow street. The stink of the river was strong, or perhaps it was the stink of the hulk beached a hundred yards down the shore.

"How ye going to do this?" Arthur asked, picking up a stick and thwacking at the cobbles. "Can't just storm the transport ship and demand hostages, can ye? Not even Walden could pull that off."

The how of the whole business wanted thought. "The convicts are rowed out in batches to the *Tantalus*?"

"Aye, and the shore party waves and cries and makes sure they each have a bottle and a loaf of bread. What's a single bottle going to do when the journey takes months?"

The bottle held spirits, also hope and good wishes. "Who does the rowing?"

"Tars or marines. The transport ships use both. The men at the oars won't be armed, but they can wield the oars like clubs."

A melee wouldn't do. The numbers alone made that approach untenable. By the time Ned, Walden, Lord Stephen, and Bob had been taken to anybody in authority—assuming they could still stand upright—the *Tantalus* would be long gone.

"Stealth is what's needed." Stealth and possibly a distraction. "Can you swim, Arthur?"

"No, milady, and I don't aim to learn how. Lord Stephen swims. He rows, he rides horseback. Anything that don't bother his knee. But the Thames will kill ye, as is known to all. Water is foul."

All too true. The river was the sewer of first resort for most of London.

Rosalind had chosen a path along the quay that took her in the direction of the looming ship that served as a dry-dock prison. Ragged men waited in a silent group, as did an equally grim group of women. Armed guards stood about, gaze on the river.

"Poor sods," Arthur murmured. "So glad to be shut of that hulk they probably look forward to being under sail."

The silence and stillness of the prisoners was at variance with the activity and bustle on shore generally. The sun had sunk below the horizon, and the ships anchored in the Pool were becoming dark shapes impossible to distinguish from one another.

One of the larger ships opened a beacon lantern twice.

"That's it then," an armed guard said. "Over to the quay with you lot. Make your farewells, and don't try anything stupid."

The prisoners shuffled forth, a few in chains, most appearing weighed down by despair rather than cold iron.

"Watch the women," Rosalind said. "Watch that last group of women." The little clutch of females moved more slowly than the others and included two small girls and several ladies bent over with age. One woman used a crutch. Another appeared to be without sight because she leaned heavily on a companion and moved in a cautious, sliding gait.

"That group," Rosalind said, "will be set free, and the kidnapped women substituted for them."

The guards were in on the scheme, clearly, for they kept glancing about as if expecting trouble—or another signal.

"I know how we can do this," Rosalind said, "but we have to hurry."

"Smack me," Arthur said. "Smack me. I'll pike off and you take off after me."

"I'll not strike a child."

"Ouch!" Arthur yelled, backing away on nimble feet. "Mama, ye oughtn't to treat me so cruel!" He darted off, and Rosalind chased after him.

"Get back here, you naughty boy! Get back here, and I will show you how such a mischievous whelp deserves to be treated!"

They kept it up all the way back to the coach, by which time Rosalind was out of breath.

"The women are being led to the quay now," Rosalind panted. "The guilty women. I know how we can bring this off without violence. We need a boat and two men to row it, and we need them now."

Ned stared at her hard in the waning light. "You think to effect a substitution?"

"The guilty women will be rowed halfway out to the ship," Rosalind said, "and at the same time, the kidnapped women will be rowed out from a different pier. The guilty women won't reach the ship, the kidnapped women will."

"So we intercept the boatload of kidnapped women," Ned said, "and then tell the tars there's been a change of plans. Trade them the empty boat for ours. The kidnappers row away with an empty boat, thinking their part of the job complete. We row the kidnapped women to safety."

Lord Stephen was frowning mightily. "What happens to the guilty women?"

"They very likely end up going free," Bob said. "At worst, they end up being transported when it becomes apparent nobody will intercept them. I'm off to find a boat. Does anybody have coin?"

Lord Stephen produced a shiny gold sovereign. "This ought to suffice."

"Walden and I will row," Ned said, unknotting his cravat. "Bob, you have the hard part."

Rosalind collected neckcloths and pocket watches, while the transportees and their families were permitted a final farewell on the quay.

"Rosalind?" Ned said, when Bob and His Grace had moved away in search of a boat.

"Hurry," Rosalind said. "And I know: I will not put myself in harm's way. I will not allow harm to come to Arthur if I can avoid it. I will create a distraction if I see that matters out on the water aren't going well for you, but Ned, if you don't find that boat immediately, there won't be enough light to see—"

Ned hauled her into his arms and kissed her. "I love you too. Madly."

He strode off, an impressive figure of a man determined to see justice done, while Rosalind stood by the coach, clutching a wad of very fine cravats and grinning like an utter goose.

* * *

Old skills stirred back to life as Ned trailed after Bob and Walden.

The ability to add a little swagger to a casual stroll, signaling to passersby that *this is my patch,* and *you'd best watch your step around a canny lad like me*.

The ability to take in details with a glance, such as the slight unsteadiness of one guard's gait, the woman in the trailing group whose dress was styled with an out-of-date high waist. An elderly man who stood not far from the possibly expecting woman, jingling a few coins in his pocket.

Bob approached a pair of fellows loading crates of clucking chickens into a skiff. The boat was large enough to hold a dozen women, and nondescript enough to approach the *Tantalus* without causing comment.

"We're in luck," Bob said, a few moments later. "This load of fowl is marked for the *Tantalus*. Ship oars, me hearties, and look lively."

"We don't have time to unload a pile of damned chickens in the middle of the Pool," Walden groused. "I did not part with my cuff links to—"

"We need the chickens to allay suspicion." Ned passed Bob a crate. "We need space for the women too."

They soon had half the cargo clucking on the dock, and were rowing away from the quay.

"Not so vigorously," Ned said, when Walden would have rowed them clear down to the Channel. "We're looking for a boat full of women departing from a dock other than the one where all the crying is coming from."

As he watched, the last group of women—the aged and infirm—were herded into a boat.

"What do you want to bet," Bob murmured, "they simply row them across and turn them loose on the Isle of Dogs?"

"Some of them would not have survived the voyage," Walden said, as the boat left the dock. "Transportation used to be a more carefully regulated affair, but now it's causing more problems than it solves. The colonies accepted the free labor at first, but now..."

"Now?" Ned asked, scanning the darkening water for another boat full of women. Young, strong, healthy women caught up in a vile, greedy scheme.

"Now we know that the dire threat of transportation has done nothing to reduce the incidence of crime here at home," Walden said. "Transportation was supposed to be a deterrent, a terrible fate that frightened the criminal class into a sober re-evaluation of their felonious ways."

Bob, sitting in the prow, snorted. "Some lord thought up that reasoning, some lord who believes an empty belly can sort out levels of hell according to the Crown's convenience. I ate better on the transport ship than I had in years."

"Or some lord," Ned said, "wanted another colony settled for the good of merry olde England, and to hell with crime rates, deterrents, and starving lads. Rosalind and Artie are on the quay."

"Getting ready to make a diversion?" Walden asked.

Darkness was falling in earnest, and still no little boat full of young women had pushed away from the shore.

"Tide's about to change," Bob said. "You live in a port town, you learn to feel it. You can feel the storms coming, the hot spells bearing down. I'd go inland to deliver an order, and be surprised by a passing shower, but on shore, I know what's coming, and I know from what direction."

Direction. Ned swung his gaze across the water, toward the London side of the river. "There," he said softly. "They're rowing them over from the other bank. That boat."

"Awfully quiet for a boatload of kidnapped women," Walden said, taking up his oar. "Let's treat with the pirates, shall we?"

"Let me spell you, Ned," Bob said, shifting to the middle of boat. "You'll sound like you mean business without coming off like a nob."

"Right," Ned replied, taking up the perch in the prow. "Walden, do not open your mouth unless you can summon your best Yorkshire dialect."

"Ye'll nowt hear a waird from me, sair."

As the two boats drew closer, Ned sent up a prayer that Reggie Sharp was not on the other vessel. Even in the dim light, recognition was possible.

"Ahoy, lads," Ned called when the boats were several yards apart. "Been a change in plans."

"Nobody said nothin' about a change in plans," came the reply.

"Captain of the *Tantalus* is on deck," Ned rejoined. "Checkin' off this and pokin' 'is nose into the middle of that. We'll take the ladies the rest of the way."

A muttered exchange took place on the other boat. "Says who?"

"Says the man whose job it is to get these women on board without a fuss. You either swap with us, or the tide will settle the argument and you'll be left to make the awkward explanations to himself."

The women were silent, sitting on the benches three abreast. Ned counted a dozen huddled and cloaked figures, hoods drawn up, in addition to the four men rowing the boat.

"How do I know you won't keep the ladies for yourself?" the largest of the four asked, as the tide brought the two boats into bumping proximity.

"I will keep 'em for myself," Ned said, "all the way to Botany Bay if they're pretty and willing, but I don't have time to dicker with you lot when the *Tantalus* is about to weigh anchor. Off your arses and take this load of chickens back to the dock. No room in the hold for 'em."

"This ain't the plan. We take the women to the ship, we don't hand 'em over to—"

"Stop, thief!" Rosalind's voice sang out from the quay, as Artie darted off down the shore. "He has my reticule. That boy stole my reticule!"

"Give the man what he wants," said another of the sailors. "We done our bit. Missus could use a pullet or two and now the constable will be coming around."

"Aye," said a second. "Don't fancy runnin' into the Thames police tonight of all nights."

Walden rose, and his height and muscle might well have decided the matter. He stepped from one boat to the other, making both ships rock. The rest of the exchange went smoothly, and the sound of clucking chickens was soon fading into the dark.

"The women are bound and gagged," Bob said, tipping back one woman's hood. "Drugged too, would be my guess."

"Walden, row like hell," Ned said, taking up an oar.

"If the constable catches Artie, there's no telling what will become of him. Ladies, you are safe. You are not to be transported, but we do want to know who did this to you."

Between the changing tide, the darkness, and the worry that somebody on the *Tantalus* would realize a boatload of women had gone missing, the docks seemed to recede rather than come closer.

"Taylor," Walden said, "assist your brother."

With Ned and Bob on one oar, and Walden single-handedly manning the other, the boat finally neared the docks.

"Upstream," Ned said. "Away from the quay, away from the hulk. Get us upstream."

Walden rowed as if driven by steam, his rhythm tireless, like a man who'd taken on single combat with the Thames itself.

"Thank God for well-fed dukes," Bob muttered, slumping over the oar when they finally bumped against a deserted dock. The nearest lit torch was a good twenty yards away, on the shore itself. "My arms are ready to fall off."

As were Ned's. "We're not home free yet. Get the women on shore and keep them quiet."

The ladies seemed to sense the need for haste and silence because they climbed from the boat and stumbled to shore with little prompting. They remained silent even when the bindings and gags had been removed and tossed into the river.

"The *Tantalus* hasn't gone anywhere," Walden remarked, as he, Bob, and Ned shepherded the ladies toward the coach.

"I know," Ned said, "and we still don't know who's behind this scheme, but I would love to turn the ladies loose on him in a dark alley."

"These ladies are in no fit state to..." Walden's smile was piratical. "Ah, my duchess has come to the rescue." Behind the ducal town coach stood another even larger vehicle, the ducal traveling coach. "She and Lady Rosalind will have all in hand, and we gents can stand around looking humble and harmless."

"We are humble and harmless," Ned said. "Though you missed your calling, Your Grace."

"I spent a few summers on fishing vessels," Walden replied. "Old skills come in handy from time to time, don't they? Let's report for duty, lads."

The Duchess of Walden treated Ned to a regal nod, then turned her attention to the ladies. Ned was fretting over Artie's whereabouts as Rosalind saw the last woman into the traveling coach.

"They're mostly unharmed," she said, embracing Ned tightly. "You did it. They are safe and whole and will soon come right. Artie's sister, Arbuckle, Campbell, and Miss Henderson, among them. Thank you."

Ned hugged her back. "We did it, my lady. You and I, assisted by family. We did it."

"We did. We absolutely did." Then Ned's beloved kissed him smack on the mouth.

* * *

"I sent a note to Mrs. Barnstable informing her that you will enjoy my hospitality tonight," Her Grace of Walden said, passing Rosalind a delicate silver flask.

"She replied by package, which I've had put into Ned's coach. I intimated that you and I had run across each other while shopping and decided to share supper. Your company is so congenial that I've inveigled you into an evening of cards with me, and Mrs. Barnstable should not look for you before morning."

Her Grace had seen the rescued women fed and billeted in the Wentworth town house with a dispatch Rosalind could only envy. The Wentworth family had gathered in the breakfast parlor thereafter and consumed enough food to feed the Congress of Vienna.

When the men had withdrawn to enjoy brandy in the library, Her Grace had commandeered another few minutes of Rosalind's time. They lounged on opposite ends of a sofa that was comfortable enough to put thoughts of slumber into a tired lady's mind.

Rosalind took the flask and had a nip, something she hadn't done previously outside the huntfield or the sickroom.

"Thank you," she said, passing the flask back. "For the medicinal tot, and for everything. We are very much in your debt." Though the duchess's sops to propriety would likely mean nothing in the face of the scandal about to break.

Her Grace had an imperial dignity, much like her husband. Unlike him, she smiled often and warmly. She linked arms with Rosalind, touched her sleeve, and generally comported herself like an auntie at large.

Or a mama. Her Grace had four daughters, after all.

The flask disappeared into the duchess's pocket. "I haven't had this much fun since Stephen courted

Abigail. You really must bring Ned up to scratch, my lady. Walden says the foundation has been laid, but one wants a marriage, not merely a proposal."

One wanted one's beloved to be happy. "Ned proposed and I accepted." The moment had been lovely, a little awkward, and fleeting. "He and I still have much to discuss."

The duchess toed off her slippers and propped her feet on a hassock. "He's told you about Newgate?"

"About Newgate, about attempting to starve himself, about his brother's hanging." Rosalind kept to herself the incident in the molly house. "He also told me about the Royal Navy kidnapping his father, consumption kidnapping his mother, and London itself trying to kidnap his human decency. I admire him all the more for what he has overcome, Your Grace. You need never defend him to me."

Her Grace shoved a pillow behind her back. "Good. Now perhaps Ned will realize—"

A soft tap on the door heralded the arrival of Rosalind's intended. He'd found a fresh neckcloth somewhere and reassembled himself into a natty, if weary, version of the successful banker.

"Your Grace, my lady." He bowed and Rosalind got to her feet. "The women having been settled, I thought I'd see Lady Rosalind home."

The duchess rose and stretched, a languorous, feline indulgence.

"I'll bid you good night, Lady Rosalind," Her Grace said, gathering Rosalind in her arms. "You have done a remarkable, courageous thing—many remarkable courageous things—and when next you meet with your animal welfare associations, I hope you will invite me to join you."

The duchess was a grand lady, both in terms of her consequence and in terms of her stately proportions. She didn't feel like a grand lady when she hugged Rosalind. She felt like a dear friend and the embodiment of feminine kindness.

Like a godmother, perhaps.

"Aunt Ida would like you," Rosalind said, easing away. "I know of no higher praise, Your Grace."

"Ned likes you," Her Grace replied, smoothing the sleeve of Rosalind's dress. "I know of no higher praise. Ned, don't keep her ladyship up too late. I will expect you back here in the morning. A dozen very upset women need sorting, and I am not equal to that whole challenge on my own."

"You are," Ned said, kissing her cheek. "Good night, Your Grace."

Ned held the door for Rosalind and the duchess, though Her Grace paused on the threshold. "You do know I'm so proud of you I could have Walden inflict a barony on you, Ned?"

He shuddered, and Rosalind thought the reaction genuine.

"Please do not," Ned said. "Lend your consequence to my small investors' projects or Rosalind's charities, but spare me your baronies."

She patted his lapel. "I knew you'd say that, but Walden did want me to ask."

His Grace joined them at the foot of the steps, and though he still carried himself with the severe dignity of a ranking peer, he also had a jam stain on his cuff.

"The nursery is settled," he said, "and thus the realm is safe for another few hours. Lady Rosalind, the day has been a delight." He bowed over her hand, then turned to Ned. "I was right in what I said about family, Ned. I am frequently right."

His duchess looked amused at that pronouncement. "Wish them good night, Walden. I require your escort up to bed."

The duke offered Ned his hand. "If you want to resume using the Taylor name, I'll see to the legal filings, but you will always be a Wentworth. Her Grace and I expect to serve as godparents to your firstborn. The line will form thereafter with Stephen and Abigail no doubt at its head, but I wouldn't put it past Rothhaven and Constance to sniggle in front of them."

In Rosalind's experience, when men hugged, the gesture was a fleeting sort of wrestling hold that occurred only after consumption of strong spirits. Pummeling was involved, followed by self-conscious disregard for the affectionate display.

Walden drew Ned into a hug, and Ned surrendered to the embrace, resting his forehead on the duke's shoulder. "I was terrified."

"I know, lad." The duke patted Ned's back gently. "So was I. You were willing to take on the whole Royal Navy and my money would have been on you. All's well now, thanks to ye and the lady."

There was the Yorkshire growl, and there was Her Grace, blinking rapidly as she gazed at her duke and the boy who'd saved him.

"Ned and Lady Rosalind must be exhausted, Walden, as am I. Shall we to bed?"

The duke let Ned go and took his wife's hand. "Good night, then. Thank you both for a fine day's adventure." His Grace bowed to Rosalind and processed up the steps with his duchess.

"Shall I take you home?" Ned asked. "You are doubtless welcome to stay here, and I'm sure the duchess would—"

Rosalind put a finger to his lips. "The duchess already has. The coach awaits, Ned, and yes, it's time you took me home—with you."

Ned grasped her hand. "With me?"

Rosalind nodded. "Take me to your house. Her Grace has seen fresh clothing packed for me in your coach, and she all but ordered me to avail myself of your hospitality—not that I needed her encouragement." Though having that encouragement meant worlds.

Ned linked his fingers with Rosalind's. "You are sure?"

"I am absolutely certain, and we are wasting time."

"Far be it from me to argue with a lady at the end of such a trying day." He offered his arm and Rosalind took it. No duke had ever handed his duchess into a coach with more dignity, or—once the horses were trotting along—been kissed by his duchess with more passion.

* * *

"Bob has accepted Lord Stephen's hospitality," Ned said, as the coach swayed around a corner. "They were in the thick of a discussion about the challenges of growing cotton in New South Wales when they departed."

And seeing Bob casually climb into Lord Stephen's coach had been daunting. Bob had climbed right back out, punched Ned on the arm, and promised to have lunch with him at the club the next day. Once an older brother, always an older brother—thank the Deity.

"Did you want to run after Lord Stephen's coach to make sure they went no farther than his lordship's residence?" Rosalind asked.

"Yes, and to pitch his lordship to the cobbles for stealing my brother." Except, Stephen had been right to offer Ned a respite from Bob's company. "I haven't asked if Bob is home to stay, or whether he'll return to his shop in the Antipodes. Our father is there. Papa never remarried, and he's minding the shop for Bob. Bob nipped out to deliver an order one day and he saw this older fellow sitting on a bench, staring out across the water. After all the misery we've been put through, they just bumped into each other on the other side of the world. That was years ago, and all this time, they talked of looking for me."

Rosalind snuggled closer. "You are overdue for some miracles, Ned, and there's time to sort it all out. Bob didn't come all this way only to jump on the next outbound ship."

Rosalind was asking Ned for a respite too, from all that still required sorting out. "I want you to know something, my lady."

"Hmm?"

"I do love you. That was not bravado or heat-of-the-moment dramatics." Though love, contrary to the maunderings of the poets, did not make life's hard decisions any less painful.

"I trust your love, Ned Wentworth, which is why I am planning to spend the night with you."

Now, when Ned needed the clarity that always came with detaching himself from his immediate experiences, the distance refused to come. He was too delighted with the feel of Rosalind nestled against him. Too intrigued by her use of trust and love in the same sentence. Too worried about all the discussions he and Rosalind would face in the morning.

"My house is nothing grand," Ned said. "I did not want the usual bachelor lodgings, and Jane found this place for me. I'm close enough to the bank, but not so close that I'd be tempted to nip back into the office at all hours."

He was babbling, and about the damned bank. "I've thought about offering Artie a place here," he went on, "though I suspect he'll want to stick with the other badgers."

Rosalind bussed Ned's cheek. "In the morning, we can talk about anything you please, such as whether Artie's Sissy might accept an offer of employment as your maid of all work. Now, I would like to see your home."

As the coach came to a halt, an odd combination of pride and trepidation assailed Ned. "I love having my own place. Love the peace and quiet of it. The Wentworth household is grand and always awash with guests, family, servants, children....I was lonelier there than I have ever been in the solitude of my own dwelling."

Ned handed Rosalind down from the coach, collected her bundle of clothing, and wondered when his tendency to confide in her without notice would abate, if ever.

"I know that loneliness," Rosalind said, as the coach rolled away in the direction of the mews. "A woman assigned a companion is all but announcing to the world that nobody in particular needs her underfoot. She is extraneous to all endeavors, not even decorative. One unfortunate individual is paid to ensure the lady doesn't become a bother to society generally."

"You may bother me all you like."

Rosalind smiled and ascended the front steps. "Do you keep your front door locked at all hours against London's thieves?"

"I do not. First, no self-respecting thief marches in the front door. He or she uses a window in the garden, where nobody will see them gaining entry. Second, everything on the premises worth stealing is under lock and key. I do lock my bedroom door, though."

"As do I," Rosalind said. "Ned—this isn't necessary."

He'd opened the door and scooped her into his arms. "Yes, it is." He set her on her feet in the foyer and closed the door. "Welcome to my home, Lady Rosalind, and I hope to your new home as well."

She leaned into him. "You are so romantic. Whatever shall I do with you?"

Before Ned could suggest she make wild, passionate love with him, she was whisking off her bonnet—one of Jane's, unless Ned was mistaken—and unbuttoning her cloak, also Jane's.

He hung them up, placed his hat on its customary

hook, and then he was trailing Rosalind up the steps, her bundle of clothing in his hand, and a sweet sense of anticipation crowding out most of his worries.

Though not all of his worries. Not quite all.

Rosalind tarried in his sitting room long enough to admire his framed embroidery. "You truly have a talent, Ned."

"I stitch when I need to think through a complicated problem, and living with the Wentworths presented a fair number of those." He wanted to watch Rosalind inspect his sitting room, and he wanted to toss her over his shoulder, pitch her onto the bed in the next room, and fall upon her like a ravening beast.

"What was this problem here?" she asked, pausing before a particularly profuse rendering of roses. "Thorns and all."

"I'd come upon Lady Constance in tears. She'd had a letter from Yorkshire—from Abigail, I'm guessing, but before the rest of us knew Abigail—and the news was apparently discouraging. Constance was the quietest Wentworth, the one who never caused any drama, and her tears were heartbroken. I did not know what to do."

"What did you do?"

"I told her that I was available to render her any aid she needed, no questions asked. She nearly started crying again, but we never spoke of it after that. Years ago, much went unspoken in that household."

Ned did not want the same sort of silences and delicate evasions with Rosalind. He wanted only the truth, however difficult.

Truth, though, could wait a few hours. "Shall I unlace you?"

Rosalind left off wandering about the room. "Please, and I will valet you, and then we will fall into bed, likely too exhausted to do justice to our hard-won privacy. The duchess really is a treasure, Ned. The duke is a darling fellow as well."

Ned let Rosalind precede him into the bedroom, where the covers had been turned down and the fire banked. He knew of no other person save Jane who would refer to Walden as a darling fellow.

"The tea tray is for the morning," Ned said. "I build up the fire, heat the water, and begin my day without intrusions."

"Nobody valets you?"

"No."

"Then I am honored to fulfill that office." Rosalind began by removing his coat and slipping his sleeve buttons from his cuffs. She was efficient but also affectionate. When she unwound his cravat from his neck, she paused to rub his nape. After Ned had taken his shirt off, she fluffed his hair back into order.

"Your hooks, my lady."

She turned and swept her hair off her neck. "I am honestly exhausted. I did not sleep well last night."

Her dress had less than two dozen hooks. Her stays were the work of a moment. "You get first crack at the privacy screen," Ned said. "I'll deal with the warmer."

He'd also deal with the novel prospect of sharing a bed throughout the night with another person. He hadn't done that since Bob had been arrested, and the prospect now should have been unsettling, if not alarming.

Except that his bedmate was Rosalind, and he was more alarmed to contemplate letting her out of his sight than sharing the blankets with her. She emerged from the privacy screen a few moments later, her hair a thick braid over one shoulder.

"That dressing gown never looked half so fetching on me," Ned said.

"Mrs. Barnstable packed me a nightgown. I don't believe I'll be needing it. I did use your toothpowder."

Rosalind was so composed, so cheerful about taking a step that could not be untaken. Yes, they were already lovers, but an interlude on a picnic blanket was an order of magnitude less apt to cause scandal than a night under a man's roof.

Under his *blankets*. "Rosalind, we need to talk about who was responsible for kidnapping the ladies."

"I spoke with the women, Ned. I know we need to talk, but it can wait until morning. In fact, I insist upon it."

Ned hadn't questioned the ladies, hadn't wanted to subject them to that ordeal when they were still dazed and upset. He also hadn't felt it necessary to seek their confirmation of the obvious.

"What did the women tell you?"

"Enough to know scandal looms. Do you intend to come to bed wearing your boots, Mr. Wentworth?"

"I do not," Ned said, strolling past her to the privacy screen. "Did you just pat my bum?"

"I might have. You have a very fine bum. Shall I crack a window?"

I love you, I love you, I love you. "I'll tend to it just before I climb into bed. If you'd lock the doors, I will see to my ablutions."

Two locks snicked—the sitting room and the bedroom—and the covers rustled, a beautiful, cozy sound.

"After my mother died, I was afraid of the dark for years," Rosalind said. "My father refused to allow me a candle, so I learned to open my draperies after the nursery maids put me to bed. The nights of the new moon were hardest, but my nurse would crack the bedroom door, allowing me a sliver of light from the fire in her sitting room."

Ned emerged from the privacy screen. He'd donned a pair of silk trousers lest he shock Rosalind with the extent to which he anticipated the lovemaking. "Would you like me to light a candle, my lady?" He'd light entire chandeliers if Rosalind asked it of him, and he hoped she never lost the habit of sprinkling their conversations with confidences.

She sat against the pillows on the side of the bed away from the window, the covers tucked up under her arms. She was at once prim and wanton, Lady Rosalind, the houri of his dreams.

"If I awaken in a fright," Rosalind said, "I will reach for you, and you will banish my fears."

Ned blew out the candles on the mantel. "Will you perform the same service for me? I'm unused to sharing a bed."

"I will love you so passionately that you cannot waken from your slumbers until next Tuesday at the earliest. Ye gods, what a day. If we ever have a dog, we must name him Nelson."

Of all the details she might have seized upon.... But then, Rosalind loved the mute beasts, which was fortunate, because Ned was fresh out of words. He would, though, send a note to Mr. Willow Dorning, purveyor of fine canines, about procuring a birthday puppy for Rosalind. Or a wedding puppy. Possibly a next Tuesday puppy.

Ned laid his silk trousers across the foot of the bed, climbed under the covers, and wrapped Rosalind against his side.

"Tomorrow will be complicated," Ned said, tucking an arm around her shoulders. "Messy even, but we shall contrive to endure it."

"Tonight will be lovely," Rosalind said, shifting to drape herself over him. "Magnificent, even."

Ned did not argue with his lady.

Chapter Eighteen

Ned had been diplomatic, in Rosalind's estimation. Tomorrow would be hellish.

The scandal would be all over London, and probably reach the Continent by nightfall. Rosalind had no intention of keeping mum about a wrong of such magnitude. Aunt Ida would agree with her about that, and so too did Ned apparently agree with her.

"I have missed you," Rosalind said, curling down to Ned's chest. "Ever since we folded up that picnic blanket, Ned Wentworth, I have been longing to unfold it."

He was wonderfully aroused. Had been when he'd sauntered out from behind the privacy screen in his nearly transparent pajama trousers.

"You chose today for my birthday," Ned said. "I know exactly how I'd like to celebrate it."

"As do—gracious, Ned." He'd threaded himself into her body, not a full penetration, barely more than a tease in fact.

"Ride the waves, Rosalind. We'll go slowly next time."

Rosalind tried an experimental undulation and, thundering chariots of heaven, the pleasure was exquisite. "We might not. We might not go slowly for at least a dozen...I like that."

Ned palmed her breasts in a warm grasp. "If you try to draw out your pleasure, I won't last. I will spend inside you, and while the bliss of that indulgence boggles my—Rosalind?"

She'd recalled that his nipples were sensitive, and feathered her thumbs across them. "We are engaged to be married, Ned. We are entitled to every indulgence."

"I'm trying to be..."

She sank onto him fully, and kissed him, lest he start citing Policies and Procedures for Lovemaking Couples.

"Be mine," she said, a few panting moments later. "Be passionate and all mine."

He wrested from her the fiction that she'd been in charge. Rosalind knew with a word, with a touch, she could resume control, but she was in bed with the man she esteemed and desired above any other, and nobody need control anybody.

"Rosalind, I can't hold..."

"Then don't."

He lashed his arms around her, and the pleasure became transcendent. Rosalind thrashed out her satisfaction as Ned groaned softly against her shoulder, and then she was so much sparkling joy, light as eiderdown, as peaceful as summer sunshine.

"I am slain," Ned said, his hold easing to merely snug. "I am utterly, completely…"

"You are all mine, Ned Wentworth, and I am all yours." An eddy of cool air wafted from the window, which Ned had opened a mere inch. The breeze was luscious, Ned's embrace a benediction beyond words, and sleep a temptation.

"Plain handkerchief is on the night table," Ned said. "I did not withdraw, in case the obvious needs stating."

"How are Their Graces to serve as godparents for our firstborn if you insist on withdrawing?" Rosalind levered up enough to find the handkerchief. She tended to the mess, and nearly fell asleep on Ned's chest.

Before she dozed off, Ned arranged her on her side, and wrapped himself around her. "I meant what I said, Rosalind. We'll get through tomorrow and whatever else today's mischief precipitates. I know who kidnapped those women, and I intend to see justice done."

Rosalind laced her fingers with Ned's, and even in sleep, she kept a firm hold of his hand.

* * *

The entire Wentworth family, even Rothhaven and Constance, gathered as a jury of the whole, and agreed with Ned that the villains had to be confronted lest the scheme simply resume. Francine Arbuckle and Catherine Campbell had agreed to give sworn statements and even testify if need be, as had several of the other women.

Two of the ladies had done little more than weep since being rowed to safety, and another hadn't spoken a word. She had gazed at Ned with furious, tormented eyes, and he had promised himself she would have justice.

"We don't have to try a peer to stop further kidnappings," Rosalind said, for the third time, as the ducal town coach rolled along in the direction of the Woodruff residence. "George inveigled those women into captivity. George benefited financially. Francine was very clear about that. The ladies all identified him from the sketch I showed them. George is most clearly at fault."

"What of Lindhurst?" Ned asked. "Do you believe George acted on his own?" The question was delicate, because Rosalind, so far, was staunchly of the opinion that only George was culpable. Ned suspected Rosalind's brothers had acted at the direction of the earl, which would mean a trial in the House of Lords, and a gargantuan scandal.

"If Lindhurst was involved," Rosalind retorted, "then why was he constantly borrowing money from George?"

"Because, Rosalind, Lindhurst cannot manage his funds."

Her gaze was on the busy streets and pretty houses of Mayfair. "Lindhurst cannot manage *anything*, Ned. Witness, he's lit upon the brilliant scheme of marrying Clotilda Cadwallader to improve the family fortunes. I suspect he has pressed his suit to the point that the lady must accept him or suffer undeniable disgrace."

The duke and duchess exchanged a glance. They

were, as was their habit, holding hands despite the seriousness of the errand, or perhaps, because of it.

"Why not confront George, Lindhurst, and Woodruff at the same time?" Her Grace of Walden suggested. "They might get to pointing fingers at one another and solve the dilemma for us."

The dilemma was whether to set off the scandal of the decade or the scandal of the century. An earl sent to the dock—or whatever the equivalent in the House of Lords was—would take precedence with the gossips over every straying wife, rolled-up baron, or outrageous wager for the next four generations.

"George will scarper," Rosalind said. "But his scheme will be unraveled, and that matters."

Walden held his peace, though Ned knew precisely what His Grace was thinking. Two large, fit, exceedingly loyal footmen rode at the back of the coach. Two grooms rode up on the box with the coachman. George would not scarper unless Walden permitted him to scarper.

And in that regard, Walden would heed the guidance of the ladies, and of Rosalind in particular.

"I'm nervous," Rosalind said. "Woodruff is the only father I've known, and his temper is cold and ruthless."

Ned, by contrast, was calm, as far as confronting Rosalind's family went. "Woodruff is cold and ruthless out of arrogance," he said. "His lordship believes himself entitled to behave like a horse's arse. I learned to be ruthless as a matter of survival. I will not allow the earl to disrespect you, Rosalind. Not ever again."

Rosalind's fingers curled around Ned's. "He can tie up my funds."

Bugger your funds. Except that they were *her* funds, willed to her by *her* mother. The point was not that Ned could provide well for her. The point was that Rosalind deserved access to her own money.

"He won't dare," Ned said. "I will put out the word that I'm buying up every unpaid bill, every marker, every IOU Woodruff owes, and before nightfall, you will own him."

"That's very good," Her Grace said. "Efficient and simple. Walden, I can see why Ned manages our bank."

Rosalind was looking at Ned as if he'd invited her on a five-day picnic in the land of perfect spring days.

"You can do that?"

"The shopkeepers talk to one another, from shop door to shop door, and bootmaker to bootmaker. The apprentices share a nightly pint, the clerks lodge together. Mercantile London knows who is bad custom and who pays reliably. Walden pays immediately, to the penny, as do I. I have reason to know that Woodruff does not. Lindhurst used up the last of his credit two years ago. George pays, but not promptly."

The coach came to a halt before the Woodruff town house, and Walden handed the ladies down.

"A word of advice?" Walden said quietly as the footmen escorted the women to the door.

"I am all ears." In Ned's experience, Walden never handed out advice. The duke was a firm believer that experience was the best teacher and often the only effective teacher.

"Be Lady Rosalind's intended before all else, Ned. Be worthy of her regard first, and let proving yourself to the world take a distant second."

"I have no need to prove myself to anybody."

Walden's smile was crooked. "Of course you don't. Neither do I. Perish the thought. We are gentlemen in good standing with our ladies, after all." And to His Grace, this was obviously all that should ever matter.

Ned and the duke joined the women at Woodruff's front door. One of the footmen banged the knocker three times, then withdrew as far as the steps.

"Ivor," Her Grace said to the second footman, "you will accompany us."

"Of course, Your Grace." Ivor's smile would have done credit to a plundering Viking.

The door opened, and Rosalind sailed past a venerable butler. "Cranston, please inform my father and brothers that Their Graces of Walden and Mr. Ned Wentworth have come to call. I will escort our guests to the formal parlor."

Cranston had likely never greeted such exalted personages, but he clearly realized that a visit at such an early hour was not social.

"I don't believe Lord Lindhurst has come down yet, my lady."

"Then please wake him," Rosalind said, passing over her bonnet and cloak. "I insist."

Cranston's brows rose.

"As do I," Ned said, adding his hat to the heap in Cranston's arms. "As do Their Graces. Please have Woodruff, Lindhurst, and Mr. George Kinwood in the formal parlor at once."

"And no perishing tea tray," Rosalind added.

"Very good, your ladyship."

Rosalind led them down a corridor that could have done with a good dusting and into a parlor that clearly saw little use. The room hadn't been aired in some time, the hearth was not only unlit, but also hadn't a fresh fire laid, and nary a single bloom graced either of the vases on the mantel.

"Rosalind." The Earl of Woodruff paused just inside the parlor door some moments later. "You will explain yourself."

Rosalind flinched under his lordship's peremptory tone, then stood straighter. "Good morning, my lord. I believe you know Their Graces and Mr. Wentworth?"

"I know Their Graces, and I have had the dubious honor of meeting Wentworth. Why have you inconvenienced a duke and duchess and upset the peace of my household at this hour?"

"It's no bother," Her Grace said. "We've come to hear you explain why you should not be arrested for kidnapping, bribery, interfering with the king's justice, wrongful imprisonment, and a few other felonies. His Grace will provide details when your sons have joined us."

Woodruff inhaled through his nose, the sound approximating a windbroken coach horse. "Your Grace surely jests."

"She does not," Rosalind countered. "And you cannot bluster your way out of responsibility, Papa."

"I do not bluster, Rosalind. Persist in this farce and I will disclaim any further connection with you."

Ned was ready to pummel the old windbag for that, but Rosalind merely looked intrigued.

"Is that supposed to be a threat? If so, I must inform your lordship that the prospect of being disowned looms rather like a temptation."

"You impertinent, disrespectful, ungovernable..." Woodruff took a step toward Rosalind. She stood her ground, while Ned took the place at her right, Walden at her left, and Ivor at her back.

"Your lordship should sit down," Rosalind said. "You will give yourself an apoplexy if you yield to a fit of choler now."

"I'd listen to her," Her Grace added. "The discussion will be trying for all concerned, most of all for you."

George chose then to stride into the room, looking quite well put together if a trifle wary. "We have exalted visitors, I'm told. George Kinwood, at your service. Roz, if you'd see to the introductions?"

"That's Lady Rosalind to you," Ned said. "Your Graces of Walden, may I make known to you Mr. George Kinwood, brother to Lady Rosalind. Mr. Kinwood, the Duke and Duchess of Walden. They are here as witnesses to a discussion of criminal wrongdoing."

George smiled coolly. "Has somebody been naughty? Not dear Roz, I hope?"

"In company, you will address your sister as Lady Rosalind." The duchess's tone was arctic. "If you presume to address her at all."

Lindhurst strolled into the room next, his cravat off-center, his curls looking more disheveled than stylish, and his pink boutonniere at an odd angle.

"Are we entertaining callers at the crack of doom

now?" he asked, making a leg at Her Grace. "Lind-hurst, at your service. I believe we were introduced last Season. Walden, good morning. Wentworth, didn't expect you to show your face here ever again. What on earth could be of such moment that I must be seen barely dressed and without having broken my fast?"

"Be patient," Ned said. "His Grace will explain the nature of our errand, and you lot will listen. Your ladyship, should we be seated?"

Rosalind took a wing chair at the end of the sofa. Their Graces appropriated a love seat, and Rosalind's brothers settled onto the sofa. Ivor was in position by the door, while Woodruff remained on his feet.

As did Ned.

"I've a mind to absent myself from this display of disrespect," Woodruff snapped. "Rosalind, have you taken leave of your senses?"

"I have not," she replied. "His Grace will offer a brief recitation of the facts."

Walden lounged on the little love seat, duke of all he surveyed. "Mr. George Kinwood has been implicated by witnesses in a scheme that begins with young ladies offered false overtures of gentlemanly interest. When the women, all of good character but of humble standing and without family in the metropolis, have placed their trust in Mr. Kinwood, he lures them into situations from which they can be spirited away. They are then held against their will for weeks."

"This is preposterous," Woodruff said. "George is the son of a peer. He has no need to coerce young women to do anything."

"He has no coin and less honor," Ned said, taking

the place beside Rosalind's chair. "Walden, if you'd continue."

"When a transport ship is ready to depart for the Antipodes," Walden went on, "the captives are substituted for married women, or women more aged or infirm. The female convicts are set free, which is one perversion of justice, while the innocent women are consigned to transportation, with a premium paid to Mr. George Kinwood for providing the younger, healthier, unmarried women, and effecting the switch. That, I believe, constitutes several more perversions of justice."

"I say." Lindhurst peered at his brother. "Not the done thing, George. Is this true?"

"Lindhurst, shut your mouth," Woodruff bellowed. "This is slander, nothing more than Rosalind's unbalanced imaginings. If I hear that a word of this fantasy has been repeated in polite circles—in *any* circles—I will bring suit in a court of law."

Rosalind stared at the carpet, and in the ensuing silence, Ned feared that she'd lost her resolve. He wanted to plead with her—the women were owed justice, the public paying to support transportation was owed justice. Some part of Ned himself felt a yearning to see Woodruff held accountable, but not at the expense of Rosalind's well-being.

"What do these so-called witnesses want?" George drawled. "A few pounds? Passage to Italy? I'm not saying a word of Walden's fairy tale is true, but to avoid unpleasantness, sometimes a little generosity goes a long way. Wouldn't you agree, Woodruff?"

A tacit negotiation ensued between father and son.

George's tone was that of a casually interested by-stander, but his gaze was worried, and Woodruff's complexion had turned the same shade as the carnation on Lord Lindhurst's lapel.

"To avoid the shame of a daughter bringing scandal down on her own family," Woodruff said, "I am willing to entertain terms here. What are your demands, Wentworth? For despite the august company you keep, I sense the tantrum of a spurned suitor in these lies."

Rosalind looked up. "I beg your pardon?"

Woodruff stalked halfway across the room, as if he'd make a grand exit, then seemed to recall that Ivor would prevent such histrionics.

"I said"—Woodruff positively glowered at Rosalind—"that just as I did when dealing with your wayward mother, I will school myself to discretion in the face of these fabrications and insults that you and Wentworth have concocted. You are a disgrace to the Kinwood name, Rosalind, and I wash my—"

Rosalind rose slowly, an eruption of feminine dignity that had Woodruff stepping back.

"Fabrications and insults, my lord? Shall we descend to the sort of cruelty you showed me when I was a mere child, innocent of adult machinations, grieving the loss of my mother and clinging desperately to familiar surrounds? Shall I inflict on you the hurt caused when a stammer is made into a source of ridicule? When my brothers were encouraged to condescend to me by your sneering example? A man who would treat a helpless child thus would not flinch at exploiting honest women for his own ends. George might well have executed your orders, but now I see that the greed and arrogance behind this scheme have your stamp all over them.

"The scandal here," she said, more quietly, "is that men of enormous privilege stooped to criminal exploitation of defenseless women, and for so paltry a consideration as coin. You had me kidnapped as well, the better to frighten me into docility yet again. You disgust me, sir, and *I am glad you are no blood of mine*." She aimed her next words at Walden. "See him tried in the Lords, Your Grace, and I will testify against him gladly."

Ned stopped himself from applauding, but only just. He held out a hand to Rosalind, thinking to assist her back into her chair, but she bundled in close and treated him to a fierce hug.

Woodruff, Lindhurst, and George all started babbling at once, with Woodruff prevailing by dint of excessive volume.

"Tried in the Lords? Don't be preposterous. If George got up to some misguided bit of mischief, that is no concern of mine."

"Papa!" George was on his feet, no cool smile to be seen. "What do you mean, no concern of yours?"

"Why don't we all have a spot of tea," Lindhurst murmured, "and just calm down?"

"He'll see me hanged!" George retorted. "See me packed off to Newgate like a footman purloining the silver."

Ivor seemed to gain three inches in addition to his already considerable height and another four stone of menace.

"If a footman steals a fork," Ned said, "you're

happy to see him hanged. You stole lives, Kinwood. You stole peace of mind and liberty from women who never offered you a moment's disrespect. You turned them into goods on offer, and worse, tossed their good names—the only treasure they had—into the river."

"It wasn't my idea," George wailed. "I only charmed them a bit, and they were willing to be charmed. I had nothing to do with snatching Rosalind. Papa, tell these people the truth before it's too late."

Woodruff shot his cuffs. "Best mind what you say, George. Rosalind has already admitted she'll testify against her own family. I would hate to be called upon to do likewise."

George sat forward. His mouth worked. He ran a hand through his hair. "Papa, how can you do this to me?"

Rosalind eased away from Ned, but kept hold of his hand. "Now you know exactly how I've felt for years. Betrayed, belittled, and bewildered, but unlike you, I was innocent of any crime save being my mother's daughter."

"I only did as I was told," George said, turning a mulish stare on his father. "Papa, you either find a way to intervene on my behalf, or I will tell the authorities everything I know."

"Tell them anyway," Ned said, "and Rosalind might prevail on Their Graces to see you transported rather than hanged. And when that transport ship catches the tide, and fourteen years of penal servitude stare you in the face, you might know the magnitude of the harm you so casually planned for innocent women."

Rosalind linked her arm with Ned's. "All so you

could afford a little more lace on your cravats. Not well done of you, George, and more fool you, you let Woodruff set you up to take all the blame."

"But he's my father!"

Lindhurst passed George a flask. "Mine too. Don't fret, George. At least you aren't engaged to Clotilda Cadwallader. I'll write to you, and fourteen years will pass before you know it."

George began to cry.

"Ned," Rosalind said, "let's be on our way. I don't believe I'll be coming back here ever again."

Ned bowed his farewell to the duke and duchess, and then he and Rosalind were out in the pretty midday sunshine, strolling arm in arm all the way home.

Epilogue

"Lady Dinkle is expecting," Rosalind said, wanting to hug the letter to her heart. Amelia Barnstable had been an ally all through George's trial and sentencing. Lord Dinkle, after proving that he could moderate his consumption of port, had been permitted to pay Mrs. Barnstable his addresses, and Mrs. Barnstable had become Lady Dinkle six months after Rosalind had married Ned.

"I will send a note around to Dinky offering congratulations and commiseration," Ned said, knotting off a bright green thread. "He has a difficult few months ahead if Walden's experience is any indication."

Ned's embroidery had become yet still more brilliant since he'd become a husband. He worked at small tapestries full of butterflies, flowers, napping cats, and colorful birds. They decorated the house, and two hung in the bank, one in Walden's office, one in Lord Stephen's. Arthur had asked to be shown a few stitches, as had several of the other children.

"Lady Dinkle faces more than a difficult few

months, Ned. Her Grace says the lying-in is only the beginning."

Ned wrapped his current work in progress around his embroidery hoop and tucked it into his workbasket. "Will you attend Lady Lindhurst if she asks?"

Rosalind looked about her family parlor, a smallish space where she and Ned spent most of their evenings. They socialized little—George's disgrace was still fresh news—and loved much. George had taken all the blame for his father's scheme, hoping Lindhurst might benefit from having only a black sheep brother rather than a black sheep brother and a scoundrel for a father.

George was on his way to New South Wales, the disgraced younger son about whom the family would not speak in public.

Ned had seen George off with some funds and a trunk of decent clothing. Bob had offered what advice and introductory letters he could, but George would face at least several years of hard work under harsh conditions.

If there was a silver lining, it was that the Earl of Woodruff's children, by mutual agreement, no longer associated with him. Lindhurst was attempting to manage on Clotilda's settlements and his own portion from his mother's estate, and Aunt Ida had offered him and Clotilda a home on her property in Derbyshire.

Woodruff had departed from Town for the family seat the day after George's arrest, and had not been heard from since. Polite society had apparently decided that banishment was to be his fate, and Rosalind found that judgment fitting. Fourteen years or so of exile should suffice, if Woodruff's drinking didn't do him in sooner.

"Are you up for a journey to Derbyshire?" she asked.

"I will cheerfully escort you there, but don't go unless you genuinely want to."

Ned did this frequently—asked Rosalind to pause and consider her true wishes and needs. She returned the favor, and they were slowly acquiring a habit of greater self-examination. Lord Stephen was more in evidence at the bank, Ned spent more time on his new project—turning the bank's approach to the badgers into a plan for a school that took in the children of prisoners and transportees.

"Autumn in Derbyshire is beautiful," Rosalind said. "Could we bring along a few of the children?"

Ned shifted from his wing chair to take the place beside Rosalind on the sofa. "I would rather have you all to myself, to be honest. We never had a wedding journey, and I believe Francine and the staff would manage without us well enough for a few weeks."

Rosalind had made the choice to remain in London while the whole scandal of George's arrest and trial were ongoing. Her Grace of Walden had been a stanch ally, as had the ladies who shared Rosalind's concern for ill-treated animals.

Part of Rosalind's motivation had been to ensure that Francine, Calliope, and the other ladies were all settled back into a decent life, inasmuch as that was possible. Francine had taken an interest in Ned's project, and had turned out to have a way with upset children.

Several of the other women had taken on various roles, and Hope House now provided a home for two dozen children in addition to the eight teachers and staff who looked after them. Two of the older children assisted in Bob's new shop several days a week, two were badgers, two assisted in the Walden stables.

The small-investor businesses had proved to be a fertile source of posts for the remaining older children, though duties were always light and secondary to basic education.

"Do you ever think of leaving the bank to make the school a full-time venture?" Rosalind asked, snuggling up to her husband.

"Yes."

Ned's answer should not have surprised her—he was a ruminating sort of fellow—but the alacrity of his response did.

"And?"

"And now is not the time," Ned said. "Maybe after Papa arrives from Port Jackson, maybe in a few years. We are still in the learning-as-we-go phase, which never quite ends, and the school needs patrons if it's to thrive. My personal fortune is sufficient to get the venture off on sound footing, but we want to establish an institution that will thrive well beyond our steward-ship of it."

"Would the bank become a patron?"

"Possibly."

"What about Rothhaven? He's a bright fellow and apparently quite the wizard with investments."

"I hadn't thought of him."

People tended not to think of Rothhaven. He was the quietest, most unassuming peer Rosalind had had the pleasure of losing a hand of cards to. He was also devoted to his duchess, fond of children and animals, and shrewd without trumpeting his insights for all to admire.

Rosalind adored him and suspected he would gladly take a place among the school's sponsors.

"He'd advise an endowment," Ned said. "A fund that produces income, one that can grow gradually as the school's alumni go forth into the world and prosper, perhaps adding a little to the fund themselves in the years to come."

"I like that plan, Ned Wentworth. I like that vision."

"I like you," Ned said, squeezing her in a one-armed hug. "I was prepared to adore you, to desire you madly, and to give you my heart for all time, but Rosalind…"

Oh, how she treasured this courage of his, this honesty. "Ned?"

"You are my friend," he said, kissing her fingers. "You have become my best, most intimate friend, and that is…I know now why Walden would die for his duchess. Why he has put aside arrogance and old hurts, along with all the mistakes that can make a man small. You do the same for me, you make me brave enough to grow past what holds me back."

"The courage is your own, Ned, and I would still be bracing myself for Woodruff's next insult were it not for you. I would not have a school to manage, two duchesses among my friends, and two dozen birthday parties to plan."

The children were quite keen on birthday parties, as was—oddly enough—the staff.

"Do you know that today is a very special day?" Ned said, nuzzling Rosalind's temple.

"Today is Thursday."

"Not just any Thursday. Today is my birthday, Rosalind."

"This is your second birthday this week, sir. At this rate you will soon be older than Methuselah."

"I know why he lived so long," Ned said, rising and offering Rosalind his hand.

She came to her feet and allowed Ned to escort her from the parlor. "I'm sure you will enlighten me."

"First I will kiss you."

By the time Ned had completed that task, Rosalind's knees were a bit unreliable and her insides were fluttery.

"About Methuselah?" she asked, as Ned scooped her up against his chest and carried her to the stairs. This was a frequent part of the birthday celebrations. Rosalind had learned to enjoy it.

"He lived so long because all those birthdays made him a very joyous fellow. Mrs. Methuselah saw to that. And do you know what else?"

Ned set Rosalind on her feet in their private sitting room. "I'm sure this was not part of any Bible history that Vicar taught at Sunday school, sir."

"This part is for grown-ups," Ned said, locking the sitting room door. "Mrs. Methuselah had a lot of birthdays too."

And so, as it turned out, did Rosalind, and all of them were very, very happy indeed!

Author's Note

One of the greatest joys of writing historical romance is hopping down one rabbit hole after another. The Duke of Chandos met his second duchess when she was a chambermaid enduring the ignominy of a wife sale, for example. How loudly does that beg to be used as a story premise?

When I was pondering Ned and Rosalind's tale, I came across a wonderful book, *The Floating Brothel: The Extraordinary True Story of an Eighteenth-Century Ship and Its Cargo of Female Convicts*, by Sian Rees. This tome recounts the voyage of the convict ship *Lady Julian*, which set sail from England in 1789. The ship's steward, one John Nicol, dictated a memoir in his later years that details the tribulations and day-to-day life on board that very long voyage.

One anecdote in particular caught my eye: Apparently, the night before embarking on a long journey, it was customary for a ship's crew to hold a send-off celebration on board. The *Lady Julian*'s crew, along with the transportees, adhered to that tradition, and somewhere amid the drinking and revelry on deck, four women escaped and were never recaptured.

My, my, my. I got to thinking about the logistics of that escape, as the last of the supplies were being loaded, and the last of the onboard visitors were saying their farewells to the convicts and crew, and...then I started writing.

Transportation continued well past the Regency period, though the practice was always controversial. His Grace of Walden mentions one argument that contributed to its eventual abandonment: The thought of being shipped halfway around the world was supposed to be so horrific that the crime rampant in London in later Georgian years would magically subside, because harsh punishments are supposed to be a deterrent to crime, right?

The Victorians noticed that after decades of employing transportation as a deterrent (in addition to centuries of capital punishment), crime in London was roaring along more vigorously than ever. By the mid-nineteenth century the notion that rehabilitation might figure into criminal justice had also taken hold, and some of the sociological origins of crime were finally getting serious attention.

Such fascinating stuff to a lawyer turned author of happily ever afters! I hope you enjoyed Ned and Rosalind's story, because clearly, I had great fun writing it, and writing the whole Rogue to Riches series.

—Grace Burrowes

About the Author

GRACE BURROWES grew up in central Pennsylvania and is the sixth of seven children. She discovered romance novels in junior high and has been reading them voraciously ever since. Grace has a bachelor's degree in political science, a bachelor of music in music history (both from the Pennsylvania State University), a master's degree in conflict transformation from Eastern Mennonite University, and a juris doctor from the National Law Center at George Washington University.

Grace is a *New York Times* and *USA Today* bestselling author who writes Georgian, Regency, Scottish Victorian, and contemporary romances in both novella and novel lengths. She enjoys giving workshops and speaking at writers' conferences.

You can learn more at:
GraceBurrowes.com
Twitter @GraceBurrowes
Facebook.com/Grace.Burrowes

*Get swept off your feet by charming dukes,
sharp-witted ladies, and scandalous balls in
Forever's historical romances!*

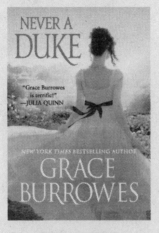

NEVER A DUKE
by Grace Burrowes

Ned Wentworth will be forever grateful to the family who plucked him from
the streets and gave him a home, even though polite society still whispers
years later about his questionable past. Precisely because of Ned's connections in low places, Lady Rosalind Kinwood approaches him to help
her find a lady's maid who has disappeared. As the investigation becomes
more dangerous, both Ned and Rosalind will have to risk everything—
including their hearts—if they are to share the happily-ever-after that Mayfair's matchmakers have begrudged them both.

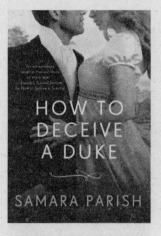

HOW TO DECEIVE A DUKE
by Samara Parish

Engineer Fiona McTavish has come to London under the guise of Finlay McTavish for one purpose—to find a distributor for her new invention. But when her plans go awry and she's arrested at a protest, the only person who can help is her ex-lover, Edward, Duke of Wildeforde. Only bailing "Finlay" out of jail comes at a cost: She must live under his roof. The sparks from their passionate affair many years before are quick to rekindle. But when Finlay becomes wanted for treason, will Edward protect her—or his heart?

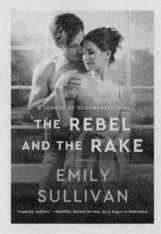

THE PERKS OF LOVING A WALLFLOWER
by Erica Ridley

As a master of disguise, Thomasina Wynchester can be a polite young lady—or a bawdy old man. Anything to solve the case—which this time requires masquerading as a charming baron. Her latest assignment unveils a top-secret military cipher covering up an enigma that goes back centuries. But Tommy's beautiful new client turns out to be the reserved, high-born bluestocking Miss Philippa York, with whom she's secretly smitten. As they decode clues and begin to fall for each other in the process, the mission—as well as their hearts—will be at stake...